Dear Maggie,

onwards & upwards

Best Wishes,

Rann Loya

CHAIRMAN-X

by

RAMI LOYA

authorHOUSE®

AuthorHouse™
1663 Liberty Drive, Suite 200
Bloomington, IN 47403
www.authorhouse.com
Phone: 1-800-839-8640

First published by AuthorHouse 10/31/2007

ISBN: 978-1-4343-2753-6 (sc)

*Printed in the United States of America
Bloomington, Indiana*

This book is printed on acid-free paper.

CHAIRMAN-X

a novel by

RAMI LOYA

SEPTEMBER 2007

DEDICATION

This book is dedicated to the memory of my parents, Uzi (Aziz) and Shulamit (Salima) Loya, whose battle for freedom, unconditional love, and relentless dedication to their family serves as an inspiration for future generations.

PROLOGUE

MIDDLE EAST, 1992

The Chairman awakened to the loud ringing of the red phone next to his bed. This was the private line, reserved for only the most pressing emergencies. He glanced at the clock: 7 a.m.

He picked up the phone. "Yes?"

"Good news, Chairman. We got them — all the sheep and the three spotted lambs — just as planned." It was his chief of staff.

"That's good, Ebrahim. And..."

"Abu Yasin has given them the ultimatum: release sixty of our freedom fighters or the bus and young hostages will be blown to pieces."

"Excellent job," the Chairman said. "Make sure the bus is wired with explosives, and demand an Air France A-320 jetliner be fully fueled and ready for takeoff by 10 a.m."

"Yes, sir."

"The next step is to get Ben Ari on the hostage bus. They won't do anything crazy with him there."

"I'm right on top of it. It shall be done." Ebrahim had personally selected and trained the men in the assault group. One of the group's combatants had grown up in Israel and knew his way around the country. He had been designated as the driver for the hostage bus. Another was a veteran Airbus A-320 pilot who had formerly worked for Algerian Airlines. His job was to fly the plane to Beirut.

"When our prisoners are released, we will order them to be driven to the airport by bus right up to the jetliner. There they will wait for the school bus to arrive."

Ebrahim's mood seemed to change abruptly. "But what if the Israelis refuse to cooperate? They say they will never negotiate over hostages."

"You know exactly what to do," the Chairman answered firmly. "There is no room for haggling. We have to prove we mean business from the outset."

* * * *

The Chairman recognized that the secret to success in any dangerous mission was to put yourself into the enemy's mind and think as he did. He had spent many years studying the Israeli way of thinking while analyzing the tactics behind their bold actions. What contingency plan would they come up with this time? What were the weak points of the PLO plan?

He knew exactly what worried Israelis most. They would do anything to avoid any harm coming to the children. Children were their Achilles heel, and his well-calculated, aggressive plan had been designed to take full advantage of it.

PLO intelligence operatives inside Israel had studied the timetables and travel patterns of school buses along the Israeli coastal highway. They had discovered that Ben Ari's three grandchildren and other privileged youngsters were being transported daily to their private school south of the city of Netanya. This knowledge sealed the planning phase of the operation. It was a sword to the throat of the Israeli Defense Minister.

The Chairman picked up the red phone again.

"Ebrahim! Call CNN's Beirut bureau. I want CNN's crew on the scene as soon as possible. The Israelis will absolutely hate a live broadcast. They're not likely to attack the bus with the entire world looking on. Live coverage will add extra confusion. It will limit their response options.

"And I want an open link established with Harel's office to transmit our demands. I will be joining you in the war room shortly."

* * * *

At 7:30 a.m., the sun was just rising above the horizon.

The voice of Abu Yasin, the operation commander, came clearly through the loudspeaker in the war room.

"All the children are handcuffed with their hands behind their backs, and the explosive charges have been distributed throughout the bus."

"Excellent work!" the Chairman spoke loudly. "Please

pay close attention to every detail. There is no room for error."

"Allah is with us! I will see you in Beirut in a few hours." A burst of static indicated Abu Yasin had broken the connection.

The Chairman addressed the PLO intelligence chief. "Put all the TVs on and start scanning the international news channels. Let's see if anybody is picking up on the action yet."

He turned to Ebrahim. "Did you get Harel's office on the line? I want you to speak directly with Ben Ari. I'm sure he is conferring with the Prime Minister right now, trying to find a way out of their crisis. I don't want the Israelis to have the opportunity to plan a response. I want Ben Ari to join the hijacked bus without further delays. The sooner we get him out there, the more havoc we can create on the Israeli side. They have three hours to get the plane with the freed prisoners into the air."

The communications officer reported that all the lines to Israel were jammed — overloaded by calls spurred by the hijacking.

The Chairman picked up the phone and called his close friend, the Russian ambassador in Beirut. He briefed him on what was happening and requested his help in establishing contact with the Israeli Prime Minister's office. Within minutes, the ambassador called back and provided the Chairman with a highly secure phone number to the PM's office, one that had been used by the United States and the former Soviet Union during major Middle East crises.

The Chairman watched Ebrahim closely as he held

the phone tightly to his ear and spoke to Ben Ari in fluent English. The chief of staff conveyed his instructions in meticulous detail. Finally he said, "Mr. Ben Ari, we guarantee the safety of all the children on the bus. As long as we are not attacked or provoked by your forces, nobody will be harmed."

Ebrahim listened for a moment and then said, "Time is running out, Ben Ari. The lives of thirty young children hang in the balance. Don't screw with us, or the blood of the children will be on your hands. The families of the hostages will never forgive you, and your government will be in ruins."

Ebrahim listened again for several seconds and then hung up the phone. He turned to the Chairman.

"What did he say?" the Chairman asked.

"He said, 'It is not my decision.' Then he hung up." Ebrahim looked up toward the ceiling, took a deep breath, and bowed his head.

There was a flurry across the room.

"CNN is on," the intelligence chief called out excitedly, "but they can't get close to the bus. It's surrounded by police."

"Abu Yasin," the Chairman's voice roared, "order one of your men to grab a hostage with a gun to his head, and order the Israeli police to let the CNN crew through."

Within minutes, Abu Yasin was live on CNN detailing demands to the Israeli government. "No one will be harmed if our demands are met, and all the hostages will be returned to Israel safely within twenty-four hours," he declared. The camera focused on the pale, frightened faces of young boys and girls huddled on the bus with explosive charges spread around them. Media coverage started paying off almost immediately. Most international news channels were broadcasting the operation live worldwide to millions of riveted viewers.

* * * *

Shlomo Harel banged on the table in deep frustration. "We need to buy some time here," he said firmly. "No rash decisions. Our response has to be well planned and executed."

A heavy layer of whirling cigarette smoke coated the ceiling of the large conference room, where for the past hour the Israeli general staff had been arguing over how to resolve the hostage confrontation with a minimum of casualties.

"Shlomo," Ben Ari said, "I ordered the chief of staff to mobilize the anti-terrorism unit and place the Army, Air Force, and Navy on the highest alert level. One can never be sure what else the PLO could be plotting."

Harel rose from his seat. "I will see you at my office when a consensus is reached," he ordered as he left the room.

David Ben Ari joined him several minutes later in the Prime Minster suite.

Harel's face was beet red, his balding forehead dripping profusely. "David," he said, "I just learned your grandchildren are on the school bus. The terrorists are demanding that you join the bus without further delays. These bastards are getting smarter and bolder. Only the prophet Mohammed knows what they'll come up with next."

"I'll report back to you as soon as I get there," Ben Ari said. "As soon as I see what choices Allah will be offering us." He forced a quick smile.

"David, this is a serious crisis. I don't want you on that bus. It will be very hard for you to control your emotions with your grandchildren on board, and these damn terrorists have planned this just so they can take advantage of your situation. I would be a higher profile hostage. I want to take your place. The Chairman will never authorize any action that will endanger my life. He knows that would be signing his own death warrant."

"That's not an option," Ben Ari answered firmly. "I must be with my grandchildren. That's the way they want it. That's the way I want it. So be it."

"I respect your decision," Harel said. He placed his hand firmly on the Defense Minister's shoulder. "Our commanders will come up with a creative strategy to get us out of this quagmire. For now, we'll have the Palestinian prisoners loaded onto prison buses. We should be able at some point to substitute buses loaded with our commandos. Take your secure radiophone to the hijacked bus. I will be in touch with you shortly to update you on our plans."

Ben Ari paused momentarily. "I'm willing to go along with this under one condition, Shlomo," he said. "It doesn't matter what happens to me, but you must give me your word of honor that you will not order any actions that will bring harm to the children on the bus."

"You have my word," Harel said firmly. "This is going

to be extremely difficult for you. These savages are going to test you to the utmost human limits. You will have to be strong in the face of the enemy. May God be with you and all of Israel."

A few minutes later, Ben Ari hopped into the back of his car and slammed the door forcefully. He thought of his young grandchildren, cowering before the vicious gunmen.

He knew he had to cool down. It was an inevitable part of his job to confront such horrors as this.

"Drive me to the school bus," he commanded his driver.

Ben Ari called his wife to update her on the most recent developments. "I am going to be with our *kindalach*," he told her. "I will protect them with the last breath in my lungs."

All he could hear through his receiver were her loud whimpers.

* * * *

At 8:45 a.m., Ben Ari arrived at the scene and was escorted to the hostage bus by Israeli police. He was searched for weapons, listening devices, and gadgets from the Mossad arsenal. He was clean. Abu Yasin held on to Ben Ari's portable radiophone.

* * * *

"The shepherd is on board," Abu Yasin's voice came clearly through the speaker in the PLO war room.

"Excellent," the Chairman said. "You and your men need to remain on the highest level of alert. The Israelis are in the process of plotting an elaborate response. They will take high risks and gamble with many lives before yielding to our demands. We must always stay two steps ahead of them, do the unexpected, and catch them off guard."

"Yes, Chairman," Abu Yasin responded.

Ebrahim's loud voice was directed at Abu Yasin. "Check the status of the prisoners and the airplane. We need to start moving, he ordered"

* * * *

Abu Yasin sat next to Ben Ari in the front of the bus. Ben Ari got on his radiophone and contacted the military headquarters of the Israeli Defense Forces in Tel Aviv. "The jetliner will be ready by ten a.m., and the prisoners are boarding their buses in the prison camp near the town of Atlit," he reported. "It will take them about an hour and a half to get to the airport."

* * * *

At 9:30 a.m., Harel's intercom buzzer startled him out of his deep thoughts. "Your much anticipated call is on line one," his director general informed him.

Harel picked up the receiver in a hurry. It was his chief of staff.

"Two buses loaded with special operations forces dressed in prison jumpsuits will be arriving at the airport in about thirty minutes. They will park next to the jetliner. I will order the PLO prisoner buses to turn east when they reach Netanya and return to the prison camp via the old Tel Aviv-Haifa road."

"How are you planning to rescue the hostages?"

"The school bus will have to pass through an airport entrance gate to reach the jetliner, which will be parked in an open area near the runway. This gate is normally closed. As the school bus approaches the gate, we will open it slowly. This move will force the bus to slow down considerably. As soon as it passes the gate, we will fire charges at its tires and explode several shock bombs overhead. This will bring the bus to a halt while the shock waves should stun the occupants for several minutes. Our elite troops will rush to the scene and force their way into the bus through the doors and emergency exits."

"What if the charges detonate the explosives on the bus or ignite its fuel tank?" Harel asked

"Shlomo, you are well aware that this is a very high risk operation where anything can happen. I have no doubt there will be casualties. How many is very hard to predict. I will have the airport fire trucks on standby at the closest possible location. If the bus catches fire, they will soak it with fire retardant chemicals.

"My men will first eliminate all the terrorists on board and then rush the children and Ben Ari to safety. We will also have several ambulances on standby at the airport. I ordered the Sheba medical center in Tel Hashomer on the highest readiness level."

"You put a lot of thought into this operation, and it appears that you have a very solid, daring plan in place," Harel commented. "I hope and pray for the best outcome. Keep me informed of any new developments. I will give you the green light when the bus gets closer to the airport."

* * * *

At 9:45 a.m., Abu Yasin reported that the two prison buses were going past the city of Hadera, heading south. He estimated they would arrive at the airport in an hour.

"Order the prisoner buses to join you at your location," Ebrahim commanded. "Have the first bus stop three hundred yards behind the school bus, and the second a hundred yard behind the first."

* * * *

Abu Yasin repeated the instructions to Ben Ari. Beet red, Ben Ari burst out uncontrollably, "You can't keep switching the goddamn plans. I'm trying to follow your instructions, but you are driving me insane!"

"We will keep changing plans until we land in Beirut," Abu Yasin answered calmly. "Don't make me remind you again who is on the bus with you!"

Ben Ari reluctantly transmitted the orders, knowing they could jeopardize the planned rescue operation.

* * * *

Fifteen minutes later, the prisoners' buses pulled up behind the school bus and came to a halt as instructed. The CNN crew descended from the school bus followed by two heavily armed gunmen. They walked briskly toward the first bus.

Ebrahim's face was glued to the large TV monitor, his eyes threatening to pop out of their sockets. The war room, filled with the spicy aroma of dark Turkish coffee mixed with cigarette smoke, fell silent.

The group of men was very close to the first prisoner bus. If the buses were filled with Israeli commandos, this was the time for them to pour out. Abu Yasin and his men were keeping very close tabs on the situation, ready to react in a fraction of a second.

The front door of the bus opened slowly. One of the PLO gunmen edged the CNN cameraman with the butt of his assault rifle to climb onto the bus. Soon the anxious faces of men in prison jumpsuits gazed vividly from the monitor. Their eyes restless with concern, they seemed confused about their whereabouts, unaware of the reasons behind their sudden mobilization.

The cameraman started filming close-ups of the prisoners on the bus. Each prisoner was instructed to say his name and country of origin as a gunman checked them off a crumpled list he had pulled out of his side pocket. Before long, anxious expressions turned into jovial smiles, and loud cheering was heard.

The gunmen dismissed the prison guards and ordered them to walk toward the police roadblock half a mile north. Soon extra weapons and explosives were being distributed among the freed prisoners. A commander and a driver were designated for each bus, and several hostages were moved from the school bus to the prisoners' buses. Each bus commander was given a radio and instructed to follow Abu Yasin's orders.

"I can certainly use sixty rested fighters to bolster my forces." Abu Yasin sounded enthusiastic. "That was a brilliant move."

"Get your convoy on the move!" Ebrahim yelled. "Demand two police cars with sirens to lead the convoy and one to follow behind."

* * * *

Shlomo Harel sat on his high-back leather chair in his chamber, coughing intermittently. The ashtray on his bureau was filled with squashed cigarette butts. He got up and increased the fan speed of the air conditioner, hoping it would help dissipate the heavy smoke. He wiped his sweaty palms with white napkins, leaned back on his chair, and took a long, deep breath.

His door opened abruptly. "Shlomo," his director general said in a tense voice, "I have been watching the hijacking broadcast on CNN. I just saw the prisoner buses pull to the scene of the hijacked bus. They have joined forces. They moved hostages and explosives to the prisoners' buses. We are now dealing with a convoy of three buses with hostages and explosives."

"Get me the chief of staff," Harel commanded

In a moment, the chief of staff was patched in.

"How are we going to deal with three buses loaded with hostages and explosives?" Harel asked

"We just completed revising our plan, Shlomo. This unexpected change forces us to do something riskier that can cause more casualties. I ordered the removal of our two buses from the vicinity of the jetliner. Our men will now take concealed positions in the area surrounding the entrance gate to the terminal.

"As the school bus approaches the gate, we will roll it open slowly, which will force the convoy to slow down considerably. We will stop the gate halfway through and inform Ben Ari that the gate is jammed and that we are trying to open it ASAP. This will force all three buses to come to a complete halt. Before they have a chance to respond, we will attack the three buses with shock bombs and blow their tires. You know the rest."

"You have my authorization to proceed," Harel said in a somber tone, "but tell the men to take the utmost precautions to preserve the life of the children."

* * * *

At 10:45 a.m., the convoy started moving south toward Tel Aviv. Abu Yasin ordered the CNN truck to the front of the convoy behind the police cars to scan the surrounding areas continuously. He reported that the Air France Airbus was ready and that it would take approximately forty-five minutes for the convoy to reach the airport.

"Make sure Ben Ari orders the roads to the airport cleared," Ebrahim warned. "I don't want the convoy to stop until it reaches the aircraft."

Trying to secure prime viewing positions, news crews were now flocking to Ben Gurion Airport near Tel Aviv. Reinforced Israeli border police units struggled to keep order. A flurry of military activity could be seen in the airport vicinity — military trucks, command and communications vehicles, vehicles of senior military personnel, and several buses.

The Chairman viewed the ominous signs on the large monitor. His mind was racing. The Israelis were not simply going to play their parts in the script he had written. They were most certainly preparing a firewor reception for the convoy. He signaled Ebrahim to join him for a private consultation.

Ebrahim agreed with the Chairman. "The airport zone doesn't look too promising," he said. "What do you think Harel is up to?"

"If he orders his troops to storm the buses, the young hostages, Ben Ari, and his grandchildren will most surely die, but if he doesn't act aggressively, his government will surely collapse, and he will lose power. We have him in a very tight spot."

"We should order Ben Ari to evacuate all military forces from the airport at once," Ebrahim suggested.

The Chairman looked pensively into the far distance. "Maybe we can help Harel come out of it in one piece. His political rivals vehemently oppose negotiating a peaceful solution. At least he and Ben Ari are open to the idea of a dialogue with us. I want to keep them in power."

"What do you have in mind?" Ebrahim asked.

"Let's talk to Abu Yasin. I need to ask him a couple of questions."

Ebrahim raised Abu Yasin on the radio.

"What other planes can our pilot fly?" the Chairman inquired.

There was a short pause before Abu Yasin answered. "He flew C-130 transports in the Sahara a few years ago."

The Chairman looked at Ebrahim inquisitively. Ebrahim nodded. "Can he still fly one?" the Chairman asked.

The answer was affirmative.

The Chairman marched back to the war room, where he asked Ebrahim to display on the main board a map of Israeli air force bases.

Ebrahim was not only an expert on Israeli military bases but also well versed in regional geography. He identified Tel Noff, a large air force base southeast of Tel Aviv, and Ramat David, a base in the northeast near the town of Afula.

"How far are they from the convoy's position?" the Chairman inquired.

"About an hour either way."

The Chairman took a close look at the map. Ramat David was much closer to the Lebanese border, which meant less airtime to Beirut and thus less time for the Israelis to intercept the flight. He also noticed there weren't any infantry bases close to Ramat David.

"Let's switch to the northeast route and direct the convoy toward Ramat David airbase," he announced. "The Israelis won't have enough time to redeploy to the northeast, and their airmen aren't trained to handle guerrilla warfare. This is our best chance to pull this mission off. Let's go for it!"

"What about the jetliner?" the PLO intelligence chief interjected. "How are we going to get it to the airbase?"

"Forget the jetliner," the Chairman responded. "We will use a C-130 from Ramat David."

Ebrahim looked at the map. The convoy was heading east on Route 5 toward the junction with Route 4, where they would turn right and continue toward the airport. He quickly raised Abu Yasin on the radio and started relaying his instructions.

As the convoy approached the junction, there appeared to be some confusion on the part of the police car drivers, who seemed to be about to go along the original route. Abu Yasin's voice in the background screamed, "Tell them to turn left...left, not right!"

The traffic lights turned red, and the police cars stopped. When the lights turned green, they made a left turn onto Route 4. Without warning, a police helicopter appeared above the convoy, attempting to track its new course. "Tell Ben Ari to make the chopper disappear," Ebrahim shouted furiously.

In a few seconds, the helicopter made a turn to the west and vanished.

* * * *

At 11:40 a.m., the convoy was getting closer to the town of Afula. Abu Yasin briefed Ben Ari on the changes and ordered a C-130 fueled and ready for takeoff on the Ramat David runway at noon. Ben Ari passed the orders on. Minutes later, he informed Abu Yasin that the Israeli air force did not have any C-130s in Ramat David. It was a fighter jet base with no transport planes and only very short runways.

"Order them to fly one from Tel Noff," Ebrahim instructed Abu Yasin. "It should take about twenty minutes to get there."

Abu Yasin reported what Ben Ari had told him. "The Israelis are not sure whether the runway at Ramat David is long enough for a transport to land or take off. Our pilot says that he knows a few tricks for taking off from short runways, but he needs to see the runway before he can be confident it's long enough."

"If they don't get the bloody plane to Ramat David in twenty minutes, start executing hostages." It was the Chairman's voice, and Abu Yasin could hear it clearly through his earpiece. "I am sick of their games. This mission will not fail — do you hear me? I don't care if you have to execute every damn hostage. Am I making myself clear? Do it now! No excuses."

Abu Yasin ordered Ben Ari's eldest granddaughter to the front of the bus next to her grandfather and pointed a handgun at her head. "Order the C-130 to take off from Tel-Noff now or she goes!" he yelled.

Distraught by the terrified look on his granddaughter's face, Ben Ari asked for Harel to be summoned to the radiophone. After a short delay, Harel came on.

"Shlomo, I urge you to get the C-130 to Ramat David right now, or it's going to be a slaughterhouse here. Nothing will stop these savages from blowing us all to pieces. Shlomo, I am pleading for the life of these youngsters. Please don't make them victims."

"Tell him that if the C-130 doesn't show up by twelve-fifteen, we will execute a hostage every five minutes, starting with your granddaughter." Abu Yasin's voice was eerily calm as he waved his handgun in lazy circles, sometimes catching the little girl in its range.

"He is not kidding, Shlomo," Ben Ari called out as Harel went off the air.

* * * *

At 12:15 p.m., the convoy entered the airbase and

drove to the end of the main runway. An amazingly crisp image of the runway nestled between the surrounding low hills covered in thick green foliage was revealed through the monitors in the PLO war room.

CNN live coverage was a gift from Allah.

The C-130 was nowhere on the horizon.

Tiny sweat pellets covered the Chairman's forehead as he paced the floor of the war room.

"Ebrahim, call the PM's office on the red phone and give them a final ultimatum," the Chairman said solemnly. "I am not going to screw around with them much longer. They have ten minutes to get the plane there, or the hostages' blood will be on their hands."

Ebrahim was patched through to central command in Tel Aviv, and soon Harel's director general was on the line. "The C-130 took off a few minutes ago," he informed Ebrahim. "It should be there within ten to fifteen minutes at the most. We had to get it fueled, but I assure you it is on its way."

"No more games," Ebrahim threatened. "This is your last chance."

The Chairman slumped down into his chair. He wiped his clammy forehead with the cuff of his sleeve. The war council members sat motionless, eyes transfixed on the monitors. Clouds of smoke rose like strange messages from the copious cigarettes lit in the room. Nothing interrupted the eerie silence.

CHAPTER 1

BAGHDAD, 1948

Ali Samara was sitting in a crowded classroom at the suburban Baghdad high school he attended. The heavy heat wave of early spring seemed to settle permanently in the steamy classroom with no relief in sight. Ali found it difficult to concentrate on his math teacher's words and scribbles on the blackboard. Sweat poured out of the teacher's forehead, and he kept wiping it with a handkerchief that was in urgent need of washing. His white shirt had heavy sweat marks under his armpits, which seemed to contribute to the unpleasant odor in the room. An occasional burst of wind from the wide-open windows brought refreshing relief from the intensity of the hot oppressiveness.

There was a loud knock on the classroom door, which opened instantly to reveal a middle-aged woman.

"I came to fetch Ali Samara," she announced to the teacher. "He is needed at home on an urgent matter."

Ali stared at Halima, his family's next-door neighbor

and his mother's closest friend. "What does she want with me?" he wondered.

"Ali Samara!" the teacher declared. "You are dismissed for today, you lucky young man. This heat wave is getting unbearable."

Ali exited the classroom in a hurry, following Halima quietly.

"Why do I have to go home now?" he inquired. "It's still early, and I'm going to miss many classes."

"Be patient, *ebni*. We'll be home soon," Halima said calmly.

"Is something wrong?" Ali pressed on. "Why is *ummi* taking me out of school? She always says how important it is for me to stay in school, listen to the teachers, and do all my homework."

"You are right, ebni. Your mother wants you to do well at school and become a successful businessman."

As they drew near the Samara home, Ali detected the loud pitch of his mother's lamentations.

"What happened?" he peered in panic at Halima. "Why is ummi crying so bitterly?"

Halima wiped the corners of her eyes with her fingers. She took Ali's hand and led him into the house.

Ali rushed to the living room. His mother Jamila was standing in the middle of the room pounding her chest with her fists. She pulled at her hair in seeming desperation. Clumps of it lay by her feet.

"Salim! Salim!" she cried. *"Fedwa-el-Eyunak* Salim! How can you leave us so suddenly? We are lost without your love and wisdom. I can't live without you, my precious angel." She fell to her knees. "How have I transgressed, dear Allah, to deserve this miserable fate? What have I done to draw your wrath to my family? How will Ali bear this horrible crisis?"

Ali rushed to his mother and held her in his arms as tightly as he could. Shuddering uncontrollably, she leaned her tear-covered face against his chest.

"Alla achatha'ha el abuk, ebni, Allah has taken him away. I wish I could go in his place."

"Ahh...*Yumma,* what happened to *Babba?"* Ali asked, stroking his mother's head.

Jamila wailed in agony and wept in her son's arms. Finally, she was able to speak again. "He had his favorite breakfast before going to work at Abu Razi's clothing store. He looked his usual self, neatly dressed and closely shaven, just like every morning. I was going out to the market when one of his co-workers came running."

She paused for a few seconds, clinging to Ali as if she were the child, and he the parent. Another outburst of screams filled the small living room.

"The man told me, 'Abu Ali collapsed at work. We rushed him to the hospital as fast as we could. You must go to the hospital quickly.'

"When I got to the hospital," she continued between gasps, "the doctor told me he had done everything he could. Oh, Salim, Salim, it was a massive heart attack."

She collapsed to her knees and clung desperately to Ali's legs.

"You're all I have left, ebni. I pray Allah will have mercy on us."

Ali wrapped his arms around her shoulders and rubbed her back gently, unable to utter a word.

* * * *

Several days after the tragic loss of his father, Ali returned to school. However, he was behind in his schoolwork and found it very hard to concentrate on his studies. He realized that he might have to leave school soon, get a job, and help his mother earn a living.

When his mother came home from work one evening, she hugged and kissed him as she always did. They sat down to have a light meal she'd put together quickly.

"I have good news, ebni," she said, trying to appear cheerful.

"Abu Reuben gave me a very generous raise today. He said it was very important for you to continue your studies at school. He didn't want me to worry about the loss of income from your father or take you out of school to get a job. At least Allah is watching over us since your father has gone."

This was a great relief to Ali. "I was worried about that, ummi. I really want to stay in school."

"Thanks to Abu Reuben and Um Reuben, you will be able to finish high school and then go to university, just as your father desired for you."

"I don't know if we will be able to afford it, ummi. We'll have to wait and see."

"Allah is watching over you, ebni. Last night I had a dream. I saw you all grown up, a successful businessman dressed in an immaculate, beautiful suit. You were glowing with happiness, and there was your lovely wife and my young grandchildren were clinging to you, calling *Babba, Babba,* please take us to the amusement park. Allah works in miraculous ways, ebni. You'll see."

* * * *

As the school year came to a close, Ali continued having difficulties focusing on his studies. His mother worked all day and was often late coming home.

One day after school, his classmate Fuad asked if he wanted to join him and other *jama'a* at the movies. "I have an extra ticket for you," Fuad said, dismissing Ali's monetary concerns.

Fuad was one of the least capable students in his class. On occasion, he was disruptive, got in trouble with the teachers, and was sent to the principal's office. Ali wasn't too keen on him, but a movie sounded like a helpful distraction from the reality of his loss.

"Sure," he responded. "I would love to see a movie."

They joined Fuad's friends, who were two or three years older. Ismail, the apparent leader, bought everyone candy and nuts to enjoy during the movie. Afterwards Ali thanked Fuad for the good time and went straight home.

The following week Fuad asked Ali to join him and his friends for another movie. Ali agreed without hesitation. This time when it finished, Ismail invited Ali to come with them for dinner at a famous Baghdad restaurant.

"I'm afraid I can't afford it," Ali said. "Also my mother's expecting me for dinner, so I have to get home."

"Don't worry about the money." Ismail's confident tone was very convincing. "Tell your mother you went to a friend's house to do homework. You'll have a wonderful time with us."

Ali nodded reluctantly, not wanting to offend his generous new friend.

After they had enjoyed a delicious meal at the restaurant, an orchestra started playing, and two belly dancers appeared on stage to entertain the audience. Their bodies were round and full in all the right places, and their provocative moves drew loud cheers from the male audience.

One of the dancers approached their table, wiggling her hips and clapping the bells attached to her fingers. She stopped in front of Ali's chair and wrapped her silk sash around his neck, twisting it from side to side. As the volume of the music rose, she leaned forward, shaking her breasts vigorously. Ali was transfixed by the amazing scene unfolding before him. The beautiful dancer ran her long fingers through his dark, curly hair as she rolled her hips up and down and side to side. All the time, she looked directly into Ali's eyes.

Ali felt excited in a way he had not experienced before. Never had he been so close to a woman so skimpily dressed or seen such beautifully molded, succulent breasts. Before his imagination could travel further, the dancer was on her way to the next table, but not before Ismail stuffed several dinars into her sparkling top.

When Ali arrived home, his mother greeted him with a terrified look.

"Where have you been, ebni? I've been worried sick about you. You've never come home so late."

"I am very sorry, ummi," Ali said, feeling guilty. "I went to Fuad's to do homework. We were working hard all evening, and time just flew by. I didn't realize it was so late."

"I'm glad you're so diligent about your homework, ebni, but you must come home first to tell me where you're going. I've had enough pain this year. I wouldn't be able to cope with a second tragedy."

"It will never happen again, ummi. I promise"

* * * *

As the school year ended and summer vacation began, Ali enjoyed more freedom and less supervision from his busy mother. However, on occasion he went with her to her job at the Sasson's home and spent the day helping her. He enjoyed playing with the Sasson's young boy, Reuben, who took a liking to the teenaged son of his caregiver.

Reuben was a smart, energetic little boy, who loved kicking a ball around or playing hide and seek. When the Sassons hosted parties for government dignitaries in their mansion, Ali helped serve the delicacies lavished upon the honored guests. For the first time in his life, he saw the familiar faces of cabinet ministers he'd read about in the newspaper. He was awed by how well connected Mr. Daniel Sasson appeared to be with the Iraqi leaders.

* * * *

Ali continued to hang out with Fuad and his friends. They took trips across town to the modern, upscale neighborhoods, roamed the bustling street markets, took boat rides on the river, and went often to the movies.

On their way home one evening, Fuad told Ali that they would be going on a very special trip the following day. Ali should dress nicely and meet him outside the school at noon.

Fuad was waiting when Ali arrived. They boarded a horse-drawn carriage and headed across town. After crossing the river, Ismail and another friend joined them. When the coachman swung his whip high into the air and cracked it, the horse picked up its pace. After they had ridden for twenty minutes, the carriage stopped in front of a large, arched stone gate, which was the main entrance to an old Baghdad neighborhood Ali had never seen before.

Ismail paid the carriage driver, who was quick to pick up new passengers and disappear in the opposite direction. Ali noticed other young men in the promenade in front of the gate. They walked around restlessly looking sideways and behind them. Ismail led the way through the gate into a narrow street lined with small stores and outdoor coffee houses. As they walked farther down the street, they reached a residential neighborhood of small houses.

On the porch of one of the houses, Ali noticed a young woman lounging on a faded armchair. Her face was made up, with black eyeliner surrounding her eyelashes and crimson lipstick decorating her narrow lips. She was wearing a light satin dress accentuating her attractive body contours. Her long, thin legs were crossed, and her dress was gathered way up her thighs.

She caught Ali's gaze, smiled, and parted her legs slightly.

"Come on in," she called out to the passing boys. "Have a nice cool glass of lemonade. Only two dinars, gentlemen. You will enjoy the most amazing time of your lives."

Ali felt a strange sense of compulsion. His eyes were riveted to the tiny panties that barely covered the triangle between the woman's legs.

"Let's go, Ali," Ismail said. There was laughter in his voice.

As they walked deeper down the narrow street, Ali saw more women on display on their porches, some announcing discounted fees in an attempt to lure them inside. The sight of so many women selling their bodies in public overwhelmed him.

Ismail turned into a narrow alley and walked up the steps of a house with a distinctive red roof. A tall, attractive woman greeted them at the entrance. She was wearing a long, see-through dress held up by two tiny strings tied over her shoulders. Underneath Ali could see a red top decorated with shiny gold beads and matching bikini bottoms. She walked toward the boys, her thighs swaying provocatively and her breasts spilling over her tight top. A pleasant odor of perfume filled the small foyer.

"Ali, this is Fatima," Ismail said. "She is the best, not like the inexperienced young girls you saw on our way here. She will teach you everything you need to know."

Ali felt his hands and face become hot and then cold as ice. His friends burst into loud laughter.

"You have nothing to worry about, Ali," Ismail said. "Fatima will rid you of your virginity, just as she did for the rest of us."

Fatima took him by his hand and marched him into a small room with dimmed, red lighting. She closed the door behind them and latched it.

Ali felt overpowered by intense desire as Fatima slid the thin straps from her shoulders and let her dress fall to the floor. She moved close to Ali and began unbuttoning his shirt and pants. He tried to move backward, but her warm breath and intoxicating scent wrapped around him like a magical cloud. She pressed her naked body tightly against him. He was in a daze; the room twirled around him as if he were ascending to the heavens.

Suddenly, he felt a pulsating explosion that left him paralyzed for several seconds. His knees were about to buckle. The pleasure was indescribably great. Fatima held him firmly in her arms until his tension faded away and a feeling of sweet exhaustion engulfed his body. He lay back on the large bed.

"You came very fast," Fatima said, "but you have nothing to worry about. There is nothing wrong with that. It is quite normal for young men the first time."

Fatima served him a cup of tea and freshly baked crackers. They sat down and chatted for a while.

Before long, Fatima started caressing his body, and the powerful tension was back.

"This time you will experience it all," she assured him. "Before you leave my doorsteps, you will become a real man."

CHAPTER 2

The following week Fuad told Ali they had an important engagement that night. Ismail had asked them to meet the group at midnight.

"You can sneak out of your home after your mother is asleep." Fuad suggested. "That's what I do when we have late night engagements."

They traveled to a wealthy neighborhood of Baghdad. Ali was told to stand watch at a street corner. If he saw anybody approaching, he was to blow the whistle Ismail had given him.

While Ali was standing guard on the corner, Fuad did the same outside the store as his friends broke into it. They cut the locks with large steel cutters, went inside, and closed the door. Within minutes, they came out, each carrying a backpack filled with merchandise. They loaded the goods into a small truck waiting around the corner and disappeared from the crime scene.

"Excellent execution," Ismail said. "Everything was timed perfectly. We were in and out in fifteen minutes exactly as planned. Ali, Fuad, you did a great job as sentries. Next time I will assign you a greater role in the action."

Ali realized that what they had done was wrong, a criminal act that could carry severe consequences. He wished he could walk away from Ismail and his gang, but he couldn't without risking serious reprisals. He was hooked on the fun, the money, the nice clothes, and especially the sex. Soon he became a full-fledged member of the gang, participating actively in many robberies and enjoying the high life.

One night they robbed a large department store in central Baghdad. While they were loading the stolen goods onto a truck, they were surprised by police detectives who had set a trap for them. Some of the boys were able to get away, but Ismail, Fuad, Ali, and two other gang members were caught red-handed. They were handcuffed, kicked, punched by the police officers, and taken to the police station for questioning. There they were thrown into separate cells in a dark dungeon, stripped down to their underwear, and shackled with chains.

The following day Ali was dragged from his cell for interrogation. He was hung by his wrists for hours until two police investigators arrived to question him and the others. They kicked and punched him, tossed insults and slurs at him, and lashed his bare body with their belts. They demanded that he admit to crimes, reveal the identities of the rest of the gang members, and give them details of all the robberies in which they had been involved.

When the interrogators were not satisfied that

he was cooperating, the torture intensified, and they started burning his skin with cigarettes and irons. He was tortured for three days and three nights. They gave him little water and no food. He had no sleep. Finally, he broke down, told them everything they wanted, and signed a confession.

Ali was sentenced to five years in jail. He had just turned sixteen, which meant that he would go to an adult jail that held hardened thieves and murderers from all over Baghdad.

His mother was devastated. Everything she worked for so hard all her life to secure a better future for him had been in vain. He had turned into a thief, a criminal, whose fate was sealed.

"Once you get into one of those jails, you're doomed," a policeman at the station told him. "You're going to be the sex slave of one of the jail lords. Those guys bribe the guards and rule the jail ruthlessly. You don't have a chance."

His mother in total desperation told her mistress, Mrs. Salima Sasson, all that had taken place. Mrs. Sasson told her husband, who said he would look into it. He just wanted to know two simple things: where Ali was detained and who had been the presiding judge.

The day Ali was to be taken from the police station to jail, he was called before the judge again. The judge announced that due to his cooperation with the police and his assistance in convicting other gang members, he had been granted amnesty and was free to go home. Ali couldn't believe what he was hearing. One minute his life was ruined forever, and the next he was free as a bird. He ran home without questioning the judge's decision.

When his mother came home that evening, she was astonished to see him. "How did you get out, ebni?" she asked between hugs and kisses.

"I have no idea, ummi. It was a miracle. One moment I was going to *jehanem,* and the next thing I knew, the judge called me and told me I was free to go. Bless Allah's name. He has his ways of working wonders for a righteous woman like you. I am a sinner, and I don't deserve to be saved. Allah did this for you, ummi, not for me. I didn't think I would ever see your gracious, loving face again, or get out of that jail alive. Once you are in there, you are as good as dead."

* * * *

When Jamila Samara came home the next day, she told her son that Abu Reuben had asked that he come see him. Ali was scared of Abu Reuben, an influential businessperson who knew all the important people in Baghdad. Why would Abu Reuben want to see him? Was Ali in trouble again?

The next morning, Ali went to the Sasson mansion with his mother and was quickly ushered into Mr. Sasson's study. Mr. Sasson was sitting on a high back, leather-upholstered chair reading the morning papers spread over a fine-looking, polished, mahogany desk.

"Sit down, Ali," he began. "You and I need to have a man-to-man talk about you and your future. You know that your mother has been working for us for over fifteen years. She has been very loyal to my wife and has taken excellent care of Reuben since he was born. We consider her as close as family, and we very much care about her and her family. We have always welcomed you to our house as a guest, and my wife has told me that you have been very helpful playing with Reuben and serving food at our house parties."

Mr. Sasson paused for a minute, looking at Ali with his piercing, hawk eyes.

"Ali, I am very disturbed by the recent events in which you were involved. Your behavior has brought a lot of pain to your mother, who has been trying so hard to secure a bright future for you. Since the untimely death of your father, she has had to work very hard to make ends meet and support your needs. She trusted your judgment, and you have disappointed both her and me. Do you think this is what she deserves in return?"

Mr. Sasson's loud voice seemed irritated, which scared Ali even more. "Please forgive my sins, Abu Reuben," he mumbled in desperation.

Mr. Sasson paused for a moment to calm his nerves and sip from a glass of chilled water resting on his desk.

"Ali, very few people in this world get a second chance in life," he resumed his rebuke. "You are one of the fortunate ones. Now I have a question for you — do you want to be a thief, a criminal preying on society all your life, or do you think there are better ways to live your life and become a productive member of this great nation that brought the wisdom of Abraham into this world?"

Ali started stuttering. "I am very sorry to cause so

much trouble for my mother and you, Abu Reuben. I learned my lesson; I will never do those things again. I don't want to be tortured by the police or end up abused and dying in jail, a disgrace to my family. My mother deserves better than that. I am ashamed of what I did and the humiliation I brought onto my family. I promise you that I will stay away from the friends who coerced me into this trouble and focus on my studies in school."

Mr. Sasson seemed more at ease now that he had heard Ali's response.

"What you just said sounds much better," he continued. "However, it's much easier talking about something than doing it consistently. This is the real test of your life, Ali. You must change your ways and be determined in your desire to improve your education and skills so that you can become a successful and productive member of society. There are not going to be any more chances or pardons. This is your last opportunity to make something of yourself and be a source of pride for your mother.

"I would like to tell you something my grandfather taught me when I was your age, and I hope you will remember it and use it as your guiding principle for the rest of your life. Everything we want to build in our lives needs to have a solid and strong foundation, whether it is our education, our home, our family, our job, or our business. Without a solid foundation, built by arduous labor, determination, and strong willpower, the first desert wind will blow everything we built into the wilderness, and we will have nothing left.

"The same thing applies to you. Good education achieved with honesty, hard work, and dedication is the foundation for your success in life and a bright future. Without this solid foundation, you will struggle all of your life, like a nomad without a home. Is that the kind of life you want for yourself, your future wife, and your children, Ali?"

"Allah forbid, Your Excellency, Abu Reuben," Ali replied in awe. "From now on, I will do only what you say, and I will listen only to you and my mother and to no one else. I want to succeed in life."

"I will grant your wish, Ali, but this will be your final chance. If you fail, I will not be able to help you ever again. You will have to deal with the consequences on your own.

"I am going to move you and your mother to a new home in a better neighborhood away from the influence and possible vengeance of your misguided friends. I will register you in a new school where my friend is the principal. He will keep a close eye on you, help you get adjusted, and keep me informed of your progress. "

"Thank you a thousand times, Abu Reuben." Ali stood up and kissed Mr. Sasson's hand in gratitude.

"You are my redeemer. I will never forget your generosity and wisdom, and I will study very hard to make you and my mother proud of my accomplishments. I don't know how I can ever repay your kindness, but I hope that one day I will."

* * * *

The following week Jamila and Ali moved to a new

house in a middle-class neighborhood close to Ali's new school. It was nicely furnished and spacious. Ali had a quiet, private bedroom where he could study and do his homework.

Ali loved the new school. It was clean, well organized and had great teachers. The children were very well behaved, which was something Ali wasn't used to. The principal took Ali under his wing and helped him adjust to the rigorous curriculum. Ali came home from school every day and studied diligently to try to catch up with his bright classmates.

After several months, his hard work paid off. He started earning the respect of his teachers and fellow students who had not been so welcoming in the beginning. He was able to befriend some of his new classmates, socialize with them, and see an entire new world that turned his life around.

CHAPTER 3

BAGHDAD, 1952

The streets of Baghdad overflowed with jubilant, festive crowds with car horns blowing, coachmen urging their horses on with long bamboo whips, and street vendors announcing their great bargains. People dressed in holiday clothing crowded the streets and sidewalks leading to Bab-el-Mu'athem, the city's central square. Old, young, families, and passersby — all gathered for the big event.

Sounds of hammering and sawing filled the air. A construction crew was putting the finishing touches on a large wooden stage located in the square's center. In the middle of the stage, two tall wooden poles and a sturdy cross bar had been erected. The crowds, filling the square to its capacity, waited eagerly for the show to begin. Within minutes, two heavy-set, muscular men wearing black *kafiyas* over their heads walked onto the stage and attached two braided ropes to the thick cross bar.

The crowd cheered the two men, chanting in steady, piercing voices:

"Hang the Zionist traitors!"

"Slaughter the conspirators!"

"Slay the infidels!"

"Alaahu-Akbar, Alaahu-Akbar." God is great! God is great!

The crowd started singing Iraqi national songs, stomping their feet steadily on the ground and swaying from side to side. Fathers hoisted young children onto their shoulders to get a clear view of the unfolding scene.

Only a few blocks away at the notorious Abu Greib jail, two men were being readied for their final journey. Just a few hours earlier, they had been convicted of treason against the Iraqi government and its people after being accused of three bombing incidents in Baghdad during the past year — incidents in which they vehemently denied any part. However, after enduring many days and nights of torture by the brutal Iraqi secret service, they'd been promised their passports and a quick deportation to Israel if they signed a so-called confession. That promise was never kept: their fate had been sealed by an order from the high echelons. The Iraqi leadership had to give the public answers to the unresolved bombings. The Iraqi secret service needed to cover up its failure to identify and arrest the leadership of the Jewish underground movement, which was working diligently to help Jews flee Iraq into their newly formed, independent state of Israel.

All last minute efforts to save them in return for a

heavy ransom for their release failed. They had to pay with their lives for the freedom of thousands of their fellow people who had left Iraq by choice, abandoning most of their possessions behind. Most had emigrated to the young state of Israel during the past twelve months. As the two men believed the cause worthwhile, death seemed a small price to pay for the freedom of so many.

The tiny death-row cell could barely accommodate the two inmates. Its dingy, peeling walls cast threatening dark shadows on the men hunched over in the corners of the cell. Their ankles were shackled with heavy chains permitting only minimal movement, while their arms were wrapped in chains attached to a metal rod to prevent them from attempting suicide.

Rumors had been circulating inside the jail walls that their execution was nearing. The sounds of hammering and sawing in the nearby square confirmed them.

At 9 a.m., a group of officials marched towards their cell. The heavy door was unlocked and opened to the sound of creaking metal. The stench of urine blended with mildew radiated from the dusky cell and overwhelmed the officials. Unaffected by the distinct odor, the jail master entered the cell and removed the chains. Then he provided the men with water to wash their hands and faces and head covers for reciting their last prayer. Their final request was that their bodies be reunited with their families in the Holy Land.

The only rabbi left in Baghdad after the exodus was there to prepare them for their final journey. He brought them messages from their loved ones and read them comforting excerpts from the Book of Psalms.

"Though I walk through the valley of the shadow of death, I fear no harm, for You are with me. Your rod and Your staff, they will comfort me," the rabbi's voice reverberated throughout the jail walls.

It was time for the men to perform their final prayer according to the laws of Moses. The rabbi handed them his prayer book. They stood tall, heads raised, reciting together:

"Hear, O Israel, the Lord our God, the Lord is one."

Their final words echoed loudly in the dark cell, sending shudders through the rest of the inmates still awaiting their fates.

Upon hearing the word "Israel," the jail master stared at the two men with piercing anger. He brushed his forefinger across his throat indicating what awaited them. Alarmed by the threatening gesture, the rabbi apologized, saying that the word was simply part of the prayer.

It was time to go. The jailers wrapped the inmates' bodies tightly in long, thin leather straps and covered their heads with black sacks. Dressed in the traditional death-row brown jumpsuits, they walked proudly to their final destination.

Accompanied by the cheers and screams of the crowd who filled every inch of the square, the hangmen escorted them to the wooden structure in the center of the stage. Bowing gracefully to the crowds, they positioned the two men under the dangling ropes and stood next to them.

An official wearing a long black robe stepped onto the stage and read aloud the verdict against the two inmates.

"For crimes of treason against our beloved country, Iraq, Daniel Sasson and Daud Selman were convicted of their transgressions by the high court of the Iraqi justice council and are hereby sentenced to death by hanging until their souls depart from their bodies."

"Death to the Zionist dogs!"

"Kill the traitors!"

"Alaahu-Akbar, Alaahu-Akbar."

The crowds chanted raucously.

The hangmen sprang into action, carefully examining the necks of the condemned men as if they were cows in a slaughterhouse. They slipped the thick ropes over the men's heads with meticulous motions, constricting them in a tight grip around their necks. Finally, they secured two heavy weights on the men's ankles.

The official in the black robe gave the signal.

In their final seconds, as if by a sign from above, the two men screamed at the top of their lungs with a sudden burst of energy, *"Tehyii Eisraeel!"* — long live the state of Israel.

The trapdoors released with a loud snap, and the weights dropped swiftly, dragging the two men with them. The ropes stretched under the heavy load, squeaking distinctly, and the sturdy wooden crossbar crackled with tension as the two bodies slammed to a sudden halt in midair.

They fluttered momentarily in the bright scorching sun of a typical summer morning in Baghdad. Then they rested motionless as the spirits of the two men soared into the tranquility of the vast Heavens.

The crowds roared with exhilaration.

"Long live the King."

"Long live the Iraqi nation."

"Long live the Iraqi People."

The singing and dancing in the streets of Baghdad lasted until dusk.

* * * *

The two bodies were left on display until the late hours of the night for the enjoyment of more crowds making their way to the center square from all over town. At 10 p.m., the crowds finally dispersed into the narrow alleys, and calm returned to the city. The two bodies were removed and turned over to the local synagogue for burial.

CHAPTER 4

Her husband's execution for treason left Salima Sasson totally devastated, banished, and isolated in a hostile land.

All her relatives had gone from Iraq in the preceding months, but she had refused to leave her beloved husband's side until his trial was over and his fate known. She'd hired a prominent criminal lawyer to defend Daniel, but his otherwise persuasive arguments were ignored by the judges who had to comply with strict orders from high above. Knowing Daniel was innocent, she had hoped for a last-minute miracle that would set him free. She'd pleaded relentlessly with the remaining community leaders to use their connections with high-ranking Iraqi officials and had paid large sums of money to try to commute her husband's sentence, but to no avail.

She'd heard the horrific news of her husband's sentence announced on the official Iraqi radio the previous night. Before long, the Iraqi secret police would be knocking at her door to apprehend her and her young son, so she'd decided to flee before it was too late. She woke her seven-year-old son, Reuben, and left her house in great hurry.

The world was collapsing on her. Who could she turn to at this terrible time? The Iraqi government had confiscated all the family wealth and property. The remaining Jewish community in Baghdad was only a shadow of the well-oiled machine, the sophisticated society that had flourished in Babylon for almost 2,500 years. Her mere presence could put her people at high risk of retaliation from the Iraqi government, and she didn't wish to inflict additional pain on a community that had been subjected to so much oppression and suffering in the past decade.

Walking aimlessly in the streets of Baghdad like a homeless beggar, she felt a strong sense of despair and helplessness. She glanced at her young boy, who seemed oblivious to the turn of events that was going to change his life forever. He looked up at her and asked, "When are we going home, Mama? Where is Babba? Why isn't he coming to get us now?"

"Don't worry, *galbi,* my heart. Mama will take care of you," she comforted him with her soft voice.

It was past 1 p.m., and the sight of her weary young son invoked her motherly instincts to shake off her desperation and focus on the immediate need to provide him with food and shelter. Her mind was probing for possible solutions to her pressing problem. Jamila, her loyal maid of more than twenty-five years, was first to come to mind.

When Salima was a young girl, Jamila had worked in

her home helping Salima's mother with housework and taking care of her children. Jamila had taken a special interest in Salima, the oldest daughter. She tailored beautiful dresses for the growing Salima, helped her dress up, and put on her makeup when she was invited to special events. Jamila had always been there to give Salima sound advice on boys and the facts of life. They'd conversed frequently, developing a close, trusted relationship that solidified with time.

When Salima married, she asked her mother if she could hire Jamila herself. Reluctant to give up the talented woman, her mother agreed, for she realized her daughter would need Jamila's help to face the challenges of starting a new family.

Jamila worked diligently, prepared delicious meals daily, and managed the Sasson household affairs with skill and efficiency. After Reuben was born, she had helped Salima take care of him like a second mother. Salima and her husband, Daniel treated Jamila generously, always praising her immense talents, dedication, and wisdom. When tragedy stuck and Jamila's husband died unexpectedly of a heart attack, they'd taken it upon themselves to provide for Jamila's family, including Ali, her son.

Jamila lived in Waziriya, a Moslem suburb of Baghdad. Although Jamila was her only hope, Salima wondered if she actually could help her through this misfortune. After all, Jamila couldn't even come to work lately because she was in fear for her life. Any association with the accused could prove detrimental. Nonetheless, Salima covered her head and face with a large *abaya,* took her son by the hand, and started marching briskly toward Jamila's neighborhood.

They walked through Rashid Street at the heart of Baghdad's commercial district, overflowing with businesspeople rushing about in light suits and ties. Sharply dressed waiters stood outside the famous restaurants along the busy street, tempting passersby with trays of exotic Middle Eastern dishes, and inviting them to enjoy the delicious meals and exciting entertainment offered inside. From the street could be heard the swirling music of an orchestra and the roar of the crowds applauding belly dancers bopping on stage and clapping their bells. The smoky aroma of barbecued meats and spices filled the air, arousing Reuben's appetite.

He wished they could just walk into one of these restaurants and fill his hollow belly. He noticed a patron sitting by an open window and being served a large plate of steaming lamb kebabs soaked in peppery spices. The man took his time wrapping the kebabs in warm pita bread, topping it with chopped garden salad, and pouring thick white tahini sauce on top. He then sank his teeth into the soft, delicious creation. Reuben's mouth was watering, and he could barely refrain from sharing his agony with his mother as she picked up her stride to clear the busy street.

Reuben was relieved when they reached the end of the street and started walking down the narrow winding alleys that led to the open markets of eastern Baghdad. When they entered the market, the entire scenery transformed dramatically. Wide, gleaming streets turned into winding, semi-paved pathways, fine stores turned into shabby-looking vendor stands, and western-style dress suits turned into plain cloth *dishdashas,* long robes, and black head coverings.

The market was very busy with women shopping for various foods, bargaining with the vendors, and making their final deals so they could get home in time to cook the evening meal. Reuben was enamored with the displays of shiny fruits of all colors and shapes arranged artfully on store counters. Miraculously, these displays survived intense handling by fussy shoppers, never rolling off the shallow wooden counters. Vegetable stands reflected all shades of the rainbow in mystifying silhouettes he had never witnessed before.

Soon they passed through a section of the market filled with the distinct scent of bountiful spice displays. Pungent spices in an assortment of shapes and earthen colors were packed in large brown cloth sacks lined in perfect rows. Reuben paused to inhale a deep breath of the intoxicating aroma that seemed to soothe his hunger for a few precious minutes.

As they walked deeper into the market, the noise caused by hammering and blowtorches intensified. Artisans in this new section were standing inside their shops in front of the flickering fires forming beautifully decorated trays and coffee sets that had distinctive, curved Middle Eastern designs. Their assistants stood in the doorways, attempting to lure the next buyer with freshly made cups of dark coffee that had a sweet, inviting tang.

Because Reuben had never experienced the market before, he was fascinated by everything: the excited voices of the street vendors, the diverse crowds of people marching up and down the narrow alleys, the colorful, traditional clothing worn by women shoppers, and the variety of merchandise filling vendor stands.

When they reached the end of the market, Salima asked for directions to a certain street. It was getting late in the afternoon, and the activity in the market was winding down. They walked out of the market and into a wider street of a relatively new neighborhood. Breathless, and with his feet dragging along the black asphalt, Reuben called in a frail voice, "Are we there yet, Mama?"

Salima paused until he reached her. Grabbing his arm firmly, she said, "We are almost there, galbi. Very soon Jamila will treat you to some of your favorite foods."

They finally arrived at an enclosed circular court that had several semi-detached cottages scattered around it. Salima recognized Jamila's house from the numerous times she and her driver had driven Jamila home after a hard day's work. It was dark already. Salima looked around, and then gently tapped on the door, which opened momentarily. Jamila didn't seem to recognize the heavily covered woman or notice the little boy hiding behind her.

"It's me, Salima," she whispered, uncovering part of her face.

Looking distraught, Jamila pulled them into the house. At the sight of her, Reuben sprang into her arms. Jamila hugged and kissed him, surrounding him safely with her comforting arms just as she had done when he was a baby.

"Did anyone see you coming?" she inquired.

"No," Salima responded. "I waited until it got dark. Nobody was around, and I was fully covered with my abaya so no one could recognize me."

"Thank Allah for that," Jamila responded. "They will slaughter all of us if they find you here." Jamila looked frazzled. Worry lines flooded her narrow, aging face. Her long black hair streaked in white was in disarray as if someone had been pulling on it, and her bloodshot, light green eyes gave the impression she hadn't slept for several nights.

"I was frightened to come to your house the last few days not knowing what would happen to Abu Reuben," she said apologetically. "I have been crying all day for him and you. You are my family, and I love Reuben just as I love my own son. I will never turn you away, but please understand my place is too dangerous for us. It won't take the neighbors long to suspect that you are here. The police may have already placed detectives to watch us. We need to think quickly of a way to find a safe place for you and Reuben.

"Abu Reuben was a wonderful, generous man. He always found time to make sure my son had a superb education and a good paying job. Why did they have to pick on him? They are returning Iraq to the dark ages, *'insha'allah ismuhum yinmihee min hay il arth,'* may their names be erased from this earth."

"Please sit down and rest for a while," Jamila continued, realizing how exhausted her visitors must be. "I will bring you and Reuben something to eat and drink."

"Thank you a hundred times," Salima murmured gratefully. "I don't know what I would do without your help."

Jamila quickly closed the shutters and disappeared into the kitchen.

Salima sat on the comfortable sofa in the living room with Reuben stretched out next to her. She looked around the room decorated tastefully with traditional furnishings and familiar-looking accessories. Salima recalled that every time she'd had her mansion redecorated, she'd had her old furnishings delivered to Jamila's house. A large family portrait decorated the wall opposite the sofa. The vivid images of Jamila, her late husband Salim, and young Ali looked as if they had been taken only a week earlier.

After a short while, Jamila returned with a steaming pot of mint tea and a plateful of circular sesame crackers and round cookies filled with sweet dates. She placed them on the coffee table in front of her guests. Reuben dove into the plate and started wolfing down the cookies. Jamila had baked them often at their house, and he always followed her around begging, "More cookies, Jamila. More cookies, please, please."

Jamila went back to the kitchen and returned carrying a large glass filled with lemonade. "The poor little boy is starving. He must have had nothing to eat or drink the whole day," she said placing the glass in front of Reuben. "Come, euni, rest on my bed upstairs. You look very tired." Jamila patted his head and kissed his forehead. "Your mom and I have important work to do."

With Reuben tucked safely in the upstairs bedroom, Jamila quickly explained her ideas to Salima. "My son, Ali, has been scouting the old Jewish neighborhoods vacated during the mass exodus from Baghdad. Most families had to leave their belongings behind as well as their property, and my son purchased many such things from their owners at a very low price. He has been taking these furnishings and selling them in the flea market to try to make a living. Many Palestinian refugee families who fled Palestine because of the war are now moving into these empty neighborhoods. I will ask Ali to try to find a place for you for the time being. I am sorry, Salima, but there aren't many choices. You will need to pretend that you are one of them for a while in order not to raise suspicion. When things settle down, we will try to find you a better place."

Salima was grateful. As long as she had shelter for Reuben, she was willing to suffer through anything. They could live in hiding until the right opportunity came along, and they could both leave for their true homeland.

"I am going to see Ali now to let him know what needs to be done," Jamila told Salima. "I will lock the door from the outside so nobody can get in. Please don't answer the door for anybody until I return."

"Thank you, Jamila. I will be forever indebted to you for saving us," Salima whispered as Jamila's shadow vanished into the dark night.

Jamila returned after two hours. "I explained everything to Ali," she told Salima in a breathless voice. "He will try to find a place for you within a few days, but for the time being, you and Reuben will have to stay inside the house."

CHAPTER 5

Several days later, Ali came to fetch them after sunset. He greeted Salima warmly and lifted Reuben, twirling him up in the air just like old times when he'd accompanied his mother to their house.

"I found a friendly place with young children who can play with Reuben," he informed Salima. "Both of you will have to pretend you are refugees from Palestine. Your husband was killed fighting the holy war to drive the Zionists out of Palestine. Fearing for your lives, you escaped with your son and came to Baghdad. You heard that Iraq was welcoming Palestinian refugees and helping them settle down in properties Jews left behind.

"I came up with new names for you and Reuben," Ali continued, handing Salima two brand new identity cards. "A friend of mine who works at the Ministry of the Interior owed me a big favor. Your new names have been recorded with the Ministry as refugees from Palestine. Please memorize your new names and practice with Reuben until he responds only to his new one."

Salima nodded in agreement, not uttering a word.

They followed Ali down dark, winding alleys for almost an hour before entering a small courtyard with a few shacks scattered around it.

"This is it," Ali said, pointing to one of the shacks. "This is your new home for now. It has an iron door with a bolt to protect you at night from the infamous thieves of Baghdad."

They entered the shack, which held one large room with peeling, yellowish walls. In one corner was a small kitchen with an open-fire stove, the walls blackened all around it. Scattered on the stove were a few pots, pans, and dishes that had known better days. In the other corner of the room stood a wide wooden bed with an old straw mattress and two blankets. A small rectangular wobbly table and two chairs stood in the middle of the room.

"I tried to get as much stuff as I could with short notice." Ali sounded apologetic. "I will see what else I can get you tomorrow."

"Thank you a hundred times," Salima exclaimed. "You gave us more than I expected. Reuben and I have shelter now, and we don't have to wander the streets. Allah will bless your soul and reward your generosity."

"The communal bathrooms and washrooms are outdoors on the far right side of the court," Ali pointed out as he was leaving.

* * * *

Salima woke Reuben first thing in the morning and said to him in her soft, gentle voice, "I have to talk to you, ebni, to explain how our life has changed in the last few days, and how you must behave from now on to help me keep bad things away from to us.

A very bad king is ruling our country now. The evil king ordered his soldiers to take Babba away from us, and we will not see him for a very long time. Babba will not be able to help us as he always did, so we have to be brave and do many things on our own. I tried very hard to bring Babba back home, but the bad king was very angry and did not want to let him go. Reuben, you are a very clever boy. You must listen to what I say very carefully and do as I tell you."

Reuben looked dumbstruck, peering at his mother in disbelief.

"I will listen to you, Mama," he said in a fragile tone, "but I really want Babba to come home now. I miss him so much already. Can I go to the king and ask him myself? Maybe he will let Babba go."

"Perhaps I can take you some other day, galbi, but I must first teach you what to do. We will be living here until Ali can find another place for us. The people and children who live here are from a faraway country called Palestine. They speak a little differently from us. You have to pretend that we are from their country. You must learn to speak like them, play like them, and behave like them. It will be a new game for you, a pretend game. Do not tell them where we lived before because we are from Palestine, right galbi? This will be our secret — just you and I will know about it.

"Your new name is Aziz, Aziz Al-Wasphi, and my name is Farida Jafari. You must forget that your name was Reuben and that mine was Salima. We will practice our new names until we forget our old ones. This will be part of our pretend game.

"Please be very careful not to make any mistakes, ebni. If you make a mistake, something bad can happen to us, but if you are very good with this game, I will give you a prize every week."

The stuffy air inside the small shack grew unbearable. Salima paused briefly and wiped her perspiring face with an old towel left on the shaky kitchen table. She wanted to finish her private conversation with her son before opening the door to let in some fresh air.

"We ran away from Palestine because of a bad war that hurt many people," Salima continued. "The war took away your father, and that is why he is not here."

Reuben started weeping pitifully. In between loud sobs, he managed to mutter, "Please take me home, Mama, I don't like this place. I want to play in my room with my toys and wait for Babba to come play with me. Please Mama..."

Salima held back her turbulent emotions, trying hard to be a symbol of strength for her son. She stroked his head with both hands and kissed him gently.

"One day you will become a very important leader, you will see," she added in a reassuring tone. "The Almighty will guide your every step from the heavens and bless you with courage and wisdom."

The child's sobbing faded gradually, and with renewed determination, he looked at his mother with his glistening, dark brown eyes.

"I will do as you say, Mama. I like your pretend game. It will be our secret, but I will never forget Babba.

I want to be just like him when I grow up."

* * * *

At first, Aziz was very unsure of how to play his mother's game. The Arabic spoken by the kids in the court sounded strange to him, and he found it difficult to break into the already existing friendships among the boys. One morning he noticed that a soccer game was about to begin in the courtyard and decided to join in. After scoring the first two goals, he started earning the respect of the boys who ran to shake his hand and congratulate him.

After his initial encounter, young Aziz quickly adapted to his new name and environment. He came up with all sorts of street games and contests to keep the other boys playing in the courtyard, and away from their tiny homes. He went from house to house gathering his friends and organizing teams to challenge neighboring teams.

Within several months, Aziz became the leader of the children in the courtyard. He developed natural leadership skills that drew the children to follow him around and imitate his actions. Over time, he got used to their accent, which he imitated naturally. Salima kept a low profile, staying mostly at home until she could adjust to the new conditions and learn the accent from Aziz.

The food and clothes Jamila gave them lasted only a short time. Salima walked to a jewelry shop in the center of Baghdad, where after a long bargaining process, she exchanged the ring her husband had given her on their engagement night for a hundred dinars. She headed to the market and bought food and clothing. This money would last them several months at their meager consumption rate and new standard of living.

Aziz developed close friendships with two boys, Ahmed and Chaled, both around his age. Ahmed was from a village called Tarshiha in northern Galilee, and Chaled was from Akka, a town on the northern coast of the Mediterranean. They loved playing soccer using a ball made out of a bundle of old rags sewn by Salima into a sphere. Two rocks were placed at the opposite ends of the courtyard, children were rounded up from the court and its surrounding areas, and an exciting game was in full swing every afternoon.

Ahmed and Chaled played on the same team with Aziz. They soon became the Three Musketeers of the neighborhood. They were fast and sneaky and quickly improved their skills with the help of Chaled's brother, who had played soccer in his hometown. Aziz's team was unbeaten in the entire neighborhood. They were becoming so good that the adults started coming out to enjoy their games every afternoon.

Aziz and his friends played outside from morning to dusk. They took a little lunch break in the middle of the day and had to be dragged home to their shacks at nightfall.

Salima noticed that Aziz was having the summer of his life, free of adult supervision, roaming around with his friends all day long, and feeling like a full-fledged member of the gang. Occasionally, she had to remind him who he really was and who were the friends with whom he was playing.

"Don't worry, Mama," he placated her in a confident, gentle voice. "I am just playing the game you taught me. I know the rules, and I am having fun while I can. I think it's better than sitting at home all day in our sweaty room and driving you crazy, right, Mama?"

"Sure, galbi." She gave him a loving hug and a few kisses on his head. "Go have fun, my little angel," she said as she sent him back out to play, tears rolling off her cheeks, not believing how much he had matured in just a few months.

Jamila came to visit once a week bringing some of her delicious baked cookies, their favorite *Kebba* dinners, and seasoned rice dishes. Jamila's visits turned out to be their weekly feast, for Salima, who had once had a fully staffed kitchen hadn't ever really learned to cook, and the foods she prepared were basic and bland.

Jamila educated Salima on Islamic customs, religion, and prayers so that she would be able to function somewhat in the new environment and not look like a total outsider who might raise the neighbors' suspicions. They spent time together chatting and socializing just like their old times at the home of Salima's parents. Salima treasured the times she had with Jamila, her only contact with the outside world.

Summer was winding down, and soon the local Palestinian community started organizing itself to help take care of the myriad of Palestinian families living in Baghdad. They found jobs for the men, set up temporary schools for the children, converted an old synagogue into a mosque, and tried to rebuild their lives in a new country.

Because all children had to go to school by the order of the Iraqi Ministry of Education, Salima had to register Aziz.

Aziz was in second grade with his two friends and close to thirty other children. They occupied an old Jewish school that had probably existed for hundreds of years, but was still in reasonable shape after a few renovations. Classrooms were furnished with wooden tables and chairs, and the teacher distributed books to every pupil in the class. They studied Classic Arabic, the Qur'an, and history of Islam along with basic math, English, and geography. Their gifted teacher had been an elementary school headmaster in Palestine. Aziz, very eager to learn, absorbed everything, including reading, writing, and speaking Classic and Palestinian Arabic. Soon he'd started reading the Qur'an.

Aziz also had to go to the local mosque for daily prayers. The first time he went there, he walked around hesitantly, not sure of the customs and prayer routines. Despite the basic instructions Jamila had given him on Islamic prayer, he felt insecure about the way he needed to conduct himself in this new, unfamiliar environment.

He followed Ahmed, closely imitating his actions as accurately as he could. When they arrived at the mosque, Ahmed took off his shoes and washed his feet and ankles and then his hands and arms up to his elbows. He splashed water on his face, rubbed it over his ears, mouth and nostrils, and entered the main prayer hall with Aziz following close behind.

Male worshipers, perfectly lined up in rows about one yard apart, crowded the spacious hall. Aziz stood between Ahmed and Chaled, glancing constantly for clues on what to do next. He emulated the behavior of the people around him and kept a low profile to minimize attention to his inexperienced motions during prayers.

During each prayer, worshipers followed a sequence of actions — standing, bowing, kneeling, and prostrating themselves with their foreheads touching the mosque floor. At the beginning of the prayer, they recited the verse "Allah-Hu-Akbar." God is great, and at the end "Salaam-U-Aleikum," May peace be with you.

When Aziz leaned his forehead down onto the carpeted floor, he noticed it was touching a large Persian rug of rare beauty. Fascinated by the rug's mysterious geometric patterns closely woven in red, blue, and cream, he imagined following a path in one of the rug patterns into a magnificent Sultan's Palace where servants dressed in colorful satin outfits served lavish trays of scrumptious dishes and passion fruits to the Sultan and his dignitaries. When he had been a little boy, he had sat on a sofa in the large guest room of his parents' home, gazing at the beautiful Persian rug on the wall opposite him and taking an imaginary ride into the maze of neverlands hidden in its fascinating designs.

The voice of the Imam reciting the prayers brought Aziz back to reality. He repeated the prayer quickly and stood up with the rest of the worshipers. He glanced the interior of the elaborate mosque, surrounded by tall white walls that arched upwards toward the center of the structure. In the middle of the ceiling was a large dome surrounded by four smaller domes, one on each side. The domes were decorated with shiny gold-plated linings engraved by calligraphic floral writings from the Qur'an.

Toward the front, he noticed a niche in the wall of the mosque with its top shaped like a cross section of a dome ornamented by fine looking calligraphic and geometric designs. The inner portion of the dome was lined in silver with writings from the Qur'an. Next to the niche was a pulpit where the Imam stood and led the prayers. Aziz remembered reading in one of his textbooks that the niche designated the direction of the holy city of Mecca because the worshipers had to face Mecca while praying.

In the back of the mosque, he saw an enclosed section separated by a four-foot high white wall draped with opaque linens. Behind the linens, shadows of women with long head covers moved about in silence. Aziz recalled that when he had gone to the synagogue with his parents during High Holidays, his mother attended the services in the women's section while he followed his father into the main sanctuary where the men prayed.

During one of the prayer sequences, Aziz was so mesmerized by the rays of sunlight seeping through the arched high ceilings that he neglected to follow the kneeling routine. A bearded cleric in a long black robe motioned toward him frantically, pointing to the floor. Ahmed grabbed his arm tightly, pulling him down. "Put your forehead on the floor quickly, or you will be thrown out," he whispered in distress. To the relief of the fuming cleric, Aziz quickly knelt next to Ahmed and placed his forehead on the floor.

"You have to be very careful, Aziz," Ahmed warned him on their way home. "The mosque is holy, and being disrespectful will bring sins on your soul. If the Imam catches you not kneeling again, he will punish you badly."

"My family rarely attended mosque in our hometown, so I am not familiar with all the customs," Aziz explained remorsefully. "I learned my lesson today. It will not happen again."

After the embarrassing incident in the mosque, Aziz decided to learn the prayers diligently until they became second nature to him. He didn't want anyone to suspect he wasn't Moslem. He started reading the Qur'an at every opportunity, including taking it home at night until he became very knowledgeable of the prayers and text. His teacher noticed his eagerness to learn and called upon him frequently to interpret verses and explain their meanings.

* * * *

One day Aziz came home from mosque after Friday noon services and found his mother sitting on the floor in a corner of the room. With her back arched and head slumped between her knees, she was weeping uncontrollably. Aziz rushed to her side. With his arms around her quivering shoulders, he asked, "What's wrong, Mama? Why are you so sad? Have I done anything to hurt you?"

Salima lifted her pale, thinning face, tears streaming

down her chin onto her crumpled dress. Her red eyes peered at him apprehensively. "I can't stand it any more, galbi, you in that mosque praying and kneeling down with all these people. It breaks my heart just thinking about it."

"Please don't be sad, Mama," Aziz comforted her. "Now I pretend so well that everybody is sure we are from Palestine. I like your game. It's fun for me to trick everybody like that. I think you owe me a lot of prizes. Mama, remember, you promised."

Salima's expression transformed into a faint smile. "Yes, galbi, you are becoming very good at this game. I am going to go to the market next week and buy you many new prizes."

* * * *

Salima felt she had to do something to preserve her son's faith and her sanity. She had secretly hidden a Jewish prayer book and a Bible under the bed. She started teaching Aziz the Hebrew alphabet along with basic prayers and the Bible. Every night they spent an hour studying and reading. Aziz was very intrigued by the stories they read and was eager to learn more about his ancient history.

At times, the preaching from the Imam at the mosque and the Bible stories his mother taught him confused young Aziz. One night when his mother was telling him the story of the Israelites' exodus from Egypt and the powerful miracles God performed to save them from Pharaoh's slavery, Aziz turned to her. "Mama, surely our Almighty God is much stronger than the Allah everybody prays and bows to in the mosque. They keep saying, 'Allah is great, and there is no other Allah than their Allah.' Sometimes it gets very scary the way the Imam speaks about the nonbelievers and how Allah will punish them harshly for their bad sins. Do you think our God will save us from them if they find out who we are and try to hurt us?"

Salima was speechless for a few moments.

"You see, galbi," she explained after regaining her composure. "The truth is that our God and their Allah are the same. We share the same God, because we are all the children of Abraham. We just have a different way of calling and worshipping God than they do, but it's still the same Almighty God of the Heavens.

"Don't be troubled, ebni. Now you have both our Almighty God and their Great Allah to protect and guide you on your way to becoming a very important leader."

CHAPTER 6

BAGHDAD 1953

Several months flew by. Salima ran low on money. She wanted to preserve the value of her remaining jewelry to be able to pay for their future escape from Iraq. She remembered some of the stories she'd heard from people who were fleeing Iraq illegally. It was a long, arduous journey full of dangers, and the prices paid to smugglers were cost prohibitive.

She realized she would have to find a way to earn money to meet their needs, but as she had never had to face this problem in the past, she wasn't sure what to do.

Winter arrived, and the condition of their shack deteriorated. It was very cold. When it rained, water seeped in from a few leaky spots, and an unpleasant mildew filled the air. At night, loud coughing mingled with the sound of heavy rain pounding the tin roof of the shack. Salima suffered from a mild case of asthma, and the moisture aggravated her condition. Her asthma hadn't bothered her when she was living in her comfortable home, but lately it was becoming a problem, and she couldn't afford to see a doctor. She kept the stove burning all night to dry the air and provide some warmth in the small room.

During one of Jamila's visits while Aziz was still at school, Salima confided to Jamila her wish to escape from Iraq to Iran, where she could get help from the Jewish Agency to address her medical problems and arrange for Aziz and her to emigrate to Israel.

"It's a risky proposition, and I will need Ali's help to contact the right people and arrange for smuggling us out of Iraq."

Jamila looked at her pensively and spoke in an authoritative tone. "Salima, I have known you since you were a young girl. Your parents and husband always took care of all your needs. You enjoyed a very easy and luxurious life. I know it's very hard for you to deal with the bad times you are facing now, but for Aziz's sake, you must get rid of your helpless feelings and sadness. You need to get more involved with Aziz's life and the community, get out there more often, and do something about earning money. You were always very talented with sewing and embroidering. You could earn a decent living doing that.

"Your desire to leave Iraq is not possible right now. The government is demanding a heavy ransom of any resident who wants to leave Iraq, even for a short journey. You don't have the money to pay for that! You have to wait until Aziz gets older and save every *felce* for the day Allah will help you leave."

Pale, her voice quivering, Salima mumbled, "You are right, Jamila. I have been so miserable since Daniel died that I've paralyzed myself. I have to be stronger and more involved with Aziz's life. I promise you that I will start fighting my misfortune and work hard to prepare for the day when Allah will set us free, ensha'allah. Thank you for being honest. Your wise words always help me overcome my difficulties."

Encouraged by Jamila's words, Salima bought rolls of plain cloth in the market and started sewing embroidered tablecloths, bedding, and bedcovers. She ventured out to the upscale suburbs of Baghdad and offered her handicrafts to the merchants who appreciated the meticulous quality of her work and were willing to pay her decent prices.

She worked from home while Aziz was at school so she would be there for him when he returned to feed him and help him with his homework. Her work kept her occupied and distracted from the desperation of their poor living conditions while providing an income to take care of their needs.

* * * *

Another year went by. Aziz and his friends, Ahmed and Chaled, now in fifth grade, continued their close friendship. They started wandering out of their court and began engaging kids from nearby neighborhoods in games and competitions. Ahmed's older brother, who had trained in the martial arts, taught them the basic positions and moves of self-defense and offense. They practiced daily after school until they became fierce fighters.

They played a new game called seven stones. Seven fragments of cement floor tiles were trimmed and stacked in an open field. Ten yards away, one of the teams lined up on home base with three other bases evenly spread around in a diamond shape.

Each player had three chances to strike the stacked stones with a tennis ball and scatter them all around. After a hit, the player ran through the bases and attempted to return safely to home base to score a run. Runners could run the bases as long as the seven stones were not restored to their stacked position and the ball hadn't reached the opposing team's catcher before they reached a base. Runners could stop at any empty base for safety.

Opposing team members spread in the field around the bases to catch the ball after it hit the stones. A catcher positioned behind the stones had to try to block the ball after a hit, restack the seven stones, and catch the ball returned by the field players.

Aziz organized tournaments with neighboring teams and kept the games going until dusk. Ahmed, who was skinny, dark haired, dark skinned, and athletic, had great speed and agility, making him a great catcher. Chaled was taller, fair-skinned, light haired, and more solidly built, with tremendous arm strength. He threw the ball with lightning speed and accuracy that allowed their team to score many runs. Aziz played in the outer field where he utilized his superior fielding skills to organize defensive plays and hold their opponents at bay. They chased loose balls with gusto, leaping over wire fences, bushes and other obstacles and then throwing the balls quickly to Ahmed to minimize the runs scored by their opponents.

Soon Aziz's fame spread across the entire district. Kids came from distant neighborhoods to join in the games and competitions he had masterminded. At school, he was a bright student, well liked by his teachers and consistently earning high grades.

He became one of them, lived like them, spoke like them, played like them, and prayed like them. Nobody could imagine that he was a Jewish boy born to one of the wealthiest families in Baghdad.

* * * *

With Jamila's help and encouragement, Salima had gained more confidence in her language skills. She started going out of the sweaty shack, chatting with her neighbors and taking pride in the fame her son was gaining.

Still, she was anxious to leave Iraq. She was concerned that Aziz was becoming too comfortable in his environment and too close to his friends. Although Aziz was still reading prayers and studying the Bible with her every night and had agreed to go with her at the opportune time, it seemed the longer they waited, the harder it would be for him to separate himself from his comfortable environment. She decided it was time for her to do something about getting out of Iraq.

One evening, she ventured out to the old synagogue. She covered her head and face with a black abaya and went there in a roundabout way, checking periodically to see if anybody was following her. She timed her arrival at dusk to conceal her identity. She remembered that evening services were over around the same time and hoped she could see the rabbi.

As she entered the exterior gate, she noticed the synagogue and its surroundings were in a state of neglect. Wild weeds had sprung up all around the yard, and trees were growing wild with their fruit rotting on the ground. The outside walls were stained with leaky watermarks, the floor tiles were cracked, and an unpleasant odor filled the air. She recalled the glorious structure it used to be, the pride and joy of the community with beautiful gardens and flowers surrounding it and an interior filled with arched walls and exquisite carved wood furnishings and decorations. Her husband had supported the synagogue for many years with generous donations, but now it had deteriorated along with the small community left behind, for it lacked the resources to sustain it.

She removed her abaya and knocked on the heavy wooden door with her fist. A middle-aged woman opened it.

"I am here to see Rabbi Shemtov. Please tell him that Salima Naui is here," she stated firmly, using her maiden name.

"The rabbi is still in services, but he should be out shortly," the woman answered. "Please follow me to his study. When he is free, I will inform him that you are here."

Several minutes later, the rabbi entered his study. He recognized her immediately.

"Where have you been, Salima?" he asked in a trembling voice. "I had people looking all over for you and Reuben. We thought you might have escaped to Israel or London, but we found no trace of either of you anywhere."

"I had to go into hiding," she apologized, "and I did not want to subject anybody in the community to additional risks after what was done to my husband and to Daud Selman."

"I saw them just before they were taken away from us," the rabbi told her. "They were very brave and peaceful with themselves. Daniel asked me to tell you that you must go on with your life and that you and Reuben must return to the Promised Land and build your life there so his sacrifice will not be in vain."

Salima's tears poured down her face, for the rabbi's words brought back memories of her beloved husband.

"That is why I have come to see you," she said, taking a handkerchief from her purse. "I need your help to get Reuben and me to Iran so we can leave this hell and start our new lives. I am not sure how much longer I can survive under the present conditions. I haven't been well, and the cold winters are aggravating my asthma."

The rabbi stroked his long white beard and looked at Salima. "I will try to do everything in my power to help you," he consoled. "How is Reuben, and where have you been staying?"

"Reuben is doing fine, thank the Almighty. He is much better than I am. It may be better for you not to know where we are, just in case. You can never tell what these murderous tyrants are up to."

"You are right, Salima. Occasionally the authorities send someone here to inquire of your whereabouts. We always say that we have no clue, so I can continue to give them this honest answer and keep your secret safe."

"Daniel's sacrifice was not enough, *min tejmad eunem.* They are still after Reuben and me. May the Almighty turn their eyes into icicles."

The rabbi leaned across his desk and looked at Salima through the thick lenses of his glasses before he resumed speaking in very low voice.

"Now, about your wish to be smuggled into Iran: here is the situation. Ever since the mass exodus of our people, the Iraqi government has introduced very strict laws concerning illegal immigration from Iraq. These laws prohibit Jews from leaving Iraq, and any person caught attempting to escape or anybody assisting them will be sentenced to death. Due to these laws and their strict enforcement, the Jewish Agency had to suspend all illegal immigration activities until the environment becomes more favorable. This situation may not change until a new government is elected, which may take several years."

"I don't know if I can last that long," Salima said, shaking her head in frustration. "Are you sure there is no other way, Rabbi? I need your help desperately. It's a matter of survival, and I'm willing to take my chances!"

"I'm very sorry, my dear. You know that I would do anything to help you, but we don't have the means or resources we used to have. Without the Agency operatives, we are paralyzed. Please come back to see me in a few weeks. I will look further into the situation and hope to have better news for you next time."

Salima leaned back on her chair and gazed at the ceiling as she voiced her frustration. "What sins have I committed, dear Almighty, to deserve this wretched fate? Haven't I been a righteous woman who helped the poor and needy? Didn't my husband give generously to build the magnificent house that bears your name? Why are you punishing my family so severely? What have I done to deserve this wrath to come upon us?"

The rabbi remained silent for a few moments. "The Almighty acts in mysterious ways," he finally muttered. "Only the future can solve the quandary of your suffering."

He rose to his feet. "One more thing, Salima. The night before Daniel was arrested, he came to see me. A close friend tipped him off that some people in the Defense Ministry were plotting against him. He deposited one thousand dinars with me to give to you in case something happened to him and you were left destitute. Not knowing where you were, I saved the money for you all this time. I will bring it to you now."

As Salima was leaving, the rabbi handed her a sealed envelope. "Please come back to see me soon, and may the Almighty be with you and Reuben to guide you through these dark days."

"Thank you, Rabbi Shemtov. I will be back."

Salima tucked the envelope into her undergarments and disappeared quickly into the streets.

Daniel was a very smart man, she thought walking briskly, fully covered by her abaya. He left the money as an insurance policy to save our lives should his own be taken away. If all other escape plans failed, there would always be some adventurous smuggler willing to take a big risk for that much money.

When she arrived home, she loosened two floor tiles under the bed and dug a small hole in the ground large enough to hold the envelope and her remaining jewelry. She wrapped them in old rags and sealed them in a plastic bag. She placed the sealed package in the hole, replaced the tiles, and put an old clothes trunk on top of them. She felt greatly relieved. The money was in a safe place, and when the time came, she would use it to buy passages to freedom for Reuben and herself.

* * * *

Several months went by without any good news from the rabbi. Salima went to see him again to inquire about possible arrangements for leaving, but he shook his head apologetically and said no new developments were on the horizon. During the winter months, her coughing fits were so bad that she could barely breathe. Aziz, very concerned about his mother's health, urged her to see a doctor.

"Don't worry, ebni," she placated him. "I will get better soon. Spring is almost here."

* * * *

The months turned into years. As they rolled along, Aziz grew into a tall, gregarious, and handsome young teenager, with a head full of dark, shiny hair and bright piercing brown eyes. His mature appearance radiated with confidence and pride.

Chaled's younger sister, Amira, a striking beauty, loved to follow the boys around and participate in their games. She wanted to take an active role in their stimulating daily activities and thrilling competitions. Chaled didn't object to her hanging out with the boys, and over time she became an active member of the young Palestinian clan.

She followed Aziz around continually, giving him admiring looks and seeking his close attention. Her transition into adolescent maturity was evident through the physical enhancement of her body as it took the shape of a beautiful young woman.

Aziz secretly enjoyed her courtship. Every time he looked at her exotic young face, the stunning curves of her body, and her pointy breasts, an unexplained sensation ran down his spine into his groin. Yet he never acknowledged Amira's affection or allowed a hint of his interest to be evident.

Amira wanted to be known as Aziz's girl to elevate her status among the clan members and gain wider acceptance from the boys who resented the presence of a girl in their midst.

One day when they were playing a game of capture the flag away from their neighborhood, Amira followed Aziz into one of his favorite hiding places. In the dimness of the dense green bushes forming an invisible narrow bubble of space, Amira crawled in, edging closer to him.

After running for a while, they were both breathing heavily. Aziz felt the warmth of her body pressing against him when their lips met for the first time. He felt a rushing sense of excitement engulfing his body as her breasts pushed against his chest. He wrapped his hands around her waist holding her close, his lips caressing her round, beautiful face.

Amira grabbed the palms of his hands and held them tightly against her breasts. She wrapped her thighs against his groin saying, "Take me, Aziz. I am yours."

Aziz pushed back, trying to overcome his spontaneous reaction to Amira's welcomed gestures. His raging hormones urged him to unlock the mystery of life's secrets. Then, the words of the Imam flashed across his brain: "Premarital sex is strictly forbidden and severely punishable."

Grabbing Amira by her shoulders, Aziz looked into her large, brown eyes gleaming with excitement.

"We shouldn't be doing this, Amira. You know it's forbidden. We could both get into very big trouble and ruin our lives."

"But I love you, Aziz, and I want to marry you," Amira confessed as she clung to him.

"We are too young to get married now, Amira. You know that."

"Aziz, I will wait until you are old enough to ask my father for my hand. I am sure he will agree."

"We have to wait until we grow up and then request the permission of our parents. Until then, Amira, we must stay apart."

* * * *

One afternoon when Aziz and his friends were playing a game of seven stones, a rival clan of local

Shiite Moslems stole their ball, crushed their stones, and started cursing at them.

"Go back to Palestine, miserable cowards. This is not your country. We don't need you traitors here! This is our homeland. You will never be one of us proud Iraqis. You are stealing our jobs and livelihood. We won't rest until we throw you all out!"

Their leader, Suleiman, a gigantic, muscular teenager two years older than Aziz, was obviously using these slurs to draw Aziz into a fight. Suleiman's gang members cheered and waved flexible sticks of wild bamboo cane that looked like fencing swords. Bamboo swords were a common weapon used by most street gangs in Baghdad because bamboo was abundant on the shores of the Tigris River. Kids learned to make them by watching their older siblings. The cane was cut to size, stripped of its leaves, smoothed out, and sharpened at its narrow end. A handle with a ring made out of white knitted rope attached to its wide end gave it an authentic look of a fencing sword.

When the swords were swung around, they made a whirling swish, like the sound of the desert wind howling during a wild sand storm. If hit by the sword, one would experience a sharp, stinging pain that left burn marks on the skin and was excruciating for many days. Wounds took several weeks to heal and left dark, ugly scars on the skin. Rumors circulated that such bamboo swords were among the means used by the ruthless Iraqi secret service in their torture chambers to extract confessions from their victims.

Trying to diffuse the looming confrontation, Aziz

gathered his friends to leave, but Suleiman and his friends followed them, poking them with their swords and persisting in their taunting.

At last Aziz roared out the get ready signal, and his friends quickly formed a circle around him. Ahmed handed Aziz his sword, saying, "Use the tricks my brother taught us, and that monster will be eating dirt in no time"

Like hungry wolves ready to tear into their prey, the two gangs lined up and faced each other in an arrowhead formation. The two leaders faced each other with their swords at the tips of the opposing arrows. Looking at Suleiman, known as a ruthless fighter who would use any dirty trick to beat his opponent, Aziz vividly recalled the story his mother had read him about David and Goliath.

He felt like David standing in front of the solid, bulky giant. He knew he would have to keep his distance and use his street smarts and speed to defeat Suleiman. Just as David did, he would put his trust in the God of the heavens, the God who had saved his forefathers from many calamities, to give him the strength and wit to defeat this vicious monster.

Suleiman was in front of him, winding his sword in sharp moves back and forth. The gangs formed semicircles behind their leaders. Aziz heard Amira's encouraging voice: "Smash him to pieces, Aziz. Show him who the real hero is, and who is the coward who hides in dirty mouse holes."

She had a sharp tongue for a young teenager, but her cheering words and his knowing that she was there watching him gave Aziz confidence and courage.

His piercing eyes were fully focused on Suleiman, watching for his next move. Aziz skipped around, circling him, his sword gripped tightly in his right arm, tipped at an angle to maintain the strike distance. When Suleiman made a move, Aziz would have sufficient time to avoid the whipping sword and respond with his own move. His plan was to tire Suleiman and daze him by making him turn around in small circles while using his own speed and flexibility to avoid his attacks.

Aziz had practiced his moves extensively with Ahmed and Chaled every day after school. Now the two friends were right behind him, giving him advice and encouragement.

There were no specific rules or restrictions on the fight. The first person who fell to the ground and didn't get up was defeated. If one of the fighters was hurt and wanted to give up, he had to walk away from the ring and was considered defeated. As long as a fighter was on his feet inside the ring, he was considered fair game to his adversary.

Aziz noticed the glowing sparks in Suleiman's black eyes, signaling he was about to go on the offensive. Suleiman charged forward with a swipe of his bamboo sword, attempting to hit Aziz on his upper body, but Aziz skipped to his left, landing gently on the ground. He turned in a full circle and stayed as low to the ground as he could. Aziz felt a burst of air brushing his face and heard the swooshing sound of the sword to the right of his ear. Suleiman's momentum hurled him forward and he was unable to turn around fast enough. As Aziz rose from his turn, he swung his sword in a wide right-hand circle and caught Suleiman in the lower back. Suleiman grunted, but he turned around immediately to face Aziz, who renewed his circling dance.

Suleiman didn't waste time. In a quick forward jump, he tried to whip Aziz's legs. Aziz jumped high in the air, drawing his knees upwards to his chin. Suleiman's sword swiped his right ankle, sending a sharp stinging sensation up his leg. With his teeth clenched tightly, Aziz landed on his feet, slamming his sword onto Suleiman's right shoulder with the full might of his downward momentum.

Suleiman shrieked and tried to straighten up quickly and get back into the fight, but his right shoulder was hanging down, his left arm clutching it. His face was strained with pain.

Aziz stepped back, feeling the intensity of his stinging ankle, and waited to see what Suleiman would do next. His opponent turned and started walking away from the circle. As Aziz walked back to his corner, he heard Chaled's scream, "Aziz! Watch out! He is coming at you!"

Aziz turned his head slightly to the side and saw a huge pile of dirt hurled in his direction, the massive body of Suleiman following closely behind. Instinctively, he turned his head back to avoid the glut of dirt Suleiman had tossed at his face and made a quick forward somersault, jumping back to face Suleiman three yards away. Suleiman missed his target and landed on the ground with a loud thud. For a few seconds he lay motionless, stretched out in the dirt. Finally, scraped and dusty, he got up slowly and walked away awkwardly holding his right shoulder with his followers behind him.

"Aziz! Aziz! Aziz!" His friends applauded in celebration of his victory. They picked him up on their shoulders, jostling him up and down and cheering him enthusiastically.

Amira danced around him in hysterical joy. "I knew you could beat that chunky rat. You did it, Aziz! You are my hero!"

They marched to their neighborhood, surrounding Aziz who limped all the way home.

"Aziz beat Suleiman!" Amira announced to the crowds gathered to observe the loud victory march. "That double-crossing traitor was swearing at us and saying we should go back to Palestine and calling us names, but don't worry, Aziz made sure he won't be climbing out of his rat hole for quite a while."

Salima came out of her shack, a worried look on her face. "Is Aziz all right?"

"Everything is fine, Mama." Aziz reassured her. "Please don't worry. You know I can take care of myself."

"I told you not to go near Suleiman and his gang. They are bloodthirsty criminals who are up to no good, and any association with them doesn't reflect well on you or your friends."

"We were minding our own business when they started disrupting our game and using curses and foul insults to provoke us. We tried to ignore them, but they started attacking us with their bamboo swords. We had to defend ourselves, and we whipped them real good,"

Aziz told her.

"Come inside, galbi, and let me bandage your ankle. It's time for you to eat dinner and do your homework."

CHAPTER 7

BAGHDAD 1958

After the Suleiman incident, Amira's passion for Aziz intensified, and her pursuit became so obsessive he had to avoid her. Deep inside, he had enjoyed their initial encounter. It had aroused his manhood, and his body yearned for more of the tense excitement he felt when he held Amira in his arms. Lately he had been waking early with an erection after dreaming exotic fantasies of himself and Amira cuddled together in their hideaway.

One day while playing a game of cops and robbers away from their court, Aziz saw Amira crawl into a thicket. Despite his promise to stay away, he couldn't resist the temptation to follow her in. While they were kissing and caressing each other passionately, Chaled stumbled upon their hiding place and surprised them. He pulled Amira away, slapping her face and saying, "You are in big trouble, little slut. I am not done with you yet. Just wait till we get home."

He then confronted Aziz angrily, claiming Aziz was

attempting to violate his innocent sister. Aziz apologized repeatedly, taking responsibility for the incident and asking for Chaled's forgiveness.

However, Chaled dismissed Aziz's lame excuses. "I trusted you as my brother. You should have known better than to lay a hand on my sister. You are both in a horrible mess now."

"If Father hears of this, he will kill us both," Amira lamented, almost hysterical. "I love Aziz with all my heart, and he loves me. We want to get married when he is eighteen. Please, Chaled, don't ruin our lives, I beg you." She fell down on her knees, gripped Chaled's legs, and kissed his hands repeatedly.

Chaled turned away from his sister in disgust, stomping his feet and kicking her to free himself from her tight grasp. "Go home, *sharmutta,*" he commanded. "Your disgraceful behavior has brought humiliation and dishonor to our family."

Chaled looked at Aziz with a piercing stare, his voice shaking with rage: "From now on, stay away from my sister, or I swear to Allah, I will kill you with my own hands. If you truly love Amira and want to marry her, you are going to have to be very patient. You must wait for her to get older and ask my father for her hand. Until then, you are not to come near her." Chaled left in a fury, dragging his sister by her arm.

Reluctant to return home, Aziz wandered the streets of old Baghdad. If Chaled decided to tell his father what had taken place that afternoon, he would be as good as dead. He waited until after nightfall, scouting their neighborhood from afar for any unusual activity. He could hear his mother's voice calling his name, but he didn't dare respond to her worried cries. When all the lights in the neighboring homes went out, he sneaked home and went to bed.

* * * *

As Aziz became a mature young man, Salima grew more apprehensive about his future, his close relations with his Palestinian friends, and the gang fights. He was completely immersed in the new culture and seemed to be falling for Amira. Salima felt panic as she realized the urgency of getting Aziz out of this environment.

The next day, she went to see Jamila and asked her to arrange a meeting with her son, Ali.

"It's about what I discussed with you a while ago," she told Jamila. "Aziz and I need to leave now. I am not well, and I don't think I can survive another winter in our leaky shack. One of these asthma attacks may finish me off, and Aziz will be left all alone in this forsaken land. I can get proper medical attention if I get to Iran. The community there is well organized and will arrange our passage to Israel."

"Your health and the future of your son are all that should matter," Jamila agreed. "I will ask Ali to come see you tomorrow morning while Aziz is at school."

"Allah will bless you and your family with much health and good fortune," Salima thanked her before leaving.

The next morning Ali came to see Salima. She greeted him with a cup of hot, dark coffee and homemade date-filled sesame cookies.

"Ali, you have helped me so much already. I don't know how we could have survived without your aid. Now I need you to find someone who can smuggle us into Iran. I know this is a very risky endeavor, and I hate to get you involved, but I don't have anybody else to turn to, and I don't think I can survive here much longer. I will reward you handsomely."

Ali nodded his head and pondered Salima's request.

"I don't have good connections in this area. I need a few days to look into it and investigate the options available before I can promise you anything. I will come back to see you in a week and let you know what I have found."

"May Allah guide your way and bring you success in your search," Salima added as she escorted him to the door.

Ali returned the following week.

"I don't have good news for you, *Um-Reuben,*" he stated in a hushed voice. "My connections refused to discuss the matter because they are frightened. They told me I should stay away from this business as I am putting myself in great danger just talking about it. The Secret Service is enforcing the government policy harshly. Recently they executed a Kurdish rebel caught trying to smuggle a group of Communists out of the country. I am sorry, but there's not much I can do about it. You must wait and see if the new government will become less strict about illegal immigration."

Salima took a deep breath and then released a prolonged sigh.

"What crime have I committed to deserve this

misfortune? Why is Allah punishing me so severely? And what is to become of Reuben?"

"Please don't lose hope, *Um-Reuben.*" Ali comforted her by using the name his mother used to call her. "It's going to get better, I promise you. Allah will save you from this evil regime and deliver you and Reuben to freedom, *ensha'allah,* very soon. I will let you know as soon as I hear anything," he uttered on his way out.

Salima sank into a deep depression. Her breathing became heavier, and the frequency of her coughing fits increased. Aziz spent more time nursing her and kept encouraging her see a doctor.

One day she told him that she must take him to see someone very important, but he had to keep it a close secret. This person, she told him, would recommend a good doctor for her and might be able to help them flee.

On Friday, the Moslem Sabbath, after coming home from prayers, Salima asked Aziz to accompany her to see the person she had told him about. They discreetly walked out of their neighborhood and reached the main street after a few minutes. Breathless, Salima signaled a horse-drawn carriage to pick them up, naming a Moslem suburb as their final destination.

After they were dropped off, they walked through several streets and arrived at a tall, arched structure whose old yellow walls were peeling. Gasping for air, her hands trembling, Salima dragged herself up the few steps and knocked on the wooden door.

"I need to see the rabbi urgently," she told the elderly woman who opened the door.

"Who may I say wants to see him?" the woman inquired politely.

"I am Salima Naui," she answered, trying to catch her breath.

"Please sit down in the lounge, and I will let the rabbi know you are here," she said and disappeared down the hallway. Within a few minutes, she returned and invited them into the rabbi's study.

They walked into a large room where an old bearded man was sitting behind a large oak desk with books and papers scattered all around. The room was crammed with bookshelves filled with old books. On the wall were framed pictures of the young Iraqi king, Faisal II, and the Prime Minister, Nuri-Al-Said.

"Salima," the rabbi said with a concerned voice. "You look very pale and seem to have lost a lot of weight. What's going on in your life, and who is this handsome young man accompanying you? Please sit down and tell me."

They sat down on two upholstered chairs that had known better days. Salima took a deep breath. "Rabbi, please meet my son, Reuben."

The man stood up and shook Reuben's hand vigorously. "I am Rabbi Shemtov. Your father was a very close and dear friend. Without his help and generosity, this synagogue would never have been built. This community suffered a great loss when he was taken away from us. Blessed be his memory.

"How old are you, son? Do you know our Holy Scripture?"

"He is fifteen years old, and I taught him everything I

know about the Bible and prayers," Salima interrupted. "He can read the words, but he can't write or speak any of them. I did my best to keep him aware of who he is and where he needs to go.

"This is why we came to see you. As you noticed, I have gotten much sicker, and I need urgent medical attention. I don't know who to turn to. I am beginning to lose hope, Rabbi." Salima couldn't hold in her emotions. "Our condition is becoming hopeless. We must get out of this hell — I can't stand it any more."

Reuben put his arms around his mother and rubbed her back gently with the palms of his hands.

The rabbi's baffled expression turned hopeful.

"One of our congregants is a renowned lung doctor. I will arrange for you to see him this afternoon. You will get the best care. Please don't worry about the money. He will not charge you a penny."

"More importantly, Rabbi," Salima continued, "Reuben and I need to leave Baghdad. His future belongs in Israel with our people, not with the ruthless traitors who murdered his father. You must do something about it now, Rabbi, or it will be too late."

"You must get better first, Salima. You cannot endure the journey in your present condition. Let me worry about arranging your passage, but you need to go and see Dr. Basri now."

The rabbi picked up the phone and spoke to someone.

"It's all arranged," he announced. "Here is the address of the El-Rashid hospital. You must go there now! Reuben, courageous son, you need to take your mother to the hospital now and make sure she is well cared for. Now that you are a grown man, you must bear the responsibilities of an adult.

"Come near me, son, and let me give you the blessing of the Holy Priests to protect and guide you in whatever challenges you may face."

The rabbi held both his hands over Reuben's head and recited the ancient blessing:

"May God bless you and safeguard you,

May God illuminate his countenance upon you and be gracious to you,

May God raise his countenance to you and grant you peace."

He paused after the prayer, rested his hands on Reuben's hair, and kissed the young man's forehead.

"Take your mother to the hospital now. May the Almighty grant her full recovery and healing very soon."

The rabbi put ten dinars in Reuben's hand and sent him on his way, saying, "Please let me know how your mother is as soon as you can."

* * * *

Dr. Basri welcomed them at the hospital. He immediately arranged a bed for Salima and promised to be back to see her the next morning.

Aziz went home that night, took out his mother's prayer book, and started praying arduously for her well-being and their safe passage out of Iraq. He was still very apprehensive about the outcome of his encounter with Chaled. He had difficulties sleeping many nights not knowing when Chaled's father might come knocking on their door looking to avenge his daughter's honor. Moslem law about premarital relations, even if they were innocent and superficial, was strict and uncompromising.

Every day after school, he went to visit his mother, anxiously waiting for Dr. Basri to give them the results of her tests. His close friends noticed his absence, inquiring what was going on with him and wondering why he wasn't coming to hang out with them as usual. He explained that his mother was in the hospital very ill and that he had to stay by her side to comfort her.

* * * *

Early one morning, the distant sounds of heavy explosions and chattering of heavy machine-gun fire awakened Reuben. He ran outside to find out what was going on. The neighbors had started gathering outside their shacks, speculating about the meaning of the unusual sounds. They tuned their radios to hear the latest news, but the radios kept playing national songs.

More people crowded the narrow winding alleys, engaging in heated discussions of what could be happening. Some of the fathers who had left for work earlier that morning returned home in a hurry. They reported that the military had staged an attempted coup against the monarchy of young King Faisal II, who had been crowned a mere five years earlier at the age of eighteen. The palace was under intense fire and surrounded by tanks and troops.

The palace guards fought vigorously to protect the

king, but because they were vastly outnumbered by superior military forces, their resistance dwindled. By early afternoon, the military overpowered the palace guards, seizing the king and top government officials. The 23-year-old king, his uncle, the crown prince, and the entire royal family were brutally murdered.

Their naked corpses were hung by their feet outside the palace to serve as an example for all to see and fear. Top government officials were also executed without hesitation. Nuri-Al-Said, the Prime Minister was caught and murdered, his body dragged by the rebels through the streets of Baghdad.

The military commander appointed himself as the head of the new government and proclaimed Iraq a republic.

CHAPTER 8

When Aziz went to see his mother the next day, she called him to her bedside. "Ebni," she said in her soft, weak voice, "I am afraid that I don't have very good news. Dr. Basri told me that I have an aggressive form of lung cancer. Do you remember what I told you after your father passed away? I explained that you would be called to fulfill a very important mission and that you are destined to become an important leader who will change the course of history of our people. Just as many of our ancestral leaders were summoned by the Almighty, it will be your duty to fulfill his calling. When that day comes, you will remember your father and me, and you will know that our lives have not been in vain. We had a purpose in bringing you into this world so you could make it better and safer for our people."

"I will remember that, Mama." His blurred words were mixed with choked sobs. "You are all I have left in this world, Mama. How can I live without you?"

He laid his head and arms on her bed cover.

"Please don't leave me now, Mama. I love you so

much. Please don't go. I wish I could go with you and be with you and Babba forever."

Salima pulled his head toward her, hugged him, and stroked his hair with the little energy left in her body. "You will be fine, galbi. The Almighty will watch over you and lead your way to freedom and success. It's all in His hands now, and I have to respect his wishes. Your father and I will always be there for you to light your way from the heavens and guide you through your lifetime journey."

With renewed vigor, Aziz looked at his mother and said, "I will not disappoint you and Babba. You will both be very proud of my accomplishments. When the time comes, I will gather the strength and courage to carry out the missions destined for me by my country and my people."

When her son had calmed down and seemed to accept the bitter reality of her impending death, Salima told him about the money and jewelry she had hidden in the house under the floor tiles. She instructed him to use the money to pay whatever was needed for his passage and to exchange the rest when he got to Iran for pound sterling, which would be very valuable in Israel.

The gold pearl bracelet and the diamond necklace he was to safeguard dearly for his future bride-to-be. It would be a good luck charm from his parents. Every time his bride wore them, it would remind them both of their legacy.

Suddenly Salima started coughing violently and gasping for air. She was having one of her asthma attacks, which increased more frequently each day. Aziz ran to call the nurse, who came rushing in, bringing with her a jar of misty fluid that had a sharp minty odor. She placed it in front of Salima and asked her to take a few deep breaths. Within minutes, Salima was calm again and able to renew her conversation with her son, who had remained next to her bed the entire time.

"Tonight after dark you must go to see the rabbi. You must be very discreet and let nobody see you going there. When you get to the synagogue, ask to see the rabbi and say that Salima Naui sent you. He will see you in his office privately, and I would like you to deliver this letter to him. It explains everything I discussed with you today. After he reads it, he will invite you to come back the following week to give you your final passage instructions.

"Ebni, I want you to be strong and brave. I have heard that these journeys can be very physically challenging and full of dangers, but seeing you grow to be a tough young leader in a Moslem ghetto has given me a lot of confidence. I have a strong faith in your ability to persevere and succeed in whatever you set your mind to accomplish."

With nightfall approaching, Salima put the letter in her son's hand. "You can go now, galbi. I look forward to seeing you tomorrow when you bring good news from the rabbi."

When Aziz reached the synagogue, he was told that the rabbi was still in the prayer service and that he should wait in the study for a few minutes. He sat on a chair gazing at the tremendous number of books filling the shelves of the rabbi's study. Walking over to one of the bookcases, he picked up a very old, tall book bound in a peeling back cover. When he opened it, he saw the familiar letters that his mother was teaching him: *Babylonian Talmud* by Rabbi Eliyahu Shamash, 1652, was handwritten on the first page. The book was filled with hundreds of pages in a tight, neat handwriting that he could barely read much less understand. He was amazed that someone would spend so much time writing by hand such a huge book that contained so much information. He had never before seen a handwritten book, for he had assumed that all books were printed.

The door opened and the rabbi walked in. "How are you, my son, and how is your mother?" he inquired. He looked very tired. His long beard seemed to have grown whiter since the last time Aziz had seen him. He appeared more hunched over, and his bloodshot eyes looked enlarged behind the lenses of his round glasses. The troubles of the aging remnants of a thriving and resourceful community seemed to have taken their toll on this scholarly, holy man who was trying desperately to keep the fragments of his community together.

The rabbi noticed Aziz holding the ancient book. "There are over three thousand years of ancient history, wisdom, and secrets of life buried in the books you see on my shelves, son. In a few months, I will be sending all these treasures to London, and from there they will be transferred to Israel to be kept in the central museum for Jewish History in Jerusalem. I don't think these books are safe here any longer, any more than any Jew still living in Iraq. Your mother is doing the right thing for your future, son. Don't ever doubt it."

The rabbi walked slowly to his chair and collapsed into it. He leaned back and took a deep breath, followed by a long, loud sigh of exhaustion. "So, how is your mother doing these days?" he inquired again.

"I am afraid I don't have good news," Aziz replied. "She gave me a letter to deliver to you personally." He noticed that the rabbi was having difficulty understanding him because of his heavy Palestinian accent. He tried to speak as slowly and clearly as he could.

The rabbi opened the letter and started reading. When he finished, Aziz noticed his magnified red eyes swelling with tears. He wiped his cheeks with a creased white handkerchief that he took from his pocket and then reached over to hold Aziz's hands.

"I am very sorry to hear the bad news about your mother. This is the wish of the Almighty, and we have to accept it. Be brave, dear son. You are a bright and strong young man, and your entire future is ahead of you. I have made some progress with regard to arranging your passage, but I still need time to finalize a few details. You will be welcomed in Israel with open arms, and you will have the opportunity to live freely in a country you can call your own.

"Please come back on Monday night. By then I should have everything arranged for you."

* * * *

Aziz went back to see the rabbi on Monday night. The rabbi welcomed him into his study. "It has all been arranged, son," he said in a relieved tone as he sipped from a clear, vase-shaped glass of hot tea filled with green mint leaves.

"Everything that I tell you must be kept a closely guarded secret, since it involves the lives of many people who are taking great risks to help you, including myself. You must not tell anybody the details of the plan I am about to reveal to you.

"Next Sunday afternoon you will leave Baghdad on your way north to Arbil through the city of Mosul in northern Iraq. I am in the process of arranging someone to accompany you on this segment of the trip. You will take the train from Baghdad to Mosul and from there a bus to Arbil. When you reach Arbil, you will be taken to an address I will give your escort. You will be staying with the family of Mahmud Abu Yusef, who for all intents and purposes is your 'uncle' on your mother's side. At this point, your escort will leave, and you will remain in this house until the guide comes to fetch you."

The rabbi paused when someone knocked on his door.

A middle-aged woman walked in with a small tray in her hand. She removed a steaming cup of tea from the tray and placed it in front of Aziz. As soon as she left the room, the rabbi continued.

"Reuben, for security reasons, we don't know the exact day of your departure from Arbil, but it will be within a few days of your arrival there. You must be ready for the guide when he comes and follow all his instructions strictly for the entire journey until you cross the border to Iran and reach the city of Teheran, where you will be given into the safe hands of the Agency people. Your guide is our most successful and reliable border smuggler. I insisted he be the one to take you on your journey. The Agency people in Iran will take care of all your needs and arrange for your flight from Teheran to Tel Aviv."

"If you are caught or questioned by the police, you must say that you were on your way to visit your uncle's family in Arbil. You are not to reveal any other details of this arrangement under any circumstances or admit that you are Jewish, that you were ever here, or that you know me.

"There is a death sentence awaiting anybody helping a Jew to leave this country illegally, which is the only way Jews are able to leave Iraq these days. People are taking very high risks to help you, Reuben."

Aziz used the pause in the rabbi's voice to take a few sips from the mint tea that had cooled down by then. The sweet, refreshing taste perked him up as a feeling of warmth spread throughout his body.

He looked at the older man. "I will do as you say, Rabbi, and I promise not to tell anybody any of the details of the arrangements. I am simply going to visit my uncle's family in Arbil whom I haven't seen for a few years."

The rabbi nodded. "You need to prepare warm clothes, a heavy winter coat, and a strong pair of walking boots for your journey. You may take only one backpack with all your belongings, for you must carry it all the way to Iran.

"Please come back tomorrow night, and I will introduce you to your escort. You will then meet him at the Baghdad central railway station on Sunday at six in the evening, and you will both board the overnight train to Mosul at seven."

The following afternoon Aziz went to visit his mother at the hospital.

"Mama," he said in an upbeat voice, "I found the money and the jewelry exactly as you said, and the rabbi read your letter. He made all the arrangements for me. I will be leaving on my journey next Sunday."

"Bless his heart!" Salima exclaimed in joy. "I knew he could work his miracles and save your soul. Now that your future is secure, I am free to soar into the heavens and reunite with your dear father. Oh, how I miss him — his handsome smiling face, his beautiful smooth black hair, brushed back, and his elegant, rimless golden glasses. He looked like a prince, your beloved father, and you are looking more like him every day. Lucky will be that gorgeous Israeli woman you will marry one day."

Salima was in a private room that Dr. Basri had been able to arrange for her. She had several tubes connected to her arms and a battery of monitors next to her bed. Aziz sat on a chair next to her, holding and caressing her hand.

She looked at him admirably with a faint smile and continued speaking in a muffled tone. "I had a dream about your father last night. He looked striking dressed in his immaculate, pinstriped blue suit, a white shirt, and a silky silver tie. His radiant face showed no signs of aging, and his thick, black hair had not even a hint of gray. He said that he had a revelation that you were living in Israel. You joined the army and became a military officer and a war hero. He said that he saw you in a military parade, wearing an officer's uniforms and standing proudly in a line-up, as an Israeli Army General pinned a shiny medal of distinction on your chest.

"He wanted to reassure me that your future was bright and secure, that my duties on earth were fulfilled, and that I need not worry about you any longer. He said he misses me immensely and is eagerly waiting for me to join him.

"Then he was gone like a leaf blown by the wind. Come near me, galbi. Let me hug and kiss you. Please be extra careful on the journey and kiss the ground for me when you get to the Promised Land."

"I will, Mama, and I will think of you every day for the rest of my life. I will never forget your lovely face, your soft voice, your kind eyes, and your generous heart. You sacrificed everything to give me hope for a new life, and I will forever be thankful to you for your legacy."

Aziz couldn't hold back his emotions. "This may be the last time that I see you, Mama," he said, his voice choking. "I will miss you every single day of my life."

"Go in peace, galbi, and may the Almighty guide you day and night, wherever you may be."

* * * *

That evening Aziz was back in the rabbi's study. The rabbi looked very upset. "We have a problem," he informed Aziz. "The escort is scared to death and is refusing to take you to Arbil. I couldn't convince him otherwise. He has a young family, and his wife is threatening to leave him if he continues to take such high risks. I don't know what to do now. I can't send you to Arbil by yourself."

"What about Ali?" Aziz interjected. "He can take me. He promised my mother that he would help us."

"I remember your mother mentioned his name in her letter," the rabbi commented. "Do you know him well?"

"He saved my mother and me and found us shelter when we were thrown into the streets," Aziz answered confidently. "He is very trustworthy."

"It sounds like a good idea," the rabbi said in his soft voice. "Can you get in touch with him soon?"

"Certainly, I will go to his mother's house tomorrow and tell her that my mother is in the hospital very sick with lung cancer, that her days are numbered, and that she wants Ali to take me to my uncle's house in Arbil."

"Good thinking, son. Please do that and insist on paying him one hundred dinars from the money your mother left for you. It would take him a few months to earn that kind of money working in Baghdad. This generous gesture should make him very happy."

The rabbi handed Aziz the address of Abu Yusef in Arbil, two train tickets to Mosul, and money for the bus tickets to Arbil. "When you arrive at Abu Yusef's house, he will know precisely who you are and take care of you from that point on. He is a tall, heavy-set man about fifty years old, with a balding forehead and a large, curly mustache across his face."

"Good luck on your journey. Our people in Iran will send me a coded message when you get there so that we know you are safe. I will pray for your safe journey and success in Israel."

* * * *

The following afternoon, Aziz went to see Jamila and told her about the recent events that had turned his life upside down.

Jamila, shaken by the bad news, started sobbing, pulling her hair, and pounding on her chest with her fists.

"I must see Salima at once," she said in a hysterical tone. "Which hospital is she in, and what is going to happen to you?"

"Mother is at the El-Rashid Hospital. You can visit her this evening. She will be very happy to see you, but I urgently need to talk with Ali. Mama wants him to take me to her brother's house in Arbil where I will stay from now on."

Aziz looked into Jamila's eyes. "You know, my uncle is the only family we have left in Iraq," he said with a wink.

"I will miss you and Mama immensely," he continued. "You are like my own mother. You raised me from the time I was a newborn baby, and Ali always played with me when I was little. I remember I used to love it when he lifted me up in the air and twirled me all around, taught me to kick the ball, and played hide-and-seek with me. Even though he was much older, he was always very friendly and patient with me. I always had fun when he was around our house."

"Come, ebni," Jamila cuddled him in her arms as if he were a little baby again. "I will miss you and your mother tremendously, and will never forget what your family has done for us. Please don't worry; Ali will be here soon as I am expecting him for dinner. I know he will be delighted to see you and more than happy to fulfill your mother's wishes. Please sit down and join us for dinner. I have some of your favorite dishes ready to be served."

Aziz sat down on a comfortable upholstered chair in Jamila's spacious dining room while she pulled out another set of dishes. The dining room table was covered with a beautiful handmade tablecloth he recognized as Jamila's own embroidery. Soon the table was elegantly set for three.

Within minutes, Ali appeared at the door. He was a grown man now, medium height, slim body, with cocoa brown eyes and curly black hair parted on one side. He was dressed in a sharp, white summer suit, a red tie, and elegant white shoes. Aziz had heard that he'd become a successful real estate broker and that his business was doing very well.

Ali seemed a bit surprised to see Aziz at his mother's house. Jamila pulled him aside and whispered a few sentences to him.

He walked toward Aziz and greeted him in a very friendly voice. "I can't believe how big you are getting, Aziz. You are almost as tall as I am. I find it hard to imagine you are the same kid I used to pick up and throw around like a ball just a few years ago. Well, time flies, but we sure had some fun together during those good old days at your house. I am very sorry to hear that your mother is ill. Is there anything I can do to help her?"

"Well, Ali, unfortunately she is beyond that point.

The doctors are giving her only a few more days. I am the one who needs your help now. My mother wants me to leave Baghdad without further delays. I need you to escort me to my uncle's house in Arbil. I wouldn't be able to get there by myself. I have never been out of Baghdad my entire life. It should take only a couple of days for the trip, and I will pay you one hundred dinars for your trouble."

"Don't worry about that," Ali replied. "It's no trouble at all, and you don't need to pay me anything. When do we have to leave on this journey?"

"On Sunday afternoon," Aziz replied. "We will take the train from Baghdad to Mosul, and from there a bus to Arbil. I have the tickets already."

"It's all settled, then," Ali concluded. "I will meet you at your home on Sunday at five p.m., and we will go to the train station together. Don't forget to pack some warm clothes. You know it can get very cold up north."

Aziz thanked them both and asked Jamila to care for his mother after he had gone. "I will see you on Sunday, Ali," he said as he was leaving the house.

The following day after school, Aziz went to visit his friends and told them that his mother was terminally ill. "I am very sorry, but I will be leaving Baghdad very soon. I have to move to Basra and stay with my uncle and his family. He is our only relative in Iraq. Like us, he came from Palestine after the war with the Zionists and settled in Basra. He has done well for himself and works as an engineer for the electric power company in Basra."

"You can live with us!" exclaimed Amira. "We are

one big family."

"Or with us," announced Ahmed. "We are brothers."

"Thank you! You have been my family and friends for the past eight years, and I would love to continue living here, but my mother's final wish is for me to move in with her brother's family. I don't have a choice, I have to respect her request."

"Then you will come to visit us as soon as you can?" Amira asked, unable to stand the thought of being away from him.

"Of course, I will!" Aziz blurted out without much thought. "I will come to visit you at the first opportunity I get."

Aziz used the rest of the time to prepare for his trip. He went to the market and bought warm clothing, including winter boots and a coat, along with some of his favorite snacks to take on his journey.

On Sunday afternoon, Ali picked him up promptly at 5 p.m. Aziz hugged his friends good-bye. In tears, Amira followed him around deliriously. "You must promise to come back for me, Aziz," she pleaded in a panting voice. "I will be waiting for you anxiously, my hero."

"I promise," he mumbled awkwardly.

Chaled shook his hand in a conciliatory gesture, saying, "I hope you can come visit us during the summer, and we can have fun again swimming in the river and playing games in the neighborhood."

"I will try my best to come," Aziz replied. This was the first time he and Chaled had exchanged words since their falling out.

An hour later, Aziz and Ali boarded the train and started the long journey to Mosul.

CHAPTER 9

They settled down on the comfortable seats of the relatively empty train. Apparently not too many people were prepared to face the bitter cold winter in the northern mountainous area.

Ali was very chatty, trying to distract Aziz from thinking about his mother by keeping his spirits up. The train started moving, slowly unfolding the glorious scenes of modern Baghdad before them. Aziz had never seen that part of the city with its wide avenues, tall palm trees centered in the medians, beautiful villas with modern, sleek cars in their driveways, large traffic roundabouts decorated with colorful flowers, and the towering statues of the new ruler, mounted in the center of many of them.

Soon they were riding parallel to the beautiful Tigris River, its embankment filled with people taking a refreshing evening stroll along its pristine, smooth waters and enjoying the cool evening breeze.

"Look, Aziz!" Ali pointed to a large, towering mansion nestled on a hill across from the river and surrounded by beautiful trees and gardens. A high brick wall encircled the mansion with a wide, black iron gate decorated with golden flowers at its entrance.

"What is this?" inquired Aziz. "It's so beautiful and peaceful."

Ali looked very pensive. "Don't you remember this place, Aziz? It has changed a bit in the last few years, but most of it has remained the same."

"I have no idea. It looks like the king's palace or something like that. Who can afford to live in a beautiful mansion like this but kings and princes?"

"Well, you are right. This is now one of the Presidential palaces, but do you recall what it used to be?"

"I have no idea," Aziz said in a puzzled voice.

"Well, Aziz," Ali explained, "this used to be your home. Could you believe that you lived in this palace? You can't recognize it because you have never seen it from far away. You saw it mostly from the inside. You were a young child then, and everything you needed was right there for you. I have such wonderful memories of this place. It was like living inside the Garden of Eden with every tree you can imagine and every kind of fruit your heart desired. Just name it; it was there in your orchards."

Ali continued to describe the wonders of the house in the good days, beginning with the front of the house with its very wide circular driveway lined by perfectly trimmed cypress trees amid rose gardens of all the colors imaginable. He told Aziz how in the center of the driveway stood a round water fountain with four marble lion heads spaced equally around it and a central circulating water jet that reached twenty-five feet high. "The lion heads were facing outwards, and water streams came out of their mouths and splashed down to the lower level of the fountain."

Ali leaned back on the wide seat of the train, stretched his legs on the footrest, and closed his eyes. He was focused on transitioning his thoughts into that old magical world he'd reveled in as a young teenager.

Soon he continued telling Aziz about his privileged childhood. "When you entered the house through the broad and heavy carved wooden doors, you walked onto a spacious white marble foyer covered by handmade Persian rugs.

"Down the hallway was an enormous living room, which served as an entertainment hall decorated with eighteenth century-style French furnishings and rare Chinese carpets. This room was used for the famous parties your parents used to host for the Iraqi political elite.

"The back of this great room opened into a wide circular terrace that stretched along the entire back of the house from where we could see the Olympic-sized swimming pool below, the immaculate back garden, and the orchards in the distance. The terrace was where guests gathered during the cocktail hour prior to dinner. There they enjoyed the most exotic cocktails served to their hearts' desire from a polished lacquer bar built into one of the terrace's corners. According to the Qur'an, Moslems were not supposed to drink alcohol, but most of them did anyway. These rules applied only to the clergy and the lower class population. The elite leadership seemed to be exempt from such strict regulations.

"Scrumptious appetizers were served on silver trays by impeccably dressed waiters wearing black tuxedos and white gloves. The air was filled with the intoxicating scent of the citrus trees sprouting in the orchards.

"At night, the pool and the back garden were lit by series of spotlights shining in all directions, an incredibly breathtaking scene."

Aziz was fascinated. "I can't believe I used to live in this magnificent mansion, or that we were so rich."

"Yes," Ali replied, "those were the days of glory when King Feisal ruled this country, before the evil traitors took it over and started exploiting it for their own benefit.

"I used to love going to your house with my mother. After my father died, your parents allowed her to bring me to your house. It was just an unbelievable experience for me to go over there from our poor neighborhood.

"Do you remember how I used to play with you when you were little? I used to pick you up in the air, twirl you all around, and pretend that you were an airplane flying in the sky."

"I used to love that game," Aziz recalled with excitement. "It was so much fun. I felt like a free bird, stretching its wings and flying into the endless skies. I remember that when I didn't see you for a couple of days, I used to ask my mother, 'when is Ali coming back? I want to play airplane with him.'"

"You sure loved that game," Ali continued. "When I stopped to catch my breath for a brief minute, you used to giggle like a wild chimp and say, 'More ai-pyane, Ayi, more ai-pyane, Ayi!' You used to call me 'Ayi' because you couldn't pronounce the *L* when you were that small. You were the cutest little kid, always with a mischievous smile on your face, running and jumping around like the entire world's energy was stored in your tiny body. Then my mother would come in and say, 'Ali, be careful with the precious boy. What will I answer his mother if he falls and hurts himself?'

"'Don't worry, ummi,' I used to tell her. 'This boy is a natural athlete. Look how he throws the ball around and kicks it to me so accurately. He is going to be a famous soccer player one day.'"

"I remember that," Aziz reminisced. "I used to have so much fun playing with you around the house. You were the only one who would play with me. Everybody else was busy with the housework or so overprotective that they were afraid to do so."

"When I got older," Ali continued, "I used to help my mother in the kitchen. I was trained as a waiter to serve food to the important dignitaries who were invited to your house for the parties.

"One night, they hosted an amazing party. You should have seen your mother and father. They were dressed like a queen and king, your mother with this incredible white dress decorated with blue sashes from her shoulder to her waist, and your father with a white English tuxedo with golden stripes on its sleeves and a golden silk bow tie to match. They looked exceptionally striking together — the perfect couple. Everybody just loved them. Then the famous Baghdadi orchestra would start playing, all thirty musicians on their unique instruments, and your parents would dance together so gracefully, just like you see in the movies.

"The orchestra's lead singer was Shafika Nasari, the most popular singer in Baghdad at the time and a favorite among the political elite. Everyone loved her theatrical performances and emotional songs. She was a very attractive woman, full of energy, with a figure that filled up all the right places. She wore a low-cut, white dress decorated by glittery sequins and wrapped tightly around her astounding body contours.

"She opened with her famous song 'Our King, Our Savior,' which praised the king as the savior of Iraq from the British rulers. She danced elegantly around the stage, her incredible deep voice filling every corner of the great room. Her electrifying performance earned a standing ovation and requests for more.

"Then it was time to serve dinner. Scores of waiters paraded in with trays filled with steaming grilled meats and fish, exotic salads, rice dishes mixed with vegetables and nuts, and round pita breads straight out of the ovens. It was an unbelievable feast suited for the king's table.

"After the main course, the waiters carried trays of succulent fruits of all colors and shapes, delicate puff pastries baked in syrup and crushed nuts, a variety of layered custard cakes, and ice creams of all flavors.

"As dinner was winding down, the waiters were back carrying trays stacked with steaming white hand towels for the guests to wipe their hands and faces and refresh themselves. We promptly served coffee, tea, and fancy European liqueurs to the sounds of the soft music played by the orchestra.

"The orchestra picked up its pace at the appearance of Shahira, an exotic Egyptian belly dancer from Alexandria who'd gained much fame in Baghdad's top night clubs. She wore a white bikini ornamented with colorful gemstones and decorated with swirling golden threads. Her perfectly tanned, shiny body and wavy black hair were in striking contrast to the silky white cloth of her bikini.

"She opened with her legendary acrobatic dance, which was a combination of belly dancing and acrobatics she choreographed herself. Her incredibly flexible body was winding in gyrating movements like a python climbing out of his master's basket. She turned and spun around to the sounds of the bells attached to her fingers waving colorful scarves in circular movements. Her hips swayed up and down, and her luscious, firm breasts danced to a mysterious tune in provocative movements aimed at the center table where the highest-ranking dignitaries were seated.

"Suddenly Shahira sprinted across the stage and performed a series of breathtaking forward and backward flips, high leaps, twisting somersaults, and graceful pirouettes. She blended the acrobatic elements harmoniously, adding excitement and rhythm to the upbeat music. The guests roared with approval, clapping their hands energetically as Shahira bowed in deep gratitude for their passionate cheering.

"Yes, Aziz, those were incredible times that I will never forget. You were too young to take part in the parties, since your bedtime was before they even started. You were there on only one occasion when His Excellency, the Crown Prince, attended a ball at your mansion. Your parents decided to keep you up and dress you in a white tuxedo that was a miniature version of your father's. You looked so cute, like a little prince in the king's castle. Everybody admired your adorable smile and tried to cuddle you and chitchat with you. You were introduced to the Crown Prince, who sat you in his lap and played with you for a few minutes until you started yawning. Then your mother signaled my mother to pick you up and put you to bed."

"Tickets! Tickets!" The conductor interrupted their conversation. "Where are you two headed?

"Mosul," Ali told him.

"What business do you two have in Mosul?"

"We are going to our uncle's house," answered Ali with confidence.

"Are you brothers?" the conductor persisted.

"No, we are cousins.

"I don't see too many visitors from Baghdad this time of the year. Why go visit your uncle in this frigid weather?"

Aziz, an anxious look on his face, stared down at the car's floor to avoid the conductor's inquisitive look.

"Let me have your I.D. cards," the conductor demanded before Ali had a chance to say a word. He examined their cards with increased suspicion.

"Ali Samara and Aziz Al-Wasphi — your names don't sound like you are cousins. Are you two trying to fool me?"

"Well, sir," Ali answered in a controlled tone. "I

am sorry if I confused you, but we are cousins on our mothers' side. We are going to Mosul, and from there I have to take my young cousin to our uncle's house in Arbil. He has to stay with his uncle since his mother is very ill"

"I am sorry to hear that," the conductor said, staring at Aziz. "I hope she gets better soon. Well, I have to get on to the next car. Have a safe trip."

Aziz sat up, leaned back on his seat, and wiped his forehead with his right arm. He glanced at Ali with a relieved look on his pale face.

CHAPTER 10

Aziz was mesmerized by Ali's account of his family's lifestyle prior to their tragedy. Ali's stories took him on a magical trip to his distant past, resurrecting vague memories that had almost faded into darkness. He was eager for Ali to shed more light on this important part of his family history about which he knew very little.

Ali got up and stretched his aching muscles from the prolonged journey; Aziz followed suit. He turned to Ali saying, "Thank you for enlightening me on the wonderful life I enjoyed as a young child. My mother hardly ever talked about our past. It must have brought her so much pain that she tried to avoid it. But as I know very little about my family's past, I would love to hear more."

"Okay," Ali nodded, "but I am not sure if you will be thrilled about the next story I am about to tell you.

"One day you almost got me into big trouble. Your father had a meeting with the Iraqi Minister of Defense, General Faruk Askari. I was playing with you on the front porch when you noticed his limousine adorned with Iraqi military flags, arriving through the iron gates and parking in front of the house. His driver ran out quickly and opened the rear door. He came out dressed in a formal officer's suit, decorated with colorful medals. He also wore a gold-lined officer's cap, which seemed to impress you quite a bit. He and your father were lounging on the soft leather armchairs in the downstairs library, drinking coffee, and conversing casually. The general took off his officer's cap and placed it on a side table next to him.

"You seemed to have taken a very strong liking to the general. You followed him around and frequently looked into the library where he was sitting with your father. Then you disappeared, and I lost track of your whereabouts for a few seconds. The next thing I saw was you sneaking into the library with a large silver cooking pot you stole from the kitchen under the cook's nose.

"I froze, having no clue what you were planning to do next. I couldn't chase you into the library and interrupt your father's conversation because I would get into big trouble for that. I just stood there, motionless, as you slowly walked behind the general, lifted your arms up, and completely covered his head with the shiny metal pot, and announced proudly, 'Brave soldiers must wear helmets.' The general didn't know what hit him, but your father jumped up in astonishment, having heard your voice and realizing what you had just done.

"The general removed the pot from over his head slowly and looked at you with curiosity. Your father pounced on you angrily, attempting to reprimand you for your mischief."

"You responded with your sweet voice, 'But, Daddy, soldiers must wear helmets to protect their lives if someone shoots at them.'

"'The boy is right and very smart!' the general interrupted. Looking at you with a gentle smile, he said, 'Come here, Saed, shake my hand.'

"Saed was your Arabic name. You walked over to him timidly and shook his right hand gently. Then he swept you off your feet and sat you in his lap, showing you all his shiny medals, his golden rank stripes, and the brightly polished golden buttons on his uniform.

"You loved sitting there and admiring him, and your father's anger seemed to dissipate quickly with the general's quick response that diffused the tension. The general saved my neck from the severe punishment my mother would have inflicted on me if she knew what had happened while you were under my care."

A loud squealing noise interrupted their conversation as the train shook violently, chugging through what sounded like a long bridge. Aziz stared at Ali, a worried look on his face, thinking that any second the train was going to derail and plunge into the deep gorge below. He was reassured when the squeaking and rattling of the train returned to normal after they crossed the bridge.

"I remember that," Aziz acknowledged in a relieved voice. "I must have been four years old then. I was fascinated by soldiers at that age. My father brought me this soldiers' game for my birthday on one of his trips to England. It had two armies of soldiers dressed with shiny uniforms, lined up to fight against each other. I used to play this game in my room for hours.

"When I saw the general, he looked just like one of them, except he was missing a helmet. I guess the large shiny pot was a good alternative in the mind of a four-year-old. The general was a good sport. He took the entire incident lightly and was very nice to me. I loved sitting on his lap and playing with all his medals and the buttons on his uniform."

"Then there was the time that I really got into deep trouble," Ali resumed telling Aziz about his falling into a bad crowd and their adventures leading up to his arrest and interrogation.

Ali paused and reached for a water bottle from his suitcase stored in the overhead compartment. He removed the cap, raised the bottle in the air, and took several gulps to quench his thirst. He then offered the bottle to Aziz who repeated the process.

He looked at Aziz with a restrained smile. "You probably don't believe that I was capable of all these incriminating acts, but it's all true. I was a wild teenager, and without the discipline of my late father, my friends were able to manipulate me and drag me into this horrible mess."

"Growing up without a father can get any teenager into a lot of troubles," Aziz acknowledged. "I have lived through it day after day for almost nine years, and I am not sure when it's going to get better."

"You will do just fine," Ali reassured him. "I know it deep in my heart. Allah will guide you through your struggles and bring you happiness and success, just as he did for me.

"After my confession," Ali continued, "I was

sentenced to five years in jail. The rumors we heard were that the young male convicts became the sex slaves of the jail lords. I was scared to death of what awaited me there.

"The day before I was to be taken from the police station to the jail, I was called before the judge again. The judge announced that due to my cooperation with the police and my assistance in convicting other gang members, I had been granted amnesty. I couldn't believe it. I ran straight home.

"The next day my mother told me that your father asked to see me. I was scared of your father. He was a very influential person who knew all the important people in Baghdad. He had very tough words with me that helped turn my life around.

"The following week he moved us to a new, beautiful house and registered me in a new school. I didn't realize at the time that my new school was the best private Moslem school in Baghdad, reserved only for the rich and famous. Your father took it upon himself to pay the high tuition and make sure that all my needs were addressed.

"Years later, after I graduated from Baghdad University, my mother told me how my miraculous release from jail came about. After your father heard of my jail sentence, he called his friend Farouk El Jamali, the Interior Minister, and asked for his intervention in obtaining my release. The police captain and the presiding judge were paid five hundred dinars each, a small fortune in those days, to smooth things out and erase my criminal record.

"This revelation brought your father very close to Allah in my eyes. To me he was a true miracle maker. 'Abu Reuben must be an angel sent from the heavens to redeem me from hell and put me on the path to success,' I said to my mother after listening to her story."

"'He certainly is an angel with a kind heart,' my mother reinforced my thoughts. 'We would be lost without him.'

"Aziz, now you know the story of my life, how your father came to my rescue when I had lost all hope. Thanks to his help and guidance, I am now a very successful real estate broker, and I earn a very good living. I can afford all the things I craved as a young thief without having to be one, and now I hope to start my own family very soon."

"Bil-Afrach," Aziz congratulated Ali. "This is so wonderful. I am very happy for you. Your mother must be thrilled! Who is the lucky bride?"

"Her name is Sharifa. She started working as my office manager two years ago, and we got along well. After a few months, I gathered enough courage to ask the permission of her parents to court her, and we fell in love. She is a very sweet and caring person."

"I wish you the best," Aziz told him. "You saved my mother and me after a shocking tragedy, and here you are helping me again. I hope I will be able to repay you for your generosity one day!"

"This is nothing compared to what your father did for me. This is the least I can do for his family now that he is unable to protect his own."

Ali stood up and unpacked a container from his

suitcase.

"My mother sent some of your favorite dishes and desserts for us to enjoy on our journey," he told Aziz.

They sat and wolfed down Jamila's delicacies in no time.

It was close to midnight, and they were both yawning with exhaustion. Finally, the rattling chatter of the train rocked them into a deep sleep.

CHAPTER 11

NORTHERN IRAQ, 1959

When they woke up, the train had arrived in Mosul, and they disembarked into the northern city's chilly morning air.

Aziz followed Ali, who was walking around asking for directions to the bus station. He noticed that Ali was having difficulty understanding what people were saying to him and had to ask them to repeat the directions slowly. It turned out that the people who lived in Mosul spoke Arabic with a heavy northern accent that was very different from the way people spoke in Baghdad. They walked for several minutes to the bus station and waited for the next bus to Arbil.

An old bus pulled into the station and came to a screeching halt next to them. They climbed onto it and sat on a wooden bench behind the driver.

The other passengers on the bus were mostly country farmers who carried onto the bus large packages wrapped in cloth tied with heavy ropes. The packages contained food supplies for the winter and clothing they had purchased in the big city.

They journeyed two hours east toward the Iranian border through winding mountain ranges, climbing into higher elevations as the engine groaned and shrieked as if threatening to fall apart any minute. Miraculously, the bus made it to Arbil without any mechanical failures.

Arbil was a small town of a few thousand inhabitants nestled in the mountains of northeastern Iraq. When Aziz felt the cold breeze penetrating every bone in his body, he remembered the rabbi's warning to be prepared with warm clothing. He was glad he had done so; both he and Ali wore warm winter coats and boots. In the winter, thick layers of snow covered the town, bringing life to a virtual standstill, causing most inhabitants to stay in their cozy houses. Aziz wasn't used to the cold weather and disliked it already. He hoped his stay in Arbil would be short and that his guide would come for him soon.

Communicating with the people in Arbil proved to be even harder than in Mosul. Not all of the people spoke Arabic; some spoke only Kurdish, which Ali and Aziz couldn't understand at all. They were finally able to find someone who offered to walk them to Abu Yusef's house. They went along several unpaved dirt roads until they reached a house made out of clay and bricks. The man pointed at the house. Before he left, Ali thanked him and gave him a few coins for his troubles.

No sooner had Abu Yusef heard them approaching than he rushed outside to welcome them. *"Salaamu-Aleikum,* peace upon you, my dear nephew and his friend," he said in his deep, hoarse voice. He hugged Aziz and kissed him on both cheeks.

Ali introduced himself as a friend of the family who'd accompanied Aziz on the journey.

"Allah will bless you and your family for your good heart and generosity for accompanying my nephew on such a long trip. Please come inside and rest. My wife has lunch ready for you." Abu Yusef was a solidly built, middle-aged man about six feet tall with a balding forehead and a large, curly moustache adorning the entire width of his face. That deeply tanned face revealed many crease lines, the result of years of intense farming under the heat of the sun.

He escorted Aziz and Ali to a large room furnished with a heavy wooden sofa and two armchairs centered in front of a decorated stone fireplace. A large wooden dining table and several upholstered chairs stood on an extension to the right, next to a large window facing the green rolling meadows to the west. It looked like a living room/dining room combination where family members spent most of their free waking hours.

Abu Yusef introduced them to his wife, Nadia, who greeted Ali and proceeded to hug and kiss Aziz on both cheeks.

"Welcome, dear nephew!" she exclaimed with enthusiasm. "It's a pleasure to have you with us. I can't believe you are so grown, a tall, handsome, young man. The last time I saw you in Baghdad, you were a little baby. We haven't been able to go back since all the troubles started. We feel much safer here, tucked away in the mountains. Please wash and sit down at the table.

Your food is ready to be served."

Nadia soon returned with a steaming pot of white rice and another filled with chunks of meat cooked in okra and tomato sauce. She generously filled the three plates set at the table, brought out a basket full of freshly baked round pita bread, and then disappeared into the kitchen. Ali and Aziz were so hungry that the delicious hot meal was like a gift from heaven to warm their bodies and fill their stomachs. The cubes of meat were so soft they melted in their mouths, and the tangy taste of the sweet and sour sauce combined with the rice was scrumptious. From the loud sounds coming out of Abu Yusef's mouth, it was evident that he too was enjoying the meal immensely.

Ali and Abu Yusef chatted about the relaxing lifestyle in the country versus the crowded population and living conditions of Baghdad. "I would consider this lifestyle if it wasn't so damn cold here. I don't think I could stand this weather for more than a day," Ali concluded.

Nadia reappeared with a steaming pot of black coffee and a tray of cut fruit and pastries dipped in sweet syrup. She poured the misty coffee into their cups, its herbal aroma filling the room with a sweet scent.

"Please try my homemade pastries. I baked them this morning especially for you, our honored guests."

Ali was quick to express his gratitude. "Thank you, *Um Yusef*. The food is mouthwatering. *Ashat edich,* may your talented hands live for eternity and kings be hosted at your generous table."

"Allah will bless you with good health and prosperity," Nadia replied graciously, apparently grateful for the splendid compliments Ali lavished on her in front of her husband.

Aziz took a sip of the coffee, which was very strong and had a hint of sweetness combined with a mellow, spicy taste that seemed to sharpen his senses immediately. He remembered his mother had sometimes made it for him when he had to stay up late and prepare for his exams, but it had never tasted as good as Nadia's.

When the meal was over, Ali got up. "Thank you for your generosity, Abu Yusef. Excuse my hurry. I have to be back in Mosul tonight to catch the train to Baghdad."

Aziz got up, shook Ali's hand, and hugged him. "Thank you for everything, Ali." he said. "I will never forget what you did for my mother and me. I will always think of you as my older brother who played with me when I was a young boy and took care of my needs when I was growing up.

"This is from my mother. She insisted that I give this to you." He handed Ali the envelope with the one hundred dinars as the rabbi had told him.

"I told her that this was not necessary and that I would help you no matter what," Ali tried to resist his well-deserved reward.

"This was one of her final wishes she expressed to me. Please accept it," Aziz begged.

Finally convinced, Ali inserted the envelope into his coat pocket and said to Abu Yusef, "Whenever you decide to visit Baghdad, my mother and I will be honored to host you and your family at our home as our distinguished guests."

"It will be our great pleasure and honor to visit you

there. Thank you for your generosity." Abu Yusef replied politely.

Ali kissed Aziz on his head and whispered into his ear. "When you get to your final destination, please give my warm regards to General Moshe Dayan."

Aziz nodded with a big smile as he and Ali burst into laughter.

* * * *

Abu Yusef escorted Ali to the bus station and was back at the house within a few minutes. He led Aziz upstairs.

"This was the bedroom of my eldest son, Joseph. He is in Israel now, serving in the army," he explained proudly. "The same guide who will escort you on your journey smuggled him to Iran a few months ago. I chose to stay here with the rest of my family to keep this escape route open and help our people get out of Iraq in case of emergencies such as yours, but I don't intend to be here much longer. We will join my son in Israel next spring.

"You will sleep in this room and stay inside the house until the guide comes for you. We don't want to attract any attention while you are here. The fewer people see you, the safer you are, and the safer my family is. On the bookshelves, you will find some very interesting books about the history of our community in Babylon for the past twenty-five hundred years. I strongly recommend that you read as much as you can while you have the time so you can understand the legacy of your ancestors and be prepared for your new life."

"The Almighty will bless your courage and dedication

to our people, and keep you and your family safe from harm," Aziz said to Abu Yusef. "Please don't worry. I will do as you say and wait for my guide patiently. I am very eager to get out of here, and I will not do anything to jeopardize it."

"My real name is Shafik Kadouri," Abu Yusef said gently, "but everybody calls me Abu Yusef after the name of my firstborn son. My wife and I have two younger children. Saul is fourteen, and Samira is twelve. They should be back from school soon, and I hope they will help you pass the time while you are with us."

"I think you already know my real name," Aziz said in a low tone. "I better start getting used to it again."

"I have to get back to my work now. I will see you at dinner time, Reuben." Abu Yusef left in a hurry.

CHAPTER 12

On Saturday evening after sundown, the Kadouri family gathered around the dinner table to perform the traditional Jewish service that distinguished the departing Holy Sabbath from the beginning of the new week. Nadia lit a long twisted candle with eight wicks as Mr. Kadouri recited the prayers. He passed along a box filled with mixed spices for everybody to shake and smell. Reuben, who had never experienced this practice before, was enjoying his newly discovered tradition.

The sweet, sharp aroma from the spice box reminded Reuben of the spices he had smelled in the coffee Nadia had served when he first arrived. After Mr. Kadouri blessed the wine, they all started singing traditional songs.

As they were singing the song about the prophet Elijah, who was very famous for miraculous disappearing and reappearing stunts, they heard a soft knock at the door. Saul opened the door to a tall, thin man, who appeared to be in his early thirties. His dark sun-tanned face indicated he'd spent many years under the sun's powerful rays. He was dressed in traditional Moslem clothing, a white *kafiya* surrounding his head and draped around his shoulders and a round black *agiela* on top. When he entered, he removed his agiela and kafiya, revealing a head full of black, curly hair and a colorful *kippa,* a round Jewish head cover, clipped to the back of his head.

"Blessed be the new week and blessed those who are present," he opened in traditional biblical Hebrew.

"Blessed be you, our distinguished guest," Abu Yusef welcomed him as he handed him a cup of wine.

"Please meet Reuben Sasson. He has been patiently waiting for you and is very eager to meet you finally. Reuben, please meet Babba Mousa, the wittiest and most experienced border smuggler in Iraq, with over two hundred people smuggled to date."

Babba Mousa shook Reuben's hand vigorously, saying, "Peace upon you young man. It's a great honor for me to accompany you, the son of the Honorable Lord Daniel Sasson, blessed be his memory, on your journey to freedom.

"Did you know that your father paid for my entire nomad tribe of more than five hundred people to be transported from the western deserts of Iraq to Baghdad and then flown to our beloved Holy Land?"

"I never heard about that," Reuben answered politely, "and I wasn't aware that nomad Jewish tribes even existed in Iraq."

"Well," Babba Mousa continued, stroking his sparse goatee. "My nomad tribe lived in the desert for hundreds of years. We've kept our Jewish traditions and prayers in the desert all these years, passing them from generation to generation.

"When we heard rumors that some of our fellow Jews were returning to the homeland after twenty-five centuries in exile, my father, the tribe leader, was determined to end our struggles in the desert. He sent me on the back of my camel to the nearest town with a Jewish population to verify the rumor. When I found out it was true and that our day of redemption had arrived, I went straight to Baghdad to make all the arrangements for our departure."

Reuben noticed a glimmer of excitement in Babba Mousa's charcoal eyes as he continued detailing his tribe's miraculous journey to freedom.

"When I reached Baghdad, I went to the main synagogue, where I was introduced to the immigration coordinators from the Jewish Agency. At first they didn't understand who I was or why a desert nomad was so determined to immigrate to Israel. When I explained to them the entire history of my people, they were very enthusiastic about their newly discovered 'lost tribe' and seemed very eager to help.

"After verifying the information with the authorities, they informed me that all the arrangements would be made and that they could have the immigration paperwork done within a few days, but each member of our tribe had to pay one hundred dinars for the transportation and flight to Israel.

"I informed the Agency representatives that we had no money and very little property, that we were desert nomads living from hand to mouth day after day who did not know the meaning or value of money. They told me they had to talk to someone to see what they can do to help us.

"The next morning the Agency representative met secretly with your father to ask him for a donation to pay our transportation costs. Your father told the representative that he would not rest until the last Jew left Iraq and the prayers of over twenty-five hundred years of the exiled community in Babylon became a reality.

"'Next year in Jerusalem!' your father proclaimed the traditional aspiration recited by Diaspora Jews during the Passover Festival. 'Our young country needs new blood and brave young men to protect it from its mounting enemies and to secure its long-term future. I will send someone to your office tomorrow with an anonymous donation that should be more than enough to take care of this, but remember, as far as I am concerned this meeting never took place!'

"This is the way your father was, an enthusiastic supporter of Israel on the inside, but on the outside a proud and loyal Iraqi citizen who believed the future of the Iraqi Jews belonged in Iraq.

"With his generous contribution, our entire tribe was brought to Baghdad, housed, and fed until the silver birds spread their wings and took us to the Promised Land. Our tribe settled in Beer Sheba, where we could enjoy city life in the middle of the desert. We are growing crops in the desert, raising sheep and cattle, and living in permanent homes with running water and electricity.

"Our brave tribesmen serve as trackers in the Israeli

Army. Hundreds of years of chasing after lost sheep in the desert have become a priceless commodity in tracking Fedayin, the terrorists who infiltrate Israel and attack innocent civilians.

"All of this is thanks to the vision and generosity of your father. We are forever indebted and grateful to your family for all he has done for us."

"That's another amazing story about my father I'd never heard before," Reuben said with astonishment. "I am discovering new facts about him every day."

"Reuben," Babba Mousa continued, "you may wonder why I am here now after enjoying the taste of freedom and independence. After my intense training in the Israeli elite combat scouts, the Agency was desperately looking for volunteers to come back to Iraq to help smuggle out Jews wanted by the Iraqi authorities.

"Remembering the words your father said, 'I will not rest until the last Jew leaves the Babylonian exile,' I decided to volunteer for one year to help my brothers return to the Promised Land, and here I am."

"Thank you for the incredible insight, Babba Mousa. I never knew my father was such a passionate supporter of the State of Israel. I was led to believe just the opposite — that he was against the Jews leaving what has become their homeland, and that he believed they should remain loyal citizens of Iraq and continue to contribute to its economic and cultural development as they did for so many years."

"You see, Reuben, your father managed to fool everybody in that regard. Because of his strong and influential position with high-ranking Iraqi officials, he had to maintain a solid pro-Iraqi façade, but deep inside, he yearned for the day when he could take you and your mother to Israel to settle there. Since he couldn't abandon the diverse family business that had grown into a small empire, he did as much as he could to help others, mostly in the form of donations that were perfectly legal."

"I wish we would have left Iraq before they arrested him," Reuben told him. "We would all be living happily in Israel now."

"You will be in Israel very soon," Babba Mousa declared, guzzling the remainder of the wine left in his glass. "There, you will be able to fulfill your parents' wishes and carry on the legacy of the Sasson family."

"I feel much safer now that I know I will be accompanied by a trained soldier," Reuben said. "You are very brave to return to Iraq as a volunteer and help others escape. I am fortunate to have you as my guide.

"It doesn't feel real that I could be living in my own country, with my own people in control of our own destiny. It would be a refreshing feeling after living for so many years purely at the graces of foreign rulers who subjected our people to so many discriminating and hostile decrees. One day I hope to join the Israeli Defense Forces, just as you did, and make my own contribution to the rebuilding of our young country."

"Your father would be so very proud of you. This was his dream. The Agency people told me all about it after he was taken away from us so suddenly and with such cruelty. He would have been one of the greatest leaders in Israel.

"He planned to liquidate his businesses in Iraq slowly and transfer the family fortune through his company in London to Israel. He planned to build new industries and establish schools and housing developments to boost the Israeli economy and increase employment of the struggling young nation. He was very eager to end the strife of many new immigrant families, living in poor conditions in makeshift tent cities.

"The Agency people told me that the Iraqi government falsely accused him of imaginary crimes and fabricated testimony against him because they were determined to prevent him from using his brilliant business skills and personal fortune to boost the economy and strength of Israel.

"They have always considered Israel their most hated enemy. Did you know the Iraqi government sent their own troops to join the Arab armies to fight against Israel and prevent it from coming to existence? When they were defeated and returned home in shame, the Iraqi government had to find a scapegoat to cover its failure and prove to the Iraqi people that they were still in control.

"Reuben! It's time for you to carry the torch of your father's memory and follow in his footsteps. We need to get ready to leave now, so please gather all your belongings. Abu Yusef will drive us to our point of departure. I hope you rested today. We will travel during the night and sleep during the day to avoid attracting attention among the mountain villagers."

Reuben thanked Nadia for her generous hospitality,

said good-bye to Saul and Samira, picked up his backpack, and followed Babba Mousa.

"We will look for you when we get to Israel next spring," Samira shouted after him.

On the way out, Reuben handed Abu Yusef an envelope with the money as the rabbi had instructed. Abu Yusef stuffed it into his pocket as the three squeezed into the cabin of his old truck and headed east out of Arbil.

* * * *

Abu Yusef drove on a narrow, winding dirt road in the dim light of the full moon rising over the distant dark hills. It was standard operating procedure to switch off the headlights while driving at night to avoid attracting the attention of local police or curious villagers. Escape journeys were always timed around the cycle of the moon, for the light of the full moon was crucial for guiding travelers at night.

About thirty minutes later, they arrived at an entrance to a small village southeast of Arbil. Abu Yusef dropped them outside the entrance, wished them success, turned his truck around, and disappeared into the darkness.

Reuben followed Babba Mousa to the far side of the village into a small shack made of clay and dirt. There he noticed two saddled mules with packages hanging off their sides. Babba Mousa instructed Reuben how to ride and direct his mule. He explained that it was going to take them three nights to reach the bank of the Sirwan River, the border between Iraq and Iran.

"When we reach the border," he explained to Reuben,

"I will signal my Iranian partner on the other bank of the river, and he will cross the river in a small rowboat to fetch you. His name is Sami Arajan. We have been working together for close to a year now. He is very reliable and trustworthy.

"Once inside Iran, you will be very safe. The Iranian authorities are very sympathetic towards the local Jewish community and pretty much facilitate all our activities without causing any trouble. We pay off the village Moula — that's what they call their leader — and the local Chief of Police, and everybody is very happy. The Iranians don't trust the Iraqis and are eager to help us get our people out of there."

Babba Mousa helped Reuben climb on top of the mule, attached his backpack to the saddle, climbed onto his own mule, and started riding up a small goat trail.

It was a frosty night. Reuben felt the cold breeze caressing his face, keeping him alert and helping his body fight the lack of sleep. He was thankful for the warm clothes, boots, and woolen head cover that protected him from the chilling air.

As they were riding below the crest line to avoid attention, he noticed that the soft moonlight was casting ghostly dark shadows around them. He followed the mysterious shadows up the hill to a group of tall trees swaying in the light breeze. Growing up in the big city, he rarely spent time in nature and especially not in the middle of the night. The lengthy night ride was a refreshing and exhilarating new experience he was starting to enjoy despite the risks and discomfort.

As dawn was breaking, Babba Mousa stopped,

dismounted from his mule, and signaled Reuben to follow suit. He tied the two mules to a large tree trunk and asked Reuben to stay back for a few minutes while he scouted their designated place to make camp. Babba Mousa circled the area, cautiously looking around and sniffing the air for a while until he decided it was safe. He walked around a large green bush on the side of the mountain and entered a wide opening hidden behind it. He took out a flashlight and went into a large cave. Within a few minutes, he reappeared next to Reuben and said, "It's clear. Let's go inside."

Leading his mule by the reins, Reuben followed Babba Mousa. He was surprised by the size of the cave, illuminated by the bright light shining from Babba Mousa's flashlight. There were high ceilings with pointy gray stalactite formations and a floor of blended rock and soil. Reuben couldn't see where the cave ended, but it appeared to be quite deep. He could hear the distant noise of dripping water which must have given the cave the musty odor he had detected upon entering. From the exterior landscape it didn't appear as if anything was there, yet a small, new world opened up inside.

They led the mules into a concealed corner of the cave and unloaded the packages from the saddles.

Babba Mousa took a large leather water jug and filled two round bowls for the mules to quench their thirst. He then filled the same bowls with a mixture of dried grains to keep them fed and content. He took two thick woolen blankets and spread them on the cave's floor next to each other. "We will sleep here until sundown," he informed Reuben. "I will wake you up when it's time for dinner."

Reuben woke up to the sounds of crackling fire and the smell of light smoke. He opened his eyes and saw Babba Mousa kindling a small fire and heating some food in a saucepan.

"Good evening, Reuben," Babba Mousa greeted him. "Please wash up and join me for some delicious dinner. You will need lots of energy for our long journey tonight."

Babba Mousa was sitting on the ground with his legs crossed and two warm metal dishes set in front of him. He dipped his long fingers into a rice dish, twirling them skillfully until the rice formed into a nice round ball. He then dipped the rice ball into the second dish filled with a soupy mix of dried meat and cooked beans.

Finally he lifted his long fingers from the second dish, tilted his head up, and stuffed the entire mixture into his wide-opened mouth. He started chewing the mixture with great pleasure, mouth open, jaws clicking, and lips sucking together loudly. He then licked his fingers methodically as if he were eating a heavenly delicacy at one of the finest restaurants in Baghdad.

Reuben sat down opposite him and tried to imitate his skilled actions as best he could. To his great surprise, the mixture was very tasty. Being nearly famished, he wolfed it down quickly while watching Babba Mousa closely in an attempt to perfect the primitive eating technique. He found this ceremonial meal quite enjoyable and remembered stories of how the desert nomads never used utensils during their meals, a tale that before now he'd always found hard to believe.

"Babba Mousa," Reuben said, "I am very curious to hear about your childhood and what life was like in the desert for a lost Jewish tribe. It sounds so intriguing — it must have been quite an experience."

"It was quite an adventure, I would say," Babba Mousa started his story, "but I am glad we are out of that wilderness and back in the land of milk and honey that God promised our forefathers.

"We were a nomad tribe of about five hundred people who found refuge in the desolate deserts of southwestern Iraq, tending our sheep and camels and trying to avoid contact with the enemies who have always tried to destroy us. We lived from hand to mouth, day-to-day, uncertain where the next meal would come from or what adversary would attack us next.

"We were the remnant of a very large and glorious Jewish tribe who lived several hundred years ago in the fertile plateau of Chieber in the southern parts of Arabia. We proudly followed the ancient laws of Moses, cultivating a rich culture of poets, writers, and philosophers. Our fierce warriors were feared and respected across the land, and we lived in peace and harmony for many generations.

"With the rise of the Prophet Mohammed, we came under mounting pressure to adopt the beliefs of Islam, become part of his empire, or be subjected to extinction by his growing army of believers. Our leaders refused to abandon our heritage and tried to live side by side with our neighbors as we had for so many generations, but the Prophet rejected our attempts for compromise and declared a holy war against our tribe.

"The Prophet's armies lay siege to our city, Chieber, trying to destroy it, but our strong army defeated them in several battles. This is when the Prophet decided to change his tactics. He sent emissaries to the leaders of Chieber and offered them a peace treaty. As soon as the peace accord was signed and the city gates opened, Mohammed's armies attacked."

"But they agreed not to attack the city," Reuben interjected angrily.

"Yes, they did, but it was a dirty trick to overpower us. You see the laws of Islam permit the use of a 'treaty' as a deceit mechanism to defeat their enemies. They led us to believe that the treaty would protect us and restore peace, but when our guard was down, they took advantage of our trust and unleashed the army of Islamic believers to destroy us."

"This is similar to the treacherous trick they used to execute my father," Reuben said, his anger mounting. "In hundreds of years, not much has changed in this part of the world."

"You are right, Reuben. This is why it is so important for you to start a new chapter in your life in a free and independent county."

Babba Mousa continued his story. "We fought fiercely for days, drastically outnumbered by our enemies, our fortresses disintegrating, and warriors falling one after another until their spilled blood soaked the land and painted it bright red. We were doomed for destruction, our remnants expelled and dispersed in the lands of Arabia.

"A group of warriors took their families and escaped

into the great desert to find refuge from their pursuers. They hid in the mountains and moved around from place to place, always in fear of being discovered and killed. Gradually they adapted to the desert life and looked like other nomad tribes wandering in the deserts of Arabia. They continued to maintain their traditions and their ancestors' prayers, even though the knowledge of their origin began to fade over time.

"The remnants stuck together and trained their young in the skills of survival in the harsh environment of the desert. They were taught to use weapons and fight the ferocious nomad tribes and gangs of villains who tried to deprive them of their livelihood. They learned to grow certain crops that could survive in the desert and to feed and protect the flocks that provided their essentials of survival.

"My father became the leader of the tribe after his father passed away, and he continued the legacy of teaching our youngsters the skills of survival and self-defense. We had a limited amount of guns and rifles that we'd acquired over time. We were taught to fight with knives, swords, bows and arrows, and our own fists."

"That part must have been real fun." Reuben tried to insert his opinion while dealing with a mouthful of the rice concoction.

"It was, until we had to face real enemies in battle," Babba Mousa acknowledged, rinsing his hands and mouth with water from a jug.

"We kept the Sabbath and murmured the prayers every morning and evening, although we barely understood what our lips were muttering. We were determined to carry on our tradition and maintain our unique identity.

"This is how life went on year after year until we heard a rumor that the Jews of Iraq were being allowed to return to their homeland. My father sent me with a small delegation to the town of Ramadi, west of Baghdad, to consult with the local Jewish community leaders. We were told that indeed the rumors were true and that the community was making a mass exodus from Iraq to Israel.

"When we reported the news to my father, he quickly decided that we would all be going back to the land of our ancestors. I was sent to Baghdad to make all the arrangements and prepare the paperwork for our departure. Our entire tribe renounced Iraqi citizenship and climbed on buses to Baghdad, anxiously awaiting their final departure. It was a magical scene watching desert nomads who had ridden camels all their lives climbing into the large silver birds that spread their wings and soared over the vast deserts to reunite them with their people."

Babba Mousa got up, filled a round tall pot with water, boiled it, and added four heaping spoons of strong black coffee. He let the mixture boil again, and then poured it into two metal cups.

"Here is some fresh Turkish coffee, Reuben. It's good for you! It will keep you wide awake throughout the night. I don't want you dozing off or falling off the mule. You need to stay very alert."

The coffee tasted bitter, but it had the same aroma and sharp taste as the one served by Nadia.

"Sorry, I forgot the sugar," Babba Mousa's apologetic voice echoed throughout the cave.

)

CHAPTER 13

It was dark when they walked out of the cave. The moon was low on the horizon, and the cold breeze seemed to have grown stronger.

They rode all night through steep hills and deep valleys. Babba Mousa seemed to know his way and navigated through the mountains as if he were in his own backyard. To Reuben, all the hills looked the same; he didn't quite understand how his guide was able to determine directions and find his way to their second camping place merely by looking at the shiny bright stars of the vast heavens.

Dawn was breaking as they approached their next camping location in a nearby cave Babba Mousa used frequently during his smuggling journeys. Apparently caves were his favorite hideout since they provided shelter from the harsh environment and were avoided by locals in fear of legendary monsters hiding inside.

Reuben was nearly exhausted; the effort of riding on a mule for ten hours on the rigorous terrain had taken its toll on him.

Suddenly both mules came to an abrupt halt. Reuben looked up, trying to figure out the reason for the delay. In the dim light of dawn, he noticed two men blocking their path, pointing long rifles at Babba Mousa.

"Put your hands up and don't move, or we will kill you both," they ordered in the familiar thick northern Iraqi accent. Caught completely by surprise, Babba Mousa and Reuben complied immediately.

Babba Mousa was the first to gain his composure and attempt to open a dialogue with them. "What do you want with us, brothers? We are just poor shepherds traveling back to our village after a long journey. We don't wish anybody harm."

"We will find out pretty soon how poor you are," answered the one who seemed to be the leader. They were both wearing old, faded, dirty clothing and soiled turbans on their heads. They appeared to be local mountain bandits looking for an opportunity to get quick money.

"Take your bags off the mules and throw them toward us," the leader commanded in a loud voice. Babba Mousa did so quickly, apparently trying to appear cooperative in order to put the robbers' minds at ease and slacken their guard.

By now, the sun had started rising, and they could see the men's faces. They appeared to be in their late forties, their deeply tanned dark faces starting to show wrinkle lines beside their eyes. They wore thick beards and moustaches sparsely mixed with white hair on the fringes. The leader had an ugly long scar running down his left cheek to below his mouth line. He pointed his gun at them while his partner emptied their bags and searched through them.

He emptied Reuben's backpack and seemed to like the new clothing Reuben had bought. He picked up every garment and displayed it in front of him to see how well it would fit.

"Poor shepherds don't have money for new clothing," he announced in a loud voice. "What else are you hiding from us?" He took Reuben's backpack, turned it inside out, and patted it all around to search for hidden objects. Reuben froze. His mother's jewelry and the remaining money were hidden inside the foam padding of the backpack. These were the only items of value he had left, and he was hoping they would help him start his new life. He prayed that the robber would not cut the backpack open and discover his little hidden treasure.

Babba Mousa was at it again, trying to converse with them.

"We saved every penny all year long to buy some warm clothing for our children to keep them warm in the frigid winter months. These clothes are too small for you anyway!"

"What else did you buy in the big city?" the leader continued his interrogation.

"Just some flour and rice to feed our family in the cold winter months," Babba Mousa answered.

"Shut up already with your complaints about your family being cold and hungry," the leader snapped angrily. "I have enough troubles of my own. If you don't stop talking right now, I will make sure you will have nothing to worry about very soon."

The second robber signaled to the leader that he had finished going through their belongings. The leader looked at Babba Mousa and ordered: "Get off your mule. Then put your hands back up and lie down on the ground." He pointed to the side of the trail as he took a couple of steps forward, looked at Reuben, and said, "After your father is on the ground, you will do the same. If you don't follow my orders, I will shoot you both dead."

"We will obey your orders," Babba Mousa said softly. "We have nothing to hide from you, brothers. You can take our belongings — just spare our lives. We have young children to feed, by the grace of Allah."

"Just shut up and get on with it." The leader was becoming very agitated with Babba Mousa.

Babba Mousa started to dismount from his saddle very slowly. Reuben noticed his right hand, hidden from the robbers, quickly releasing the reins of the second mule that had been tied to his saddle. As he was slowly stepping down onto the ground, he gave a very high-pitched shriek into the mule's left ear while at the same time kneeling down next to the mule and whacking its hind left thigh with all his might.

The frightened mule suddenly charged toward the two stunned robbers. They jumped sideways to try to avoid the mule's massive body storming toward them like a freight locomotive. The leader was quick enough to avoid the mule, whose mighty chest barely scraped his left shoulder and pushed him to the side of the path. His partner wasn't so lucky: the mule slammed onto his chest and with a loud thud flung him several yards away.

Babba Mousa rolled to his left side and emerged with a long commando knife that had been strapped to his right leg under his garments. Reuben saw him kneeling forward on his right knee, his left leg bent forward in front of him. Slowly he drew his right arm backward, his long fingers gripping the handle of the knife, his knuckles tensely stretched apart. His eyes sparkled with excitement as his arm began moving forward in slow motion that appeared to take forever.

The leader attempted to get up and regain his composure and balance. He tried to raise his cumbersome long rifle to try and take aim at Babba Mousa, but the weapon was awkward to handle. As he struggled to aim it, Reuben heard the whipping sound of the gleaming knife slicing through the cold morning air.

The knife struck the bandit in the center of his chest with tremendous force, the thin blade piercing through his clothing so that only the heavy handle stuck out of his coat. He fell down instantly and lay motionless on the ground.

Babba Mousa jumped to his feet, a pistol drawn in his right hand. He ran toward the fallen robber, covered the barrel of his pistol with his coat sleeve, and put a bullet through the man's temple. He then ran toward the second robber lying several yards away and shot him in the head at close range, again covering the gun barrel with his sleeve. The coat sleeve muffled the noise of the two shots, minimizing possible attention to the drama taking place in the small valley.

The whole episode had taken less than a minute.

Reuben had never dismounted. He watched the entire incident in astonishment from the back of his mule, which remained motionless the entire time. Reuben tightened the reins firmly to deter his mule from running forward. He realized that they were in grave danger, but everything had happened so quickly that he hadn't had the opportunity to digest the implications of the events unfolding in front of him.

Babba Mousa ran back toward him and asked him to dismount quickly. "Tie your mule to this tree and hide in these bushes," he ordered. "I need to scout the area to make sure these bastards worked alone and that no one else is aware of their fate. Look out for my mule, and if you see it, pull it by its reins and tie it to the tree next to yours."

Babba Mousa scouted the area meticulously for a while looking for evidence of any suspicious activity. When he was satisfied the area was clear, he returned to where Reuben was hiding.

"For the time being everything appears to be calm. They must have been working alone, but I don't think it was a coincidence. They were expecting us, so they must have had some advance knowledge of our movements. They knew our travel route and where we were preparing to camp for the day, hoping to take us by surprise just as we were ready to enter the cave.

"Reuben, pick up your stuff and bring your mule into the cave. We will need to bury the scumbags inside the cave and cover all the tracks. I will carry their bodies inside and clean the surrounding area."

Babba Mousa carried the two bodies into the cave

and placed them in a corner away from the entrance.

"Reuben, start digging a large hole to bury them," he said in an authoritative tone. "I need to go look for my mule before it gets too far away. I don't think we can make the rest of the journey on foot and get to our destination on time. I will be back as soon as I can."

Using one of the metal saucepans as a shovel, Reuben started digging a large hole. The ground inside the cave was soft and damp, which made his eerie task tolerable. The thought of the two bodies lying not too far from him was very ghoulish. This was the first time in his life that he had seen a dead person this close, and his imagination was running wild. He was sure the two robbers were only pretending to be dead and that any second they would get up and attack him.

The calm voice of the returning Babba Mousa alleviated his fears. "I found my mule grazing near the stream. I don't think it appreciated the way I smacked it and screamed in its ear, but I think it will get over it. After all, it did a great job helping us get rid of these miserable robbers."

Babba Mousa joined Reuben in the digging. "I hope these guys didn't give you too much trouble while I was gone," he said jokingly.

"I didn't quite enjoy their dry sense of humor," Reuben joked back, "but their armed robbery stories were quite fascinating. Do you really think they were going to kill us?"

"Most certainly," Babba Mousa replied. "Mountain robbers rarely leave witnesses or evidence behind. They would have killed us for the two mules alone, but they wanted to search and question us to make sure we didn't have money and valuables hidden elsewhere."

"Babba Mousa, you were just amazing...the way you handled the situation and got rid of them in a flash. I didn't know you had any concealed weapons. The way you threw the knife right into his heart was absolutely incredible."

"My father taught me how to handle robbers from a very young age, and we practiced these techniques frequently," Babba Mousa responded humbly to the compliments. "It was part of growing up and learning how to survive in the desert. It was the only way we could endure in the wilderness with all sorts of predators fighting for the limited amount of food and shelter available.

"We were trained in knife throwing and had target practice every week. I mastered the skill very quickly and worked on it a lot in my spare time, which was plentiful. During target competitions, I was always in first place for my age group. I could hit a desert rat from fifteen yards in the blink of an eye."

"That nasty rat today didn't even have a chance to realize what hit him. He must have died instantly," Reuben commented.

"The rest of my training and weapon handling skills I learned as part of an elite commando unit of the Israeli Army. A full year of training taught me how to handle any kind of emergency. I am sure you have heard of the daring operations these elite units executed successfully during war times."

"Actually you don't hear much about these things

in Baghdad," Reuben told him. "You only hear bad things about Israel on the radio and read them in the newspapers, about how the country is so poor that most people live in tents, have no jobs, and hardly any food. But I always knew it was just propaganda from the Iraqi government to discourage more Jews from leaving and joining their families in Israel.

"Babba Mousa," Reuben continued, "I am very curious why you shot them both in the head after they were dead already."

"The golden rule is not to take any chances by making sure they are indeed dead. There were too many incidents during fighting when enemy soldiers pretended to be dead, and when our soldiers got close to them, they were shot at close range. We lost many friends to such careless mistakes, so we learned our lesson. Now we don't take any chances that could jeopardize our safety. The rule of war is, 'It's better to kill your enemy twice than let them kill you once.'

"We've got to get moving now, Reuben. It's not safe to stay here much longer, and we need to travel farther before I can find another shelter for us to rest. You never know who these guys were connected with or who may come looking for them."

They buried the two robbers and their rifles in the large ditch in the cave. Babba Mousa brushed the soil above the fresh grave with a branch and then spread dry soil and old manure over it.

"We will stop to rest at another location in a couple of hours," he informed Reuben. "I am going to alter our route somewhat just in case somebody is following us.

Please keep a close eye on the surroundings and report anything suspicious to me."

* * * *

Just before dawn on the third day, they arrived at the agreed location on the bank of the Sirwan River. The river was bordered by thick reeds that grew wildly in the water. Babba Mousa found a small path to the water's edge, took out a small flashlight, and transmitted a few short signals to the other side. Within a few seconds, they saw lights flashing back from the opposite bank.

"This is it!" he said to Reuben. "The man will be here to fetch you very soon. I wish you the best with your new life, my dear friend Reuben. I know you are going to love Israel. I am confident you will be very successful in whatever you set your mind to accomplish. Your entire future is ahead of you. Just make the best of it now that you are a free man. I will look for you when I complete my time here. After this incident, it may be sooner than I thought. Who knows? Maybe some greedy informant is trying to benefit from our zeal for freedom."

"Thank you for saving my life, Babba Mousa. I will never forget our adventure. I hope to reunite with you in Israel soon and celebrate our freedom together." They embraced.

When the small rowboat reached their bank, Reuben quickly climbed into it. He was very anxious to leave the Iraqi soil that had brought so much agony to his family and start his new journey of freedom. Babba Mousa introduced him to Sami Arajan, the Agency man in Teheran.

"Sami will be responsible for getting you to the Agency's headquarters where your travel arrangements will be finalized. Then you will participate in a short orientation program.

"Next year in Jerusalem!" Babba Mousa declared and quickly disappeared into the thick reeds.

Within minutes, the small boat reached the opposite bank of the river, and Reuben was finally safe in Iranian territory. He followed Sami up a narrow winding trail until they reached a dirt road where a small truck was parked.

"No mules here," Sami joked in fluent Arabic, although Farsi, the language of Iran, was his native language. "We drive on the highways and byways with no fear. We have the full support of the Shah's administration, which maintains a very close relationship with the Israelis. The Israeli secret service trained all the Shah's personal bodyguards and laid the foundations for establishing his own secret services to protect him and his regime.

"You can relax now, Reuben. You are a free man. Take a deep breath and smell the sweet fragrance of freedom."

* * * *

Two days later, Sami and Reuben reported to the Agency's central headquarters in Teheran.

The head of the Agency came out to greet Reuben personally. "It's our pleasure to have you with us, Mr. Sasson. We have been anticipating your arrival anxiously and are glad you are here safely. We heard about the troubles you ran into on the way here, and I am very pleased that you were in the safe hands of Babba Mousa. He is our most experienced and courageous guide who can handle almost anything that falls into his lap."

"He certainly did in the most amazing way," Reuben said with a smile. "I miss him already!"

"I will send a coded message to the rabbi's office in Baghdad to let him know that you've arrived here safely. He will get the message to your mother. I am sure she will be very happy with the good news. However, we are told that she is still in the hospital, and sadly her condition has not improved.

"Reuben, you will stay here with us for about a week and participate in an orientation program to prepare you for your new life in Israel. Upon the completion of the program, you will board an El Al flight from Teheran to Lod Airport in Israel where the Agency's Youth Director will welcome you. He will make arrangements for your settling down in Israel and for taking care of all your needs."

* * * *

Reuben had a relaxing week in Teheran. He was with a group of fifteen teenagers assembled there from several neighboring countries to prepare them for their journey to their ancient homeland. They had classes during the day that taught them the history of the Jewish nation including the establishment of the Jewish state, the War of Independence, and basic Hebrew.

During the evenings, they had social gatherings with group singing and dancing to Israeli folk songs. One evening, the group went for a night on the town where they were treated to a lavish meal at a famous kosher restaurant in Teheran's Jewish section. It was a great morale-building week with the spirits of the youngsters rising to the highest level of national patriotism.

* * * *

Salima was resting in a semiconscious state in her bed at the El-Rashid Hospital. She was heavily sedated with medications to relieve her pain. She felt someone holding her hands and shaking her arm, calling "Salima! Salima!" She turned her head in a haze and saw an elderly man with a long white beard and round-rimmed glasses looking at her and trying to talk to her.

"I must have reached the gates of heaven," she thought, "and the man must be an angel welcoming me." She muttered a great sigh of relief from the misery of the world she lived in and was engulfed with a feeling of ultimate heavenly exhilaration. "It feels so good to enter the gates of heaven and be free of all the human suffering on earth," she thought.

"Wake up, Salima. Wake up. It's Rabbi Shemtov. I've come to bring you wonderful news."

Salima opened her eyes again slowly. "Is that really you, Rabbi?" she inquired. "I thought I was in heaven already and all my troubles were over."

"Listen, Salima, I had to let you know the great news about Reuben. I just got a message from Teheran. Your son has arrived there safely and will be on his way to his final destination next week. You can relax now. He is safe and free. Your efforts have been crowned with success, for the Almighty has granted your final wish."

"Bless you, dear Rabbi. I couldn't have done it without your help and dedication. The Almighty will reward your pure heart and precious soul for all that you have done for this community and me. May you be granted entry to the Promised Land and be united with your ancestors, the holy priests of the temple in Jerusalem. Now that you have brought me the wonderful news, I can go through the gates of heaven with a pure conscience."

Salima closed her eyes slowly. She looked very calm and very much at peace with herself. She was happy to leave the desolation of earth, and eager to reunite with her beloved husband, Daniel, in the tranquility of the heavens above. Oh, how she longed to kiss his face and his eyes, put her fingers through his smooth silky hair, hug him close to her heart as hard as she could, and smell the pleasant scent of his body!

"Daniel, Daniel, I am finally here with you. I missed you so much all this time. Part of me was gone when you left us. I couldn't live without you any longer. It feels so divine to be back together and safe in your arms again."

CHAPTER 14

ISRAEL, 1960

El Al Flight 309 from Teheran to Tel Aviv landed at nearby Lod Airport. Reuben was among a group of fifteen young new immigrants arriving on that flight. The anxious passengers waited patiently until a portable stairway was attached to the plane. One by one they descended slowly, and upon reaching the tarmac, they prostrated themselves and kissed the ground, their teary eyes closed and their lips murmuring the prayer of survival, "Blessed be our God, ruler of the universe, who kept us alive, sustained us, and enabled us to reach this time."

Recalling his mother's request, Reuben kissed the ground three times and repeated the prayer for himself, for his mother, and for his father. He felt an enormous sense of relief. Now he was in his own country, with his own people, and his future was in his own hands. His fate was no longer controlled by some dictator or government that could oppress him, confiscate his belongings, or murder him as they had his father.

The Agency's youth director welcomed the youngsters warmly, handing each a bouquet of flowers and a small package of goodies all proudly made in Israel. They were ushered to the immigration authorities where they were registered and issued new immigrant identification cards. Family members flocked upon the arrival gate with anticipation and excitement, eager to celebrate the end of a long separation from their loved ones.

Because Reuben was an orphan and had no knowledge of any family members living in Israel, he needed to be placed in an environment where he would be provided with his basic needs while having the opportunity to learn Hebrew quickly and to continue his education. The youth director decided to put him in a kibbutz, a collective farming community, which was the ideal environment for a young, patriotic immigrant. There he could enjoy the life of a community of real pioneers who shared social equality and strong national values.

All kibbutz members were obligated to contribute equally toward the fieldwork and domestic duties that involved the day-to-day running of the community. At the kibbutz, he would have an opportunity to attend school, learn the language, help in planting and harvesting, assist in milking cows, and work in the communal kitchen. He would quickly learn what life was all about in a new country made of a multitude of immigrants who had fled from all corners of the earth to their last hope for safety, independence, and renewal.

The youth director decided to send him to Kibbutz Deganya, located in the beautiful setting of the fertile

Jordan valley on the banks of the Sea of Galilee. Deganya was considered an economically solid kibbutz with diversified agricultural enterprises that included fruit orchards, fields for cultivating various grains, cattle, and poultry. The youth program combined accelerated Hebrew learning, high school general studies, and a wide variety of jobs at the kibbutz. In particular it ran a very successful program for young immigrants who had no family or who were separated from family living abroad.

Some of these youngsters had left their countries and families with the encouragement of their parents or on their own initiative in search of freedom and self-determination. Most had to escape and undergo long, perilous journeys driven by a strong flame in their hearts that urged their inner strength to put an end to the humiliation, suffering, and holocausts their people had endured for centuries.

Their sheer determination to control their own destiny and fight for their human rights had brought them back to their ancient homeland.

* * * *

After a short orientation, Reuben took a bus from Tel Aviv to Deganya. His trip took about three hours with numerous stops on the way. He had the opportunity to view a large portion of the country and its landscape from the window of the bus, which traveled from the flat planes of the Mediterranean Sea through the mountains and valleys of the lower Galilee. He was surprised to notice there were large portions of the land still uninhabited and undeveloped. He realized the pioneers' work had just started, with much more needing to be done to build this young country.

Reuben fell in love with Deganya and its beautiful setting on the shores of the sea, the striking tall palm trees ornamenting its entrance, and the friendliness of the kibbutz members, who were so genuine in their welcoming.

The youth groups and their counselors were housed in wooden structures with separate quarters for boys and girls. Each room was modestly furnished with four metal beds, straw mattresses, and wooden closets. There were separate communal bathrooms and showers for boys and girls. The counselors' job was to provide the youngsters with assistance and guidance throughout their busy day and supervise them during the evening hours.

They had a hectic daily schedule. They woke up at 6 a.m. and reported for kitchen duty from 6:30 a.m. to 8 a.m. At 8:30 a.m. they started their two-hour beginners' Hebrew class called *Ulpan*. From 11 a.m. to 3 p.m., they attended classes at a regional high school nearby. They had a short break from 3 to 4 p.m., and then they reported for duty at the cowshed to feed the cows, milk them, and clean up. After a quick shower, they gathered in the dining room to enjoy a home-cooked dinner while relaxing and chatting with their friends and other kibbutz members.

However, their schedules changed frequently depending on the seasons and the type of work needing to be done. They also had the opportunity to rotate among jobs in different specialty areas and in the process learn many skills from their mentors.

During the hot summers typical of the valley, they had to get up at dawn to harvest the ripe fruits in the orchards before it became too hot to stay outdoors. They worked in the orchards from daybreak until 10 a.m. and spent the afternoons on their Hebrew lessons and general studies.

Every youngster was assigned an adopting family from the kibbutz to help him or her become acquainted with life there, provide emotional support and encouragement during the transition period, and fill the gap left by missing parents. Reuben's adoptive parents were Amnon and Yaffa Harrari. They were second-generation founding members whose family had come from Russia in the early 1900s.

Their parents were true pioneers who arrived in Israel penniless and built their life and family from the fruit of their hard work and courage. The Harrari family was an inspiration to Reuben with their undeterred national conviction, solid work ethic, and true warmth.

They welcomed him into their family as one of their own and provided him with a sense of family and belonging, a major kibbutz principle for ensuring continuity of future generations. Their eldest son, Ronen, happened to be Reuben's counselor and became a very close friend.

Since kibbutz children were expected to do a lot of work and take on the responsibility of adults from a very young age, they were extremely independent and free-spirited. This atmosphere was quite appropriate for

Reuben, who had also learned to be autonomous early on and had spent most of his childhood days playing with his friends outdoors.

The kibbutz was characterized by simplicity, lack of materialism, and deep national devotion. In one of their early study sessions regarding Jewish history, the teacher reviewed the history of Deganya. Deganya, labeled "the Mother of all *Kibbutzim,*" was the first kibbutz established in 1910 by ten men and two women in what was then Palestine.

The name *Deganya* came from the Hebrew word *dagan* for grain because of the five types of grain grown in Deganya's fields: wheat, oats, barley, corn, and sorghum. The founders' goal was to establish an independent settlement of Jewish workers on land acquired by the Jewish National Fund from Iranian landowners. They wanted to create a real commune based on member equality without owners and workers, exploiters or exploited, managers or laborers. Everybody shared in the hard work and participated in the decision-making process, which took place by democratic vote. Social life revolved around the dining room table, where members met, ate, and dialogued. Debates and discussions often continued late into the night. Members decided how to allocate the following day's work in the fields, assign shifts for guard duties at night, determine the kitchen schedule, and do other miscellaneous tasks.

Over the course of time, the group faced tremendous obstacles: scorching heat during the long summers, plagues of nature, diseases, tense relations with their Arab neighbors, and a hostile British regime. Nevertheless, despite the problems and sacrifices they had to endure, their spirits did not waver. They also enjoyed happy occasions: families were established, children were born, and agricultural prosperity became a reality. Their economic viability and the justification of their founding ideas had finally proven true.

During Israel's War of Independence in 1948, the Syrian army prepared to invade the Galilee and take over the Jewish settlements, including Deganya. On the eve of the attack, the defenders of Deganya were desperately asking Central Command in Tel Aviv for arms and reinforcements in preparation to defend against the Syrian assault. Ben Gurion, the President of the Provisional Council, replied, "The whole country is on the front line. We don't have any reinforcements for you."

The advice from the Chief of Staff was, "Since you have only light weapons and the Syrians have artillery and heavy armor, allow them to approach within twenty or thirty yards from the gates of Deganya and then counterattack them."

Because they had advanced successfully through several other Jewish settlements, the Syrians were poised to take on Deganya. At sunrise, they opened fire with all their weaponry — tanks, artillery and aircraft — and continued for nine hours. Deganya's defenses were not designed to withstand such a large-scale assault. Its defenders who had witnessed the previous successes of the Syrian army believed the fight for the Galilee was irreparably lost.

Syrian forces then launched an attack on Deganya

in three columns. Tanks, covered by machine guns and rifle fire, led the assault, A Syrian tank from the second column succeeded in breaking through the security gates, crossing the trench dug in the road, and storming through the internal security barrier. As the tank approached the compound, suddenly a young man jumped out of the trenches and ran toward it and stood facing it with only two Molotov bottles in his hands. The battle of the Galilee hinged on one brave young man against a massive metal beast.

The Syrian crew, stunned by his appearance, struggled to react. Before they could open fire, the young man hurled the Molotov bottles at the tank, igniting it instantly. Witnessing the courageous action of their comrade, the other defenders moved out of their trenches and pelted the tank with Molotov bottles until it was an inferno.

The vision of the burning tank and the fate of its crew had a devastating impact on the Syrian forces. They started retreating in total disarray, leaving heavy losses behind. The battle of Deganya was won by the heroism of a brave young man who did not hesitate to put his life on the line to save his country from destruction.

Several hundred yards inside the gate of Deganya, opposite a banana plantation stands the same, authentic Syrian tank, a memorial to the battle of Deganya and the heroic young men and women who repulsed the attack by the Syrian army. This was Israel's first significant victory in the War of Independence. News of the victory traveled fast and served as a strong morale booster for all the Israeli defenders fighting Arab assaults along four fronts. It proved that victory was within reach and that the day of redemption was rapidly approaching.

The story of the battle of Deganya had a profound influence on Reuben. He admired the devotion and the bravery of the pioneer fighters who had built the country from desolate, rocky land plagued with swamps and malaria. They had never given in despite setbacks caused by vicious attacks and murders of close friends by Arab bandits. They were hard-working farmers during the day and soldiers at night, standing guard to protect their lives and the little property they'd managed to accumulate. They were modest, never boasting about their successes and victories against all odds. They were very simple, down-to-earth people, completely free from materialistic desires. They were the role models he had been searching for all of his life.

As the years went by, Deganya had flourished with a surge of social and economic development. A stable economy had been built based on agricultural expertise and advanced technology.

Reuben adored Deganya and felt strong affection towards its people. This was one of the happiest periods in his life. He treasured the closeness to nature he never had experienced in Baghdad, including the sweet smell of fruit trees in the orchards and the relationships he formed with his new friends and new family. After a hard day of work in the hot sun, he loved dipping into the glistening cool waters of the Sea of Galilee and then socializing with his friends after a delicious meal in the main dining room.

Deganya was laid out with communal facilities such

as the dining room, social hall, and administrative offices conveniently located at its center. Members' residences and landscaped gardens were scattered around the main facilities with an educational and sports complex beyond them. On the outskirts of the kibbutz stood industrial buildings housing agricultural equipment and serving as storage facilities for fertilizers, crops, animal feed, and other farm needs. On the outer perimeter were the vast agricultural lands used for growing grains, vegetables, and fruits.

Reuben was soon attending his senior year in high school. Fluent in Hebrew by now, he excelled in his studies and starred on the kibbutz soccer team; otherwise, he was always hard at work performing many duties.

Toward the end of his senior year, there was a lot of talk among his classmates about joining the army. Most of the kibbutz's young members volunteered to join elite units in the Israeli Defense Forces. Exemplary soldiers, many of them advanced swiftly through the IDF ranks and became high-ranking officers.

After three years at the kibbutz, Reuben had learned many facts about the IDF and the remarkable attitude of the young Israeli men and women who looked forward to serving their country and contributing their fair share to the effort of keeping the young state free and democratic.

Every Israeli citizen knew that without the strength and devotion of the young men and women in the service, the country could not survive, and its population would be subjected to a second Holocaust. Young IDF recruits considered it a great honor to volunteer for an elite unit or become an officer in the military.

Frequently there was intense competition among the young candidates who tried to outdo each other by joining the highest-ranking Special Forces to prove their superior abilities. IDF general command considered this competition a healthy phenomenon, proof of the strong motivation of its young soldiers to serve their nation in even the riskiest of missions. Elite unit commanders loved it because there was never a shortage of volunteers constantly crowding their recruitment centers.

With all that pride and eagerness, most recruits didn't really know what awaited them when they joined these elite units. Such service was an endless test of physical and emotional strength, endurance, and perseverance from the first day until the three-year compulsory service term was over.

At the conclusion of the regular service, enlisted men automatically joined the compulsory military reserve services. Reservists were called for active duty an average of forty-five days a year to refresh their combat skills, receive additional training, and replace regular combat units on the various front lines. IDF reserve units constituted close to seventy percent of the entire IDF military forces and actively participated in full-scale wars or extended service periods during national emergencies. IDF reservists remained on active duty until their late forties and then transferred to lighter duty assignments.

Having been immersed in this extremely patriotic environment and remembering the words of his mother before she died, Reuben was extremely excited about joining the IDF and stamping his own unique signature on its future. He knew this was part of his destiny and one of the ways he would contribute to the success and survival of his nation. Soon he must make up his mind and choose his path into the future as many of his ancestral leaders had done when they were called to serve their nation.

Reuben heard legendary stories about the glorious paratrooper brigade that became very famous for executing courageous missions with exacting precision and minimal casualties. They were also famous for the red berets and light-brown army boots they wore to distinguish them from other IDF units. They were an all-volunteer elite unit that enjoyed an overwhelming number of applicants during every recruitment session. Candidates who met the physical profile criteria to join had to undergo rigorous physical and mental endurance tests to prove that they were worthy. Reuben heard that only fifteen to twenty percent of the volunteer applicants were accepted, and only about seventy percent of those starting the long training actually graduated from the famous IDF Paratrooper School.

He used to look at the young kibbutz members who joined the paratroopers with a mixture of curiosity and envy. They came home for short weekend visits once or twice a month, proudly wearing their distinct uniforms and paratrooper wings. Reuben listened attentively to their stories about their intense training, night jumps from transport planes, and combat encounters.

These adventures really excited him and got Reuben's adrenaline pumping. He made up his mind to volunteer for the paratrooper brigade. He felt that he was physically fit to withstand the arduous training and smart enough to advance into officers' school and continue to develop his military training and leadership skills.

CHAPTER 15

ISRAEL, 1975

After a wave of violence unleashed by the PLO on Israeli civilian targets, the Israeli Prime Minister, Shlomo Harel, summoned his Mossad Chief, Avi Shaffir, for an urgent meeting. He opened the meeting by stating, "I asked you here because I am very alarmed with the continued success of recent PLO terrorist missions and our inadequacy to contain their vicious attacks on innocent civilians.

"It is my ultimate responsibility to protect the safety and well-being of every citizen in this country, and I intend to be very vigilant in this regard. We need to do something urgent and drastic about the situation. Our population cannot continue living under the shadow of terrorism, not knowing from where the next calamity will strike. We look helpless in front of our people and the entire world, and that makes me extremely unhappy. I am moving this matter to the top of your priority list, which means you will be heavily accountable to me for the outcome of a plan of action to neutralize the effectiveness of the PLO military arm.

"I need you to think hard and long and come up with an ingenious plan. By that, I mean we need to put some mechanism in place to allow us to control the PLO military actions and political destiny over the long term, yet have an effective, pre-emptive offensive strategy against their terrorist attacks for the short term."

"What are you thinking, Shlomo?" Shaffir, the chief of Israel's secret service agency asked. "How could we control the entire organization or be able to gain access to their terrorism plans?"

"One possible way," Harel continued, "could be to bribe a high level PLO official with access to this information and provide him with the means to transmit the information to us prior to attacks. We know that some high-ranking PLO officials will do anything for money, including selling their own people."

"It's not going to work!" Shaffir was quick to opine. "We learned from many years of operating high level moles that they don't last very long. If they reveal the PLO attack plans, and we foil every terrorist attempt, they will be exposed quickly. PLO counter-intelligence will realize after only a few failures that there is a high-level traitor in their midst, and we will have another Eli Cohen crisis on our hands."

Harel stood up and started pacing his spacious office as he pondered Shaffir's compelling response. He lit a cigarette, inhaling its smoke deep into his lungs and exhaling it slowly like a jet plume. "Another Eli Cohen inside the PLO is exactly what we need!" he exclaimed as he stopped next to Shaffir.

"It wouldn't have taken Eli much longer to become the President of Syria and gain control of the entire country. If only we hadn't been too eager to pressure him to transmit his intelligence so frequently and act on his tips even before the ink dried out, I could be negotiating a real peace accord with Syria right now.

"Avi, we must learn from our mistakes and avoid the same pitfalls. This time I want a brilliant plan that can be executed flawlessly. Please refresh my memory with regard to the circumstances that led to Eli's capture in Damascus. We can learn a lot from that fiasco and perfect our scheme this time around."

"I can think of a few fatal errors off the top of my head," Shaffir recalled. "Eli was discovered because of a secret transmitter he kept in his apartment. He used it to transmit intelligence to our headquarters near Tel Aviv. He was able to gather so much intelligence that his transmissions became more frequent and longer than his prescribed strict limits. His transmissions interfered with the communications of the Embassy of India located close to his villa. The embassy communications officer complained to the Syrian authorities about the frequent interference and asked that the source be investigated.

"This incident was another indication to the Syrian counterintelligence agency that a high-level spying operation was taking place in their capital. The Syrians could not identify the source of the transmissions for quite a while and eventually had to enlist the help of the Russian KGB to bring sophisticated electronic equipment that could pinpoint the location of the transmission source.

"Another major problem was Eli's need to travel back and forth to Israel. He came home periodically to be briefed by the Mossad and to visit his wife and children. His visits complicated matters even further and turned out to be a very risky proposition.

"While Eli was on an official tour with high-ranking Syrian and Arab League military officials to Syrian fortifications on the Golan Heights, he allowed himself to be photographed in public with them. His thinking was that his appearance in public with prominent military commanders would help him build recognition in the Arab world and accelerate his political career.

"These photographs were published in numerous Arab newspapers and as a result were subjected to routine examination by Egyptian counterintelligence. The Egyptians compared his newspaper photos with their records of Eli's interrogations while he lived in Egypt as an active Zionist Jew. At the time, he was suspected of assisting the Israelis in underground spying operations in Cairo and Alexandria. The resemblance raised the suspicion of the Egyptian counterintelligence agency.

"Months later, an old Egyptian school friend of Eli who saw his photo in the newspapers reported to the secret police that he believed this was a picture of an Egyptian Jew with whom he had gone to school. Eli hadn't undergone plastic surgery prior to his mission to change his facial features. Now it's a standard Mossad practice for high profile spies. This oversight facilitated his identification by the Egyptians, who then alerted the Syrians.

"The main reason Eli was sent to Syria and not to Egypt, where he grew up and would have felt very comfortable, was the Mossad's fear of detection and exposure by people who had known him as a young man. Ironically, the Egyptians were the ones who detected his presence in Syria.

"Perhaps the biggest mistake was made by an overconfident Mossad official, who leaked bits of Eli's intelligence briefings to the media. The leak made its way to a news report on the Voice of Israel, which was closely monitored by the Syrians. From that point, it didn't take much longer for the Syrians to put the pieces together. They showed up at his villa in Damascus one morning while he was transmitting another long report to Tel Aviv and surprised him in the act.

"We took too many unjustifiable risks with Eli," Shaffir concluded, "and they bit us right in the face in front of the entire world. We lost our best spy ever along with a golden opportunity to change the fate of our conflict with Syria."

"This time it has to be a very well-thought out, iron-clad plan," Harel stated. "We can't afford to risk another failure, and I will not allow the bloodshed of innocent civilians to continue. I want you to put your brilliant scheming brain to work and come up with the best plan of your career.

"One more thing before you leave: this undertaking is to be treated with the most extreme secrecy. No one aside from the two of us is to have any idea of what we are planning here. Use other operation codes to cover up the activities and searches you need for this operation. Minimize the use of other staffers as much as you can. Also I want nothing in writing on this, absolutely no records or documentation whatsoever. I hope I am making myself perfectly clear on that," Harel emphasized as he concluded the meeting.

* * * *

Shaffir didn't waste any time. The PM was his direct superior who had appointed him to his post when he took office. Shaffir answered to no one but him. He thought the PM's idea of planting an agent who could rise through the ranks of the PLO was very clever and workable, if he could just identify an ideal candidate for the mission. The candidate would be the key to success, just as in Eli's case. Shaffir knew he would soon be looking for someone with a perfectly matched profile and exceptional leadership skills. He needed an individual who could gain popularity among the Palestinian people and the Arab countries supporting their cause. Only this time the chosen recruit would have to operate under a revolutionary set of new rules to delay his inevitable detection and prevent his eventual demise.

Shaffir decided to pursue the PM's idea first to see how far he could get with it. He knew that without the perfect candidate for the mission and a foolproof cover story, the chances of success were remote. Recent intelligence gathered by his agents indicated the PLO had finally become sophisticated in screening new recruits and weeding out planted spies. They'd learned from their past mistakes that accepting new recruits without systematic background checks allowed the Mossad and other rivals to penetrate their ranks with relative ease. Accordingly, they'd turned to the KGB spymasters to provide months of training in recruit screening processes and identity validation.

Shaffir sat down in his office and made a list of the traits his candidate must possess for this job:

> Semite appearance, looks like an Arab
>
> Can behave as a Palestinian Arab
>
> Fluent in the Arabic language, specifically Palestinian dialect
>
> Familiar with Muslim religion, customs, culture, and mentality
>
> Familiar with the history of the Palestinian people and their struggle for independence
>
> Familiar with the structure of the PLO and its rival factions
>
> Fluent in English
>
> Unmarried with minimal family ties in Israel
>
> A loner who can operate on his own for many years
>
> Physically fit and able to lead and command military operations
>
> Outstanding leadership and negotiation skills
>
> Exceptional memory to store and retrieve information rapidly
>
> Unequivocally loyal, patriotic, and dedicated

> to the cause and long-term objectives of the
> Jewish state

Such a person couldn't possibly exist, Shaffir thought as he entered the candidate search criteria into his secure terminal of the Mossad's supercomputer. He started scanning through the computerized records of his top agents. He knew he didn't have the luxury of spending five years to train and prepare a candidate for such a colossal undertaking, although that would be the normal preparation time if the level of urgency weren't so great. He was certain he would have to compromise and pick a candidate who simply came as close as possible to the long qualification list. The rest, he thought, would have to be accomplished through extensive training and preparations.

Shaffir was looking for a male in his early to mid-thirties who had grown up in an Arab state, spoke fluent Arabic, and was single. The Mossad owned one of the country's most sophisticated supercomputers that was constantly being upgraded with the latest technological advancements. It was loaded with huge databases ranging from its own personnel records to the records of both friendly and unfriendly operatives worldwide as well as records on every intelligence agency in the world, including its history. Shaffir knew that if his man existed, his supercomputer would find him.

To his surprise, his computer search yielded eight possible candidates. The Mossad was very fortunate to have a myriad of Arabic-speaking agents who had been raised in Arab countries and immigrated to Israel as young adults. He started going through each record meticulously. His sixth record, an agent known by the code name Mountain Lion, looked very interesting.

Born in Baghdad, father executed, concealed identity by living as a Palestinian, escaped from Iraq, placed at Deganya, joined the paratrooper brigade. These words were like music to Shaffir's ears. With increased curiosity, he turned to the agent's military record

An outstanding soldier, he'd advanced rapidly through the paratrooper's ranks and become a lieutenant within eighteen months. As a young captain, he'd commanded a paratrooper company of one hundred fifty men during the 1967 war Israel fought against its three neighboring Arab states. He'd been decorated with the Medal of Courage for his fierce fighting, personal leadership, and sacrifice in the battle over Jerusalem. After the war, he'd continued his career with the paratroopers, advanced to the rank of lieutenant colonel, and been appointed to command a paratrooper battalion.

While in the IDF service, he'd attended the Hebrew University in Jerusalem, entering a bachelor's degree program in Middle Eastern studies. Fluent in Arabic and very familiar with the nature of the Israeli-Arab conflict, he'd excelled in the program and graduated with distinction. His invaluable qualifications, comprehensive knowledge of the Arab world, and distinct service record had been brought to the attention of the head of Military Intelligence. The MI head had then submitted an urgent request to IDF General Command to transfer him to MI authority.

The request had been granted, and the new MI

recruit was trained and subsequently appointed Chief Intelligence Officer for IDF Northern Command. In this capacity, his duty was to assess the military capability and offensive intentions of Syria. He was responsible for predicting the intentions of the Syrians during the period of massive buildup along the Israeli-Syrian border leading to the 1973 Yom-Kippur war that took Israel by complete surprise. All his urgent appeals to the head of MI to call up the reserve IDF forces and send reinforcements to the front had been dismissed.

During the war, he'd provided IDF forces on the Golan Heights with precise intelligence on the advances of Syrian armor columns into Israeli-held territory. He'd played a critical role in halting the Syrian advances on Israeli settlements in the south of the Golan and deploying reinforcements to all fronts to repel the Syrian forces. He'd acted with extreme courage and determination during these critical hours of fighting on which the very existence of the young Jewish state hinged heavily.

After the IDF regained its control over the Golan, the agent had been immediately reassigned to the paratrooper brigade fighting the Egyptian army on the southern front. He took over the command of a paratrooper battalion whose commander had been seriously injured during the initial fighting. The mission of his battalion was to drive back the advancing Egyptian forces in the Sinai desert. His battalion played a significant role in halting the Egyptian progress in the Sinai, subsequently advancing to cross the Suez Canal and trapping the Egyptian third army in the Sinai.

For his heroism, initiative in battle, and personal sacrifice, he'd received the most prestigious medal awarded to IDF personnel, the Medal of Valor. Since the War of Independence, fewer than thirty IDF soldiers had earned such medals.

At the conclusion of the war, he'd been promoted to the rank of full colonel and returned to Military Intelligence. As the emphasis began shifting toward the PLO, he'd been appointed to lead a newly formed Anti-Terrorism Intelligence Group. The mission of his group was to collect information on the various Palestinian terrorist organizations, monitor their activities closely, and coordinate strikes at the heart of their operations. This assignment had provided him with the opportunity to gain a great deal of knowledge about the structure of the PLO political and military wings, their methods of operation, their leadership, and both their internal politics and rivaling factions.

His impact on the success of the unit had been felt within the first few months of his taking the reins. The intelligence was much more accurate and reliable. The level of success of Israeli commando preemptive strikes against terrorist organizations rose significantly, while the success of PLO raids on the Israeli population declined to its lowest level.

The agent's unprecedented success in anti-terrorism activities had captured the attention of Mossad recruiters, who submitted an urgent request through the Prime Minister's office to have MI allow his recruitment into the Mossad.

Shaffir didn't need to read much further. One of his

best skills was the ability to pick the right person for the right job, and he felt this agent could be the one. He destroyed all his handwritten notes and arranged to meet the agent the following morning.

* * * *

Agent Mountain Lion showed up for the meeting on time. The handsome, neatly dressed, young and courteous man impressed Shaffir immediately. His dark complexion, black hair, and brown eyes would allow him to pass as an Arab anywhere, anytime.

Shaffir opened the conversation in classic Arabic, inquiring about his upbringing in Iraq. The agent answered in flawless Arabic in the Palestinian Moslem dialect.

Shaffir knew from experience that most Jewish communities in Arab countries developed their own dialect of Arabic to distinguish themselves from the local Moslem majority. Such dialects meant a death sentence for spies whose origin could be identified if they maintained even a hint of that dialect. The Mossad was insistent on perfecting the dialects of agents toward the specific country of their mission in order to eliminate the possibility of their detection due to a telltale accent.

Continuing in perfect Arabic, the agent described to Shaffir the details of his childhood and family history in Baghdad. The astounding history of the man continued to please Shaffir. The more he heard, the better he felt about the man and his fit for the mission. The longer the conversation went on, the more impressed Shaffir was with his candidate. He saw sheer determination and strong will in the young man's sparkling eyes. He radiated self-confidence and displayed a deep, blind devotion to the cause of the Jewish state. His military career proved his leadership skills and exceptional courage beyond a shadow of doubt.

"It was a pleasure to meet you. Thank you for your time," Shaffir said as he wrapped up their meeting. "You will probably hear from me again soon."

Shaffir picked up the phone, called the chief of his investigation department, and ordered an urgent and thorough re-verification of background checks on the agent. He wanted every small detail revalidated, including the man's childhood in Iraq, his life on the kibbutz, and his military service. Before any individual was accepted into the Mossad ranks, he or she had to undergo a prolonged, meticulous process of background checks and identity authentication to the smallest details. Shaffir couldn't take any risks: the mission was so vital that he needed additional assurances before he would go back to the Prime Minister with his plan.

As he waited for the background checks to be concluded, Shaffir started weaving his scheme. A week later, he was informed that all checks were clear. He had his man, and now it was time to present his plan and his candidate to the Prime Minister.

CHAPTER 16

Two weeks after the initial meeting, Shaffir reported back to Harel's office to lay out his plan.

"The operation code name for the mission will be Chairman-X," Shaffir opened. "Our goal will be to place a highly qualified Mossad agent inside the PLO within twelve to sixteen months." Shaffir then described in detail the character and traits of his candidate.

"Our agent will go through a year of training and deprogramming in preparation for his mission. He will also have plastic surgery that will alter his facial features to avoid detection by his former acquaintances in Iraq, his friends in Israel, or even the agency's own staff. His mission will be to join the PLO as a new recruit, ascend through the organization ranks to a leadership position, and attempt to capture the top position of PLO Chairman.

"When his training is complete, he will be sent to London via Iraq to study for a doctorate in Middle Eastern studies. He will reclaim his Iraqi identity of Abdul Aziz Al-Wasphi, a Palestinian Arab who escaped from Palestine and grew up in Baghdad. He will be provided with full authentication of his identity, historical background, and education that can withstand the test of the PLO's and KGB's intense screening processes.

"In London he will build up his contacts with the very dynamic local Palestinian community, join the PLO, and become actively involved in its political and military wings. He will increase his recognition and influence in the local PLO chapter through vigorous campaign activity on behalf of the Palestinian people. When the opportune time arrives, he will move closer to PLO headquarters and try to secure an influential position close to the top leadership. Once he becomes a member of the PLO's upper echelon, he is to use whatever means at his disposal to capture the PLO top position.

"As the PLO Chairman, his mission will be to bolster the moderate forces within the PLO and crack down mercilessly on radical terrorist factions, eliminating them completely. As his control over the entire organization consolidates and he gains popularity amongst the Palestinian population, he is to approach the Israeli government through friendly European or American channels and initiate negotiations for a peace agreement.

"His ultimate mission will be to negotiate a peace accord with the Israeli government that will provide the Palestinians with self-determination and governorship over all civilian affairs and internal security within their territories, but not statehood. The agreement should exclude the ability of Palestinians to form an organized military force or stockpile weapons within the Palestinian territories. Israel will maintain control over its secure international borders with Jordan and Egypt and will be able to monitor movements of population and goods through checkpoints and border patrols.

"He is to develop and build an economic cooperation program with Israel to create jobs for the Palestinians and help Israel become the technological center of the Middle East.

"He is to gradually transform the Palestinian education system from focusing on hatred and aggression toward Israel and the Western world to a more moderate and tolerant value system based on justice, freedom, and individual rights."

"How will he justify to the Palestinian National Council his position on not insisting on an independent Palestinian state as called for by the Palestinian National Charter?" Harel interjected.

Well prepared for this question, Shaffir answered without hesitation. "He would simply represent it as the first step toward statehood and insist that they should take what they can get while they have the support of the Americans, Europeans, and Russians. Once they have achieved their first goal of self-governance, they will move on toward statehood as the second step.

"It may never need to go further than self-governance if enough progress is made on the economic and social fronts. When their living conditions have improved significantly, Palestinians may be content with the status quo. Our government will not negotiate on Palestinian statehood anyway, so this option is out of the question.

"He is going to have to use his best judgment under the circumstances. The situation is going to be very fluid because he will encounter fierce internal resistance to the peace process as well as enormous pressure from certain Arab states trying to influence the outcome. He will have to fight through it all and make things happen. With strong popularity and firm support from the people, he will carry a great deal of clout, and the council will have to go along with his decisions. After all, he is going to be the most popular elected Chairman of the PLO."

"You seem to have precisely the right man for the job," Harel complimented Shaffir. "Where did you find such a remarkable candidate?"

"I have my sources, but it's a state secret I can't reveal," Shaffir said jokingly in a typical response from the man in charge of keeping Israel's secrets safe.

Harel replied, "I've always admired your remarkable intuition and wouldn't hear of any other candidate when it came to filling the critical position of Mossad Chief. I know that you will never disappoint me, Avi. You are blessed with the most brilliant mind. This country needs to utilize your extraordinary talents to finally enjoy some peace and tranquility after so many years of bloody conflicts with our neighbors."

Harel looked pensive for a few minutes and then said to Shaffir, "I am authorizing you to go ahead with phase one, which includes solidifying the details of your plans and starting to train your agent. I expect to receive progress reports from you during our monthly review meetings. My final decision will be made when your agent is ready for the mission. A quick reminder: I want nothing whatsoever in writing about this operation, and no one but the two of us and the agent will have any knowledge of the true mission of 'Chairman X.'"

Shaffir's second meeting with agent Mountain Lion took place two days later. Shaffir disclosed his plan to the agent in meticulous detail and told him that he had been selected as the primary candidate. The agent listened attentively, remaining totally focused on Shaffir and absorbing every word he said. Shaffir again noticed the tough resolve in his stubborn chin and the glowing sparkle of enthusiasm in his eyes.

When Shaffir had completed his presentation, the agent looked him straight in the eye and said without a hint of hesitation, "Mr. Shaffir, I am greatly honored to accept this mission of supreme importance to our national security. You will never regret my selection for this most admirable undertaking. I am confident in my ability to accomplish the mission goals as outlined in your statement. I have been preparing and waiting for this assignment all my life. I was destined for it from birth."

Shaffir was taken aback by the agent's response and immediate acceptance of the perilous mission without any further questioning. He was very pleased though with the agent's display of blind devotion and trust in the Mossad establishment and its secret missions to protect the national interest. He was hoping to hear this response as further affirmation of the agent's resolve and unequivocal commitment to the challenges ahead.

Shaffir thanked him and without further delay

added his instructions: "You have seventy-two hours to get yourself ready and put your personal affairs in order. You will inform your friends and close acquaintances that you are taking a sabbatical to tour the world for a few months before starting a Ph.D. program in the United States.

"Your training program for the mission will commence early next week. Remember, not a word to anybody about this, and absolutely nothing in writing on paper, tape, or camera. This is one of the most vital assignments in our nation's history, and it must remain top secret. Any leaks, even internal, can jeopardize your safety and the success of your mission. One last thing, Prime Minister Harel would like to meet you for a brief introduction next week."

* * * *

Reuben left Shaffir's office with a feeling of great relief. This was the moment he had been waiting for ever since his mother first promised him that he would be destined for a great leadership role in shaping the future of his beloved nation. He had been very diligent in putting forth his utmost efforts to prepare himself for this great undertaking.

When Shaffir called him for a second meeting, he had a feeling that something big was in the making. When he heard Shaffir describing the mission, he immediately knew that this was it. This was what his mother had ingrained in his brain since he was a young child. This was the reason his parents had to sacrifice their lives. It was now his turn to pick up the torch and carry it forward to continue the tradition of his brave ancestors.

Reuben felt no fear. He was confident in his ability to carry the mission to its ultimate success, for he drew on his strong belief that a supreme power from above directed his destiny. He was convinced his mother and father up in the heavens would shield him from harm and protect him from any adversaries. His life history was so well suited for the role he was about to assume that he was convinced this plot had to have been planned by Divine power decades in advance.

Reuben recalled the ancient biblical story of how Joseph, the son of Jacob, was sold by his brothers into slavery and brought to Egypt. Joseph was called from his Egyptian jail cell to interpret Pharaoh's mysterious dreams. His accurate interpretation of the dreams paved his path to great prominence in the ancient land. His appointment by Pharaoh as his Viceroy, second in command to the supreme ruler, allowed him to save the nations of Egypt and Israel from the great famine and ultimate destruction. Joseph's role now became Reuben's role.

* * * *

Several days after his second meeting with Shaffir, Reuben joined him for a short meeting at the PM's office. Harel welcomed him with enthusiasm and lavished upon him compliments on his superb accomplishments in his service to the nation. Rueben thanked Harel humbly. He felt privileged to meet Harel, one of Israel's most legendary leaders and war heroes.

In his mid-fifties, Harel maintained the athletic build of a man who had served close to thirty years in the Israeli armed forces and reached its top rank. His receding shiny silver hair projected an image of wisdom blended with undeterred tenacity to protect his nation from its mounting adversaries.

Harel inquired about Reuben's life as a young Jewish boy, raised as a Palestinian refugee in Baghdad. This was a major issue for Harel since Reuben would have to maintain dual personality roles on his new mission. Reuben explained how he'd managed to switch roles as a child, behaving like a normal Palestinian boy during the day while learning about his true faith and ancestral history from his mother at night.

Reuben turned to Shaffir, and conversing in fluent Arabic, emulated the role of a high-level PLO official speaking publicly on his nation's aspirations for independence. His unexpected move took Harel by surprise, proving Reuben's natural abilities to switch roles without notice and to display a completely new personality.

Harel was charmed by the manner in which Reuben conducted himself, by his notably Semitic appearance, and by the sheer determination in his glistening eyes. Now that he had met the man, he felt the level of comfort he expected from a candidate hand-selected by Shaffir. He stood up, paced the room for several minutes, and then stopped next to Reuben.

"This is not going to be easy, son. Your life is going to be under constant and imminent threat, and you will have to calculate every action with caution and wisdom.

Are you sure you can handle this enormous burden?"

"I am ready to serve my country unconditionally, sir," Reuben responded without hesitation. "My destiny prepared me for this unique role, and I am confident in my ability to accomplish the goals outlined by Mr. Shaffir."

Satisfied with Reuben's response, Harel reiterated the objectives and vital national importance of the mission. "I don't want our people to live in fear within our own sovereign homeland when we did so among the nations of the world for more than 2,000 years and suffered endlessly. It's time for our people to rejoice in the fruits of our hard labor and remarkable sacrifice and enjoy well-deserved peace and prosperity. I hope and pray the Almighty will strengthen your hands and give you the courage to secure our future into the next century.

"Reuben, you have an enormously dangerous task ahead of you. I am confident Shaffir will prepare you in the best possible manner, but from that point on, you will carry the heavy load on your own shoulders. I have strong confidence in your abilities and very high expectations for you. I look forward to seeing you again before your departure."

* * * *

Although Reuben was the Mossad's most suitable and well-qualified candidate for the mission, there were still many things he needed to learn and prepare for. His plastic surgeries had to be performed in several stages and required several months of healing. As an additional precautionary measure to avoid future detection by the

Mossad's own staff, Reuben was fitted with a disguise he used for the entire duration of his training.

The Mossad's strict policy required its agents and staff to follow orders and perform their duties to the best of their ability without questioning or doubting the motives of their superiors. There was a valid reason for everything being ordered, for the ultimate responsibility of the agency was to protect the long-term survival of the Jewish state. Mossad personnel who questioned this policy or deviated from its rules were immediately ejected from the Agency.

Still, if any staff member recognized Reuben in the future as a leading PLO official, rumors could start circulating and his identity could somehow leak to the outside. Shaffir wasn't going to take that risk.

Shaffir designed a specific training program to perfect Reuben's qualifications and supplement his knowledge where needed. This program was structured into several areas of expertise and involved numerous Mossad training specialists who were not aware of each other's roles in his preparations for the mission.

The first area of his instruction involved brushing up on his spoken Arabic, perfecting his Palestinian dialect, and becoming familiar with the latest Palestinian trends in expressions and slang. His instructor was a professor of classic Arabic and Palestinian history at the Hebrew University in Jerusalem who had been recruited by the Mossad to train undercover operatives in Arabic.

He and Reuben conversed strictly in Arabic for several hours daily and studied Palestinian history in minute detail, starting from the nineteenth century and ending with current events. At the conclusion of his training, Reuben had to pass verbal conversation and written tests in both Arabic and Palestinian history.

At this point in his training, Reuben was no longer permitted to use Hebrew as a spoken language. He had to switch his mindset to the future environment in which he would be operating. He was deprogrammed from using Hebrew and trained not to respond to the mention of his Hebrew name, names of friends, and places. He had to disassociate himself from his life in the kibbutz, his adoptive family, and his military career.

His deprogramming instructor frequently attempted to catch him off guard, throwing at him a quick question in Hebrew about a popular place in Israel or a close friend. Reuben always responded with a dumb look on his face, questioning in Arabic, "I didn't quite understand. Can you repeat that please?"

Frequently he was awakened in the middle of the night and asked similar questions in Hebrew. He responded to these night attempts in the same manner until his instructor was satisfied his deprogramming had worked.

Next on the list was his English language skill development. His English teacher had immigrated to Israel from London a few years earlier and spoke with a heavy British accent. Reuben was to work on developing the British accent that was considered widely acceptable and respected worldwide. His British accent would also be instrumental in building his leadership image at the beginning of his career in London and later while speaking in international forums.

Reuben enjoyed that part of the training immensely. He had always wanted to master the English language and speak it the British way. His mother had told him many stories about Iraq under the British rule and their house had been frequently visited by British businessmen. As a young child, Reuben had admired their professional appearance, including their finely tailored suits, and he had liked to listen to their fascinating accents when they spoke to his father.

His teacher was very thorough and insistent on proper grammar and pronunciation. Reuben's natural gift for grasping languages quickly made his teacher very happy. His teacher also used the instructional time to provide him with an overview of life in London, its historical sites and places of interest, population demographics, the British higher education system, and government structure. This information would be very useful for helping Reuben envision and understand the landscape waiting for him in London at the onset of his mission.

The Mossad built a cover story for Reuben around his childhood and young adolescent life in Baghdad as a Palestinian refugee, starting his new life in Iraq with other Palestinian families in the abandoned old Jewish quarter. Shaffir loved the idea that Reuben's name was recorded at the Iraqi interior ministry as an Iraqi citizen of Palestinian origin. This record allowed him to obtain an authentic Iraqi passport without much difficulty. It also made his cover story simpler to substantiate and eliminated the risk of having to forge permanent identity documents. The Mossad arranged to verify this data with the Iraqi interior ministry records and to add his name to the graduate list of Baghdad University in Middle Eastern Studies.

Reuben rehearsed his cover story repeatedly and was questioned continually by Shaffir down to the minutest details. Because Shaffir wished to get to know Reuben well and develop a lasting personal relationship with him, he took him under his wing and became his personal mentor.

Shaffir was in his late fifties, short and stocky. He was bald except for sprinkles of short white hair above his ears. He was very patient, but extremely methodical in his directives, knowing that his vast personal experience in the espionage arena would benefit Reuben immensely. He wanted to have his own signature on the success of the mission by providing Reuben with the knowledge and experience of one of the most respectable people in the business.

He knew that the better prepared Reuben was to face the unexpected and unknown, the higher the odds of his success. Reuben needed to be able to handle any crisis, political or military, at any given moment and completely control its outcome. Shaffir constantly drilled Reuben on different scenarios, presenting him with situations where he had to make tough choices and initiate drastic measures to assure his progress in rising to the PLO top position.

Shaffir provided him with documents to substantiate his history in Iraq so it could withstand even the most thorough investigation. It was crucial for his origin and identity to be unquestionable within the PLO ranks in order to pave his way to reaching its high echelon.

Between his training courses, Reuben had undergone three separate plastic surgery procedures that required extended periods of healing. Shaffir, who had some hidden artistic talents, developed a master image of Reuben's new look. He then hired three plastic surgeons to work on separate areas of his facial transformation process. Each surgeon had his own area of expertise and performed that portion of the surgery unaware of the other surgeons' work. None were allowed to examine the final product of the new Reuben when all his surgeries were completely healed.

Reuben used the time between surgeries to read the latest intelligence on PLO strategy and tactics, learn of recent political developments, and understand the leadership structure and the roles of the major players in the organization. He received similar information on rival factions operating independently of the PLO, sometimes against it. This data provided him with a more complete picture and insight into the environment that he would face when he started his mission.

CHAPTER 17

Reuben studied the Mossad files on master spy Eli Cohen to uncover the secrets of his success and learn the lessons of his fatal errors. Eli Cohen was his ghost mentor, the only known Mossad agent able to penetrate deep into the enemy's heart and lounge in the Syrian lion's den.

Just thinking about Cohen sent chills of fear mixed with excitement down Reuben's spine. Eli had thrived on the exhilaration of high risk, just like a skydiver jumping from atop a mountain into an unknown abyss with only a mere parachute separating him from death. Eli had stared into the face of death every day and come out smiling, until the day of his execution in the public square of Damascus.

Reuben was deeply moved by the tragic, yet heroic story of Eli Cohen. Eli's dreadful execution was a distressing reminder of the pain and humiliation his own father had endured in Baghdad for allegedly similar crimes. Eli's story was a convincing example of what could be awaiting him if he were discovered during his mission. The ruthless manner in which Arab states treated their captives would be a constant reminder for him to weigh every move and not make any hasty errors that could prove detrimental to his mission and himself.

In his weekly mentoring session with Shaffir, they reviewed the lessons of Eli Cohen's mission in scrupulous detail.

Eli's success stemmed from several behaviors that worked greatly in his favor. First, his unequivocal fanaticism for the cause of the Syrian nation, specifically the Ba'ath party, had been combined with his persistent expression of deep hatred toward Israel and the Zionist cause. This was a position that could easily draw attention and a following from the mainstream Syrian populace.

Second, his lavish monetary contribution to the cause of the people and the party had been beneficial. He'd used the ample supply of money provided by the Mossad wisely to buy his way to popularity and fame. With this method, he was able to accelerate the time frame required to access the vital intelligence Israel needed so desperately.

Through his unique interpersonal skills and outgoing personality, Eli was able to gain the trust, affection, and admiration of the high echelon of Syrian leadership. "People just loved the guy and opened up to him," Shaffir explained.

"He entrenched himself in their lives, culture, aspirations, and beliefs. They felt without a shadow of doubt that he was one of them and fully identified with the ideas and actions he was advocating.

"You must emulate this type of behavior as best you can and expand it to the masses as well," Shaffir continued. "This is what will make you a great leader and a formidable contender for the Chairmanship position.

"Eli accomplished in three years what a dozen agents couldn't in ten. Can you imagine how far he would have gotten if the Mossad had used his phenomenal talents more wisely instead of focusing only on short-term intelligence-gathering objectives? We could have had a very powerful ally in Syria now if we hadn't been so destructive in the way we exploited him to milk every bit of intelligence he could gather and transmit it home immediately. The only way I can describe this type of reckless conduct is suicidal.

"Reuben, we have learned our lessons the hard way, and we paid greatly for our mistakes. This is why your mission is totally the opposite of Eli's.

"Your mission is not about collecting intelligence or about attempting to foil terrorist attacks on Israeli targets. We have a myriad of agents and military personnel charged with this responsibility day after day, all around the world. Your job is to reach a position that will allow you to influence decisions from within the PLO and provide you with some level of control over the strategic direction and future actions of our foes.

"There will be no communications, and no transmission of information at all. We cannot take the risk of blowing your cover and exposing you to bloodthirsty murderers. Quite honestly, I believe such communications would be counterproductive even if there were no risks involved. You need to be fully focused on your mission and goals without any distraction or emotions getting in your way. You have to block such feelings and eradicate them from your mind the minute they surface.

"Your job is to change the character of this murderous organization that vows to destroy our people and wipe our nation off the face of this earth. One small step at a time with incredible patience will bring you success.

"I want to re-emphasize that there will be no transmissions, no visits home, and no contact with other agents under any circumstances. You will operate entirely on your own, guided by the sacred objectives of your Divine mission. You will bring salvation to our people, not by force and not by might, but through unquestionable devotion to your Holy mission through the spirit of the Almighty pounding in your heart."

* * * *

Reuben's final course was a refresher in military planning, strategy, and tactics. Shaffir's thoughts were that Reuben's rise to the top of the PLO would have to involve significant roles in its military wing. Reuben had to be ready for this part of the mission as much as he was for the political.

His distinguished military career and IDF training had prepared him extremely well for these potential roles. The only issue Shaffir was concerned about was how Reuben could maintain a balance between the need to score successes on the armed struggle front while restraining the use of his military brilliance against the

Israelis themselves. Shaffir's solution was for Reuben's military talents to be used to consolidate his control over the entire Palestinian forces and to eliminate resistance from the extremist rival factions that would become a strong opponent to future peace negotiations with Israel.

It was clear Reuben wouldn't be able to prevent all terrorist activities against Israel. Such a move could risk his premature exposure and jeopardize his mission. He would need to act in moderation and score successes to build up his popularity and glory as a successful leader. His emphasis should always be on minimizing casualties as best he could. When he reached the top, he was gradually to taper off the armed struggle and move toward peace negotiations without raising any suspicion of his true motives.

* * * *

Within a year, Reuben's training was completed, and Shaffir reported to Harel that his agent was ready to embark on his mission. He requested authorization to proceed as planned. Harel asked for one more face-to-face meeting with Reuben.

Harel, Shaffir, and Reuben met at the PM's office a few days before Reuben's planned departure. Harel welcomed Reuben warmly. He couldn't recognize the person he had first met only a year earlier. Reuben was still as tall and handsome as before, but his facial features were completely different. His cheekbones were higher, his nose slightly wider, and his stubborn chin not as protruding as before.

"The surgeons did an amazing job," he thought. "Leave it to Shaffir. He could probably make me look like Golda Meir, if he had to!"

Harel reiterated the objectives of the mission and emphasized that Reuben was to use his best judgment and all the means at his disposal to adhere to them.

Next, Shaffir went over the rules of conduct Reuben had to follow along with his emergency operating procedures. He was to have no contact or communication with any Mossad agents, Israeli embassy officials, or any Israeli citizen anywhere. He would not be allowed to return to Israel under any circumstances until he was ordered to do so. He was to operate completely alone and not expect assistance from any Israeli agency or embassy worldwide. He was to keep his identity and his assignment in complete secrecy. Only the PM and the Mossad chief would be aware of his existence.

When new Israeli officials were appointed to replace existing ones, it would be the responsibility of the predecessors to inform their successors of his existence and the nature of his mission. The method of transmitting the information would be strictly verbal without written records.

"We will keep track of your progress within the PLO ranks through our own intelligence sources," Shaffir explained. "We will always know where you are and how much progress you have made. You will never need to jeopardize your safety by reporting anything to us. We want you to be absolutely focused on your mission and not distracted by minor details. As I said, you are not to report to or contact any Israeli official or agency worldwide under any circumstances. In the unlikely event that we need to contact you, it will be done in a very discreet manner.

"If you are discovered, or if your life is in grave danger, you are to abandon your mission without hesitation. However, do not attempt to return directly to Israel. You must develop your own contingency plan to reach Switzerland and go underground.

"A safe deposit box will be set up for you in a bank in Basel. There you will find new identity papers, cash, bank account information, and further instructions on your next move. You are to memorize the address of the bank and the numeric code of the safe deposit box without maintaining any written records," Shaffir concluded.

"Mr. Chairman, I look forward to meeting you at the negotiating table in a few years," Harel said humorously. "Don't forget! I am a very tough negotiator, but I am confident that with some mutual understanding and hand twisting, we can reach an equitable solution to the Palestinian issue.

"Before you leave, Reuben, I would like to give you some of my own personal insight that may be very useful in your future leadership career. Coming from an old and wise soldier and politician who has been around the block a few times, who knows, it may come in handy one day.

"The only way you will be completely successful in your mission is if you truly become one of them for its duration. You must live like them, think like them, act like them, pray like them, just as you did when you were growing up in Baghdad. You must totally immerse yourself in their life, culture, customs and traditions. You must always stay close to the people, earn their trust, and build your popularity.

"Ultimately, leadership is governed by popularity and trust. If you have the people's trust behind you, the rest will come naturally. However, if you behave as an outsider, or remain distant from the people, it will never work. Your mission will fail.

"Having said all that, I have to reemphasize one point again, and again. ***Never, ever forget*** who you are, where you came from, or what the ultimate objectives of your mission are."

Harel shook Reuben's hands, put his arm around his shoulders, and said, "God bless you, dear son. May you go in peace, and may you come home in peace. May the Almighty strengthen your hands and grant you success in all your endeavors. May peace and tranquility be forever granted to our beloved nation, amen!

* * * *

Air France Flight 118 from Paris arrived in Baghdad during the afternoon of an early fall day. Khalef Al-Watani, a Jordanian businessman, passed through Iraqi immigration with minimal questioning and checked into the Al-Rasheed hotel. The next morning, he visited the department of Middle Eastern studies at Baghdad University. He met senior faculty members to discuss a research project his company was interested in conducting jointly with the university. After the meeting, he walked around the busy campus and chatted with students in the cafeteria.

In the afternoon, he socialized with guests and local Iraqi businesspeople in the busy hotel lobby. That evening, as the air cooled down from the searing daily heat, he joined a group of guests on a tour of the city nightlife. They spent time at famous restaurants and popular nightclubs.

Baghdad had changed a great deal since he had left some two decades earlier. New construction activity was evident in every part of the city. He ventured to the old neighborhood where he'd spent most of his childhood years. The old crumpled houses had been replaced by modern apartment buildings. The present regime was now embarked on intensified modernization efforts fueled by mounting oil revenues. Brand new roads and highways crisscrossed the modernized city. He noticed numerous new government buildings, high-rise hotels, and upper class mansions on the western side of the Tigris River.

The following week, he went to the Ministry of Interior and applied for an Iraqi passport under his registered name of Abdul Aziz Al-Wasphi. He was told to return in several days to pick it up.

He submitted his applications for a doctoral program at London University and anxiously waited until all his papers were in order.

CHAPTER 18

LONDON, 1976

Several weeks later, Mr. Abdul Aziz Al-Wasphi arrived in London on an Iraqi Airlines flight from Baghdad. He checked into a small apartment he'd rented in South Kensington and started attending classes for a doctoral degree in Middle Eastern Studies at the University of London.

Within days of his arrival, he went to visit the office of the Palestinian student union in London to collect information on activities and get to know the local leadership. He introduced himself to Hassan Al-Nassar, the president of the student union, who invited him to attend meetings and participate in weekend rallies.

Soon thereafter, Aziz joined the Palestinian student union as a member and started attending the local PLO chapter meetings. He involved himself in committee work and actively participated in demonstrations to gather widespread attention and support for the Palestinian cause. With the sponsorship of Hassan, who was immediately impressed by Aziz's personality, dedication to the Palestinian agenda, and verbal abilities, Aziz became the primary vocal source representing the chapter in rallies, international conferences, and demonstrations.

His well-spoken English with a hint of British accent that his trainer had worked so hard to create paid off in no time. His passionate speeches attracted the attention of a plethora of foreign visitors and Londoners who always seemed to be crowding his favorite spot at Speaker's Corner in Hyde Park.

He often set up a stand and started educating his audience on the history of the Palestinians, their suffering, and the cruel and unjust manner in which the Israelis were treating them.

Occasionally he engaged into heated discussions and verbal scuffles with Israeli tourists and members of the local Jewish student union. However, with his witty tongue, he was able to come out on top and earn the cheers of the audience.

One evening he received a call from Hassan who invited him to his apartment for a social gathering. When he arrived, Hassan greeted him warmly at the door.

"Come in, please. There is someone I would like to introduce you to." He escorted Aziz into the living room, where a slim, neatly dressed individual was sitting in a comfortable armchair.

"Aziz, please meet Saleh Al-Shariff, the head of PLO operations in London."

Saleh rose to his feet. He was a fair, tall, good-looking

man who appeared to be in his mid-thirties.

"It's a great pleasure to meet you, Aziz," he opened with a friendly voice. "I watched your performance at Hyde Park this Sunday. It was quite impressive, I must say."

"It's a great honor to meet you, Saleh, *Ahlen-Wa-Sahlen.*" Aziz greeted him in traditional Arabic. They embraced and kissed each other as customary among Middle Eastern men to demonstrate close friendship.

"Please sit down and be comfortable," Saleh continued. "I asked Hassan to arrange this meeting since I thought this would be a good opportunity for us to learn more about each other."

Over the next hour, Saleh conducted an unofficial but thorough background examination of Aziz — his origins, his childhood, his education, his personal beliefs, and his commitment to the holy struggle against Israeli oppression. He gave Aziz a short synopsis of his own background and his role in the organization.

Toward the end of the evening, Saleh turned to Aziz and said, "Hassan and I are very impressed with you and your abilities, and we are confident that you can make significant contributions to our organization. After much thought and discussion, we've decided to invite you to join the PLO officially. As a full-fledged member, you could actively contribute to the advancement of our struggle for freedom."

"I always wanted to do something more productive and practical to help stop the pain and suffering of our people," Aziz answered quickly. "I would be honored to be part of this great organization, and delighted to actively participate in its campaigns."

"You need to know, Aziz," Saleh added, "that as a member of this cell you will be involved in both political and nonpolitical activities that I cannot elaborate upon at this time."

Aziz nodded. "I expect nothing less than that. We have to use all the means at our disposal to reach our ultimate goals, and with that come personal sacrifices."

"It's all settled then," Saleh concluded. "We will complete your background screening. When I get the green light from our headquarters, I will invite you for a second briefing and explain our objectives in more detail."

A week later Aziz was called for his second meeting. Hassan and Saleh welcomed him with enthusiasm. "Congratulations, Aziz. You have been accepted to our secret club. You passed your background checks without difficulty. We are ready to officially swear you in now."

Aziz jumped up with excitement, hugging and kissing them both. "I am so looking forward to working closely with both of you. We are going to be a great team, and I can feel the thrill already. We are going to accomplish so much and have fun getting back at the Israeli bastards. It's time for us to turn the table. It's their turn to suffer and be disgraced, and our turn to win and be glorified."

When the swearing-in ceremony was completed, Saleh turned to Aziz, "My brother, as a member of this cell, you will be called upon from time to time to perform certain duties ordered by our central command. You will be instructed and trained for your role in every mission. You are to follow orders and perform your duty with courage and determination, putting our people's interests ahead of your own. If you are captured by the authorities and interrogated, you are to reveal nothing about our personnel or operations."

A week later, Hassan called Aziz and asked him to meet Saleh and him at the corner of Hassan's apartment building at 9 p.m. sharp. They picked him up in a large gray van and traveled west of London while Saleh briefed him on their mission.

Two hours later, they drew near to a small marina. Hassan turned the van's lights off and approached under cover of darkness. He drove around the marina's parking area a couple of times to make sure it was clear. He then parked the van alongside the entrance to the pier and showed Aziz his observation post. Saleh and Hassan got out of the van and disappeared into the marina, returning within minutes carrying heavy boxes. They repeated this process several times until the large van was fully loaded.

From the pickup point, they drove into a built-up area and pulled into a warehouse complex. They stopped in front of an overhead metal sliding door marked *Consolidated Shipping Enterprises, Ltd.* Saleh opened the door using a small remote control device. After the van pulled into a warehouse, the door slid down behind them. Aziz breathed a sigh of relief and helped unload the boxes.

"Please handle everything with extra care and don't drop any of the boxes," Saleh warned. "There are enough explosives here to blow up this entire complex! We don't want to be sent into the heavens prematurely. We still have an enormous task ahead of us."

When the unloading was complete, Saleh explained, "We are in the city of Bath in western England. This is our operations center under the cover of a shipping company that actually exists. We built two concealed rooms where we store our weapons and make bombs."

The warehouse was full of crates scattered all around. Saleh walked to the back and pressed a hidden button. A part of the brick wall opened up revealing a narrow corridor leading to two rooms that had thick steel doors. Inside the first Aziz noticed stacks of machine guns, RPG rocket launchers, sharpshooter rifles, pistols, and boxes of ammunition. The second room had a workbench with several tools mounted on it and a locked steel cabinet.

"This is where we build explosive devices to carry out the missions ordered by central command," Saleh elaborated. "We have been stockpiling weapons and explosives to prepare for holy missions planned in England and Europe over the next several months. We buy what we need from the IRA and pay them in cash. We maintain close, but unofficial, relations with them. It works very well for both sides."

"Are there any new operations on the horizon?" Aziz inquired eagerly.

"Nothing that I can discuss right now," Saleh replied. "For now I can only involve you in minor roles, such as tonight's guard duty. I am not authorized to engage you in operations that are more serious until you pass your basic training course. I have arranged for you to attend basic training at one of our camps during the four-week

Christmas break. Hassan will provide you with the details prior to your departure."

* * * *

Several weeks later, Aziz arrived at Beirut International Airport. He was greeted by a local PLO representative and transferred to a PLO military base southeast of Beirut, where many new recruits were arriving from many corners of the world.

The course started the next morning. The trainees were housed in large tents, each accommodating ten men. They were provided with uniforms, AK-47 assault rifles, and basic military gear. Training started with teaching them the skills of handling light weapons. They learned to dismantle, assemble, and fire assault rifles and handguns, and then they engaged in target practice. Next, they were taught how to assemble and handle basic explosive devices followed by more advanced forms of high power explosives with remote detonation.

The following week, the emphasis shifted to a more physical nature, such as running through obstacle courses, group marches for several miles, and individual combat skills. Training started in small groups and gradually increased to squads of about ten fighters.

Aziz noticed the focus was on both individual and squad-level training, which was the primary format of conducting guerilla warfare against the Israeli armed forces. The more extensive explosives training reflected the PLO strategy of launching terrorist attacks on any target worldwide.

Compared to the extensive training he'd received in

the paratrooper brigade, this course was very basic and easy for Aziz. Nevertheless, he acted as if this were his first military training course and performed every task with precision and enthusiasm.

Using Eli Cohen's strategy, he became very vocal among the recruits, speaking vehemently against Israel and promoting the ideas of using local and international terrorism to turn the world's attention to the plight of the Palestinian nation. His superior performance as a soldier and his aggressive stance against Israel and the USA captured the attention of his commanders, increased his credibility in the PLO ranks, and earned him graduation with distinction.

At the conclusion of the course, the new recruits were assembled for a graduation ceremony with the commander of the base. The commander delivered an enthusiastic speech on the sacred mission of the PLO to liberate Palestine from the Israeli and American oppressors and the critical role each one of them would play in achieving this supreme mission.

* * * *

Back in London, Saleh greeted Aziz eagerly at the airport. "Congratulations!" he said, embracing him. "We have been notified of your impressive achievements in the training course. I have learned to expect nothing but the best from you, and you have proven me right every time. Your future career with our glorious organization is wide open, and I am confident you will go very far. Now that you have completed your training with excellence, I can get you actively involved in our covert operations. But first, Hassan needs your political talents to deliver a speech at a student rally we are holding in Birmingham this weekend. After the rally, I will inform you of an exciting new assignment we were ordered to carry out. I want you to be fully involved in planning this task. I am sure you will enjoy it immensely."

The following Monday, Saleh picked Aziz up and drove him to one of the PLO safe houses in London for a planning session. He didn't waste much time getting to the point. "Have you heard of a Palestinian journalist by the name of Naji Al-Karadi?" Saleh questioned Aziz. "He works for a Kuwaiti newspaper published in London."

"You mean the one who always tries to portray our faithful leaders in a negative way in his cartoons, claiming they live like kings at the expense of the poor Palestinian people?"

"Exactly," Saleh confirmed. "I am glad you are up on your reading. This fellow has given our leadership much grief, but this time he has gone too far. He is alleging in a new article that our Chairman is having an affair with a married woman. He is questioning the integrity of our leader and his dedication to our cause. He has been warned several times to refrain from his vicious attacks that try to undermine the authority of our leadership, but nothing seems to deter his continuous public assault. This time we have been ordered to eliminate him, with no more warnings. I am told this order came from the Chairman himself. He was so infuriated by the latest Al-Karadi allegations that he ordered his instant execution."

Aziz was relieved that the target was a Palestinian and not an Israeli. He realized such would not always be the case and that he had been lucky this time.

Saleh proceeded to lay out his plan to murder Naji Al-Karadi. "We will follow him around for several days to track his work habits. We need to find out when he leaves work in the evenings and in which direction he walks to the tube station. On a chosen night, you and I will wait for him at a relatively quiet street corner. When he reaches the corner, we will call his name, and as he turns toward us, we will both shoot him at close range using handguns equipped with silencers. A car will be waiting for us around the corner, and we will get into it and disappear from the scene before anybody realizes what has taken place. What do you think about this plan?"

Aziz paused pensively. "May I suggest some minor adjustments?" he finally said.

"Certainly," Saleh replied. "I would love to hear your ideas."

"I was thinking one assassin may be sufficient for this job. One person will attract less attention and raise less suspicion. I will wait for him around the street corner. We will need someone to monitor the building entrance and alert me by radio when Naji leaves the building and approaches my position. When he reaches the corner, I will call him, positively identify him, and shoot him from close range.

"A motorcycle as the getaway vehicle would also be much faster and easier to maneuver in London's narrow streets. It can easily avoid traffic jams and will be harder to follow if discovered. We will smear the plates with dirt to conceal its identification. After the shooting, I will leave the scene quickly and turn at the corner of the next side street. You will be waiting there for me on the motorcycle, with its engine running. I will hop on the back, and we will take off to our closest safe house.

"When we get to the house, we will hide the motorcycle in a concealed compartment in the garage. When things cool down and there is no evidence of our suspected involvement in the incident, we will emerge from the safe house and resume our normal routine. We will need to rehearse this sequence of events and getaway route on location several times prior to the actual shooting."

"These are excellent ideas." Saleh praised Aziz. "Let's go for it. I will make the logistical arrangements necessary to carry out our plan. I would like this job to be done within the next two weeks."

Over the next several days, Naji was followed to survey his work and commuting habits. It turned out that he left his office between six and seven every evening and walked to the same Underground station.

Over the weekend, Saleh and Aziz drove to the operation center in Bath so Aziz could practice target shooting with the handgun he was to use to eliminate Naji. Saleh introduced him to another PLO activist, Daud Al-Sharawi, who had also been following Naji around for the past several days.

"Daud will be monitoring Naji's movements on the night of the mission," Saleh explained. "He will communicate with you and inform you of Naji's exact location. After the shooting, he will board a train and return to the safe house in Bath."

The three men rehearsed their roles and tested the escape route a few times during the evening hours when Naji was supposed to emerge from his office building. Aziz was able to take a close look at Naji and observe his dressing patterns, especially the long black wool coat he wore on his way to the train station.

Saleh was concerned about the volume of pedestrian traffic on the streets during rush hour and the possibility of hitting innocent bystanders. "It will be poor publicity for us if any innocent civilians are hurt in the process. British Intelligence will realize who is behind the attack and blame the PLO publicly for carrying out an act of terrorism on British soil. Our operations in Britain may come under more scrutiny and crackdown by British security forces, so I prefer to avoid this situation."

"Please don't be too concerned," Aziz reassured him. "I will be very careful. I plan to shoot him in the head so the bullets lodge in his skull and not penetrate through and hit another person. I will make sure nobody is in the way when I do it. If it's going to be too crowded on that night, we will have to abort our mission and try again another night."

"It's settled then." Saleh seemed satisfied with Aziz's reply.

On the night of the mission, the three men took their positions and waited patiently for Naji to appear. It was past seven p.m., and there was still no sign of him. The pedestrian traffic on the main street slowly dwindled. Aziz liked the idea of less traffic, which meant less potential interference and hopefully no witnesses to the act. Daud reported that Naji had not emerged yet, but he could see that the lights in his office were still on. Probably Naji was working on another article defaming the Chairman with more accusations and frantically trying to meet the press deadline.

A few minutes past nine p.m., Aziz received word of his approaching target. The streets were almost empty by that late hour. "He is right around the corner from you," Daud's excited voice announced over his radio.

Aziz turned the radio off and waited for Naji to pass the corner. After he did so, Aziz walked closely behind him for several yards making sure nobody was in the way. Aziz was holding his handgun tightly under his short jacket. He called Naji from behind, greeting him in a friendly voice. Naji turned around abruptly, a curious look on his face as if he were wondering who was addressing him at this late hour of the night.

Aziz recognized Naji's round face and balding head without a doubt. He shot two bullets into his forehead from close range. Naji's curious look turned into a frozen expression of horror. He collapsed instantly.

Aziz turned the next corner, pulled a ski mask over his face, and rushed to the waiting motorcycle. He jumped behind Saleh, saying, "Naji's miserable soul is on its way to hell."

Saleh took off swiftly. Nobody appeared to be on their trail. It took several minutes for a passerby to realize that a murder had taken place on one of London's peaceful streets.

Twenty minutes later, two men on a motorcycle

arrived at a house in one of the quiet suburbs of northwest London. The overhead garage door rose quietly as the motorcycle rolled into the garage and quickly disappeared behind the closing door.

The next morning the story was all over the press, with a picture of Naji Al-Karadi on the front page of most of London's newspapers. There was a great deal of speculation as to who might have been behind the brutal attack, but it was clear there were no witnesses or clues as to the identity of the perpetrators. The PLO office in London issued a vigorous denial of any involvement in the Al-Karadi murder case.

Saleh and Aziz had to remain in the confines of the safe house until it was evident the British authorities weren't looking for them and didn't suspect their involvement in the incident. They spent a lot of time getting to know each other, learning each other's life histories, and building a close relationship. Aziz was able to establish a very strong bond with Saleh that would prove to be extremely valuable in the future.

Aziz knew that Saleh would be the key to his next promotion. Saleh was a rising PLO star rumored to have direct ties to the Chairman. It was known that he was due for a significant promotion in the PLO ranks. Aziz needed to prove himself to Saleh quickly to get on the PLO radar screens. This was his main reason for taking the initiative in the Naji Al-Karadi execution. It allowed him to show Saleh his invaluable operational abilities and at the same time carry out an order that came directly from the Chairman. Surely the Chairman would be curious to know who'd killed the traitor who was smearing his name in the Arab world and casting doubts on his faithfulness to the Palestinian people.

Several days later Aziz and Saleh received a prearranged phone call from Daud. After reciting the required code words, Daud provided them with the all-clear signal, indicating there were no signs the British authorities were looking for them. There was no special monitoring activity near their respective residences or wiretapping of their phone lines. The PLO offices in London were not searched, and apparently investigators had no real leads in the case.

Saleh informed Aziz that he could return to his apartment, but he needed to be very cautious and continuously aware of his surroundings. Saleh decided to remain at the safe house for a couple more days to be on the secure side.

Aziz returned to his normal routine focusing on his studies and participating in political activities. Weeks went by, and the entire Al-Karadi incident was forgotten.

CHAPTER 19

As a result of his success in the Karadi operation, Aziz was invited by Saleh to become a permanent member of the PLO operational committee in Britain.

He and Saleh continued to maintain close personal relations and socialized frequently with Hassan at popular London nightspots frequented by wealthy Arabs from oil-rich countries. They befriended many of the young wealthy students sent by their families to London to receive their higher education. Most of these youngsters were supportive of the Palestinian cause and openly expressed their sympathy for the liberation of Palestine.

Aziz approached Saleh with the idea of inviting these rich young people to a fundraising party at the student union. He explained that these students would become the future leaders of their nations, so gaining their support at an early stage might pay handsomely in the future. Saleh loved the idea and assigned Aziz and Hassan to organize the fundraiser.

The grand affair was held several weeks later with

overwhelming support from the students. Hassan arranged for a delicious meal of Middle Eastern delicacies to be served to the honored guests. A small orchestra of Arab students playing popular Arabic music followed the meal. Shortly afterwards, two belly dancers entered the stage and performed skillfully, moving around the crowded hall and teasing the young men with their bold body gestures.

Toward the end of the party, Saleh approached Aziz and congratulated him on his brilliant idea. "We raised more than ten thousand British pounds," he announced proudly. "These people think we are going to use this money for humanitarian purposes. Little do they know we have several operations on the horizon that desperately need this cash. Thanks to you, I now have the money to proceed with planning them.

"Aziz, you came up with a perfect idea to help advance our fight for freedom. You must realize that our funding resources are the most crucial element in sustaining our warfare against the Israelis and their allies. The monies we raise fuel our war machine and elevate the world's awareness of our noble cause. Without continuous funding, our years of intense effort and endless sacrifice could wither away in the wind.

"I want you to make this a semi-annual fundraising event for the benefit of deprived Palestinian children in the refugee camps. The funds we raise will support our local operations, and we will contribute a portion of the proceeds to the Chairman's fund. This is bound to capture the Chairman's attention and elevate the status of our chapter.

"One more thing, I signed you up for an advanced training course for PLO Special Operational Officers this summer. After passing this course, you will be able to run PLO covert operations in any major region in the world."

"Thank you for your generosity and kindness," Aziz said, expressing his gratitude. "I've learned so much from you. I feel you are the brother I could never have since the Zionist infidels killed my father while he was defending our homeland. I will never disappoint you, Saleh. I will continue to work diligently to promote the cause of our people and liberate our nation from the ruthless Israeli and American aggressors who evicted us from our sacred land."

"It's a great honor for me to become the brother you never had," Saleh responded. "I am very proud of you and your accomplishments. I predict a very bright future for you. You will just need to be very patient and let time and history take its course."

* * * *

Two days later, Saleh asked Aziz to meet him at his apartment.

"I just received a directive for a new, challenging mission," he told Aziz. "I want you to be involved in the planning right from the start. Your brilliant planning skills and ability to analyze all the factors involved and come up with a perfect strategy is what I need. We have an extremely important high profile mission that will send shock waves throughout the world," he confided in Aziz. "This time we will strike at the heart of the Israelis and prove to them that none of their leaders are safe anywhere in the world. I need to alert you to the fact that this is a top-secret operation. The information I share with you is not to be repeated or discussed, even with our own people. What I tell you is to remain strictly between us.

"We have been ordered to execute the Israeli Ambassador in London. He is one of the most prominent Israeli ambassadors in the world, and we are told he is the favorite candidate to become the Foreign Minister after his term is over. Our goal is to send a wave of fear among all Israeli officials worldwide, prove their vulnerability, and demonstrate our superior mission execution skills.

"We have been given a window of three to four weeks to carry out this task. I will be looking for innovative ideas in planning this challenging job. We will be provided with assistance from our intelligence department at headquarters."

"This is an unbelievable opportunity for us," Aziz said with astonishment. "I am ready for whatever challenges they send our way."

"The Israeli ambassador will be attending the annual Ambassador's Ball to honor the international diplomatic dignitaries in London. This ball is hosted by the British Foreign Ministry and will be held at the Langham Hilton Hotel in about three weeks. Our intelligence sources at the Egyptian embassy confirmed the Israeli ambassador has already accepted the invitation. One of the top security officials at the Egyptian embassy in London is working for us. He is very reliable and eager to help, especially when it comes to the Israelis.

"We now have an opportunity with a definite time and place to get to him. We need to start planning the details about how we can gain access to him and manage a clean escape after the shooting.

"Aziz, you will start by scouting the hotel, investigating the areas around it, and checking the strictness of the hotel security measures. I need you to formulate a plan for accomplishing our task in a swift and expeditious manner. We will meet in three days to review your plan and evaluate fresh intelligence."

"I will start working on it right away," Aziz reassured Saleh. "I am thrilled with the high-profile target we are going to hit this time. I can't wait to start shedding some Israeli blood and spreading horror in their midst. These bastards have been immersed in their arrogant overconfidence for too long. It's time for us to go on the offensive."

Although Aziz was secretly very distressed by Saleh's news, he showed no external emotion. He kept his composure and played the game of the zealous Palestinian terrorist eager to inflict death upon his sworn enemies at any opportune moment. He knew he had to go along with the plan and perform to Saleh's expectations. He just hoped that circumstances would somehow force the eventual cancellation of the mission.

The next day, Aziz put on a business suit and went to the Langham Hilton Hotel. He had lunch in the restaurant overlooking the hotel entrance and lobby and closely observed the conduct of hotel staffers performing their routine work. He detected two undercover security guards dressed in business suits with miniature microphones attached to their ears. They positioned themselves at opposite ends of the lobby, pacing their designated territory frequently. He also noted the locations of several security cameras positioned strategically around the lobby.

After lunch, Aziz attached to his suit a nametag frequently worn by businessmen attending conferences. He roamed freely in the various hotel meeting rooms and entered the Royal Ball Room where the lavish affair honoring the diplomats was to take place. After combing the hotel's interior structure, he exited from one of the side doors and scouted the surrounding streets.

The following day, Aziz returned to the hotel dressed as a typical tourist. He wore a concealed video camera supplied by Saleh. He ascended the stairway to the upper floor and filmed the lobby area from above, making sure he was out of the sight of the security guards. He proceeded to the meeting room areas he had visited the day before where his camera got close views of the entire lower lobby surroundings. He noticed that the lower lobby wasn't equipped with video cameras. Two short corridors led from the lower lobby to emergency exits that connected to side streets in the back of the hotel. Aziz exited the hotel and videoed the side streets connecting to the exits.

Using all the intelligence information he'd gathered, Aziz started formulating his plan. He knew he had to provide Saleh with a convincing one to continue to earn his respect and confidence.

The following day, Aziz met Saleh in his apartment

and presented his plan. He was praying that Saleh would not ask him to be the triggerman. He didn't think he would be able to point a gun at one of his prominent fellow countrymen and shoot him in cold blood. The Palestinian journalist was a different story. It wasn't something he'd taken pleasure in doing; it was something he had to do as part of his mission.

Saleh was amazed by the meticulous planning, attention to detail, and inventive ideas in Aziz's presentation. "This is absolutely brilliant!" he exclaimed, "but I will need to study the plan carefully and run it by our operations HQ to get final approval."

They met again the following evening. Saleh informed Aziz that the PLO Intelligence and Special Operations Commander thought his plan was outstanding, but there might be some minor details that would need to be finalized. The commander decided that due to the critical nature of the operation, he would have to dispatch to London a professional hit man from Force 17. An experienced special operations PLO officer who would oversee the operation's final details in London would accompany him. The two men would arrive in London separately using European passports.

"Force 17," Saleh explained, "serves as the Chairman's personal bodyguard unit and performs many covert special operations ordered by the Chairman. They have the best and most experienced special operation fighters under PLO command.

"I am happy that they are sending the professionals for this important job," Saleh said in a relieved voice. "They are much more experienced in such complex operations than we are."

The following week all the men assembled in the operation center west of London to finalize the details of the operation. Aziz was introduced to the two newly arrived men from Force 17. To his surprise, the two men looked European and spoke with German accents. When he questioned Saleh about them later, Saleh revealed that the PLO had recently started recruiting European nationals as hired guns for Force 17. With their European looks and authentic German passports, they were unlikely to raise suspicion with the British authorities.

Several days prior to the scheduled hit date, the group moved back to London and started conducting their rehearsals in preparation for the mission. The special operations officer checked into the hotel as planned, taking the time to familiarize himself with all the hotel entrances, exits, and security installations. The hit man stayed in the safe house in London and visited the hotel discreetly to familiarize himself with his area of operation and various escape routes.

As the hit date approached and the operation seemed to be moving forward as planned, Aziz was extremely torn between playing his role as the rising PLO strategist and his strong desire to save the ambassador's life. He realized that his mission was the highest priority, and he had been told explicitly not to make contact with Israeli embassy officials. He had to continue playing the role of a brilliant planner to advance his career and leave the rest to destiny. After all, this operation would have taken place regardless of his getting involved with it as a PLO insider.

However, during the nights prior to the intended assassination, Aziz had trouble sleeping. He cringed at the thought that a German hit man working for the PLO would murder the Israeli ambassador. He felt he just couldn't live with the fact that he would be letting one of his prominent countrymen die at the hands of a bloodthirsty assassin and felt compelled to do something about it without revealing his identity. Even if a failed assassination attempt would delay his PLO career advancement, he felt it was worthwhile to save the man's life and spare his family the horrible grief.

He decided to place an anonymous call to the embassy from a public phone booth on a busy London street. He knew he would be violating his orders by making the call, but technically, he wasn't the one calling. He wasn't going to identify himself, and the security people at the embassy wouldn't know who he was anyway.

When he reached the embassy operator, he requested to speak to the head of security.

"He is not available right now," the operator responded in the standard policy language intended for unfamiliar callers.

"I have a very important and urgent massage for him," Aziz insisted.

"He is in a meeting right now and cannot take any calls," was the next response from the operator.

"This is extremely important."

The operator finally yielded to his persistence. "I will transfer you to one of his assistants."

A man's voice came through the receiver, saying,

"Security. Who am I speaking to?"

"I have an urgent message for the ambassador," Aziz blurted out quickly. "He is not to attend the Ambassador's Ball tomorrow night. His life is in grave danger."

"Who are you?"

"Please don't let the ambassador go to the ball tomorrow. Someone is plotting to kill him."

"I cannot issue any warnings without knowing who you are," the man answered.

"I can't reveal my identity, but I can assure you that this is true, and you should take it very seriously." Before Aziz could finish his sentence, he heard a dial tone on his receiver. He hoped that the security guard would report the incident to his chief and that they would take extra precautions to protect the ambassador.

The security guard was disturbed by the call, although similar calls were routinely received by the embassy. He immediately went to the office of the chief of security.

"I just received another prank call stating that the ambassador's life is in danger and that he should not attend the Ambassador's Ball tomorrow night," he stated dryly.

"If we listen to every warning call we get, the ambassador would never leave the gates of this embassy," the chief responded. "Our job is to protect the life of the ambassador anywhere and anytime, regardless of being able to get advance warnings. If we always depended on advance warnings, there wouldn't be much justification for our existence as bodyguards, would there?" He dismissed the security guard, returned to the pile of papers on his desk, and thought nothing more of the incident.

CHAPTER 20

The dignified guests started arriving for the Ambassador Ball promptly at 7 p.m. The Israeli ambassador arrived at the hotel at around 7:30 p.m., a standard security procedure to try to confuse potential adversaries. He had no reason to suspect anything. His security chief had not mentioned any unusual or precautionary procedures. He trusted his security staff to be vigilant with his personal safety. Looking forward to spending a wonderful evening among close friends and colleagues, he entered the opulent Royal Ballroom.

As the ball was winding down, the PLO informant within the Egyptian security detail gave his first signal consisting of three short beeps to the hit man. In anticipation of receiving the first signal on his miniature receiver, the hit man was already fully dressed in his bellboy uniform and wearing a wig, round-rimmed glasses, and a trimmed moustache.

The Israeli security chief never liked to follow a set schedule for his ambassador. He knew that terrorists depended on close timing to execute their treacherous deeds, and he did not intend to provide them with such luxury. He informed the ambassador that they would have to leave the ball thirty minutes ahead of schedule to avoid the congestion at the hotel entrance when all the other dignitaries were departing. The ambassador nodded his head. Soon he got up to thank his hosts for the wonderful evening he had enjoyed immensely.

Noticing the ambassador's rushed departure, the informant realized what was going to happen and sent a second signal consisting of two short beeps to the bellboy.

Surprised by the early timing of the second signal, the bellboy quickly checked his handgun, tucked it under his gold-trimmed jacket, and put on a pair of soft white gloves frequently worn by bellboys in Europe. He made sure the corridor was empty and walked briskly toward the elevators holding a polished silver tray and a white envelope by his side. He bypassed the elevators and entered the emergency staircase, then rushed down through eight flights of steps to the level of the Royal Ballroom. He avoided the elevators to prevent unexpected delays and exposure to security guards monitoring elevator traffic. He expected to have to wait inconspicuously around the lower lobby corridor until the third signal arrived.

The informant was monitoring the movements of the Israeli ambassador closely, not sure what to expect next. Suddenly the ambassador started making his way toward the ballroom exit. In a panic, the informant sent his third signal of one short beep to the assassin, hoping the assassin would make it downstairs in time. However, as he realized the signals were not expected to have been that close, he knew this could confuse the assassin. The ambassador was moving so fast that the informant didn't expect the assassin to make it down to the lower lobby prior to the ambassador's departure.

As the assassin was coming down the steps, he heard the third signal. He looked at his watch — 11 p.m. The ball wasn't scheduled to be over until 11:30. He wondered if the signals were false, but he knew that he had to adhere to the original plan and improvise his moves as the situation unfolded.

When he reached the bottom of the steps, he paused for a few seconds to catch his breath and tidy his uniform. He stepped into the corridor and walked briskly towards the lobby to catch a glimpse of the ballroom entrance. As he reached the end of the corridor, he slowed down and held the silver tray in front of him in his left hand with the envelope on top.

As the ambassador, joined by his chief of security, was about to exit the ballroom, he bumped into the American ambassador to Britain, who greeted him with a big hello. The two had developed a close relationship during the frequent consultations and meetings they had held on various Middle Eastern policies.

"Why are you leaving us so early?" the American ambassador inquired. "The night is still young."

"You know how tough these security guys can be. If they had it their way, a double would be waltzing with my wife while I'm locked up in the embassy."

The American ambassador chuckled. "My guys give me this bull crap all the time. Hell, sometimes I wish I could get them off my back, but I guess it won't happen in our business."

"Not in our lifetime," the Israeli ambassador noted as he headed to the exit.

The informant was greatly relieved by the unexpected turn of events, as the last-minute delay would allow the assassin to make it downstairs in time.

The bellboy paused briefly at the corner of the corridor to assess the situation. He spotted the Israeli ambassador chatting with someone just inside the ballroom. "He must be on his way out," he thought. "I'd better get ready." He decided to start walking toward the entrance as soon as the ambassador started walking out of the ballroom.

The ambassador seemed to be concluding his conversation. He shook his colleague's hand, turned around, and started walking out accompanied by a neatly dressed tall man on his right.

The bellboy started walking in the direction of the ballroom entrance opposite the two men. He timed his steps so that he would be next to them when they were approximately halfway through the lobby. He glimpsed the two men walking toward him. The ambassador was dressed in a sharp, black two-button, single-breasted tuxedo jacket and pleated satin-striped trousers. He wore a white ten-pleat wing collar shirt, black bow tie, and shiny black shoes. His escort was dressed in a dark pinstriped blue suit, a blue shirt, and a modern, shiny gray tie. The bellboy knew that the escort was the ambassador's chief of security and that he would have to deal with him after he shot the ambassador.

Nobody seemed to pay much attention to the innocent-looking hotel bellboy on his way to deliver an important message to one of the many dignitaries in attendance. The ambassador was conversing with his bodyguard and wasn't paying attention to his surroundings.

As he drew near, the bellboy looked straight ahead to avoid eye contact with the two men walking opposite him. As soon as they were past him, he slowly sneaked his right hand under his jacket and grabbed the handle of his handgun. Suddenly, he turned around, dropped the tray onto the heavily carpeted floor, and drew his weapon. He aimed his gun at the back of the ambassador's head and squeezed the trigger once. A soft shriek from the silenced gun accompanied the shooting.

The ambassador collapsed instantly, falling onto the lobby's floor. His bodyguard, not realizing exactly what had taken place and thinking that the ambassador had tripped, tried to catch the ambassador and cushion his fall, He immediately noticed the ambassador's wound and turned around to face the assailant, a short handgun in his right hand. Another soft shriek sounded as the bodyguard was hit in the chest and flung backward by a second bullet fired from the bellboy's handgun.

The bellboy sprinted back toward the corridor and disappeared out of the hotel's side exit doors. Outside in the cool dark night, he turned the corner into the first side street, running toward the location of his getaway vehicle. He spotted the white mist emitting from the exhaust of the motorcycle ahead and heard the steady ticking of its engine. He leaped onto the back seat, tapped the driver on the right shoulder, and said, "Go! Go! Quickly, I got him!"

Saleh's motorcycle took off like a fighter jet, and before anybody realized what had occurred inside the hotel, the two men were a mile away from the crime scene.

Aziz waited restlessly in the driver seat of the getaway car, not knowing if or when the motorcycle and its riders would show up. They had agreed to refrain from any communication throughout the operation to avoid the risk of detection by the British Secret Service monitoring operations. He hoped the attempt had been aborted and that the two men on the motorcycle would not show up that night.

To his great disappointment, the motorcycle appeared before the expected time. The assassin jumped off the motorcycle and leaped into the back of his car. Aziz drove away while Saleh raced his motorcycle in the opposite direction.

The hit man in the back of the car was catching his breath and settling down.

"Did you get the bastard?" Aziz inquired, anxious to learn of the fate of the ambassador.

"I hit him right in the head," the assassin bragged, "and I got his bodyguard, too. I don't think either will survive, definitely not the ambassador. The plan worked almost flawlessly, except the ambassador decided to leave the ball early, and I barely made it down there in time."

"Outstanding job." Aziz tried to sound as upbeat as he could while hiding his deep disappointment. "It's great news! Now we will earn the respect of the entire world, and terror will reign over the Israelis. They will have to hide deep in their rat holes to escape our wrath."

Aziz turned into a major road leading to the railway station. He was continually scanning the area for the presence of police cars and roadblocks. He needed to get to the railway station ASAP to drop his passenger before all the security alerts were posted by the London police. If he were caught with the assassin in the back of the car, he would be finished.

He noticed in his rearview mirror that the man was peeling the evidence off his body and starting to change. "Stuff the uniform, the gun, and all the accessories into the duffle bag and zip it," Aziz reminded him. "We should be arriving at the station momentarily."

"I am almost ready," the man assured Aziz.

"Your suitcase is in the trunk of the car," Aziz continued. "In it you will find a pouch with your passport, wallet, train ticket, the address, and keys to the safe house in Edinburgh. You also have clothing for several days. I will drive to a side entrance of the station and release the trunk lock. You will pick up the suitcase, enter the station, and board the train as soon as you can. We reserved for you a private sleeping compartment so you can get a good night's rest. You will find the rest of your instructions at the safe house in the bedroom desk drawer."

The drop-off went without incident, and the hit man disappeared into the station. Aziz drove off, stopping shortly thereafter on a side street to stuff the duffle bag into a hidden compartment under the rear passenger seat. With the incriminating evidence tucked away, he drove toward the motorway leading west of London.

He turned the radio on to a news station and picked up live coverage from the Langham Hilton hotel. The reporter stated that the two men shot at the hotel had been rushed to the trauma center of a nearby hospital. They were listed in very critical condition undergoing emergency surgery to try to save their lives. "There may still be hope that they will survive," Aziz thought, remembering that the hit man had bragged as if they were both dead.

The following morning while tucked away in the PLO safe house in Bath, Aziz turned on the TV to listen to the latest news update on the previous night's events. The incident had captured heavy media attention in Britain and throughout Europe. Reporters at the hospital were constantly updating the condition of the two men struck by the assassin, and news flashes regarding the investigation's progress were accompanied by police appeals to the public for information leading to the capture of the perpetrators.

A small splinter group of the Popular Front for the Liberation of Palestine took responsibility for the treacherous act. The group, which had split from a PLO-affiliated Marxist group several months earlier, had close ties with Syria. Aziz recognized the technique used by the PLO to isolate itself from its acts of extreme violence and to preserve its outward posture of a peace-seeking partner. Some of the organizations that claimed responsibility for terrorist acts did so at the PLO Chairman's request, which was accompanied by a generous donation for their holy cause.

The condition of the two men was still unclear, and the police seemed to have no clues to the identity of the actual group that had carried out the attack or to who was behind it. Two days later, it became apparent the head wound suffered by the ambassador had left him almost completely paralyzed. His chief of security was more fortunate: he was listed in serious condition, recovering from multiple surgeries resulting from his chest wound, but he was expected to recover fully.

Aziz felt very saddened by the news of the ambassador's condition. He understood that this outcome would only cause more suffering to the ambassador's family and the State of Israel. He felt helpless about being unable to prevent the attack. He knew that his emotional involvement in the case had clouded his judgment and led him to break the rules. Because of his emotional impulse, he could have blown a mission of supreme national importance.

Now he understood why Shaffir and Harel had insisted on no communications during his mission and that his identity be fully obscured. Frequent, lengthy communications caused Eli Cohen's downfall. He'd been so eager to protect his country and transmit every bit of intelligence he'd gathered that his transmissions were too frequent and too long. His emotions got in the way and trapped him.

Aziz was determined not let his own emotions get in the way again. He vowed to remain totally focused on his mission and objectives.

Two weeks later, he was back in London. There was no evidence that the authorities suspected his or Saleh's involvement in the incident, nor were they able to discover a link to the men from Force 17 who had come and gone like two ghosts.

Saleh emerged from the safe house and invited Aziz to celebrate the success of the operation at a prominent restaurant in London. Saleh welcomed him warmly as they sat down for a long relaxing meal. It was a strict rule not to discuss operational issues in public places, so they spent their time chatting about international politics and reminiscing about their childhood days.

At the end of the evening, Saleh drove Aziz home. In the privacy of the car, the other man took the opportunity to praise Aziz for the meticulous planning and congratulate him on the success of the operation. "Your plan worked like clockwork, you are an operational genius," he commended Aziz.

"The PLO Intelligence and Special Operations Commander has his eyes on you already. This is the second successful mission we've carried out in the last three months, and we're being noticed. The men at headquarters are eager for you to get there to attend the Special Operations Officer's course. They predict an important promotion for you after its successful completion.

"I plan to be there at the same time for an advanced Special Operations training. We will have a great time together in Beirut. I know the city inside and out, and the nightlife there is fabulous. After a tough week of training, we can have great fun.

"We control large portions of the city, and we can pretty much do as we wish in these areas. Our men police the streets and control all the businesses. We practically run a mini-Palestinian state in Lebanon, and the authorities are helpless against the might of our forces. We will soon turn Lebanon into a sovereign Palestinian state and start expanding southwards and claim our homeland back from the Zionist traitors."

"I can't wait to get there," Aziz responded passionately. "I am so happy that you will be there at the same time. It will be amazing to work hard training all week and play hard during our weekends off in this jewel of a city."

Saleh dropped Aziz several streets away from his place. "I will see you at our next meeting," he told Aziz and drove away.

The next few weeks passed in relative calm. Aziz used the time to focus on his studies and complete his course work and papers due for the school year. He was diligent in keeping his academic career on track despite the continuous distractions and his deep involvement in PLO political and covert activities.

CHAPTER 21

LEBANON, 1977

Shortly after the conclusion of the academic school year, Aziz landed at Beirut International Airport. Saleh, who had arrived there two weeks earlier, went to the airport to welcome him. He whisked Aziz through immigration and customs and ushered him to a waiting taxi. "I am glad you came a few days early," he told Aziz. "This will give us the opportunity to catch up and go around town. I am eager to show you our beautiful city and celebrate your arrival at one of the prominent nightclubs in town."

They drove to the hotel where Aziz was going to spend the next three nights before starting his officer's training course. After checking in and freshening up, Aziz joined Saleh for their outing.

It was a hot summer day, typical for Beirut that time of the year. The strong rays of the sun caressing his face and body felt very rejuvenating. It reminded him of the hot summers he'd spent in Deganya, which was only about a hundred miles southeast of Beirut. However, unlike Deganya, Beirut was located on the Mediterranean coast and enjoyed a cool evening breeze that provided much-needed relief from the heat of the sun.

In contrast to London where Saleh was always reserved and on guard, he was very cheerful and gregarious in his local environment. In Beirut, he was on his own turf with his own people, and very much in control.

He drove Aziz along the Mediterranean coastal road where he could enjoy the breathtaking view of the glistening blue waters of the sea and the white sandy shores. They stopped at a famous landmark called Pigeon Rocks, a huge rock formation nestled like sentinels in the deep blue waters just off the coastline. They sat down and relaxed at a cliff-side café, enjoying an ice cold drink and admiring the beautiful panoramic view.

As they continued the tour, the grand architecture of the enchanted ancient city surrounded by hills, the steep cliffs along the sea, and the majestic mountains rising to the east impressed Aziz.

The city conveyed a sense of radiant energy that was immediately apparent to any new visitor. The streets were bustling with people walking along the sidewalks, merchants announcing their special offers, and street vendors bargaining with their clients. "No wonder Beirut is called the Paris of the Middle East," Aziz thought.

On the way back to the hotel, Aziz noticed several structures damaged from bombing attacks. Saleh explained the structures had been hit by mortar exchanges between rivaling factions battling for the control of Beirut suburbs. "It's quiet for the time being, but you never know when the next flare-up will occur," Saleh said as he dropped Aziz at the entrance of his hotel. "I will pick you up tonight at eight. We are going to have a wonderful evening," he promised and waved goodbye.

That evening Saleh took his guest to the hot spots for clubs and bars and the latest fad restaurants on Rue Monnot in Ashrafieh, one of the most renowned districts of Beirut that was famous for its old houses and colorful streets. They dined at one of the most exquisite French restaurants in the area and then went on a nightclub-hopping spree, dancing to great hip-hop and Arab-Latin music until the wee hours of the morning. Saleh was warmly welcomed in all the places where they dropped in. He seemed to know people in every nightspot and was popular with the young, exotic women who surrounded him as soon as he appeared.

Saleh made use of his good looks, particularly his piercing blue eyes and smile that could captivate any young woman's heart. He introduced Aziz to many of his male and female friends and made him feel very welcome in the social circles of the city.

Aziz appreciated why Saleh was so happy in Beirut. There he was a freedom fighter during the day and a playboy at night. He loved the worry-free lifestyle, the openness and warmth of the people, and the atmosphere of a modern city in the heart of an ancient Middle Eastern society.

After enjoying three days of unprecedented Middle Eastern hospitality by his host, it was time for Aziz to report to training camp to start his special operations officer's course. The camp was located in the northern Bekkaa valley, about a ninety-minute drive from Beirut.

The facilities at the officers' training camp were by far superior to those at basic training. The structures consisted of several brick barracks, a large dining hall, an administrative building, and separate instructors' quarters. The camp had formerly been a Lebanese army base that had been taken over by the PLO.

The makeup of the officers' course was modeled after the curriculum provided by the Soviets, who used it for their own training of special operations officers. With the curriculum came several Soviet advisors who oversaw the training regimen and made sure the PLO instructors, trained in the Soviet Union, strictly adhered to the program.

Thus, officers' school training was very professional and rigorous. It started with intense physical fitness training to whip all the recruits into shape and reinforce strict discipline. Next, they learned the most effective use of miniature machine guns and handguns. Various advanced weapons techniques were taught, ranging from accurate firing position and actual firing of the weapon to overcoming weapon jamming and switching weapons in action. The weapons training was accompanied by many hours of practice at several target ranges with short breaks occurring only to count the hits and mark the targets. They were also taught creative ways to conceal weapons and explosives in hand luggage and ways to plant weapons on board airliners so that they did not have to be carried on.

Small weapons training was followed by an airline hijacking course that built on the skills learned during the first phase of training. They used an old Boeing 707 aircraft purchased as scrap from Middle East Airlines, the Lebanese national airline. The airplane was hidden in a large camouflaged hanger to keep it from the eyes of Israeli and American spy planes.

They learned how to take over a jetliner, overcome the crew, and commandeer the cockpit. Handguns were to be fired only if plainclothes air marshals were on board and tried to resist the hijacking attempt. They practiced firing and maneuvering in tight spaces such as the airliner's aisles and cockpit along with controlling the partitioned sections of the plane with remote-controlled miniature explosive devices.

They conducted onboard drills in which some of the recruits acted as the hijackers while others served as onboard security guards, crew and passengers. Roles were switched until everybody was fully trained in the hijacking process.

In the final hijacking simulation exercise, each team was presented with a complex hijacking scenario with varying incidents taking place along the way. The team and its commander had to prove their ability to react to a crisis in a rapid and effective manner, improvise quick solutions, and maintain overall control of the situation on the aircraft at all times. To make the final exercise as practical as possible, they used special paint rounds fired by the recruit's standard weapons.

An integral part of the course involved teaching

skills in conducting negotiations with local authorities, insisting on their demands, and executing hostages if the demands were not met.

Select recruits were assigned to basic flight training and navigation of commercial aircrafts. They used a commercial flight simulator confiscated from an MEA flight training school near Beirut. The main purpose of flight training was to make sure the hijacked pilots were following orders and navigating the craft to its intended destination. In the event pilots were shot in the struggle to take over the plane, there could be an urgent need for an individual with basic flight skills to maneuver the plane, direct it to the closest airport, and possibly land it. The flight training instructor was a former Algerian airlines pilot who'd decided to join the PLO as a freedom fighter and contribute his expertise in the field.

Aziz loved the flight training portion of the course, for it had always been something he'd dreamed of doing. Ironically he was learning it in a terrorist training course.

The following week they received training in sniping and sharpshooting using long-range sniping rifles equipped with a telescope, night vision aids, and a silencer. They learned to dismantle and assemble collapsible Soviet-made rifles that fit in a hand-carried briefcase. They were also taught camouflage techniques for positioning themselves prior to firing at the target. This training was intended for high-level assassinations ordered by PLO central command.

The toughest part of the course was contact combat training, which turned out to be a brutal, no-

nonsense, highly effective technique that combined all the nasty elements found in martial arts. Contact combat instructions reflected intense aggressiveness and decisiveness with the single objective of quickly disarming and incapacitating the enemy. Its purpose was to intensify the aggressive nature of the recruits and prepare them physically and mentally for absorbing and sustaining heavy beating. During drills, the trainees encountered violent situations in which they had to demonstrate extreme brutal aggressiveness to overcome their enemy.

At the end of the week, they held one-on-one, tournament-style combat between the trainees. Each trainee was eager to prove his superior aggressiveness and ability to crush his opponent so as to advance his career prospects. As a result, the combats were very vicious, and many participants had to be carried away for medical treatment due to injuries sustained during combat.

Aziz faced a young, aggressive, but inexperienced recruit who was trying to show off his violent aptitude. Aziz blocked the recruit's assault attempts with relative ease, waiting patiently for him to become careless. As soon as he did, Aziz inflicted on him several blows with all his might, and the battle was over in no time.

In the final phase of the course, they trained in the assembly of explosive devices. The course head instructor was a renowned PLO bomb-making genius, dubbed "the engineer," who had received extensive bomb-making training in the Soviet bloc. He demonstrated miniature explosives made of thin plastic layers that were integrated into the lining of carry-on luggage. The detonator and batteries were concealed in the suitcase handle, so the entire device was virtually undetectable by airport x-ray machines. These devices were equipped with barometric detonators that could be set to go off when an airplane reached a certain altitude. The recruits were taught to assemble explosive charges of various sizes that could be detonated remotely by radio signals. Such devices were used during hijacking of airplanes or buses to frighten the passengers and deter rescue forces from storming the target in an attempt to free hostages.

Next they moved on to bigger bombs that could be used as large-scale destruction tools against civilian or military targets. The engineer demonstrated how to construct powerful car and truck bombs, roadside charges, and large explosives that could be placed at selected targets. This training was accompanied by supervised workshops where recruits followed written instructions to assemble various devices and then explode them in the field.

As the course came to its conclusion, Aziz was impressed by the quality of the training instructions and the knowledge he had acquired. Many elements of the course were new to him because he hadn't been exposed to terrorism training during his IDF career. The course earned his respect for PLO capabilities and provided him with insight into PLO strategy to prepare its future officers to conduct a wide range of operations.

He understood the PLO's strong commitment to its long-term objective of fighting Israel to the end unless a respectable and peaceful settlement could be reached.

It was clear they were in it for the long haul, and that over time they would grow into a formidable force Israel and the world would have to reckon with. Hence, the PLO leadership steering the organization would play a major role in determining whether to favor the peace negotiations route or continue the bloody struggle.

He suddenly realized why Harel and Shaffir had insisted on his total focus on the mission and avoidance of any distractions along the way. Although they were both frustrated by the continued terrorist attacks on Israeli targets at home and abroad and the mounting casualties, they knew these were short-term problems. They were smart to realize that to protect the long-term survival of their beloved nation, they would need to penetrate the high echelon of PLO leadership and try to guide its decisions toward a negotiated settlement with Israel that would bring stability and economic prosperity to the region. This purpose was the reason for the supreme importance and urgency of his mission and the need for strict adherence to its objectives. He had to focus on the big picture and ignore the minor diversions along the way.

Aziz completed the course with high merit, winning the praise of his instructors and the school commander. After the graduation ceremony, he traveled back in Beirut to spend a few days relaxing on its beautiful sunny beaches. He spent most of his time with Saleh, who had also completed his arduous advanced training and was ready to have real fun.

Saleh told Aziz that the Chairman had invited him to a private meeting to discuss his future leadership role at the PLO. The Chairman informed Saleh that he had been slated for a major promotion and would not be returning to London. He was to continue his advanced training in Pakistan and return to PLO headquarters in Beirut for his new high post in Force 17. Saleh revealed that because Aziz had proven his abilities in the field and in the commander's course, Saleh had strongly recommended him as his successor to command PLO operations in Britain. Aziz's new appointment was to be confirmed the following day.

Aziz was elated by his promotion. This was going to be his first command position within the PLO and a major step in his quest to advance in its ranks. He jumped up in excitement, hugging Saleh and thanking him repeatedly for his help in reaching the crucial milestone. Saleh responded by saying that Aziz was very deserving, and he hoped Aziz would soon join him at PLO Command HQ.

The following day Saleh took Aziz to visit the PLO headquarters in West Beirut to introduce him to his new superior, the Commander of Intelligence and Special Operations. Next, Saleh asked Aziz to follow him down the hall. They entered what appeared to be a highly secure area with several armed guards who waved them through. Saleh entered a lavish office suite with Aziz following closely behind. Without warning, the Chairman appeared right in front of them with a big smile. He greeted Saleh warmly, blessing him as if he were his own son, then hugging him and kissing him on both cheeks.

"I came to thank you for my new promotion, your

Excellency," Saleh stated. "I leave for advanced training in Pakistan next week and will return to Beirut to assume my new responsibility within six months. I appreciate your confidence in me. I will always make you proud of my accomplishments in advancing the cause of freedom and honor of our people."

"Well done, son. I know you will never disappoint me," the Chairman said. "I have strong faith in your abilities to help me make this organization a major force in shaping the future of this region and regaining the lost pride of our people. But who is the handsome gentleman accompanying you, Saleh?"

"Your Excellency, it is my great pleasure to introduce you to Abdul Aziz Al-Wasphi, my dear friend and your chosen new commander of PLO operations in Britain. Aziz is the man who took care of Naji Al-Karadi, the traitor who tried to defame your name and insult your character. Aziz planned the entire operation and personally eliminated Naji with his own hands, leaving no trace behind."

"Thank you, Aziz, for your excellent service to the cause of our people," the Chairman acknowledged. "I am glad you took Naji out of the picture. His vicious character attacks and disrespect became too much of a distraction for me. He wouldn't relent despite all the warnings we gave him."

"Aziz also started a fundraising drive in London and donated half of the proceeds to your Special Fund," Saleh continued praising his friend.

"Excellent idea, Aziz. We need to intensify the effort of contribution collections to keep our war machine and political campaigns going strong. I am always looking for creative ideas to increase our revenue stream. It's the most vital factor to our ultimate success."

Aziz managed to sneak in a few words. "It's my great honor to meet you, your Excellency. Just like Saleh, my talented mentor, I will continue working diligently to advance the cause of our people and spread wrath and terror over the double-crossing Israeli traitors until we throw every one of them into the sea."

"Well said, son," the Chairman acknowledged. "I am sure I will be hearing of your acts of courage in the near future. Please come to see me when you are back in Beirut."

As they left the Chairman's office, the close relationship between Saleh and the Chairman amazed Aziz. Saleh was the Chairman's wonder boy, slated for a promising future in the organization's high ranks. There were rumors that Saleh was related to the Chairman, but nobody knew exactly how. Aziz was thankful for his good fortune to have been recruited by Saleh and for his ability to establish very close relations with him. He knew Saleh and his vast connections within the PLO would be the key to his own future success in rising to the top.

CHAPTER 22

The following week Saleh embarked on his journey to Pakistan while Aziz began his way back to London. Shortly after arriving there, Aziz convened a meeting with his staff to brief them on the leadership changes and prepare them for the challenges ahead. He had been instructed to organize a series of hijackings of European airlines en route to Israel and land them in friendly Arab nations. They were to offer to exchange the hostages on board the airlines for Palestinian prisoners in Israel.

European airlines were relatively easy prey for the well-trained and experienced PLO operatives. Responsibility for carrying out hijacking missions was always attributed to obscure Palestinian organizations used as the cover for the identity of the hijackers. Airline security in Europe was very lax because the responsibility for the expenses to maintain it lay mostly with the airlines' already stretched budgets, while government agencies tried to ignore the problem. There were no sky marshals onboard flights, not even those to Middle Eastern destinations.

As a secondary alternative to the PLO prisoner

exchange, Aziz came up with an ingenious scheme to spread fear of hijacking among major European airlines. After several successful hijackings, passengers' fear was certain to affect airline occupancy rates and hurt the airline business. The PLO was then to approach top executives of European airlines and offer them hijacking protection services, insuring that their planes would not be targeted for future hijackings. This scheme was to be used to extort several million dollars of protection money from each airline every year and disguise it as donations to humanitarian funds.

Their first target was a flight from Paris to Tel Aviv. Aziz received his orders and a detailed plan from his new commander in Beirut. Four PLO European operatives, including two Germans, were to board the airline using falsified passports. In the interim, a PLO recruit working for the catering company servicing the plane was to smuggle a handbag with hidden handguns and plastic explosives on board the plane. He was to place it in a luggage compartment in the back of the plane above the designated seat of the group leader and his men. The hijackers had assigned seats next to each other in the last row of the plane.

Thirty minutes after takeoff, the German group leader was to remove the bag from the compartment and discreetly distribute the guns and explosives to the men. They were to assume their positions: two in the front near the cockpit, one in the middle, and one in the back of the plane.

At the agreed moment, they were to put their masks on, draw their guns, and announce to the crew that the airliner was being hijacked. The group leader would then enter the cockpit, hold guns to the pilots' heads, and instruct them to fly the plane to Algiers. His men were to place explosive devices with remote detonation at each section of the plane and patrol each section to ensure that the passengers remained in their seats throughout the rest of the flight. Upon landing in Algiers, the non-Israeli and non-Jewish passengers would be released while the crew and the Israeli and Jewish hostages would remain on the plane. The hijackers would then demand that one hundred Palestinian fighters held in Israeli jails be released, flown to Algiers, and exchanged for the Israeli hostages.

Aziz was resolved to stay focused on his mission and go along with whatever he was ordered to carry out. He would use his skills to execute his missions successfully while doing his best to preserve innocent human life.

He made all the preparations for the mission, including traveling to France over the weekend to coordinate the activities and brief the men on their roles in the operation. The Algerian authorities, who were strong PLO supporters, were expected to cooperate fully with the hijackers and assist them in achieving their objectives. Aziz returned to London on Sunday night to avoid any suspicion by the French authorities of his association with the hijacking.

The following Wednesday morning, the French jetliner took off from Paris on its way to Tel Aviv without any suspicion of what was about to take place. The hijacking operation was executed without any resistance. The crew and passengers were taken by complete surprise, and within two hours, the hijacked plane landed safely in Algiers.

The hijacking received the immediate attention of the international media, spurring around-the-clock coverage of the incident. The Israeli government, known not to yield to terrorism demands, mounted a massive political campaign with the help of its Western allies to pressure the Algerian government to release the hostages and not become an accomplice to international terrorism. The Algerians stalled for a while, not sure how to react. They were upset with the PLO for choosing Algeria as the hijacking destination and placing them in the midst of an international incident. With mounting international pressure, they detained the hijackers and moved the passengers to temporary quarters until all issues were resolved.

Realizing that the prisoner exchange was not going to take place, PLO Command under the cover of a splinter group resorted to its contingency plan and demanded ten million dollars from the airline for the release of the jetliner and its passengers. The airline officials, eager to end the negative media attention, agreed and transferred the money to a designated Swiss bank account.

The jetliner and its precious human cargo returned to Paris, and the terrorists disappeared without a trace.

Aziz was very pleased with the outcome of the operation. The media coverage was a strong boost to the world's awareness of the Palestinian cause, the Chairman's fund had been boosted by ten million dollars, and the Israeli hostages had escaped unharmed. Not a bad return on a few days of work, he thought.

Aziz knew the Chairman would be very happy with the media attention, which was worth millions by itself. He loved seeing his private fund growing, and the Palestinian prisoners in Israeli jails would be an excuse to mount another operation in the near future.

Subsequent to the incident, the PLO contacted the airline and offered their protective services from future hijackings. The airline secretly agreed to pay the PLO ten million dollars annually for the service. This fee was only a fraction of what it would cost them to install all the security equipment needed at the airports and hire the security personnel to operate it. The economics of the deal worked in favor of terrorism.

After a string of a few more successful hijacking operations that demanded the release of terrorists held in European jails, several European airlines signed up for the PLO's hijacking protection services and the Chairman's fund swelled to record levels.

One evening Aziz received a call from Saleh, who was in London for a few days after completing his six-month advanced training program. They met for dinner that evening in one of their favorite nightspots. Afterwards, Saleh invited Aziz to his hotel suite. He congratulated Aziz on his continued success in aviation-related operations and praised Aziz's brilliant planning and execution abilities. He then revealed to Aziz that the Chairman had appointed him, Saleh, to become the new Deputy Commander of Force 17. His training in Pakistan was specifically for providing security and personal protective services for the Chairman and other high-ranking PLO officials. In addition, he would be responsible for covert special operations against Western targets worldwide.

Saleh went on to tell him that the PLO command was going to promote Aziz to oversee PLO operations in all Europe. "We concluded that you would be the best choice for the job," he added. "You have been heavily involved in European operations already, and this is a natural progression in your career. The Chairman is very impressed with your innovative ideas and sophisticated planning skills. Seeing his personal fund grow so nicely in the past few months has definitely elevated you on his radar screen.

"The best news," Saleh continued, "is that your new command will fall under my direct responsibility, and we will be working together again. You will remain in London and continue your studies, which is a great cover for you. You will travel to Europe using a counterfeit Tunisian passport to avoid attracting the attention of the European authorities."

"This is the most superlative news yet, my dear brother," Aziz responded enthusiastically. "I have missed working with you so much this past year. We make a great team, and we are going to have lots of fun blasting the arrogant Israelis and battering the pathetic Europeans who start trembling the minute they hear our name. The European governments haven't changed much over the years — they remain susceptible to terror, always preferring to cooperate with us to avoid retaliatory actions. This is a perfectly fertile ground for our operations. We can dictate pretty much any terms we want, and they'll comply without putting up too much resistance. They'll try to avoid arresting any of our men or keeping them in jail, since they know we will mount more operations to free them."

"You are quite right about that," Saleh acknowledged, "but my ultimate goal is to get you to join Force 17. There you will be close to the real action and be part of our operational planning activities. You will be close to the top echelon of PLO leadership, including the Chairman, and be able to start establishing close relationships with the powerful men who will forge the future of our beloved nation."

"I would love that." Aziz again expressed his gratitude to Saleh for advocating his career advancement within the organization. "In several months, I will be completing my doctoral studies, so the time may be ripe for my next move."

"It does sound like the perfect moment," Saleh agreed. "With a Ph.D. in Middle Eastern studies under your belt, you can become active in the political wing of the PLO. We can always use brilliant strategists like you in our foreign and public relations departments."

CHAPTER 23

ISRAEL, 1977

In his monthly review with the PM, Mossad Chief Avi Shaffir updated Harel on the progress Reuben had been making in climbing the PLO ladder. "Believe it or not, he is now in charge of all PLO operations in Europe," Shaffir told Harel. "Quite an impressive performance, I would say. The man is one of the Chairman's favorite PLO rising stars.

"Our senior Middle East intelligence officer, who doesn't know Reuben's true identity, is recommending that we keep a close eye on him as a potential new threat to our national security. What do you think of that? Is the man a genius, or what? One of the methods he is using to promote himself within the PLO is a firm voice against Israel, voicing radical opinions to use all means to redeem the respect of the Palestinians and advance the creation of an independent entity within the Israeli-held territories. His strategy is working so well that it captured the attention of our own watchdogs, who think we may need to target him for a hit down the road."

"How far is he going with this strategy?" Harel voiced his concern. "Should we be alarmed about what operations he will initiate in Europe to build up his power and popularity? I don't want more casualties on my hands. We've suffered enough already this year."

"I discussed this matter with him at length before his departure," Shaffir responded. "On the one hand, he needs to build up his success and popularity to get where we need him to be within several years. On the other hand, he needs to preserve Jewish lives. We agreed that he would do his utmost to balance this paradox by focusing on high-profile European targets."

"Avi, I am sure you are aware that the elections are drawing near, and I need all the support I can get to maintain my popularity for re-election. More bloodshed will not work in my favor."

"I hope you will win with a comfortable majority," Shaffir said. "The last thing this country needs is yet another change in leadership. I too have concerns about the elections. If for some reason, you are going to lose the electoral power during the coming elections, you will need to inform the incoming PM of the Chairman-X mission.

"A new PM is likely to reconsider the entire project and may decide to call it off. I don't think we can take that risk and lose the remarkable progress our agent has made in the past few years. He is our best chance for future stability in the region and an end to the bloodshed. We can't afford to lose this golden opportunity after the huge investment we've made."

Shaffir leaned back in his chair, waiting for a reaction from Harel.

"My strong recommendation to you, Shlomo," he continued staring at Harel's stonewall expression, "is to keep the existence of this mission between us for the time being. Even if you are not re-elected, I will remain the head of the Mossad until the new PM decides whether he wants to replace me. If I am replaced, I will have to inform the new Mossad Chief of the mission. However, I should be able to persuade him to explain to the new PM how critical this mission is and that it must be kept a closely guarded secret. The fewer people have knowledge and involvement in this mission, the better our chances of success.

"I would also strongly recommend removing all of Reuben's records and files within the Israeli Interior ministry, IDF, and the Mossad, as if he never existed," Shaffir added. "This will ensure his safety from internal leaks and increase his odds of success."

"You may be going too far with this." Shaffir finally had drawn a reaction from Harel. "I don't want him to become the victim of his own mission."

"My main fear, Shlomo, is our inability to predict the nature of the Israeli political landscape over the next few years. We must shield Reuben from internal politics and let him continue his mission uninterrupted. The mission's objectives are unlikely to change in the next two decades. Therefore, the seed we planted should continue to grow and flourish with only minimal interference."

"This was not part of the plan," Harel countered.

"We have no way of informing Reuben of these changes. Would that be fair to him?"

"These changes are irrelevant to him or his mission," Shaffir said in a passionate, defiant tone. "They are designed to protect him more than anything else."

"I will go along with your recommendations on one condition," Harel told him. "You must establish an infallible system to ensure that Reuben's true identity is maintained at the very top level. You and I will have to continue our communications throughout the next several years, either in an official capacity or as private citizens. We have to make absolutely sure that this continuity is maintained until the mission is complete."

"Consider it done." Shaffir shook Harel's hand vigorously and left. He was anxious to get to bed after another exhausting day of work into the early hours of the morning.

Shaffir's driver was waiting for him in the secured parking garage of the PM's office. He slipped into the backseat and told his driver, "Take me home. I need to get some sleep and rest my brain."

While he sat in the back of his official car, Shaffir continued mulling over the entire Chairman-X scheme. His experiences with past failures made it clear that the best chance for success would be if no one else knew about Reuben. It wasn't a short-term mission; the longer it went on, the more benefits would be reaped from it. The more people knew about it, the higher the chances of it going amiss. He recalled that too many people had known about Eli Cohen's existence, and in the end that had caused his downfall. Eli could have operated for many more years in Syria undetected if he'd been instructed to operate on his own with a set of predefined guidelines that excluded frequent transmissions. Of course, there was the issue of Eli's family in Israel, which was another obstacle.

Reuben didn't face any such restrictions. He was a loner who thrived on risk and success and could build an entire new way of life during his assignment. Even if nobody knew of his existence in Israel, the outcome should not change. If he were discovered and able to flee, he would have his original identity authentication papers in the Swiss bank safe deposit box. If he returned to Israel, he would have all the documents to reinstate his identity and receive the great honors he deserved. If his success was so great that his mission would be prolonged, no one would really need to know his true identity until the time that he would rise to a PLO leadership position.

The following day Shaffir arranged for Reuben's personal documents to be removed from their respective records while other documents were added to the safe deposit box in the Swiss bank.

CHAPTER 24

In the national elections held in Israel that fall, Shlomo Harel lost by a narrow margin. The opposition party formed a new government. Shaffir kept very close tabs on the election results and realized that his days in office might also be numbered because new administrations always favored the loyalty of their own appointees to key positions. The Mossad Chief reported directly to the Prime Minister, and the new PM was expected to place his own confidant in this very sensitive and critical position that had access to the most intimate secrets of the country.

Shaffir was determined to keep the Chairman-X mission a secret as long as he possibly could. He didn't see any benefits from relaying the information to the new Mossad Chief or the new PM. With the instability of Israeli politics, the shaky new coalition might not last very long. If yet another new government had to be formed, the secret would be revealed to more people.

Shaffir knew that Reuben needed several more years to reach the PLO top spot. At the average rate at which

Israeli governments changed hands, this meant that by the time Reuben reached the top, there would be dozens of people aware of his mission and identity. This fact was unacceptable to Shaffir. Chairman-X was his baby, and he was going to protect it as long as he was still around. He had learned from his long service with the various Israeli secret agencies that the statistics of human nature didn't work in Reuben's favor. With so many people privy to the secret, his identity would surely be leaked out somewhere along the way. The only people Shaffir felt had to know about it were the PM and the Mossad Chief in office at the time when Reuben would become Chairman — if and when that finally happened.

Shaffir knew that Harel wasn't going to bail out of the political scene anytime soon. There was a good chance he would be back in the government in some capacity, and perhaps one day return as the victorious PM.

When the new Mossad Chief took office three months later, Shaffir did not inform him of the Chairman-X mission as he had promised Harel he would. He was going to monitor Reuben's progress through his loyal confidants inside the Mossad and keep Harel updated periodically on the progress Reuben was making inside the PLO.

* * * *

Over the next several months, Aziz and Saleh mounted a series of successful terrorist operations in Europe and the Middle East against Israeli targets, non-sympathetic Arab targets, and Euro-American targets.

They attacked the offices of the Jordanian National

Airline in Rome, assassinated a Jordanian diplomat in Turkey, attacked the US embassy in Cairo, assassinated a British diplomat in India, and attacked El Al Israeli airline offices in Amsterdam.

One of their bloodiest and most successful operations was a simultaneous and coordinated attack mounted near airline counters in both Rome and Vienna international airports. Terrorists armed with automatic machine guns and hand grenades opened fire on passengers seated in lounge areas of flights bound for Israel, inflicting heavy casualties and wounding scores of civilians.

At the request of the Chairman, Saleh instructed Aziz to carry out death sentences ordered by the Chairman for several Palestinian political figures who'd initiated political contacts with the Israelis without the Chairman's knowledge or approval. These assassinations were to serve as a stern warning to liberal elements within the PLO that the Chairman was in full control and that he was the only one who would decide when, where, and how to initiate contacts with the Israelis and the Americans.

Saleh's and Aziz's fame within the ranks of the PLO was gaining strong momentum. The men under their command revered them, and the signature of the terrorist operations they mounted was becoming the pride and joy of PLO fighters and their leadership. With the remarkable publicity generated from the relentless operations, sentiment about the plight of the Palestinian refugees was growing daily in the Western world. More and more European leaders were joining the call for a just and respectful solution to the Palestinian problem and initiation of negotiations to address the pressing situation and find acceptable solutions.

At the request of the Chairman, Saleh invited Aziz to come to Beirut to attend a special awards ceremony hosted by the Chairman and the Palestinian National Council. Saleh and Aziz, among others, were being honored for their outstanding service on behalf of the Palestinian Nation and its struggle for independence.

After the ceremony, Saleh asked Aziz to join him for a private meeting with the Chairman. The Chairman welcomed Aziz with a warm embrace and the traditional kisses. "Saleh is always singing your praises to me and keeping me informed of the incredible work you have been performing," he opened the conversation.

"Thank you, Your Excellency," Aziz responded humbly. "This is just the beginning. We will continue our vicious attacks until we bring the Israeli traitors and their American puppets to their knees, begging you to start a dialogue with them on your terms.

"My dear brother and mentor, Saleh, has been guiding me on this path since the first day we met in London. I owe everything I have accomplished to his incredible devotion and constant guidance."

"Saleh and you, Aziz, are the pillars of our future," the Chairman told them. "With young, energetic, and brilliant commanders such as you under my leadership, the future of our beloved nation can be steered to great success and a bright future.

"I spoke to Saleh about you, Aziz, and we both feel strongly that you belong here with us, at the heart of our operations. Here you will be able to contribute your great mind to advancing our cause, both on the armed and political fronts. I will order your immediate transfer to Beirut. You will split your time between working closely with Saleh at Force 17 and serving on my Strategic Planning Committee.

"Welcome home, fearless warrior. There are many challenges ahead of us, and we will prevail, *ensha'allah,* God willing, very soon."

Aziz rose and kissed the Chairman's hand in gratitude for the honor bestowed upon him. "Your Excellency, I will continue to work very diligently to support your objectives and wishes until the day that all our brothers and sisters live in dignity and prosperity in our true and only homeland."

* * * *

After attending his graduation ceremony and receiving his doctorate from London University, Aziz was ready to move on. He packed his belongings, and within a few days, he moved to western Beirut into a nicely furnished small apartment located within the protective jurisdiction of the PLO forces.

Once settled in Beirut, he went through an orientation period to familiarize himself with the broad PLO organization, its various operating departments, its functions, and its decision-making process. He worked closely with Saleh on pressing operational, security, and funding issues. Saleh trained him extensively on security procedures for protecting the Chairman and other high-ranking PLO officials. Saleh told him that the Chairman was extremely fanatic about his personal security and trusted only a handful of men with his safety. He always had his mini-submachine gun strapped to his waist or placed by his bedside. He worked late into the night, sleeping at most only four or five hours. He liked taking short catnaps in the afternoons whenever possible to get extra rest and improve his stamina in the evenings.

Saleh informed Aziz that the Chairman had requested Aziz be appointed as one of the commanders of his security detail. He revealed that the Chairman was so impressed by Aziz's accomplishments, devotion to the Palestinian cause, and hatred for the enemy that he felt he could trust him with his own life.

The two men spent a lot of time together on the job, with Saleh filling Aziz in on the most intricate details of safety procedures and precautionary measures to ensure the Chairman's safety. Potential adversaries to the Chairman came mostly from rival Palestinian factions that had ideological differences with the Chairman and had split off from the PLO. Some of these factions were closely supported and funded by Syrian intelligence. They'd plotted several attempts on the Chairman's life because of his disagreements with the Syrian President and his taking control over most of Lebanon. The Syrians were upset by the PLO's actions in Lebanon and viewed the organization as a potential threat to their national security.

Ironically, the threat to the Chairman's life from the Israelis wasn't considered as forthcoming as it was from the Arab side. It was well known from reliable intelligence sources that the Israelis did not wish to target the Chairman. Israel considered the Chairman an acceptable choice who had the backing of most Palestinians. When the right opportunity arrived, the Israelis felt and hoped he would be the only Palestinian leader with a mandate from his people to negotiate a durable peace accord with Israel. Compared to the much more fanatic militant rivals who would not accept any compromise and wanted only the total destruction of the Jewish state, he looked the most reasonable, at least on the surface. These were the notions that guided the Israeli strategy toward the PLO.

"Don't you think it's ironic," Saleh asked Aziz one evening after a long day of working on security arrangements for the Chairman's trip to Libya, "that we are protecting the Chairman from our own and not from the real enemy? If the Israelis really wanted to take out the Chairman, we couldn't stop them. We could die as martyrs trying to protect him, but eventually they would get him, just as they have so many others. I know they've had several opportunities, but for unknown reasons, probably political, they never took advantage of them. They must think the next leader could only be much worse, so they'd rather stick with the known rather than the unknown."

"That is a very interesting angle of thought," Aziz responded. "I always believed the Israelis would be after him big time, but what you just said makes absolute sense. It's impossible for them to predict who will succeed him, or how many more-extremist militant groups will emerge in the vacuum that would be created if something happened to him, Allah forbid.

"Nonetheless, we are not going to let anything

harm our esteemed leader," Aziz continued. "On your watch, Saleh, not even a tiny hair will be shed from the Chairman's head. He considers you the rising star of the revolution and is planning a gleaming future for you."

"Yes, Aziz, but I need you there by my side every bit of the way. I am counting on your continuous support and brilliance to help me clinch some major victories and rise to the number two position at the PLO one day soon, *ensha'allah.*"

"Your word is my command, Saleh. I trust that by now you know there isn't anything I wouldn't do to support you and the Chairman in achieving your personal goals and the freedom of our people from our Israeli enemies."

"I know you will never let me down, my dear brother Aziz. I feel I have known you all my life and that you are my own flesh and blood."

Aziz continued to cultivate his close bond with Saleh, who had been the key to his rapid ascent through the PLO ranks and the link to establishing close relations with the powerful Chairman. It was evident that nothing would pass without the Chairman's blessing, and Saleh definitely had his ear when it came to Aziz.

Whenever the two men had the night off, they went around town enjoying the diverse nightlife of Beirut's famous nightclubs. Saleh was popular among the young attractive women who gravitated to him every time he showed up in one of the nightspots. He introduced Aziz to many of his female acquaintances who found his tall, handsome friend very gracious.

During the next several weeks, Saleh spent a lot of

time training Aziz in the Chairman's personal security details until he was satisfied that Aziz was ready to take full control. The security procedures they followed were the result of extensive training by the East German Secret Service, strongly influenced by KGB practices.

For Aziz, who had never been taught this type of job, it was an eye-opening experience. He gained the inside knowledge of every detail of the Chairman's security arrangements, hoping this valuable information might serve his self-interest very well in the not-too-distant future.

Being so close to the Chairman allowed Aziz to solidify his relations with the man and impress him even more with his extensive knowledge of the international political landscape surrounding Middle Eastern affairs. He knew that Saleh had recently been appointed to the Chairman's Executive Committee, which was, for all practical purposes, the forum where all the important decisions affecting the PLO were made. Aziz's next critical step would be his appointment by the Chairman to this prestigious committee. Serving on it would expose him to all its influential members and allow him to start building strong relations with them. However, he knew this would take more time and effort, and that he would have to continue making significant contributions to the success of the organization to earn this prestigious appointment.

Since Aziz was already actively serving on the PLO strategic planning committee, the Chairman invited him on occasion to make certain presentations to the Executive Committee on his behalf.

Several weeks later, Saleh told Aziz that the Chairman would like to see them both urgently on an important matter. They reported to his office at once.

"Gentlemen, we've had pledges of financial support from many of our so-called friends in the Arab world," the Chairman began, "but most have not kept their promises and are far behind in their payments. We need to intensify our fundraising efforts due to a shortfall in our operating cash reserves that is reaching an alarming level.

"I need you two to come up with creative ideas to make up our shortages fairly quickly. I am talking about two to three months at the most. You can use any methods you deem appropriate to get this money, for without it some of our most important programs will come to a grinding halt."

"We will take care of it without delay," Saleh reassured the Chairman. "Please rest your mind and leave it to Aziz and me. We will have the funds in your bank accounts on time, as you requested."

"Thank you, gentlemen. I am counting on you two to make this happen. By the way, if the media gets wind of your efforts, I know nothing about this, and this conversation never took place."

Saleh and Aziz left the Chairman's office in a hurry. This serious problem needed to be addressed urgently. Without proper funding, the organization's future was at risk, and failure wasn't an option. The money had to be acquired by any necessary means and without delay.

Aziz asked Saleh which countries were delinquent or had reneged on their PLO pledges and what other possible sources of funds could be accessed quickly. Saleh called in the Chairman's fundraising chief advisor to consult with him on the situation. The advisor provided them with a list of the countries that were behind on their payments along with a second list of several very wealthy Palestinians who had pledged large sums for the PLO but had broken their promises, giving only various lame excuses. He also indicated the shortage was in the range of five hundred million dollars, which was a colossal amount to make up.

Aziz's mind was racing: how could they get so much money so quickly? He had to come up with some ingenious method. Saleh was also churning the wheels of his brain to come up with an answer. They exchanged many ideas and considered quite a few options until they finally came up with two plans, each addressing the form of debt to be collected.

After the particulars of each plan were formulated in detail, several weeks of intense training for the missions ensued. At the designated times, each team left on the way to its target.

On a breezy spring night, teams of PLO fighters accompanied by hired underworld robbery experts sprang into action. They were positioned in several oil-rich Gulf states. In each area, a specific bank known to hold large cash reserves was targeted. Each team disabled the bank's security system, entered the bank, and blew its safes open using specially designed plastic explosives. They broke into the bank's safe deposit boxes and emptied as many as they could. The loot was stashed into large duffle bags and loaded onto a waiting van.

Before dawn, several motor yachts were steaming out of the Gulf of Oman into the Arabian Sea.

Local police authorities in multiple Gulf states were trying to make sense of the crimes and their perpetrators. They didn't make the connection between the strings of multiple robberies that took place in their countries almost simultaneously. The robberies were attributed to a crime cartel that had launched a few bold robberies in the Gulf region from time to time, but the PLO was not in any way even near being considered a suspect.

Several days later, PLO bank accounts started swelling to record levels.

Two weeks after the night of the bank robberies, a series of kidnappings took place in several countries around the world. Palestinians had found their fortunes in many parts of the globe and settled in many countries that permitted their entrepreneurial spirit to soar into new heights of success.

The kidnappers used a very low-key approach to avoid attracting the attention of the media or local authorities. Their goal was to try to keep the matter strictly between the family and the PLO without the involvement of the local authorities. Each team tracked a close family member of a rich Palestinian donor from the list, primarily young children or grandchildren. When the right opportunity presented itself, they seized the child from school, home, or a busy public place without the immediate knowledge of the supervising adults.

The kidnapped children were whisked to a local safe house and placed under house arrest in sealed rooms. Each child was provided with food, drink, books to read, and games to play. Their caregivers wore disguises at all times.

Shortly after each kidnapping, the team informed PLO command that the "golden egg" was in their possession. Within several hours of the kidnapping, a PLO official from the finance department placed an urgent telephone call routed through an unlisted number in Europe to the head of the family on his private line. The official informed him of the situation and demanded that the designated amount of money be wired to a PLO Swiss bank account within twenty-four hours, or the delinquent would never see his child or grandchild again. The official stressed avoiding contact with the police or local authorities, or the child would face grave consequences.

Because the people they were dealing with were very wealthy and had quick access to substantial financial resources, they were expected to comply promptly without putting up too much resistance. They were well aware of how desperate PLO leaders could get when they were in a jam as well as the atrocities they were capable of committing. They would have no doubt that noncompliance would lead to the ultimate demise of their loved one and that the affair would not reach a favorable outcome until the PLO demands were fully met.

The official explained that after their current debt was paid, their annual contribution would return to its normal level and that the PLO would not initiate any actions against them or their families as long as the payments were made on time. The purpose of the last statement was to ensure a continued flow of funds into the PLO coffers long after the operation was over.

Saleh loved this concept since it taught the Palestinian "fat cats" a valuable lesson for all to witness and fear. They would learn not to mess with the future of the Palestinian nation and to do their fair share of advancing the just cause of their brothers.

Most of the kidnapping operations went smoothly. Some of the teams ran into unexpected snags, but nothing they weren't trained to overcome. Very shortly PLO Swiss bank accounts were swarming with a wave of new donations from its loyal, wealthy members who'd just needed a little convincing. The combined revenues generated from both operations exceeded six hundred million dollars, surpassing the amount needed to float the PLO accounts by over one hundred million.

The Chairman was so elated by the influx of cash that he decided to throw a private party to honor Saleh and Aziz, the masterminds behind the operations. He'd had doubts about Saleh's promise to obtain all the funds since he knew it was close to impossible to raise such an inordinate amount of money in such a short time. He praised the two men's ingenuity in front of the hand-selected group of PLO dignitaries invited to celebrate and thanked them for allowing PLO payrolls to continue into the distant future. The two men were glowing from the compliments showered upon them by the noted officials who were greatly relieved that the future of the organization was back on track, and more importantly, that their personal paychecks would not bounce.

As a result of the huge success of the two operations,

the Chairman authorized their incorporation into ongoing fund-raising efforts of the PLO. Cash was the blood flowing through its veins. Without it, the organization was doomed for extinction. The means of obtaining the cash were of secondary importance, with the victims being considered taxpayers who had to put forth their fair share of the effort for the supreme mission of the PLO.

CHAPTER 25

Several weeks later, Saleh informed Aziz that he would be spending a few weeks in Europe to oversee new covert operations. Aziz was to take over the command of the Chairman's security detail while Saleh was away. He reviewed with Aziz the latest information gathered by PLO counterintelligence services. The Chairman's security guard detail had been placed on a higher level of alert due to increased indications that the Syrians through one of the PLO's strongest adversaries were planning another assassination attempt on the Chairman.

The Syrians vowed to take more control of the PLO and its actions. The Syrian leadership was very upset by the manner in which the Chairman had managed to take over major parts of Lebanon, Syria's neighbor. The Syrians wanted to control Lebanon themselves, and they were not happy with the independent manner with which the Chairman had managed to muscle the territory away from them. Given the history of PLO conduct against Arab regimes, first in Jordan and then in Lebanon, the Syrians viewed the PLO as a serious threat to their national security.

Their goal was to try to replace the PLO with a Palestinian militant organization they supported and controlled. Their first step was to get rid of the Chairman.

Abu Zayad, the leader of the Palestinian Liberation Front, a rival Marxist organization aligned with and supported by Syrian intelligence, led the opposition to the Chairman. Abu Zayad despised the Chairman's ideological principles, which he considered limited in scope since they were focused solely on the objective of creating a new Palestinian state. He considered Chairman Hackim a sycophant, serving the principles of the conservative oil-rich states that provided much of the PLO funding. In his view, the Chairman was a weak and compromising leader, not a true revolutionary maverick dedicated to the supreme cause of Arab unity and the destruction of pro-Western Arab regimes.

Abu Zayad fiercely hated Chairman Hackim. He was rumored to say to his followers that he would squeeze the last breath of life from the Chairman's body with his own bare hands.

Aziz knew that the Chairman's enemies were desperate and would use elaborate measures to try to kill him. The Chairman's safety was essential to Aziz's own career advancement. He'd managed to cultivate very close relations with the Chairman which he knew would help promote his own interests. With the Chairman gone, the organization could fall in total disarray and the leadership succession might become a struggle that could bring more waves of violence.

Aziz devised several schemes to camouflage the whereabouts of the Chairman. He hand-selected several men from Force 17 who had body builds similar to the Chairman's. They were dressed in the same distinctive attire the Chairman wore and were used as his doubles.

Aziz also beefed up the security of the Chairman's quarters. He personally chose all the security guards posted close to the Chairman and added sophisticated electronic scanning devices for identity authentication. Concealed video cameras were placed at sensitive locations with twenty-four hour monitoring.

All the areas surrounding the Chairman's quarters were secured to make sure no large-scale explosive devices could be planted in close proximity. Aziz had the records of the Chairman's entire security detail reexamined and re-verified to make certain none of the rival factions were able to plant a mole inside Force 17. He briefed all the security guards on the reasons for the high alert and ordered them to be extra watchful and ready to sacrifice themselves if anybody got within shooting distance of the Chairman.

Even with all the extra precautionary measures in place, Aziz was still concerned about the Chairman's safety because he knew that armored cars furnished only limited protection when it came to sophisticated roadside explosives or car bombs. For those extreme risky situations, Aziz had a different solution.

He ordered from the PLO's armored vehicle supplier in France construction of a special vehicle that looked like a normal large delivery van, but was equipped with a reinforced steel cage several inches in thickness installed in its center. The cage was completely sealed with internal provisions for ventilation. Only the Chairman and his most trusted bodyguards could open it via a programmable identity authentication mechanism using fingerprint and retina scans. Access to the steel cage was through the back door of the van.

The cage was padded on the inside and could accommodate up to four people seated opposite each other. It was equipped with a two-way audiovisual system that enabled the people in the cage to maintain close communication with the driver and have a visual display of the areas through which the van was traveling. The vehicle was equipped with a high-powered V12 turbocharged engine that could take off like a rocket in case of an emergency. It was painted with the name and logo of a local food delivery company that was a member of the PLO enterprise development program. Because of the immediate need for the special van, the supplier was paid a premium to deliver it expeditiously.

Aziz waited anxiously for the delivery, for he felt the van was the only foolproof method to preserve the Chairman's life. All the other measures were prone to some level of risk since Syrian intelligence had access to unlimited resources, special operations personnel, and sophisticated Soviet weapon systems. If they decided to deploy all these resources in a concentrated effort against the Chairman, it would be very difficult to stop them. The only way to protect the Chairman from his enemies was to outwit them.

When the van finally arrived, it was kept in a secured

PLO warehouse and used only with Aziz's explicit orders. He kept its existence secret, and only a handful of the Chairman's most trusted bodyguards were trained in its operation. The fewer people who knew about the new secret weapon, the longer it would serve its purpose.

Early in the spring, the Palestinian National Council or PNC held its annual meeting with most of the Palestinian militant factions in attendance. The Chairman was to deliver the keynote opening speech.

The next morning, the Chairman's entourage left PLO headquarters and traveled to the PNC meeting at a hotel in central Beirut. There were several cars in the convoy with the Chairman's limousine traveling in the middle. The atmosphere was very tense, and all the men were ready to spring into action.

The commander of the convoy switched routes continuously to try to avoid a potential ambush, but this proved to be a difficult task considering the number of vehicles jamming the streets of Beirut during the morning rush hour. When the convoy reached an intersection close to the hotel, a large maintenance truck entered the intersection and blocked the street. Several maintenance personnel appeared to be performing urgent roadwork at the intersection. The convoy came to a dead halt with the heavy truck blocking its way.

Two bodyguards jumped from the first convoy car with machine guns in their hands and ordered the truck and maintenance men to move out of the way immediately. The maintenance men complied and started walking toward the back of the truck.

Suddenly a huge explosion rocked the entire street.

There was smoke, fire, and shattered glass everywhere. A passenger car traveling two lanes from the Chairman's limo detonated with tremendous force. The Chairman's limo was on its side, engulfed with smoke and flames. The side panels of the maintenance truck suddenly dropped to reveal two heavy machine guns that started spewing deadly fire at the convoy, spraying its vehicles relentlessly.

The guards tried to jump out of their vehicles to return fire, but they were killed instantly. Several explosions rocked the street as rocket-propelled grenades fired from the truck hit the jammed vehicles and ignited their fuel tanks. Loud screams were heard from the trapped vehicles between the gunfire rounds, but they faded away gradually.

Within a few minutes of the explosion, the heavy truck pulled away, leaving behind it four heavily charred vehicles and no survivors.

* * * *

The Chief of Syrian Intelligence Services was in his Damascus office waiting anxiously for a report from his commander of special operations. His patience paid off. He soon received a message containing the code word, "Dead Rat," which meant the operation in Beirut had been successful and his long-time rival, the PLO Chairman, was history.

The slaying of its leader would disrupt the PNC meeting, shock its members, and throw the PLO into turmoil. In the chaotic aftermath of the Chairman's death, he planned to gain control of the PLO and

Lebanon forcibly with the help of Abu Zayad and his militia.

He turned on the TV monitor in his conference room to enjoy the chaos he expected to view at the PNC meeting in Beirut. To his great surprise, a clear, crisp picture of Chairman Hackim delivering his keynote speech came through the large monitor. He turned the monitor off in a great rage. "Someone's head is going to roll for this disastrous failure," he thought to himself as he left his office to submit his report to the Syrian President.

* * * *

The night before the PNC meeting, Aziz had moved the Chairman from his headquarters to an alternate location. The van was ordered to deliver food products to PLO HQ. While it was docked at the delivery bay, the Chairman and Aziz sneaked into the secure cage unnoticed. The driver and a second bodyguard, dressed in the food company uniforms, got into the van and drove to the designated location without incident.

The following morning as the Chairman's decoy convoy left PLO HQ, the van left its undisclosed location on its way to deliver food to the hotel where the PNC meeting was convening.

The van arrived at the hotel delivery entrance without incident. Aziz and the Chairman disembarked discreetly and entered the hotel side entrance. All the dignitaries greeted the Chairman with fervor. He proceeded to deliver an electrifying keynote speech that captured the enthusiasm of the entire audience.

The assembly hall rocked with clapping as the audience gave the Chairman a standing ovation for his heartwarming speech on achievements and hope for the future. The Chairman gloried in the limelight, a wide smile on his round face.

Aziz learned the news of the vicious attack on the Chairman's decoy convoy during the Chairman's speech. After the speech, the Chairman stepped down from the podium and returned to his seat. Because Aziz wanted to shield the Chairman from the bad news, he waited until the conference ended for the day before informing him of the tragic event that had taken the lives of one of his doubles and many of his brave bodyguards.

When the Chairman was back safely in his headquarters, he was furious over the incident. "I will show these double-crossing bastards who is in charge." His voice trembled with anger. "The Syrian traitors and their puppets will pay heavily for this. They are concerned only with their own selfish interests. They couldn't care less if our Palestinian brothers and sisters rot in the refugee camps for another fifty years, just as they let them suffer in subhuman conditions in Syrian camps to this day.

"The PLO is the one and only true savior of the Palestinian people! This hasn't changed over the last four decades. The Arab regimes only want to exploit us for their own interests, never concerned with our own endless suffering.

"Aziz, I want you to start planning my revenge against them. This time I want you to hit them viciously, without mercy and with all our might."

He pulled Aziz into his quarters for a private conversation. "You have been doing an outstanding job here. I cannot imagine how events would turn out without your continuous diligence to protect my safety. Without your ingenious schemes, I would probably be dead by now, and our supreme mission in jeopardy.

"As soon as Saleh returns, I am going to promote him to commander-in-chief of Force 17, and you will be appointed as his new deputy. With you two at the helm of my security and special operations, I will sleep much better at night.

"Aziz, it feels as if you can read the minds of these double-crossing traitors and outmaneuver their attacks every time. Although I am not crazy about that safety cage you built for me since I get a little claustrophobic and dizzy riding inside it, it is surely an innovative lifesaver."

"Your Excellency, thank you for your confidence," Aziz responded. "Your safety is my supreme purpose for being. I will protect you with the last breath in my lungs and the last drop of blood in my veins. We always have to read the minds of our enemies and prepare for the worst. This is the only way to avoid catastrophic surprises. I will start planning our response to the brutal murder of our slain brothers without delay."

Over the next several weeks, special operation units of Force 17 carried out a series of attacks on Syrian targets in Lebanon. They ambushed Syrian supply convoys and destroyed vehicles and supplies. They used car bombs to attack Syrian roadblocks and kill the soldiers operating them. They went as far as launching car bomb attacks in the heart of the Syrian capital, Damascus, to spread fear in the hearts of the Syrian leaders who'd thought they were shielded from the long arm of the PLO.

When Saleh returned from his European mission, he and Aziz planned several attacks on Syrian interests in Europe, including Syrian embassies in several European capitals, Syrian airline offices in Italy, and high-ranking Syrian diplomats in Switzerland.

The Chairman was thrilled by the success of the action against the Syrians and the PLO rival they supported. He felt more at ease with the two men he trusted most looking after his personal security and carrying out his orders.

With Saleh at the helm of Force 17 and Aziz his deputy, the force had undergone a major overhaul to improve combat readiness, utilize modern weapon systems, and streamline internal operations. Over the next two years, the force reached an unprecedented level of success against the PLO's internal rivals and continued mounting operations against Israeli targets inside Israel and abroad.

The Palestinian issue was gradually moving to the top of the agenda of the United Nations Security Council, sponsored by European governments constantly suffering attacks at the hands of Palestinian terrorists.

CHAPTER 26

Several months after the new Mossad Chief replaced Shaffir, he received orders from the incoming Israeli PM. Upon taking office, the new PM had formed a highly secretive counterterrorism committee to address the continuing terrorist assaults on civilian targets within Israel and abroad. The committee, consisting of intelligence and terrorism experts, was to recommend to the PM effective strategies to combat terrorism.

With the approval of the PM, the committee issued explicit instructions to the Mossad Chief to implement its decisions to target the assassination of several high-ranking PLO terrorist leaders involved in the planning and execution of bloody massacres against Israeli civilians. The committee concluded that the only way to curb terrorism was to hunt down the terrorist leaders, make their lives a living hell, and terrorize them in hopes of leading to their eventual execution by special Mossad death squads. The committee felt that such actions would send a clear signal that Israel would not tolerate terrorist activity against its population and would authorize the assassination of any terrorists involved in such activities. This directive included a list of names of high priority targets to be eliminated over the next several months.

At the top of the list was Saleh Al-Shariff, the PLO new commander of Force 17. He was targeted due to his role in the assassination attempt on the Israeli ambassador to London, the massacre of innocent passengers in the coordinated attack on El-Al check-in counters at the Vienna and Rome airports, and several raids on civilian targets inside Israel. The Mossad had previously made several attempts on Al-Sharrif that had gone astray. It was common for the Israelis to focus on commanders of Force 17, for the only way to reach this prestigious post was to plan and execute high profile operations against Israel.

The Mossad Chief appointed his deputy, Uzi Granit, to oversee the formation and training of special death squads to carry out the new orders. Granit formed several squads, each with specific targets and operating procedures. The new orders were so secret that the squads were not made aware of one another and did not share information or resources.

It was common knowledge among Force 17 members that their commander was always a high-profile target for the Israelis. For this reason, the commander had his own security detail.

Deputy Granit knew that Al-Shariff's weakness lay in his affection for young, attractive women. He realized this was the best way to get close to him, study his pattern of movements, and plan his demise. The deputy's first priority was to recruit an attractive female who could pose as a Palestinian or Lebanese woman, plant her in Beirut, and have her be introduced to Saleh at one of his favorite nightspots.

Granit used the Mossad supercomputer to try to identify a potential female candidate and other squad members for what he termed his Beirut death squad. This high-level squad was to be based in Europe, but it was to launch most of its operations in and around Beirut where the high-level targets resided.

He was looking for an attractive female in her late twenties with an exotic Middle Eastern look, fluent in Arabic, and very familiar with the Lebanese culture and surroundings.

The Mossad often recruited young attractive women who'd completed their service with IDF Military Intelligence, which was an excellent training ground for future Mossad agents. There they received an extensive education in Arabic and intelligence gathering and analysis along with in-depth knowledge of the enemy and its intentions.

He knew the perfect candidate for the mission, an exotic Mossad agent by the name of Carmit Arazi, code name "Desert Fox," a former intelligence officer with MI who had been recruited by the Mossad several years earlier. When Granit had been in charge of operating the Mossad cell in Beirut, he had worked closely with Arazi on several missions. She'd caught his attention right from the start with her meticulous mission preparation and lethal executions. Many successful operations were credited to her ingenuity and ability to improvise quick actions when mission plans went astray. Considered very intelligent and extremely aggressive in the manner in which she pursued wanted terrorists, she had earned several commendations from her superiors.

She was also a striking beauty he found hard to resist. Although Mossad regulations forbade romantic relations between its agents to avoid conflicts and distractions, it had been extremely hard for Granit to forego the opportunity to get romantically involved with her. When they were back in Israel, he'd secretly asked her out on several dates and their romance had blossomed into a serious love affair. He fell in love with her astonishing splendor and fiery personality charged with deep emotions. She apparently admired his mature, confident personality, and his brilliant tactical planning abilities. Sometimes after they made passionate love, she shared with him the stories of her childhood as a young Jewish girl growing up in Beirut.

Their love affair came to a sudden halt when the word got out to Granit's superiors that he and Arazi were romantically involved. Granit was warned behind closed doors that their affair had to end or they would both be ejected from the Mossad without further warning. In order to keep them apart, Arazi was immediately dispatched on new missions to Europe.

Granit was devastated by the abrupt disruption of their intimate relations. He couldn't keep Arazi off his mind, and he never lost hope of reuniting with her at a later stage in their lives. He thought this would be a rare opportunity for him to see her again, even if it was only for a short while.

He turned to his large computer monitor and flipped

quickly through her familiar dossier. Her original name was Claire Najar, family roots Lebanese; father a successful merchant in Beirut. She had an older brother, Akram, and a younger sister, Vivian. They were brought up with close observance of Jewish values and strong secretive affinity to the young Jewish state of Israel. They also maintained close ties with the prosperous Christian community that controlled the political and economic landscape of Lebanon for many years. She'd enjoyed a happy childhood growing up in an upscale suburb of Beirut, attending a private school, and having a great social life in this modern, vibrant city.

However, at the age of twelve her peaceful childhood ended with the PLO rise to power in Lebanon. The conflict escalated into a full-scale civil war between Muslims and Christian factions battling in the heart of Beirut. The PLO actions shattered the peace and tranquility she'd enjoyed in this small haven of progressive society, turning her family and friends' lives into turmoil.

When internal conflicts and PLO dominance started plaguing Beirut and the fighting was getting closer to her neighborhood, her father decided to move the family to a safer haven in London and settle there.

In London, she'd continued attending school, but she never felt that this was where she belonged. She'd told him she longed for the day she would be with her people in a free country she could call her own. When she reached the age of eighteen, she'd decided to move to Israel despite strong objections from her parents.

She'd spent several months in a new immigrant

absorption center in Tel Aviv attending intensive courses in Hebrew, becoming familiar with Israeli culture, and touring the country extensively.

Granit recalled that she'd also told him how delighted she was when she finally received her eagerly awaited summons to report to military duty. She was hoping her unique background, qualifications, and language skills would come to the attention of Military Intelligence recruiters. Several interviews later, MI enlisted her into their ranks.

After completing an intensive training period, she'd been assigned the task of collecting and analyzing information on terrorist organizations in Lebanon and Syria and submitting a weekly report to her commanding officers. Her superb performance earned her admission to the prestigious Intelligence Officer's school, which she completed successfully in six months. She followed it with six years of distinguished service in MI rising to the rank of a major, at which point the Mossad had recruited her.

In the Mossad she had gone through rigorous training for combat agents trained to operate in hostile enemy environment. Since then, she'd had close to five years of operational duty as a combat agent sent on several missions, including a few to Beirut, her familiar childhood ground. The feedback from her commanding officers had always been very encouraging.

In particular, she displayed a very militant stance against the PLO and terrorism, having personally experienced the mayhem they had caused in turning the life of the peaceful Lebanese population into a nightmare. She pursued known terrorists with cunning aggression and did not hesitate to use brute force in their elimination process. She was known to use her beauty and charm to trap some of her victims.

Granit turned to her enlarged color photo. She had an exotic, pretty face with high cheekbones, sea-green almond-shaped eyes, and silky brown hair down to her shoulders. She was slender and tall, yet filled out all the right places to form an almost perfectly sculpted figure. Her skin was on the fair side, yet lightly tanned, giving her body a bright, shimmering glow.

He longed to hold her tightly in his arms and to fill his lungs with the distinct scent of her sensual body that was once an inseparable part of him. Ever since they'd been separated, his heart had ached for her endlessly. He had lain sleepless many nights in his lonely bed, yearning for her desperately and wishing she were next to him.

Granit knew she was someone Saleh would undoubtedly fall for and was confident in her ability to bring him down even after the long and unsuccessful pursuit by the Mossad.

During their private meeting, Granit briefed her in painstaking detail on her new mission. As she was about to leave, he couldn't hold back his turbulent emotions. He grasped her hand tightly, reaffirming his passionate feelings for her and expressing the hope that she would be able leave the Mossad after her upcoming mission. He told her he hoped they could renew their romance, get married, and start a family.

Arazi caressed his hand softly, confirming her

desire to continue their relations despite the mounting difficulties. She also expressed the hope that she would be able to settle down after carrying through the next series of anti-terrorism missions.

Granit moved quickly. He ordered the Beirut death squad to commence several weeks of specific mission training under his direct supervision. In the interim, the Mossad security division prepared verifiable identities and cover stories for each member. Granit was encouraged by the turn of events and eager for the mission to conclude rapidly with the desired results. A triumph over Al-Shariff would add to his rising reputation within the Mossad and advance his prospects of settling down with Arazi.

He gathered the members of the squad for a final briefing before they departed on their new assignment. He rehearsed their operational plans repeatedly until he was convinced the squad members could perform their roles flawlessly.

Within days, Arazi arrived in Beirut on an MEA flight from London under her new identity and moved into a rented apartment strategically located in a complex several blocks away from the PLO headquarters in West Beirut. Her apartment overlooked one of the main streets used frequently by leading PLO officials for their daily travel to and from their residences.

She slowly familiarized herself with the areas surrounding her apartment and started frequenting Saleh's favorite nightspots. To legitimize her presence in Beirut and introduce her to Saleh in a more formal manner, the Mossad used the services of one of their most guarded Palestinian agents inside the PLO. He was one of the Chairman's closest confidants. The Mossad had recruited him while he attended a university in Paris. His greed knew no end; he was always eager to perform more services for the Mossad to earn more cash.

The Mossad arranged for the agent and Arazi to meet at a nightclub where Saleh loved to hang out during the weekends. Upon spotting Saleh, the agent invited him to join their table and formally introduced the two. Saleh knew the agent well from his frequent sessions at the Chairman's quarters. The three sat down and chatted for a while, sipping the alcoholic drinks Saleh kept ordering. Shortly thereafter, the agent excused himself, saying he had to prepare for a meeting with the Chairman the following morning.

Saleh invited Arazi to dance, and they spent a lovely evening together socializing and reminiscing about each other's childhood in Beirut. After midnight, she told Saleh that her brother was picking her up because she had to be at her job early the next morning. Saleh seemed a little disappointed by her early departure and said he hoped to see her again soon.

She responded by saying she would be back at the club the following weekend, and they agreed to meet again. Arazi left the club and was picked up by a member of the Beirut cell who drove her home.

Arazi was pleased by her first encounter with Saleh and encouraged by his expressed desire to see her again. She was confident that Saleh would fall for her and start planning his conquest of her soon. She liked playing hard to get and prolonged the courting game as long as she could without having to give in to intimate sexual overtures.

Saleh took a strong liking to her. He invited her on several dates and seemed to enjoy her company. He escorted her home accompanied by his security detail that always followed him around. They were driven in the backseat of a brand new armored black Range Rover, sandwiched between two cars loaded with bodyguards. Saleh would kiss her good-bye at the entrance to her apartment building and leave with his men. His heavy guard detail didn't allow for much privacy for the two, which worked well for her.

Saleh was also enjoying the challenges of pursuit. He admired Arazi's unique beauty and unparalleled intellectual abilities and longed to enjoy her luscious, ripe body.

Although the Chairman's trusted aide had introduced her to him, Saleh had her background checked by his chief of security. To his relief, everything appeared fine.

Arazi was able to track Saleh's movements in and out of the PLO headquarters and gather solid intelligence on his habits. On one occasion, he told her that he usually visited his mother on Wednesday afternoon, but that afterwards, he would like to take her out for dinner. Arazi watched closely from her apartment as the black Range Rover escorted by two cars zoomed out of the PLO headquarters on Wednesday afternoons.

Saleh's overtures became bolder, and she could barely hold him off any longer with her religious excuses.

Soon other members of her cell joined her, arriving on a flight from Paris using French passports. They rented cars at the airport and checked into a local hotel.

One Sunday after midnight, two of the cell members rendezvoused with an Israeli naval commando unit at a deserted beach south of Beirut. The commandos came ashore in a rubber dinghy launched from a naval missile boat lurking two miles offshore. They delivered two hundred pounds of powerful plastic explosives with remote control detonators and then disappeared into the dark night. The explosives were packed into the trunk of one of the cars, which was driven back to the hotel and parked in the indoor parking garage.

On Wednesday in the early afternoon, the explosive-laden car was driven out of the hotel and parked on the main street outside PLO headquarters. Arazi was in her apartment watching the busy street through the lenses of her powerful binoculars. Her mind suddenly drifted to a scene of another early afternoon years earlier...

* * * *

A large mortar shell exploded just outside her Beirut childhood home. That afternoon there was the usual sporadic exchanges of fire near her neighborhood, which had become somewhat of a routine. Without warning, the PLO had mounted an offensive against the local Christian militia to try to gain ground in the battle and put the Christian population under siege. A barrage of shells started exploding indiscriminately around her neighborhood, sending people running everywhere, scrambling for shelter.

Her young sister, Vivian, was on her way home from school and unaware of the immediate danger. Trying desperately to reach the safety of their home, Vivian had been caught in the crossfire. Crouching and looking through the window for Vivian, Clair tried to help her sister navigate her way home. Vivian managed to get closer. She lay flat on her stomach at the edge of an open field across from their home. When there was a break in the fire exchanges, Claire opened the front door and screamed to Vivian, "Run home now! Quickly!"

Vivian ran through the last bit of open field. Suddenly an explosion rocked the area in front of their home, raising a large cloud of smoke and fire. When the smoke dissipated, Clair saw Vivian lying on the charred ground.

She ran to her sister through the smoke and fire, ignoring the shells that continued to explode around her. She was able to reach Vivian and carry her bloodstained body home where she tried frantically to control the bleeding. She called for an ambulance, but it was unable to get close to their home because of PLO barricades blocking the streets and PLO fighters shooting at it indiscriminately. Their objective was to maximize civilian casualties so the people would abandon their homes and allow the PLO to move further into Christian territory.

With no help in sight, Vivian's bleeding slowly drained the life from her body. With the last breath of air remaining in her lungs, Vivian whispered, "Claire, I want you to get them for me...don't forgive or forget... you can do it...you are brave... and strong."

"Shhhh," Claire said. "You are going to be fine, my angel. The ambulance is on its way. It will be here soon," but Vivian lay motionless in her arms.

"I will never forget you, Vivian," she cried in desperation," or forgive your murderers. They will pay a very heavy price for what they did to us today."

The trauma of her sister's cruel murder and her last words never left Claire's mind. Frequent nightmares continually disrupted her life. Without her beloved sister, life would never be the same for Claire. She vowed not to rest until her sister's blood, crying to her from the bottom of the earth, was fully redeemed.

When the civil war had broken out, she recalled her mother's constant pleas to her father to take the family out of the country. He'd started arranging to relocate the family to England where he had numerous close business associates and relatives. However, his efforts had been delayed by the continuous hostilities until it was too late for Vivian. Shortly after the seven-day mourning period for her sister ended, her father moved the family to London.

* * * *

Suddenly the familiar Range Rover with its escorts entered her view as they exited the gate of the PLO headquarters and turned into the street opposite her apartment. As the convoy pulled closer to the parked car and the Range Rover positioned alongside it, she detonated the powerful explosives using a remote control device.

The fierce explosion rocked the entire street, sending shock waves all the way to the PLO headquarters buildings. Several PLO security guards rushed to the scene to try to determine what had taken place. They discovered the burnt remains of the Range Rover together with its escort cars and several other vehicles that had been completely destroyed. The surrounding office buildings and retail stores located near the explosion had also been severely damaged, and a number of pedestrians caught by the blast suffered serious injuries.

Arazi used the ensuing chaotic environment to sneak out of her apartment after clearing away any evidence of her involvement in the incident.

Now she felt as if an enormous rock had been lifted off her aching heart. She was engulfed by a euphoric feeling of elation, a clear image of her sister's graceful, innocent face vividly in front of her. Vivian was smiling at her and whispering ..."Claire, I knew you wouldn't disappoint me, you are my hero, I will always love you..."

Arazi never imagined she could ever feel such a sense of joy after the tragedy that had struck her family. There was nothing like the feeling of great exhilaration from sweet revenge. "This is only the beginning," she thought to herself, "The PLO leadership will be reduced to ashes by the time I am done with them."

She moved into a safe house on the east side of Beirut for a few days, waiting for the fallout from the incident to settle. All the cell members, except the one who had driven the car, left for Paris that morning to avoid any suspicion.

Several days later Arazi was back in London for a briefing on her next target.

CHAPTER 27

When Aziz heard the immense explosion, he felt that something had gone terribly wrong. He knew Saleh had just exited the compound, leaving him in charge of the Chairman's security. He immediately ordered the highest level of alert and whisked the Chairman into an underground bunker adjacent to his quarters, sealing it off as soon as the Chairman was safely inside. He ordered additional guard reinforcements to report to HQ immediately.

Without leaving the Chairman's side, he ordered his company guard commander to take a contingent of guards to investigate the explosion and report their findings to him right away. He felt the Chairman's life could be in danger and wanted to stay by his side to protect and placate him. Within a few short minutes, Aziz received the gruesome report that the blast had taken away his best friend's life, together with all the bodyguards and several innocent bystanders.

Aziz was very saddened by Saleh's sudden death. He had become very close to Saleh over the past several years, and they'd been virtually inseparable. His relationship with Saleh was the only close human one Aziz had developed since embarking on his long, lonely mission. He liked the friendly, outgoing personality of Saleh and his courage and devotion to the cause of his people.

However, he realized his thoughts were entirely unrealistic. Saleh was a high-ranking terrorist wanted for the murder of many innocent people, both in Israel and abroad. Aziz knew that his emotions were getting in the way again, a factor that could lead only to disaster. He recognized that this incident could bring him much closer to achieving his mission's objectives, but for the time being, he couldn't help being overcome by a deep feeling of sorrow.

The Chairman's voice interrupted his thoughts. "What's going on, Aziz? Did you find out what the big noise was all about? Maybe it was just a sonic boom from the Israeli jets exercising their scare tactics again."

"I will be getting a report very shortly, Your Excellency," Aziz answered softly. "I hope you are right and this was just a sonic boom of a low-flying F-15 jet." Aziz was trying to buy time in order to figure out how to break the shocking news to the Chairman. He knew the Chairman loved Saleh like a son, and that his sudden death was going to break his heart.

Aziz asked his company commander to reconfirm the initial report and check for any survivors. He was hoping that perhaps the armored Range Rover had saved Saleh's life.

The company commander returned shortly thereafter with an explicit affirmation of no survivors and reconfirmed that Saleh was among the dead. The Range Rover had simply not been designed to withstand the magnitude of such a powerful blast.

Aziz had no choice but to tell the Chairman.

"Your Excellency, I am afraid I don't have very good news," he addressed the Chairman in a somber voice. "I just received confirmation that our sworn enemies have murdered my dearly beloved brother and commander, Saleh. The blast we heard was a very powerful car bomb that went off just as his car was passing by. He and all his brave bodyguards were killed instantly. This is a very dark day in our history," Aziz continued, tears rolling down his cheeks.

"That's not possible, Aziz," the Chairman responded. "He was just here with me a few minutes ago. Are you sure? I want you to go out and see for yourself."

"Captain Majid just reconfirmed this information," Aziz replied. "I wish it were just a bad nightmare. I thought I had better stay close to you in case these traitors were planning another attack, but if you insist, Your Excellency, I will call Captain Majid back to take over command of security and go out myself to verify the information."

"That will make me feel much better," the Chairman replied. "You know that I trust only Saleh and you with the absolute truth."

Obviously the Chairman was in denial, refusing to accept the bad news. He had incredible survival instincts that had kept him as the unchallenged leader of the PLO for more than two decades. He had always been suspicious and had trusted only a very few close aides who had unequivocally proved their loyalty to him, putting their own lives on the line to save his. Now he had lost one.

Aziz arrived at the scene shortly after Captain Majid had returned to assume command of the Chairman's protection. The shocking sight revolted him. Half the street was charred by the remains of the torched vehicles. The air had a nauseating odor of burned human flesh, and body part fragments were scattered all over. The fire and rescue crews had started washing everything away with their powerful water hoses. Aziz identified the remains of the Range Rover, which had been reduced to a scrap of metal. There was no way anybody could have survived.

He returned to the Chairman's bunker as fast as he could. He knew there was nothing he could do to bring Saleh back. "Someone just gave us a big chunk of our own medicine," he thought to himself, wondering who was behind the daring attack. Was it Syrian Intelligence retaliating for the many assaults on their forces planned and executed by Saleh, or was it the long arm of the Mossad that had finally gotten to him after many years of marathon chases and several failed attempts on his life?

Aziz entered the Chairman's bunker and reaffirmed the enormity of the tragedy to the Chairman, saying in a solemn, loud voice, "Our dear brother Saleh and nine of the most courageous men of Force 17 have joined the Palestinian martyrs in the peaceful heavens above. They always fought fiercely and relentlessly for the cause of our nation. Their deeds of courage and sacrifice will be the torches that spark the fighting spirit of our young generation to lead us to our ultimate victory. They are the glorious heroes of our people. May Allah and His Prophet welcome them in the heavens with open arms and shield their families from suffering and pain."

Upon hearing the dreadful news, the Chairman was panic-stricken. He felt that if the assassins could get to Saleh, they could target him as easily and that his days on earth were numbered. He grieved enormously over the death of his favorite PLO commander. He considered Saleh the son he'd never had, the crown prince next in line to the throne of Chairmanship when he was finally ready to retire and hand over the reins. He had trusted Saleh more than he had trusted anybody else in the entire organization. Saleh's sudden death tore a large hole in his soul that would never heal.

The Chairman ordered an immediate investigation into the bombing be conducted by the PLO counterintelligence services. He doubled his bodyguard detail and refused to leave his bunker for days except for attending the very emotionally charged funeral of Saleh and his men.

Aziz stayed constantly by his side to console him and provide him with emotional support and reassurances of his personal safety. He also kept trying to present the situation in a more positive light, persuading the Chairman that the struggle for freedom was still in full force and that the Chairman must continue to lead the people by personal example.

The Chairman anxiously awaited the results of the investigation into Saleh's death. The PLO's second highest-ranking official after the Chairman, the Chief for Intelligence and Security Services, handled the investigation personally. The investigation was going nowhere due to the lack of clues left behind by the attackers or further intelligence about the perpetrators.

The investigation, which was concluded in two weeks, blamed Syrian Intelligence for the deadly attack. The investigators knew that the Chairman needed closure in order to get on with his life and continue leading the people. They had to provide him with such finality, even though they lacked any conclusive evidence.

The Chairman reviewed the investigation's conclusion in Aziz's presence. "I knew the Syrian conspirators were behind this treacherous act," he muttered in a shaky voice. "They won't rest until they destroy our aspirations for freedom and independence. We are spending a lot of time and resources fighting them without advancing our national goals. It's a continuous distraction from focusing our efforts on our real enemy, the Zionist State.

"How do you feel about it, Aziz? How do you think we should react to this cowardly Syrian act?" the Chairman asked.

"I fully agree with you, Your Excellency," Aziz reaffirmed the Chairman's opinion. "While we closely guard against the Syrian double-crossing traitors and their followers, we must advance our struggle and focus all our efforts on our sworn Israeli enemies who brought this calamity on our people."

"Aziz, you have always been blessed with very sharp intellect and the witty talent of a master tactician," the

Chairman acknowledged. "With Saleh having left us prematurely, you are the only person I would trust with my personal safety and astute advice. I have decided to appoint you as the new Commander of Force 17. You will also inherit Saleh's seat on my executive committee. I know that your contribution to both will be invaluable.

"I am aware that the new appointment will put your life at even greater risk, so I would like you to double your bodyguard contingent and use very discreet means to travel, just as you did for me."

Aziz got up and kissed the Chairman's hand. "Your Excellency, thank you for your confidence and trust in me. I will never disappoint you nor spare any effort to fulfill your sacred commands. Under your supreme leadership, our people will, one day soon, *ensha'allah,* fulfill the ultimate dreams of freedom, independence, and prosperity in the land of our ancestors."

* * * *

As soon as Shaffir received the news from his loyal Mossad contact that Aziz had been appointed as the new commander of Force 17 with a permanent seat on the prestigious Chairman's Executive Committee, he decided to call Harel and arrange a meeting to update him on the latest development with the Chairman-X mission. Harel was still very active in the leadership of his party and heavily involved in recent negotiations to join a national unity government.

They met at a beachside café outside a Tel Aviv oceanfront hotel overlooking the glistening blue waters of the Mediterranean. They chatted for a while, sipping on cups of hot cappuccino and enjoying freshly baked pastries. They continued their conversation strolling in the privacy of the beautiful seashore promenade, which was deserted on the cool fall morning.

"Shlomo, it's been almost ten years since Reuben left on his mission," Shaffir finally came to the point of the meeting. "He has just been appointed by the Chairman to the helm of Force 17. He is the number three man in the PLO military leadership chain and a permanent member of the Chairman's executive committee. Give him another four or five years to build up his power and popularity, and he will be there before we know it."

"That's a remarkable accomplishment," Harel responded. "Is your source reliable?"

"My sources are as good as gold," Shaffir reassured Harel, "although they are not aware of his true identity. Our people were finally able to eliminate his bloodthirsty predecessor after a manhunt that lasted almost ten years. Reuben was his deputy and promoted to replace him."

"This is great news!" Harel said. "Our plan has worked incredibly well so far. We saw it coming — we predicted that the PLO would emerge as the most hostile challenger in our struggles with the Arab world. Now we are closer than ever to being able to control its actions and its future."

"I agree," Shaffir continued. "All we have to do is help Aziz get rid of number two and then let him figure out a way to eliminate number one."

"Avi, I have some news I think you are going to like," Harel confided in Shaffir. "We are in the final phases of negotiations on a national unity government. It's almost certain I will hold the post of Defense Minister in the new government. We will be voting on it within a couple of days. Listen closely to the news reports. It should be formally announced sometime next week."

"This is wonderful! Once you are back in the political saddle, you can navigate the mission to a successful conclusion."

"I will push as hard as I can," Harel told him. "The Mossad still reports directly to the PM, but I will certainly have strong input and influence on our policies towards the PLO."

"I hope your appointment comes through soon, Shlomo, and I wish you a lot of success with the challenging new position. Please keep me apprised of any new development and I will do the same for you."

Two weeks later, the formation of a national unity government in Israel was announced. Shlomo Harel was appointed as the new Israeli Defense Minister.

Shaffir was very pleased by the appointment. Through Harel, he would again have some measure of influence on policy and actions against Israel's main opponent. He still did not feel the present Mossad leadership needed to know about the mission and his agent. He didn't think the Mossad would target Aziz in the near future because Aziz wasn't directly linked to plotting and executing operations against Israeli civilians. However, although he knew Aziz wasn't on the Mossad target list for the time being, he would certainly ask his contacts to let him know if and when Aziz was added to that list. He decided to stick with his original decision that only the PM and the Mossad Chief in office at the time that Aziz reached the PLO leadership would be informed of the mission and his identity. The mission was at such a critical stage that any leaks could jeopardize it and put Aziz's life in grave danger.

CHAPTER 28

During their monthly briefing, the Mossad Deputy, Uzi Granit, updated the Mossad Chief on the progress the death squads were making in the hunt for the terrorists on the target list. The Chief congratulated him on his recent success in eradicating Saleh Al-Shariff, the infamous terrorist leader long wanted for several brutal attacks on defenseless Israeli civilians.

"We reduced him and all his bodyguards to ashes," Granit bragged. "I am always happy to send their martyrs on a one-way express shuttle to hell.

"The key to our success was this amazing agent in the Beirut death squad. It's a she, and she is absolutely lethal. Carmit Arazi is her name. Her squad members have dubbed her the Black Widow. She attracts her victims with her exceptional beauty, reels them in with her charm, and exterminates them with her lethal poison. She took care of Al-Shariff, who was chasing her like a horny dog with his tongue hanging out. Beautiful women were the Achilles heel of the Beirut playboy. His lust for them led to his demise.

"He no longer needs to chase all the gorgeous virgins left in Beirut. There will be at least seventy-two of them waiting for him at the gates of heaven. Now he can enjoy the pleasure of all the virgins he was chasing all his life without having to worry about a thing. Personally, I hope he is burning in hell.

"I have unleashed our Black Widow and her cell members on the next victim on the list. The other squads have made good progress in Europe. The Prime Minister should be very pleased with the results so far, for the list is getting shorter every month."

"The Prime Minister is thrilled with the progress we've made," the Chief acknowledged, a smile spreading over his round face. "Keep up the good work."

"Thank you for the confidence," Granit noted. "The man replacing Al-Shariff as the new commander of Force 17 is Abdul Aziz Al-Wasphi, a new PLO rising star who grew up in Baghdad, of all places. He has been Al-Shariff's deputy for the past two years. After the incident, the Chairman promoted him to the Commander's position. Prior to that, he was in charge of PLO operations in Europe.

"Our analysts predict that in the absence of Al-Shariff, who was considered the Chairman's golden-boy, Al-Wasphi will rapidly rise to the top echelon of the PLO and become a major player in its leadership. He is known to openly express radical opinions against Israel and an uncompromising desire to build a new Palestinian state on our ruins."

"It sounds like you are going to have a new target on your list pretty soon," the Chief said pessimistically.

"Every time we erase a name from that list, two more are added. There never seem to be a shortage of radicals who want to destroy us."

"I am going to keep a very close eye on this man and determine at what point he will become a serious threat to our national security," Granit reassured the Chief. "When the time arrives, I will submit my recommendations on how to deal with him. For now, I will continue to focus on the hit list and on gathering intelligence designed to prevent future terrorist attacks."

"Tell me more about this Arazi woman. She sounds very promising." The Chief's curiosity was evident.

"First of all, she is exceptionally attractive, but more importantly, she is very intelligent and devious. She is strong-minded and unequivocally focused on accomplishing her goals. She uses all her means, skills, and even her natural gifts to bring her missions to decisive, successful conclusions. We have also been able to establish an irrefutable cover story for her that has withstood the test of time."

"Go on, go on," the Chief encouraged Granit. "This woman is starting to fascinate me."

Granit continued unraveling the history of Arazi in front of his Chief.

"In my experience agents with strong motivational forces such as hers can go a long way." Granit concluded. "She is fearless, yet confident. She is audacious, yet deceitful in a very intelligent way."

"This is a captivating story." The Chief expressed his amazement and pride in the superior performance of the agents under his command. "Maybe we should put this mind-boggling talent to task at much higher elevations. It could pay us high dividends in the not-too-distant future. I will develop some ideas around this premise. Please arrange for us three to meet for a couple of hour next week."

"I will make the arrangements," Granit promised as their meeting concluded.

On the way back to his office, Granit realized he had made a grave error in his overzealous praising of Arazi's talents to the Chief. He planned to summon Arazi home soon, reassign her locally, and finalize their personal plans for the future. He'd been carried away by his love for her, trying to prove to the Chief how gifted she was. He never dreamed that the Chief would get involved in Arazi's operational plans. He feared the plans the Chief would envision for her would keep them apart much longer and exacerbate his agony.

Several weeks after the three met in the office of the Mossad Chief, Arazi departed to an undisclosed location with new orders at hand. Granit's disappointment was devastating; he felt she was slowly slipping out of his reach, this time by direct orders of the Chief. Her blind devotion to the Mossad did not permit her to decline the new assignment directed by the Chief. Like most Mossad agents, she placed the interests of the country well above her personal desires.

* * * *

Aziz's first task as the commander of Force 17 was to secure the safety of the Chairman and other high-ranking officials. The Chairman was terrified of another attack on his life and demanded a great deal of attention and assurances from Aziz. He ordered Aziz to be focused solely on his protection and remain always by his side.

Nonetheless, Aziz managed to reorganize the entire force, improve the guards' skills through extensive training, and intensify counterintelligence gathering. This new focus limited the involvement of Force 17 in planning and executing new terrorist attacks on Israeli targets, with that task being delegated to other PLO factions.

Aziz was pleased with this new arrangement, for it kept him out of the direct planning of assaults on Israelis. This arrangement also provided him with the opportunity to become more deeply involved in the political landscape of the PLO. He accompanied the Chairman to all the executive committee meetings, stayed by his side continuously, and participated actively in discussions and consultations.

The Chief of Intelligence and Security Apparatus, Abu Selman, the Chairman's right hand man and number two in the organization, took over most of the planning and ordering of the terrorist attacks on Israel. Over the next several months, he planned several daring naval commando operations against Israeli targets. The PLO had executed several such operations in the past, and his aim was to repeat these successes.

His plan was to use a merchant ship to unload naval commando squads in international waters off the Israeli coast. The commandos were to use high-speed rubber boats loaded with weapons and explosives to reach the Israeli coastline during the night and land onshore. Their objective was a daring attack on IDF's central command complex in Tel Aviv. They were to capture hostages, secure some form of transportation, and then force their way into the IDF complex. Inside the complex, they were to use the hostages to secure the capture of high-ranking military officers and specifically target the Israeli Defense Minister.

Abu Selman personally instructed the departing commandos in the details of executing his plan. He encouraged them to fight fiercely and inflict as many casualties as they could on the hated enemy. They were not to surrender, but rather die as martyrs for their national cause, bringing down as many of the enemy as they possibly could.

However, Israeli intelligence was tipped off as to the impending attack and intercepted and sank the mother ship before it was able to unload its lethal cargo. Most of the commandos drowned. Several survivors were captured and turned over to the Israeli Intelligence Services. Under interrogation, they revealed the nature of the plan and Abu Selman's active involvement in its preparations.

Abu Selman was not deterred by setbacks. His relentless attacks continued. He was linked to direct involvement in operations carried out by PLO agents in the Israeli-held West Bank and Gaza territories. He was strongly promoting and supporting civil unrest and an organized uprising against the Israeli authorities in these territories. His strategy was to sacrifice the lives of unarmed Palestinian youths fighting with rocks and stones against heavily armed Israeli soldiers. The impact of Western media coverage of such incidents was priceless in terms of gaining worldwide sympathy and support for the Palestinian cause. He even went as far as mounting an attempted assault on Israel's nuclear facility in the south, a move that greatly angered Israeli officials.

Abu Selman became very powerful and influential within the PLO ranks. The Mossad warned that his popularity was gathering steam and that he was being promoted as a potential successor to the Chairman. His immense operational experience, high intellect, and strong influence in the territories were considered a much higher threat to Israel than the leadership of a secluded Chairman suffering from assassination phobias.

Shlomo Harel, the former Prime Minister who was now the Defense Minister in the new coalition government, was angered by the revelation that a major terrorist mission planned by Abu Selman had been aimed at him personally. Abu Selman was breaking the unwritten code of both sides of not targeting top leadership.

Abu Selman lived in a villa located on a hill two miles off the Mediterranean coast. Several of his PLO high-ranking comrades lived in this quiet, upscale neighborhood.

On a dark winter night, just before midnight, two high-speed rubber crafts loaded with heavily armed elite commandos were launched from a Corvette class missile boat positioned a mile off the coast.

The commandos came ashore swiftly where they were met by two Mossad agents who led them to

Abu Selman's villa. The villa had been under constant surveillance by other Mossad agents nearby. It was a quiet night. Nobody seemed to suspect anything as the commandos readied themselves for the assault. The agents in surveillance positions informed the raiding party that their target hadn't arrived home yet. Abu Selman was attending an executive committee meeting that usually ended around midnight.

The commandos waited patiently while Abu Selman was caught up in heated discussions with other committee members over finalizing their strategy of escalating the civil war in the occupied territories. Abu Selman was the formal PLO minister in charge of the territories and the ultimate authority on directing their struggle against Israel.

The raiding party had a short window of opportunity, for they had to be back on their mother ship before dawn. If Abu Selman was delayed much longer, they would need to abort the attempt.

However, at 2 a.m., they spotted the lights of a car approaching the villa. The car slipped into the villa's enclosed garage as Selman's bodyguards took their positions inside the house. At 2:30, the house returned to its quiet, dark state.

Equipped with night vision goggles, the commandos moved in like bats, forcing their way into the villa through the back door. They quickly secured the lower floor and garage area. Three members of the team rushed to the master bedroom where Abu Selman slept. The two bodyguards stationed in the area leading to Abu Selman's bedroom were caught by complete surprise and eliminated instantly by silenced weapons. The commandos burst into the bedroom, positively identified their victim, and shot him several times in the head.

Except for several flashes barely visible through the shaded bedroom windows, there were no signs of the violent act taking place inside the villa, which remained dark and quiet throughout the short but deadly assault. Within minutes, the entire area was cleared and the raid team was on its way to their rubber crafts.

The following morning, the housekeeper reporting to duty at the Abu Selman residence discovered the bodies of the PLO leader and his bodyguards.

* * * *

Shaffir was pleased with the news he'd received from Harel that morning. He felt the way was paved for his agent to reach the number two slot. The rest was up to Reuben to figure out. Because Reuben had proven his resourcefulness and ability to make things happen consistently, Shaffir was confident Reuben would not fail him and would eventually justify Shaffir's incredible intuition in selecting him for the mission and in protecting his identity.

Harel was closely watching the developments in the aftermath of Abu Selman's death. For a while, it wasn't clear what actions the Chairman would take to fill the void created by the departure of the PLO's most brilliant military leader. It also wasn't clear whether the Chairman might have welcomed the Israeli act due to the perceived threat Abu Selman posed to his own leadership. It appeared that some sort of struggle could be taking place inside the PLO for the prestigious number two spot.

The Chairman did not immediately appoint anybody to replace Abu Selman. Israeli Intelligence reports indicated the Chairman had decided instead to increase his personal involvement in directing the struggle against Israel while continuing to rely heavily on Aziz for his protection.

There were difficulties finding a successor for Aziz because the Chairman was reluctant to trust anybody else with his personal safety. Finally he instructed Aziz to handpick a superior candidate and train him as his own successor.

Harel waited patiently for further intelligence regarding the new appointee to command Force 17 and the promotion of Aziz to the number two spot. Without direct access to the Mossad's latest intelligence that he'd been used to receiving when he was the PM, Harel decided to tap into the reliable resources of his close friend Avi Shaffir.

On his way from home to the defense ministry, Harel called his friend's residence to set up a time to meet in the evening. There was no answer. He left a message for Shaffir to call him back at his office and gave the matter no further thought.

After a long busy day at the Defense Ministry, Harel realized that Shaffir had never called back. It was almost 11 p.m. At the second attempt to reach his friend, an unfamiliar feminine voice answered the phone. He asked for Shaffir. The woman's voice hesitated, asking who he was. After identifying himself, the woman said she was Shaffir's daughter.

"My father suffered a heart attack early this morning," she informed Harel. "He is hospitalized in critical condition."

Harel expressed his surprise and sorrow. After getting the name of the hospital, he instructed his driver to rush him to his friend's side.

When he arrived at the hospital, he was directed to the intensive care unit. He entered a private hospital room where his friend was stretched out on a bed with multiple tubes hooked to his body. Mrs. Shaffir was by his side, holding his hand firmly. At the sight of Harel, she rose and burst into tears. Trying to calm her shuddering body, Harel hugged her and comforted her with gentle words.

Shaffir lasted until the early morning hours. Harel joined the family at his bedside as Shaffir's soul soared to the tranquility of the vast heavens.

Harel felt deep sorrow for the departure of his close friend and loyal ally. He had always admired his brilliant, scheming mind that remained sharp to the very end. Shaffir's departure left a deep gap in Harel's life. He was the only person who shared the Chairman-X secret. Harel knew that he would greatly miss their conversations and frequent meetings to discuss the progress of their joint creation. Shaffir had strongly encouraged Harel to make another bid for the country's premiership. "You are the only leader who can deliver peace to our nation," Shaffir had told him on several occasions. "Our people will trust only a person of your stature, a decorated general, an IDF Chief, and a veteran politician."

Harel was determined to continue the vision and legacy of his dear and gifted friend and carry on his challenging aspirations with renewed strength and vigor.

CHAPTER 29

Aziz learned of Shaffir's death from the routine intelligence reports he received and reviewed daily. He was deeply saddened by the news. He had grown fond of the tough, brilliant man he had worked so closely with during the preparations for his mission. He admired his leadership skills and the warm personality concealed under a thick layer of outward coarseness.

Aziz was in the midst of training his successor to take over the command of Force 17. After long deliberations, he'd decided to appoint a highly respected veteran military officer to the vacant post. Colonel Ebrahim Bartawi was a professional soldier who had shown immense courage and intuition on the battlefield. He disliked the dirty games of politics and avoided them like the plague.

Aziz wanted a military leader who was used to obeying orders without question. He needed a person shielded from the pressures and influences of political maneuvering. He was very impressed with the professionalism of Ebrahim, who had been a high-ranking officer with the Jordanian Legionnaires prior to the eruption of the civil war in Jordan that had driven the PLO out. Ebrahim, a Palestinian reared in Jordan, had decided to join the ranks of the PLO after its war with the Jordanians. He had received his military officer training at an elite British academy.

Aziz spent endless hours working with Ebrahim and filling him in on every little detail of the Chairman's security arrangements and the extreme precautions exercised in handling his travel plans. After three painstaking months, the Chairman finally approved Ebrahim's appointment.

As the Chairman had promised, he appointed Aziz as the Supreme Military Commander of all the PLO forces.

The Chairman didn't like stagnation in the armed struggle and wanted to keep the pressure on the Israelis continuously in order to gain concessions from the Americans and the European Union. The plan was to wear out and frustrate the Americans and Europeans to a point where they would pressure Israel to join a peace negotiations summit with the PLO under the auspices of a joint Euro-American umbrella. The Israelis would have to be prepared to announce major concessions to allow for such a summit.

The PLO launched a new offensive against Israeli military forces, attacking border patrols and firing rockets into heavily populated civilian targets. PLO guerrilla squads operating under the cover of newly formed terrorist groups launched multiple hijacking operations against European and American airlines.

The Israeli Mossad Chief was angered by the new wave of attacks. He knew that the flurry of newly launched PLO assaults would very soon lead to criticism of his organization's inability to predict and prevent the attacks. He was also very well aware of the recent appointment of Abdul Aziz to the number two PLO position. He attributed the escalation of the armed struggle to an effort by Aziz to show his immediate mark on history and prove his ultimate dedication to the advancement of the Palestinian cause.

He summoned his talented deputy Granit for an urgent consultation. Granit had been able to pull off several successful operations against PLO military leaders.

"This new Aziz character is flexing his muscles against us and causing a lot of havoc," he posed the matter to his deputy. "I think it's time to cut off his wings before he gets too far off the ground. I don't want to wait until the PM and his counterterrorism committee are all over us and put us on the defensive. We need to take a more proactive role in achieving our objectives and not allow our foes to gain ground on us."

"I've always advocated the same doctrine," Granit replied. "It's the politicians who can never make up their minds. When things are relatively calm, they want us to keep our hands off the terrorism perpetrators and leave a door open for peaceful negotiations. When all hell breaks loose, we get blamed for not predicting and then preempting their actions."

"I agree," the Mossad Chief reaffirmed his deputy's view. "Politicians waver with the winds of opportunity, but we are the rock entrusted with protecting the existence of our nation."

"We concur then," Granit replied. "I just need you to say the word, and I will put the wheels of Aziz's funeral arrangements into high gear."

"You have it," the Mossad Chief replied. "Please update me when your plan is finalized."

Granit didn't waste any time. He assembled his veteran operation planners to come up with a scheme to eliminate his new target. He thrived on new, exciting challenges. For him, this was a high stakes game. He had to win every time. Now he had to start collecting his trump cards and prepare for the final bid.

He knew that Aziz often flew to Europe on the Chairman's private jet, seemingly on official missions. In fact, his trips were designed to coincide with final briefings for attacks on European targets. Aziz, who was revered by his men, insisted on instructing them before their missions and giving their actions his personal blessing.

Intelligence reports confirmed that Aziz, who had a passion for flying, had renewed his private flight instruction classes. There were rumors that during some of the flights, he took the copilot seat of the Chairman's jet and helped in flying and navigation.

Granit's plan was to wait for Aziz to take off on one of his trips, track his jet after takeoff, and shoot it down over the Mediterranean. To execute this plan, the Mossad would use the unmatched services of the Israeli Air Force, a frequent partner in complex Mossad operations.

An air force fighter jet would track the private jet, wait for it to be well on its way, and deploy an air-to-air missile to its target from several miles away. The Chairman's jet would be reduced to ashes and disappear into the deep Mediterranean waters without a trace.

Granit tapped into his resourceful PLO informant to learn of Aziz's travel itinerary. The well-connected informant provided Granit with a detailed listing of Aziz's travel plans to Europe and other Middle Eastern destinations. The deputy selected a scheduled flight to Greece that was well within the operating range of the Israeli fighter jets. The flight path was perfect for a staged accident.

To avoid blowing up the wrong jet, the deputy put safeguards in place to verify that it was indeed the correct aircraft and that the target was on board.

The informant was to place a miniature transponder on the Chairman's jet so that it could be identified and tracked by the fighter jet. Upon verifying that Aziz and his detail had boarded the plane, the informant was to send a pre-agreed signal giving the green light for the operation to move forward. The deputy submitted the plan for approval by his chief and received the authorization to go ahead.

However, the day before the scheduled operation, the Mossad Chief instructed Granit to make a change to the plan. Instead of shooting the plane down, it was to be intercepted and forced to land at an air force base in southern Israel.

"The PM is looking for a morale booster for his shaky coalition government," the Chief explained.

"He wants to bolster his government's popularity by proving that Israeli intelligence services can outsmart the enemy and strike at its heart anytime. The captured terrorist mastermind and his accomplices are going to be formally charged with atrocious crimes against defenseless civilians."

* * * *

Aziz kept the Chairman's and his own travel itinerary extremely confidential. He even issued multiple trip itineraries due to apparent leaks in the system that had allowed the Israelis to track down his predecessors' travel plans. The takeoffs and landings of the Chairman's jet often coincided with the departure of other private jets to cause confusion and make it hard to track a specific jet. He even ordered frequent changes to the craft's color scheme so there would never be a distinctive way of identifying it. Actual flight departure times and exact destinations were kept in secrecy until the last minute.

The Chairman was petrified of being intercepted by the Israeli Air Force and being forced to land in Israel, where he could face a criminal tribunal. To make it even harder to pinpoint the Chairman's jet, Aziz reached an agreement with a local executive jet charter company. The company operated several planes, one of which was identical to the Chairman's. Often Aziz arranged to switch jets just prior to takeoff.

Aziz suspected that a high-level informant was operating in the midst of the PLO leadership. Someone with intimate knowledge of the movements of top PLO officials was passing information to its adversaries.

Somehow their enemies knew where and when to strike their top leaders: this information could come only from an inside source.

Aziz wasn't concerned about the Israelis targeting him. Shaffir had reassured him there would be continuity in tracking the progress of his mission by top officials. He was more concerned with the actions of radical Palestinian organizations who wanted to topple the PLO leadership and take control of the organization.

He didn't think the Israelis would attempt to target the Chairman directly. Such an act would conflict with the unofficial rule of not targeting heads of state, as the Chairman occupied the equivalent leadership position. Moreover, the timing was not ripe yet for Aziz to take over the PLO leadership. He needed more time to consolidate his new position and garner support within the Chairman's Executive Committee and the Palestinian National Council.

Aziz was determined to uncover the identity of the informant without alerting anybody. He kept close tabs on how classified information was handled, and on occasion passed specific information to people in the Chairman's close circle to see if it leaked out.

The following day, Aziz and his detail boarded the Chairman's jet on their way to Greece. The jet taxied to the runway through an area populated by large service hangars and proceeded to take off to its destination.

* * * *

Two Israeli air force pilots in an unmarked F-16B Falcon fighter jet were cruising at 40,000 feet over the Mediterranean coastline in anticipation of a signal indicating the imminent departure of their target. The F-16B Falcon circled around several times under the clear blue skies waiting patiently for its prey to arrive.

Finally, the long-awaited signal was received, and the pilots started scanning their radar screens for the blip of their target to appear. Within several minutes, a steady blinking spotlight appeared on their radar indicating the position of an approaching plane.

The pilots waited for the plane to complete its ascent, turned sharply to the east, and dove down to around 30,000 feet.

The F-16 flew over the plane, gradually positioning itself in front of it and clearly conveying its unfriendly intentions. The pilots used international signaling methods to instruct the pilots of the private plane to turn around and follow them. They waved the left wing up and down several times and started turning northwest in a wide circle. They then used an electronic device to jam the frequency of air traffic control and prevent radio contact between the private jet and the outside world.

However, there was no response from the private plane. It maintained its course and speed, trying to ignore the fighter jet.

The F-16 soared sharply into the sky, making a circular loop and reappearing in close proximity to the left of the plane. The F-16 pilots made visual contact with the private plane's pilots, signaling them to turn around and follow. When their actions didn't bring the desired response, they fired several rounds of warning shots in front of the plane from the F-16's 20 mm multi-barrel cannon, making their intention unmistakable.

Their menacing action seemed to persuade the pilots of the private plane to comply. The two planes made a wide, circular turn in a southeasterly course with the F-16 leading the way. Shortly thereafter, the two planes landed at an air force base in southern Israel.

The Mossad deputy was eagerly waiting for the landing of the Chairman's private jet. He could sense the sweet smell of victory in the air and could hardly wait to break the great news to his boss. His plan had been executed flawlessly. The informant had provided confirmation that the party was on board, and the transponder had identified the plane without a trace of doubt. His prized big fish was going to step down onto the tarmac any minute.

A squad of armed counterterrorism troops surrounded the private plane with their weapons pointed at its doors. They opened slowly and two uniformed pilots stepped out. Speaking in clear, accented English, they asked who was in charge. The squad leader immediately asked them to raise their hands in the air and submit to a search for concealed weapons. They were not armed.

The squad leader asked the pilots to order all the passengers, without exception, to disembark immediately with their hands up. The pilots tried to protest, saying that the passengers were a group of Italian and Lebanese businesspeople on their way to Milan and that the interception was an illegal act of piracy.

The pilots were handcuffed without further warning;

with guns pointing at them, the orders were repeated.

One by one, eight passengers wearing business suits and ties stepped off the plane and were escorted into a private conference room where several Mossad interrogators were waiting.

The deputy had closely scrutinized the men walking down the short folding steps of the private plane. He could not identify Aziz or any of his bodyguards or aides.

He started sweating profusely. Something had gone terribly wrong with his operation. Instead of a sweet victory, he was facing the embarrassment of an international incident.

It appeared that Aziz had somehow outwitted him and landed him in big trouble with his superiors.

After a short investigation, it was concluded that the intercepted jet was truly a charter flight carrying a group of Italian and Lebanese executives to Milan. The operation turned into an embarrassment for the Israeli government and the Mossad, who appeared to have intercepted the wrong plane.

The Israeli Prime Minister's office issued a short statement to the media claiming a private plane that had violated Israeli air space had been intercepted by the IAF. Israeli authorities had been concerned about the plane being loaded with explosives on a kamikaze mission to a high profile target inside Israel. After making sure that the plane didn't pose any danger and that it had been an innocent navigational error, the authorities allowed its departure.

* * * *

Aziz learned of the interception when he arrived in Greece. Ebrahim called him as soon as his private plane landed in Athens and briefed him on the details of the incident.

"They were after you big time, Aziz," Ebrahim said in a somber voice. "From now on, I am going to have to take even greater precautions in protecting you and the Chairman. I am so relieved that you arranged the switch with the chartered jet. It saved your life and prevented a major blow to our organization. I suspect a mole within our ranks is responsible for the release of sensitive information to our enemies. I will order an investigation into this matter immediately."

"Thank you, Ebrahim," Aziz responded. "I will deal with it when I return. Please don't let the Chairman travel anywhere until I get back and don't release any statements on the incident to the media."

* * * *

After the private jet incident, Deputy Granit was enraged by the major blow Aziz had dealt him. He felt humiliated in front of his superiors, the Israeli cabinet, and the entire world that had come to expect perfection from the Mossad. His aspirations to reach the top Mossad position, which with his immaculate Mossad record had otherwise been almost certain, would now be tainted by the actions of the conniving swine, Aziz, who'd managed to outmaneuver him.

The conflict between Granit and Aziz had escalated to a personal level. Granit now had an additional material motive to get rid of Aziz. "Next time," he thought, "I will get personally involved in the operation and make absolutely sure that Aziz will be eliminated."

Aziz was quite confused by the skyjacking incident. He was guarding himself heavily from the Syrians and their accomplices, but it appeared instead that it was the Israelis who were targeting him. He recognized the fact that the Israelis did not simply shoot the plane down, as was expected in assassination attempts, but rather had wanted to apprehend him for some unknown reason.

He knew that Shaffir had died recently, but Harel was the Defense Minister in the present Israeli government. Surely he and Shaffir had passed the information about Aziz and his mission to their successors as promised. The current PM and the Mossad Chief should clearly know who he was and what he was trying to accomplish. The question was whether the incident was an error by lower level officials unaware of his mission who were targeting him in his PLO capacity or whether the skyjacking had been intentional.

He wondered if the Mossad wanted to apprehend him in order to call him in for an urgent consultation or possibly cancel his mission. Still that rationale didn't make much sense either because the Mossad could have done it in a more discreet manner without causing an international incident that drew more positive attention to the PLO.

If the new people at the helm of the Mossad didn't really know his true identity, they could have been targeting him because of recent PLO missions in Israel and Europe.

Whatever the reason, it was still a puzzle that didn't have a logical solution. He decided that from that point on he would be even more cautious with the Israelis. "Who knows?" he thought. "Maybe something has gone wrong with the internal communications system Shaffir set up, and they've lost track of me."

Upon his return, Aziz ordered a search of both private planes for any electronic positioning and listening devices. Trained technicians used special electronic gear to scan the interiors. They discovered the hidden transponder in the bathroom of the Chairman's jet.

Aziz discerned the identity of the informant beyond a shadow of doubt. His last act had proved his treacherous conduct. Aziz had proof that the informant was passing top secret information to the Israelis and potentially to other foreign intelligence services. His motive appeared to be pure greed: selling information to the highest bidder with total disregard for the consequences.

However, Aziz kept this highly sensitive discovery to himself. He decided to wait and think of the best way to deal with the traitor. He planned to exploit him by letting him feed misleading information to his handlers. Obviously, someone in the Mossad was one of his handlers, and it was clear that at least that person wasn't aware of Aziz's identity.

CHAPTER 30

Over the next several months, Aziz shifted his focus and emphasis from operational to political activities. Ebrahim turned out to be an excellent choice as his successor. He brought professionalism and strong discipline to Force 17 by enlisting the help of several colleagues who had served with him in the past as officers with the Jordanian Legionnaires.

Ebrahim took over the bulk of the operational activities and consulted with Aziz only on major actions. This arrangement allowed Aziz to cut down significantly on his travel, which had turned out to be hazardous.

Aziz accompanied the Chairman to all the PLO Executive Committee and Palestinian National Council meetings as his chief advisor. He started delivering passionate speeches on behalf of the Chairman when the Chairman was too busy or too tired. He developed close relationships with influential members of the PNC who controlled the decision-making process of the PLO. His gregarious personality and exceptional social skills made him extremely popular among the PLO leadership echelon. His prominence among the armed forces was unmatched by any PLO leader.

Aziz joined the Chairman's close circle where most decisions were secretly made before they were put in front of the PNC rubber-stamp vote. He continued to gain the respect and confidence of the Chairman and the members of the circle for his brilliant analytical mind. He provided them with detailed proposals founded on solid historical facts with analytical insights into political and military ramifications of each position they were to take. Upon learning of his Ph.D. in Middle Eastern studies, some of the members started calling him Dr. Aziz.

There were more frequent discussions of the need to open a communication channel with moderate Israelis and to try to reach a point where more advanced talks could take place. The PLO had proven itself a capable enemy with whom the Israelis would have to deal over the long term. After over twenty-five years of armed struggle, the Israelis might realize that the only way to resolve the Palestinian problem was through peaceful means, not continuous bloodshed.

The Europeans were enthusiastically supportive of such talks and willing to host and mediate initial unofficial discussions to try to reach a baseline for more official meetings in the future.

Most of the members of the Chairman's circle, including the Chairman, wanted to see progress in this channel. Many had been involved in the organization for over thirty years and wanted to start enjoying the fruit of their endless sacrifice. Some even dreamed of realizing the goal of establishing a form of an independent Palestinian entity within their lifetime. They prayed they would be able to pass on a legacy of freedom and independence to their children and grandchildren.

With all the Executive Committee members voting unanimously to authorize low-level talks with Israeli moderates, the signal was sent to the Europeans to approach the Israeli side.

Initial meetings were held in London between two Israeli university professors with close ties to the Israeli Foreign Ministry and the PLO chief economist. As talks progressed, more rounds of secret talks were held with the sponsorship of the Norwegians. The Chairman directed the talks remotely, while the two sides waited for a breakthrough that would justify the involvement of high-ranking officials from both sides.

However, some of the radical elements within the PLO felt left out of the decision to initiate contact with the Israelis and were furious with the move. The Palestinian National Charter clearly called for the utter destruction of the state of Israel and the establishment of a sovereign Palestinian state in the same geographical areas on which the state of Israel existed. Their position was that there had been no vote on deviations from the charter or approval of any amendments to its standing language. Therefore, the Chairman, or his executive committee, should not have authorized any contacts with the Israelis without formally proposing an amendment to the charter and obtaining a majority vote on it.

Abu Zayad led the opposition to the Chairman. He was determined to continue his vicious attacks until the

Chairman was forcibly removed and out of his way. The failed attempt on the Chairman's life during the last PNC meeting was a great disappointment that wasn't going to deter Abu Zayad.

Abu Zayad and his followers sensed that the Chairman was abandoning the Palestinian legitimate claims for the entire land of Palestine that ran from the Jordan River in the east to the Mediterranean Sea in the west. The Chairman's perceived acceptance of a Palestinian entity to be established within the limits of the West Bank and the Gaza Strip was interpreted as a treacherous appeasement of the Americans and Israelis and a crime against the Palestinian people. They felt the Chairman was running the organization like a dictator, always forcing his will on them without giving anyone else's opinion a fair consideration.

Yet this had been the Chairman's ruling style for many years, and nobody was able to challenge or change it. The Chairman was accustomed to hearing the occasional grumbling from various groups who were not in total agreement with his policies or decisions. He always shrugged off their grievances, which tended to dissipate as quickly as they appeared.

Abu Zayad called for the leading groups resisting the Chairman's policy to hold a secret meeting to plan a daring revolt against the Chairman and his loyal supporters. His ideas gained strong support from equally frustrated factions within the PLO and most importantly, from the Syrian authorities.

Aziz vigorously supported the Chairman's peace negotiation efforts because they were in line with his mission objectives. The more progress the Chairman could make in negotiating a comprehensive peace agreement with Israel, the easier it would be for Aziz to build on this trend and navigate the negotiations within the guidelines he'd received from Harel and Shaffir.

The Chairman seemed to realize at last that peace negotiations could lead to normalized relations, ensured by economic prosperity that would greatly benefit the Palestinian people. It was time to focus on the emerging peaceful alternatives and rest the weapons until and unless it became clear that a comprehensive peace accord could not be concluded.

Aziz got wind of what Abu Zayad was plotting behind the scenes. If the Chairman were to be assassinated and the rebels took control of the PLO leadership, all the progress he had made in the past several years would be lost, and his life would be in great danger because he would be the second target on the rebels' hit list after the Chairman. The rebels considered him a potential successor to the Chairman and had no doubt where his loyalty stood. He frantically thought about how he could turn the impending event he considered inevitable into a breakthrough for promoting his mission goals.

He suspected the rebellion was very near, but he had no timetable for its onset and only limited information on the scale of dissension within the ranks of PLO military forces.

Without explicitly discussing the situation and his suspicions with Ebrahim, he used the excuse of new intelligence on impending threats by Syrian forces to order the men of Force 17 to a high level of alert. He called all the units conducting field training back to their bases and ordered additional reinforcements of loyal forces and heavy artillery deployed strategically in areas surrounding the PLO headquarters.

He visited the troops to prepare them for a possible imminent encounter with Syrian regular forces. He encouraged his men and lifted their morale by stressing that the Palestinian people were the only ones in control of their future. They would fight fiercely, prevail over their enemies, and reach the ultimate goals of victory, freedom, and independence. The intervention of the Syrian traitors was entirely unwelcome and would be met with a crushing blow to their forces.

Aziz reviewed his personal contingency plans and made sure that all the resources he'd prepared for such circumstances, including a private jet from the charter company, were in place and ready. He checked and polished his personal arsenal of weapons, always keeping his automatic Magnum within close reach.

The Chairman didn't seem too troubled by the opposition's demands to cease all negotiations with the enemy, renew the guerrilla assaults on Israel, and relinquish some of his powers to their leaders. He dismissed their demands, promising to institute sweeping reforms in the movement, crack down on corruption, and include all PLO factions in the decision-making process.

The Chairman was always able to muster the votes and support he needed for major decisions through arm-twisting maneuvers and fear of retaliation. He masterfully controlled every aspect of the organization, including a tight control over its finances, the appointment of every political official and military commander, and the judiciary process. People who tried contradicting him or dared to stand in his way quickly fell from grace or mysteriously disappeared from the scene.

He was confident that this crisis would also blow over and normalcy would soon return.

CHAPTER 31

One late night Aziz received a call from his intelligence chief.

"We intercepted a communiqué from the head of Syrian Intelligence," he said in an alarmed tone. "He ordered the rebel forces to initiate a surprise attack on our headquarters tomorrow at dawn. He has given strict orders to eliminate our leadership and destroy our organization.

"Very good work!" Aziz complimented him. "We have been preparing carefully for the traitors' attack, and this time we will decimate them with no mercy."

"This is what I wanted to hear," the intelligence chief said in a relieved tone. "Best of luck tomorrow."

The following morning at 5:45, Aziz marched toward the private quarters where Chairman Hackim and his chief political advisor, Anwar Asadin, were having their usual early planning session. Aziz entered the Chairman's quarters, closed the heavy door behind him, and proceeded to the conference room, where the two men were having a heated discussion. He greeted the Chairman and proceeded immediately to draw his handgun from its holster.

He pointed it at Asadin and said, "You miserable, double-crossing traitor. How long did you think you could fool us with your sleazy schemes of betrayal? You are responsible for the murder of many of our most talented leaders and brave brothers, including my brother and hero Saleh and the Chairman's right-hand man, Abu Selman. You also almost put me in the hands of the Israeli conspirators. Somehow I suspected it was you. I didn't tell you that I was going to switch the jets on the day I flew to Greece. We found the transponder you planted on the Chairman's jet after it was returned from Israel. If I hadn't been careful enough to make the switch, I would be rotting in an Israeli jail right now."

Asadin, speechless with a horrified look on his blood-drained face, stared at Aziz who continued his relentless verbal assault, his outstretched hand tightening its grip on the Magnum.

"All of this for the love of money. Selling our brothers into the slaughterhouse for the Zionists' dirty dollars soaked with our martyrs' blood. Didn't the Chairman treat you like royalty, caring for all your family's needs? But that wasn't good enough for you. Your greed knew no end, and you couldn't care less who was the next victim or how you were slowly eliminating the courageous leaders who held the torch of hope for our people."

Asadin waved his arm in protest, trying to interrupt Aziz's onslaught.

"Well, your doomsday has come, Asadin, you miserable, greedy rat," Aziz's voice pierced the heavy tension in the conference room. "I am not going to let your treacherous acts ruin the hopes of our people."

Before Asadin could utter another word, Aziz pulled the trigger of his powerful, Magnum. One shot of the bursting munitions into Asadin's forehead silenced him forever. He collapsed with a shocked look on his face, his head enveloped with blood.

The Chairman was stunned by the events that had unfolded in front of him. He slowly rose to his feet, shaken and protesting Aziz's execution of Asadin. "Why did you do that, Aziz? How can you be sure that Asadin was behind all these acts? You should have consulted me before killing him."

Before the Chairman could finish his sentence, the sound of several explosions rocked the PLO compound, followed by heavy machinegun fire. It was 6 a.m. The revolt against the Chairman had begun.

The Chairman was even more confused. "What's going on?" he questioned Aziz in a shaking, worried voice. "First you shoot Asadin, and now I hear explosions and heavy gunfire. Are we under attack?"

Aziz put his gun back into its holster, as if attempting to reassure the Chairman. Then without warning, he pulled a small-caliber handgun from the back of his belt and fired three shots at the Chairman. The Chairman collapsed instantly, a look of disbelief on his face, blood gushing from three chest wounds. Aziz had aimed for his heart to shorten his agony and ensure his immediate demise.

Aziz wiped off the handle of the .22 and then placed it in Asadin's hand. He took a second look at the

Chairman, who lay on his back motionless in a pool of blood. He was dead.

He pulled the emergency alarm lever in the Chairman's office to summon the bodyguards. The sound of automatic weapons firing and shells landing around the compound buildings intensified as bullets started hitting the fortified walls of the Chairman's quarters.

Ebrahim burst into the Chairman's suite, his fingers clasping the trigger of his AK-47 and his eyes bulging with intensity. Several of the Chairman's bodyguards followed him.

"We are under intense attack by the Syrian traitors and their cowardly followers," Aziz announced. "Deploy your men to the top floor and the roof of the buildings and return fire immediately," he ordered. "They are to shoot anybody attempting to get close to the building. Use rocket-propelled grenade launchers to fire back at any vehicles approaching the compound."

Ebrahim quickly glanced at the two bodies lying on the floor.

"Who killed the Chairman?" he asked in astonishment.

"We are in the midst of an attempted coup, Ebrahim," Aziz told him. "Asadin was working for Abu Zayad and his Marxist traitors. He shot the Chairman. I heard the shots as I was entering the conference room. I found Asadin standing over the fallen Chairman with the gun in his hand, cursing him relentlessly. I shot him without a second thought. I had suspected for quite a while that he was betraying us, but I didn't have the proof.

"Unfortunately, the Chairman is dead now, and we must fight back to restore order and keep his legacy alive. We must defeat Abu Zayad and avenge the Chairman's blood or stand to lose all the outstanding progress he brought our people over the past twenty-five years."

Ebrahim hesitated, taking a second hasty look at the two bodies. The room was starting to fill with smoke from the constant barrage of heavy machine gun and rocket fire.

"Yes, sir," he blurted out. "We will fight back fearlessly until we eradicate the last of the traitors from the face of this earth." He ran out, shouting orders to his men who were returning enemy fire.

Aziz ran back to his quarters, picked up his communications radio, and ordered the commander of the closely stationed elite troop brigade to counterattack the rebels from the outside perimeter of the compound. "You need to deploy your brigade rapidly and secure positions all around the headquarters," he commanded in a firm voice. "We have to deal a crushing blow to Abu Zayad and his treacherous rebels before it's too late. I will provide you with additional instructions once I get an assessment of the enemy forces. "

"Yes, sir!" the brigade commander responded. "I will order our men to move on the offensive without delay and wait for further orders from you and Ebrahim."

Aziz grabbed his AK-47, his portable RPG launcher, and a backpack filled with munitions and ran through the smoky corridor and up the emergency stairs to the roof. He needed to position himself where he could have a clear view of the battlefield and the scale of the enemy forces. With this information, he could then assess the situation and direct the counterattack.

He saw Ebrahim ordering his men into positions all around the roof and urging them to fight back. Ebrahim was a courageous leader who led his troops by personal example without fear or regard for his own safety.

Aziz took out his RPG launcher and fired several rockets at armored vehicles attempting to breach the building's perimeter. Ebrahim ran toward Aziz with several men to secure his position and provide him protection.

"Guard the stairwell with several men so no one comes up to the roof," Aziz shouted to Ebrahim. He got back on the radio with the brigade commander to brief him on the rebels' attack. "The Syrian traitors with the support of Abu Zayad's Marxist puppets launched a coup attempt against the Chairman," he informed him. "They killed the Chairman and launched an offensive on our headquarters. We must quash them immediately to restore order and maintain our leadership.

"You are to advance your forces and eliminate any sources of resistance around the compound. Don't shoot at the HQ building and don't try to enter the compound until I order you to. Your troops are to create a tight, ironclad ring around the building. Let nobody out alive.

"Ebrahim and his men will try to secure the HQ building from within, and you will secure the perimeter around the compound and drive the rebels out."

Abu Halim, the brigade commander, was a professional soldier and one of Ebrahim's loyal commanders. Aziz very much wanted to believe that Abu Halim had remained faithful to him and Ebrahim and not conspired with the rebels. His forces were the main hope of defeating the enemy. Without their heavy weaponry and expert soldiers, all could be lost.

"We will follow your orders and crush the enemy," Abu Halim's confident voice came across the radio. "We will annihilate these bastards in no time and restore the pride of our people and the sacred memory of our beloved Chairman."

Hearing the soothing words of Abu Halim, Aziz felt a great relief. He hoped that his words would translate into the immediate action urgently needed to repel the rebels closing in on the compound.

Suddenly Aziz noticed two rebels who had managed to climb up the windows of the top floor onto the roof. They did not notice Aziz, who was hidden in the corner of the building. Ebrahim was running back toward him, unaware of the imminent danger.

"Get down!" Aziz shouted toward him, firing a sweeping hail of bullets from his AK-47 toward the intruders. The two men were violently flung backward, tumbling off the roof as the bullets aimed at Ebrahim missed their target and rose into the sky.

Ebrahim lay flat on his stomach. He rose awkwardly; he was scratched but unharmed. "I owe you one, Chief," he said in a low voice.

* * * *

After three days of intense battles with the rebels, the combined forces of Ebrahim and Abu Halim crushed the uprising, decimating the rebel forces who retreated into Syrian territory. It took several more days to clean out the last pockets of resistance and restore order. Abu Zayad managed to flee back to Syria and take refuge under the protective umbrella of the Syrians.

The Palestinian National Council convened several days later to hear testimony about the uprising, elect a new Chairman, and decide on the future direction of the movement. The Council unanimously elected Abdul Aziz Al-Wasphi as the new Chairman of the PLO.

Aziz immediately appointed Ebrahim as the Commander in Chief of all the PLO military forces. Aziz trusted Ebrahim as a father would trust his own son. From that day on, Ebrahim became his right hand man and the second highest-ranking official of the PLO.

Chairman Aziz urgently convened the Palestinian National Council to review the present state of affairs resulting from the revolt. He initiated new strategies to focus on the true fundamental objectives of the PLO and to advance the process of accomplishing them. He proposed to the Council an agenda that strongly advocated new initiatives to solidify unity within the PLO ranks and accelerate the momentum toward establishing self-governance and independence.

His first and most urgent initiative was the unification of all the various Palestinian factions under the PLO umbrella, thereby, creating one central body with a single doctrine and goals — in other words, one central voice and address for the struggle of the Palestinian people. Rival factions tearing the nation apart with internal conflicts and armed clashes were to be banned and disbanded. The PLO would no longer tolerate the behavior of noncompliant factions who conducted their own terrorism operations and deviated from the PLO's unified strategy. Any faction or group not complying with PLO central command policies and orders would be outlawed and forcefully eliminated.

The PLO focus was to remain on the main enemy, Israel. It would use its entire available means to pressure Israel for far-reaching concessions that would lead to advanced high level negotiations toward a comprehensive peace accord. To support this initiative, the PLO would rally political support from influential Arab nations to pressure the USA and Europeans to insist that Israel join the negotiation table or face political and economic isolation.

Fund-raising efforts to increase incoming revenues from rich, oil producing Arab nations and wealthy Arabs would be intensified significantly to support increased budgets for social services, public relation campaigns, and military spending.

A professional public relations campaign would be launched to upgrade the image of the Palestinians to that of a nation struggling for independence rather than a terrorist organization murdering innocent civilians. The campaign would be designed to sway public opinion by emphasizing the pain and suffering endured by the Palestinians for more than four decades with no relief in sight. It would serve as an integral part of the strategy to pressure the Israelis to yield significant concessions at the onset of the peace negotiation process.

During the period of attempted dialogue, there would be a temporary halt to all terrorist activities in order to increase support in the Western world and prove the genuine intentions of the PLO.

The Chairman's revised agenda represented an enormous shift in the PLO strategy that aimed to open a new chapter in its history and focus on attaining more realistic and immediate goals. The Chairman wanted to bring quick relief to the civilian populations in the West Bank and Gaza Strip and to the masses of Palestinian refugees spread in numerous camps around the Middle East.

Following several days of an intense and often heated discussion and the inclusion of minor language changes, the new agenda was ratified by a large majority and incorporated into the Palestinian National Charter. Chairman Aziz invited the leaders of all the independent Palestinian factions to a summit where he presented the approved amendments to the charter and gave a thorough explanation for the shift in PLO strategy.

He requested all the leaders to comply with the council's decision, join the PLO peacefully, and receive proper representation on the Council and its operating committees. He warned that factions that refused to comply with the new doctrine would face the full PLO might and would be pursued vigorously until their complete elimination.

"Without the complete unity of our people, we will not be able to accomplish the ultimate goals of our beloved nation," he declared. "Whoever chooses to stand in our way of achieving this holy mission will suffer grave consequences."

He then announced a reshuffle in the leadership of the armed forces and the promotion of several key, loyal commanders who would not hesitate to clamp down on noncompliant rival factions.

Several leaders of the more extremist organizations were not happy with what they heard. They walked out of the summit, declaring their refusal to comply with new council policies.

Chairman Aziz knew that Abu Zayad was fueling the opposition from behind the scenes and continuing his relentless attempts to take over the PLO. He used the hiatus in the fighting to reorganize his forces and gain reinforcements from his Syrian allies.

Aziz made several peaceful attempts to persuade the renegade groups to reconsider their decisions and adhere to the new policies, but they rejected all his overtures. Without any further hesitation, the Chairman ordered the use of PLO elite troops to crush the traitors, destroy their infrastructure, and arrest their leaders. Over the next several weeks, a bloody civil war erupted between the PLO and its opposing factions.

Ebrahim, the PLO's newly appointed Chief of Staff, ordered the highest level of security alert to protect the Chairman and top PLO officials from assassination attempts. It was clear that Abu Zayad was going to launch desperate attempts to hit high profile targets and strike at the heart of the new regime.

Aziz quickly shifted the organization into a war mode, continuing operations from secure underground locations. Ebrahim masterfully orchestrated the crushing of the rebels by the superior PLO special operations forces. It was part of a contingency plan developed by Ebrahim in anticipation of resistance to the Chairman's new initiatives and attempts to undermine his leadership.

Precise intelligence was gathered in advance about the locations, numbers, and capability of all the extremist groups. Special operation forces were prepared for attacking targets as soon as the Chairman gave the order.

The rebels were attacked mercilessly with devastating force. They suffered heavy losses, with their leaders and surviving members fleeing for their lives. Ebrahim managed to capture most of the leaders, but some like Abu Zayad who had prepared their own contingency plans escaped unharmed. Ebrahim knew this would not be the last time they would hear from Abu Zayad and his gang. He had learned from experience that they would be back someday with great vengeance and that he would have to continue his vigilance to protect the Chairman every minute of every day and night.

Within four weeks, the civil war ended with an overwhelming defeat to the rebels. Chairman Abdul Aziz was able to consolidate his rule over the entire nation and create a central leadership that could control both political and military agendas. His power over the organization was supreme and uncontested. With the fresh example of the rebels' fate, no one dared challenge the leadership of the new Chairman.

After several months of intensified effort, the strategy instituted by the new Chairman started paying off.

The PLO image improved in the world's media, while internal resistance waned. The Chairman formed a government in exile and appointed ministers to all the key offices. The new government worked diligently to start managing the day-to-day affairs of the Palestinian people, from education to social services, finance, foreign relations, and internal security. The PLO became the only recognized official representative of the Palestinian people.

CHAPTER 32

BAGHDAD, 1964

Ali Samara's real estate business was thriving. New construction activity in Baghdad was evident in almost every part of the city. The Iraqi government had embarked on an intensified modernization effort fueled by mounting oil revenues and provided new construction companies with attractive incentive packages. Ali's entrepreneurial instincts recognized the tremendous opportunity.

He'd founded his own construction company to develop residential properties for the growing middle class. Naturally, his real estate company would handle the sales of the properties he developed.

The first apartment building complex was a great success. Most of the apartments were sold before they were completed, and his company's profits soared to record levels. Ali was constantly looking to acquire new properties to build on the momentum of his company's growth and immaculate reputation.

Ali knew Baghdad inside out, for he'd been roaming the streets and alleys of its vast neighborhoods from a very young age. His experience in the real estate business combined with prudent business acumen guided him in selecting ripe properties for his construction projects.

He recalled the old Jewish neighborhood where he'd started his real estate dealings. He was confident he could turn it into a bustling, fashionable project that would attract the burgeoning upper-middle-class families.

His challenge would be to resettle the mostly Palestinian population occupying the old decrepit homes into one of his projects across town. After Aziz's departure five years earlier, Ali continued to visit that neighborhood from time to time, taking candy to Aziz's old friends, kicking the soccer ball around with them, and encouraging them to do well in school.

He decided to pay another visit to the old neighborhood and see what people were up to now. He timed his arrival in the early evening when most of the people were outdoors watching the young kids playing their games. He noticed Ahmed and Chaled coaching soccer players on competing teams. They were screaming from the sidelines, instructing their players how to outmaneuver their opponents and gain an edge in the game.

As darkness fell over the makeshift soccer field, the teams had to settle for a 3-3 draw. Ahmed and Chaled walked off the field exchanging exciting highlights of their team's accomplishments. Ahmed, who became a very talented soccer player, was playing on the young Iraqi national team and was predicted to become a national soccer star.

They immediately noticed the sharply dressed Ali and greeted him warmly.

"What brings a successful businessman to our old neighborhood?" Ahmed asked curiously.

"Where else can you catch an exciting soccer game coached by a rising soccer star?" Ali was quick to compliment Ahmed.

"*Ensha'allah!* From your mouth to Allah's ears. I still have a long way to go and many skills to master, but I am going to give it all I have, just as you used to tell us when you came to visit," Ahmed replied.

"I have great confidence in your ability and promising future," Ali replied handing Ahmed and Chaled bags of candy to distribute to their teams.

"What have you been up to lately?" Ali questioned Chaled

"I will be graduating high school this summer and I am hoping to be able to continue my studies at the university, but my father said that I might have to start earning a living to help support the family."

"Now that you mention your father, I wanted to have a word with him. I'm working on a business proposition that will greatly help your entire community and solve your education quandary," Ali told him.

"My father must have just gone home after watching the game. I'm sure he would love to hear what's on your mind."

Ali shook Ahmed's hand enthusiastically, wishing him success in his career and promising to attend his games. He and Chaled walked towards Chaled's home in the courtyard.

Ali knew that Chaled's father was the leader of the local Palestinian community and that his word carried great weight among its members. If he could persuade him that this was a very attractive proposition for the community, Ali would have a strong advocate for his lucrative project.

"Tfadal," Chaled's father welcomed Ali with enthusiasm. "It's always a pleasure to see you in our neighborhood, encouraging our youngsters and treating them to candies."

"Shukran," Ali responded, thanking him for his compliments.

Chaled's mother appeared with a tray consisting of a steaming carafe of dark Turkish coffee and a plate of home-baked cookies for the honored guest.

Ali got to the point. "I have a business proposition for you and the community. I am offering to relocate the community to a brand new apartment complex in a modern suburb of Baghdad. In return for the sale of your homes, I will provide you with very attractive financing and generous discounts that will make it possible for your community to start a new chapter in your lives.

"My company will apply for government subsidies on behalf of every family in the community, so you will not need to pay a penny to move into the new apartments, and you will have a very low monthly payment. After fifteen years, each family will own their apartment free and clear."

"Where are the apartments and how large are they?" Chaled's father's interest seemed to be piqued.

"I will arrange to pick you up tomorrow and take you for a tour of our new development. I am confident you will fall in love with it.

"One more very important point," Ali continued. "I will establish a higher education scholarship fund for the community and will start by granting a scholarship for Chaled to attend university and for Ahmed to receive advanced soccer training in Europe."

"Thank you for your generosity, Ali." Chaled's father voice sounded very emotional. "We need an angel like you to save our community from hopelessness and despair. Our prayers to Allah have been answered."

Six months later, the massive relocation of Palestinian families from the old Jewish quarters to a new, modern apartment complex was completed to the delight and elation of the new residents.

Chaled's parents were very appreciative of Ali's generosity. They invited him, his wife, and young family to festive meals in their new home during Muslim holidays. Ali became Chaled's mentor, encouraging him to excel in his higher education and providing him with financial support.

After Chaled's graduation from a University in Egypt with a degree in civil engineering, Ali hired him to work for his booming construction company. Chaled became a successful civil engineer and advanced to become one of Ali's key executives.

CHAPTER 33

BEIRUT, 1988

With Aziz becoming the unopposed Chairman with consolidated power and immense popularity, close friends and fellow leaders told him he should consider starting his own family. His colleagues stressed the need of the people to see their leader as a family man with a wife and children as a symbol of the evolving new future of the Palestinian nation. Just as his family would evolve and grow, so would the future of his people. They convincingly explained that as the internal conflicts were over and the organization was attempting to enter a peaceful stage, he should have time to devote to this very important duty. Aziz reluctantly agreed to consider an introduction to several eligible women.

One evening, Ebrahim approached him about a wonderful lady he thought Aziz should meet.

"She comes from an affluent Palestinian family that left Palestine during the 1948 war. Very well educated, with a degree in political science from Beirut University, and extremely attractive," Ebrahim added. "She is an active and vocal PLO advocate who works as a director at the Palestine Department of Social Services.

"I have met her personally," he continued, "and believe me, Mr. Chairman, she is an absolute gem. I think I know your taste by now, and I'm confident you will be very impressed by her in every way."

Aziz met Leila several days later. He was astounded by her natural beauty and bright intellect. They spent a very enjoyable evening together, and unlike other women to whom he had been introduced, Aziz felt he would like to see her again.

When Ebrahim inquired about his date the next morning, he was pleased to learn that Aziz was impressed by the lady. "Your Excellency, if this works, it will be a marriage from heaven," he enthusiastically commented. "A wife with Christian blood will consolidate your power further by creating a strong unity with our Christian brothers."

"Slow down, Ebrahim." Aziz tried to downplay Ebrahim's farfetched prediction. "I've only met the woman once, and you want me to marry her already. I promise you that I will see her again, but nothing beyond that."

However, Aziz couldn't keep Leila out of his mind and decided to invite her for a private dinner at his closely guarded villa. She looked as gorgeous as before, dressed in a striking long black shiny dress that emphasized her slender body contours, yet was modestly designed to cover her neck and arms. Her shoulder-length, smooth light-colored hair rested gently on her narrow feminine shoulders, surging like ocean waves every time she moved her head from side to side. Her large greenish eyes had a piercing inquisitive look that didn't seem to miss even the most minor of details. She had the face of a porcelain doll, one that Aziz could hardly take his eyes off.

They got along well, developing a pleasant conversation regarding many common interests. Leila told Aziz about her family history in Palestine and her childhood growing up in Lebanon. Aziz learned that her family had been confined to the poor conditions of a refugee camp for several months before her father was finally able to move them to a suburb of Beirut. After she graduated from the University of Beirut, she'd decided to devote her life to helping the refugees move out of the camps and build a new rewarding lifestyle. Aziz told her about his adventures in the narrow alleys of Baghdad and about the great time he'd had growing up with his Palestinian friends.

Aziz admired her unique beauty, her diverse knowledge of the local and international political scene, and her devotion to providing the deprived refugees with a gleaming hope for a better life. He recognized the sacrifices she made on their behalf every day, fighting for increased budgets for housing, medical care, and educational facilities.

Leila in turn expressed strong support for Aziz's efforts to conclude the armed struggle and negotiate a rewarding solution to the Palestinian refugee problem. She hoped he could end the bloodshed and advance the negotiations to a successful conclusion.

Aziz felt he was falling in love with this nurturing, beautiful woman, but he was besieged by mixed emotions. How could he marry a Palestinian woman and have Moslem children with her? It was against all the beliefs his mother had instilled in him from when he was young.

"You must marry only someone Jewish to build a family with," his mother's words reverberated through his mind. "You cannot marry someone who is not Jewish, unless she first converts to Judaism."

Then the words Harel spoke to him before he left on his mission echoed in his memory: "Reuben, you must become one of them, live like them, think like them, pray like them. This is the only way you will succeed in your mission. If you behave as an outsider, it's not going to work, and you will fail in your mission."

Only now had he come to realize what Harel was trying to tell him. Unless he fulfilled the people's expectations that the Chairman would become the role model for his entire people, build a family, and be one of them, he would not be accepted into the mainstream Palestinian population and would eventually lose his grip on power.

The more he thought about it, the more he realized there was no way around this issue. Although Harel and Shaffir hadn't said so explicitly, it had been expected of him if and when he reached this advanced stage of his mission.

Aziz tried to compare his situation to that of Eli Cohen, the Israeli master spy in Damascus who had reached the high echelons of Syrian leadership. He recalled that Eli had never married in Syria, even though he was considered a very eligible bachelor and was approached continuously by his Syrian friends and their wives with very prominent women for a match. Using various excuses, Eli always declined.

Eli could not marry a Syrian woman, no matter how bright or beautiful she was, for a very simple reason: Eli had a wife and three very young children living in Israel to whom he was very closely attached. He could hardly wait to get home to see them, even for quick, short visits. Aziz realized that Eli couldn't fully immerse himself in the life of the Syrian elite unless he was ready to abandon his family forever. Eli hadn't considered this ultimate sacrifice an option.

For this and other reasons, Eli's mission had been doomed for eventual failure. It had been just a question of when he would be discovered and whether he would be able to escape from Syria in time. There was no room for error, but his destiny took him to the gallows in the public square of Damascus.

Aziz did not have the same limitations Eli faced in Damascus. Shaffir, learning from past errors, had a very strong motive in selecting a candidate who was single and had minimal family ties. Aziz's lack of attachment maximized the flexibility in which he could maneuver on his mission and adjust it to the realities he would be facing.

Clearly to accomplish what Harel and Shaffir expected of him, Aziz had to start his own family. There was no way around it!

Aziz recalled the story of Joseph, son of Jacob, and his

rise to supreme power in ancient Egypt. Joseph married an Egyptian wife, Osnat, the daughter of an Egyptian high priest, with whom he had two boys. Through his marriage, Joseph integrated his life with that of the Egyptians, became part of the nation, and was widely accepted by the Egyptian people. He hadn't separated or isolated himself from his new surroundings; instead, he'd immersed himself into the Egyptian culture and lifestyle in order to build on his success. Aziz noticed that many elements of his own destiny were analogous to the life of Joseph in Egypt. Joseph's rise to prominence in Egypt allowed him to save his family from famine and keep the Israelite nation alive and thriving for several generations.

Joseph's success in Egypt brought Aziz much comfort and confidence that he too could reach extraordinary levels of success in caring for his nation from his position of power within the PLO. If this was his destiny, and there was no way of avoiding it, Leila would be the one he would choose to share his life with until his mission was accomplished and he could be the master of his own will again.

He felt that Leila wasn't merely a beautiful Palestinian woman who'd accidentally crossed his path. Leila was more of an angel sent from heaven to make his daunting mission tolerable, enrich his life with love and affection, and placate his cravings to return home to the land and the people he loved. After spending more time with Leila, he was convinced his theory was real.

As he'd determined that his union with Leila was essential to his mission's success, and it was highly regarded by his close friends, he decided not to wait any longer. He would propose to Leila the following week.

Under the Moslem faith, marriages had to be arranged through agreements with the bride's parents and her own consent to the match. However, since Leila's family lived abroad and she was considered a modern and mature woman capable of making her own decisions, Aziz decided to propose to her directly. After spending a very pleasant evening with her at his villa, he gathered the courage to ask for her hand in marriage.

Leila seemed to be completely surprised by his move. Because her mother was Christian and she had been raised in a very modern household, she knew that as the Chairman's wife, she would have to adopt the more strict Moslem ways and that their children would have to be reared as Moslem according to the laws of Islam. She understood that this marriage would also help the Chairman increase his popularity and support within the Palestinian Christian community.

She smiled at Aziz gracefully and thanked him for the great honor he'd bestowed on her. Then she asked him if she could have a few days to think about the enormous commitment of becoming the Chairman's wife and to consult with her family.

Aziz had been confident of an immediate positive response from her. Now he was lost for words by her unexplained hesitation. He slowly gained his composure, saying to Leila in a gentle voice, "I understand this will be a colossal undertaking on your part. Take as long as you need to think about it and make up your mind. I will be waiting patiently for your answer."

He escorted her to the waiting limousine in front of the villa and waved goodbye, wondering if he would ever see her again.

He paused briefly at the entrance to his villa to enjoy the cool evening breeze and take a deep breath of the pure, crisp mountain air. Although he was somewhat disappointed by Leila's initial response, he was relieved in a way. If it wasn't meant to be, he thought, he would be less restricted and better able to keep his options open. He was hopeful that one day, he would be able to make it back home to find the woman of his dreams. However, Leila had captured a soft spot in his heart, and it was hard to keep her off his mind.

* * * *

A week later, Leila was back. She told him she would be delighted to accept the great honor of marrying him and would stand by his side, supporting him in building a new future for their beloved nation. Aziz lifted her off her feet, holding her closely in his arms and kissing her gently on her cheeks. "I will be thrilled to share my life with the wonderful, caring person that you are," he said with a sigh of relief.

Three months later, the Chairman and his bride were married amidst very tight security in a well-publicized, lavish affair that drew many dignitaries from the Arab world.

The bride looked stunning in her ivory floor-length wedding gown ornamented with shiny, pure pearls followed by a long wavy cathedral train. Her face was covered with a floor-length lace veil, giving her an aura of graceful romantic beauty.

The bride's lovely ivory ensemble culminated with a perfect headpiece made of a shimmering V-band surrounding her beautiful hair and flaring with lace at the back of the head. A large, pear-shaped shining diamond attached to the band rested on her forehead, centered above her perfectly shaped eyebrows.

The handsome Chairman was dressed in a long black tailcoat with matching striped black trousers paired with a wing-collared white shirt, white vest, and white bow tie.

Radiating with happiness, the bride and groom, danced the night away in a most elegant affair that would be remembered in Beirut for years.

CHAPTER 34

During the time preceding the rise of Abdul-Aziz to the helm of the PLO, international pressure had been mounting on the Israeli government to open peace negotiations with the Palestinians and accept an initiative by the U.S. Secretary of State to meet with a Palestinian delegation and begin a dialogue with them. However, the Israeli PM refused to respond to American overtures and continued a policy of ignoring the problem and avoiding direct talks with the PLO.

Shlomo Harel, serving as Defense Minister during the time of the Palestinian uprising in the Israeli-held territories, tried repeatedly to crush the uprising by using brute force to bring law and order to the territories. However, civil disobedience and violence increased, forcing Israeli regular troops to fight a long civil war against stone-throwing Palestinian youths. Harel noticed the negative impact of the civil war on the young Israeli soldiers trained to fight against professional armies, not kids. Morale was down, and reluctance to serve in the territories grew rapidly.

Harel was determined to pursue the avenue of a peaceful solution to the conflict and to determine how much progress could be made with the Palestinians. Israeli public sentiment was growing impatient with the continuous conflicts that brought the number of Israeli casualties to record levels and caused high unemployment and economic uncertainty.

Harel started preparing for the upcoming elections. He was determined to revolutionize the government's approach to peace and make a significant impact on progress toward direct dialogue with the Palestinians. However, the only way he could achieve this objective was by recapturing the top leadership position and becoming the new Israeli PM. He decided to enter the race for his party leadership and run for the PM post. His campaign, which strongly promoted peace, gathered steam with the Israeli public that appeared more than ever eager to give peace a chance.

In the subsequent national elections held in Israel that summer, Shlomo Harel was successful in beating the opposition by winning the majority vote in the Israeli Parliament. He returned to the powerful position of Prime Minister fifteen years after he'd left the post. Harel now held the people's mandate to restart the peace process and attempt to bring it to a favorable conclusion.

Harel was aware of the internal struggles and rebellion that had taken place within the PLO ranks. He followed the developments very closely, receiving daily reports from the Mossad on the situation. He waited patiently for a positive outcome and a prevailing leader who was willing to pursue the road to peace.

To his great delight, he learned of the emergence of Abdul Aziz Al-Wasphi as the newly elected Chairman of the PLO. He was ecstatic with the wonderful news and wished Shaffir were still alive to enjoy the fruit of his ingenious scheme.

Chairman Aziz was equally thrilled with the news of Harel's election as the new Israeli PM, for he saw an excellent opportunity to negotiate a peace treaty with Harel. Harel was the initiator of the Chairman-X mission, and now his vision had materialized. Aziz recalled the words Harel had spoken to him before he left.

"Mr. Chairman," he had said, pretending that Reuben had reached the PLO top leadership, "I look forward to meeting you at the negotiations table within a few years. Don't forget that I am a very tough negotiator, but I am confident that with some mutual understanding and hand twisting, we can reach an equitable solution to the Palestinian issue."

Aziz viewed Harel's re-election as a signal to push forward with peace efforts and open the door for dialogue with the Israelis. With the help of influential Arab and European leaders, he initiated low-level contacts with Israeli officials. These lower level meetings were successful and gradually led to higher-level meetings that culminated with Foreign Ministry-level negotiations under the sponsorship of the Europeans.

However, at a critical point in the negotiations, the two sides reached a deadlock. The Palestinians demanded more concessions, but the Israeli opposition objected strongly to yielding to further demands and threatened to topple Harel's narrow coalition government with a no-confidence vote. Harel, realizing that he could lose control of the situation and suffer a major defeat by the mounting opposition, decided to back off and wait for better timing.

Chairman Aziz was frustrated by the deadlock in the negotiations with the Israelis and his inability to break the stalemate. His continued attempts to renew the dialogue and meet with Harel encountered stern refusals and public statements that the Palestinian new demands were unacceptable.

Under mounting internal pressure, Chairman Aziz convened the Palestinian National Council to discuss the situation and formulate new strategies to address the impasse in advancing the peace negotiations with Israel. Frustration at the lack of progress was building up among PNC members, and many voices were in favor of the resumption of violent acts to shake the Israelis out of their hard-line position.

Two days of frenzied and passionate discussions yielded two resolutions.

On the political front, it was decided to dispatch envoys immediately to prominent Arab countries that maintained close relations with the West. The envoys were to meet with the foreign ministers of these countries and use their influence with the Americans and Europeans to pressure the Israeli Government to resume the peace process. They were to work diligently toward reaching a UN resolution threatening to impose economic sanctions and an arms embargo on the

Israelis.

On the armed front, PLO military command was ordered to start planning a high profile, daring operation inside Israel. If political maneuvers proved unsuccessful, there would be no choice but to exercise this violent option. A successful operation at the heart of Israel would demonstrate Israel's vulnerability, sway public opinion, and exert public pressure on the Israeli government to return to the negotiation table.

Intense political maneuvering by the PLO, its Arab allies, and the Europeans ensued. Several weeks of mounting effort failed to yield progress. The slim coalition majority held by the Harel government had left its hands tied.

CHAPTER 35

ISRAEL, 1992

Prime Minister Shlomo Harel was an early morning person. He arrived at his office at 7 a.m. daily ready to face the never-ending challenges that seemed to have become a routine part of his brutally demanding job.

At 7:15 a.m., his director general burst into his office.

"I was just informed by the police that a school bus has been hijacked by a group of terrorists south of Netanya."

"Were there any children on the bus?" Harel shot back at his director.

"About thirty of them, I'm afraid," the director responded.

"Goddamn cowards! They never dare facing real soldiers. They are big heroes against defenseless women and children. Summon my security cabinet for an emergency meeting at once."

The hours since he'd received word of the hijacking

had been the most difficult in Harel's career, with the lives of thirty youngsters hanging in the balance, his Defense Minister on board the hijacked bus with his grandchildren, and the entire world looking on. The terrorists were on the edge; one wrong move and all hell could break lose. He didn't want the blood of the youngsters on his conscience; however, yielding to terrorism was not an option.

At 12:15 p.m., his director general entered his chambers. "Ben Ari is on the radiophone," he announced. "He is asking to speak to you."

Harel picked up the phone and listened attentively for about a minute. Soon the sound of the phone slamming on its cradle shook the large chamber.

"Damn this Aziz. He has gone too far this time. He is going to pay dearly for this fiasco. Tell the IAF Chief to order the C-130 to fly to Ramat David right now," Harel shot at his director. "As soon as it takes off from Ramat David, I want two fighter jets on its tail. They are to redirect it to Ben Gurion airport, but not, I repeat, not to shoot it down."

"Right away, Shlomo." The director general left in a hurry.

CHAPTER 36

At 12:40 p.m., the loud roar of an approaching aircraft broke the silence at Ramat David air force base. A C-130 transport appeared overhead. It made a wide circle and made its approach for landing from the southwest. It came in over the hills at very low speed, the pilots cautiously navigating it toward the short landing strip and then bringing it to a screeching halt at the end of the runway. Loud cheers could be heard from the three buses parked on the opposite end of the runway.

Ebrahim radioed Abu Yasin and asked him to put the pilot on.

"Now that you see the runway, does it look long enough for a takeoff with over one hundred people on board?" he inquired.

"I think we should be able to make it," answered the pilot.

"What do you mean you think you can make it?" Ebrahim's voice quivered with fury.

"With the help of Allah and a few tricks I learned in the Sahara Desert, we should be able to clear the hills in time. I will remove nonessential loads from the aircraft to reduce its weight. I have taken off from shorter runways in the desert, so I should be able to make this one, *ensha'allah,* by the grace of *Allah.*"

The C-130 turned around, taxied to the southern tip of the runway, and came to a complete stop. Abu Yasin told Ben Ari to order the pilots not to open any of the plane doors or move the plane until a thorough check of the aircraft was completed. Four blindfolded and handcuffed hostages were led out of the school bus. Two gunmen followed them with machine gun butts edging their backs. They approached the aircraft slowly and asked the pilots to open the side door.

Abu Yasin was tensely watching the large cargo door in the rear of the aircraft. This door was used to load and unload large vehicles or troops onto the C-130. If the Israelis planned an assault, their commandos would emerge from this door. He had two men with heavy machine guns aim at this door.

Two Israeli pilots emerged from the side door. They were searched and ordered to walk to the base. The gunmen, with the hostages in front of them, boarded the plane cautiously and proceeded to conduct a thorough check of the inside. Several minutes later, one of them emerged with a thumbs-up sign. Abu Yasin sent the PLO pilot to check the plane and prepare for takeoff. Soon the heavy cargo door slid down slowly, revealing an empty cargo hold.

Abu Yasin ordered boarding to start immediately. First, explosives and detonators were moved from the buses and set in designated areas on the plane. Next, the blindfolded and handcuffed hostages were seated in fold-down seats attached to the plane fuselage and buckled in with seat belts. The freed prisoners were dispersed between the hostages to keep a close eye on them. Ben Ari was moved to the front of the aircraft to help Abu Yasin maintain communications with Israeli central command.

The pilot asked Abu Yasin to instruct his men to walk through the plane and remove all nonessential loads to minimize takeoff weight.

"We are doing so as we speak," responded Abu Yasin.

"Can you tell me how you plan to make this beast take off from such a short runway? If you don't make it, we will all die in a hell of a fire! Are you confident it will work?" Abu Yasin asked nervously.

"How do you think I took off from the short bumpy runways of the Sahara?" the pilot asked, attempting to calm Abu Yasin. "This workhorse of an aircraft can do incredible stuff if you know some tricks I was taught by a veteran pilot. Let me take care of the plane while you prepare everybody for takeoff."

It was 1:45 p.m. No special activity was noticed around the airfield. Abu Yasin's voice could be heard screaming, "Let's get the hell out of here, now! We are behind schedule. Everybody sit down and don't move until we are airborne."

The pilot completed his takeoff checklist. "Everything is in order," he reported.

Soon the roaring sound of four turboprop engines revved to full speed disrupted the afternoon tranquility of Ramat David.

Abu Yasin sat in the cockpit next to the pilot. "Roll away, tiger," he proclaimed his signal for takeoff. "Let's see how you are going to get this mammoth up in the air."

"Sit back and watch my magic," the pilot exclaimed confidently.

The CNN truck moved backward, its cameras fully focused on the C-130 positioned at the end of the runway with its four propellers spinning at an increasing speed. The Chairman's eyes were riveted on the C-130. Ebrahim stood next to him, his rapidly pounding heart threatening to leap out of his chest.

It was 2 p.m.

"Clutch the brake levers as hard as you can!" the pilot yelled toward Abu Yasin. "Hold them down tightly until I give you the signal to let go."

The engines roared into high speed. The plane shuddered violently, its heavy body seized by the pressure on the brakes. The cabin started filling with the strong odor of burning rubber while white smoke swirled in the air. Abu Yasin sweated profusely as he clasped the brake levers as hard as he could. The noise was becoming unbearable, and the plane shook so hard it seemed about to explode.

"Let go!" the pilot yelled over the immense howl of the engines. Suddenly like a raging bull unleashed from its gate, the plane leapt forward with great force.

The hazy black asphalt runway disappeared rapidly while the plane accelerated hurriedly, as if it knew that time wasn't on its side.

"I don't think he is going to make it," Ebrahim exclaimed in a panicked voice as the plane approached the end of the runway.

At that instant, the pilot activated the turbo-boosters on all four engines, and in a thundering roar, the plane started lifting. All eyes were glued to the monitor, watching apprehensively as the plane barely cleared the low hills to the northeast of the airbase.

"The eagle has spread its wings," the pilot radioed in a very excited voice. "No wonder they call this beast Hercules! It's an immensely powerful and amazing machine that can perform wonders. I told you I could make it, your Excellency! I would never dare to disappoint your Highness."

"Outstanding job. We will see you here soon. Just stay calm and bring the eagle home safely."

The war room turned into a wild party. Everybody was screaming and jumping with joy, hugging and kissing each other.

Ebrahim jumped on the Chairman like a kid on a soccer team that had just won the championship. "You are a genius! You made it happen. This is our biggest victory since we started our struggle!"

"Please calm down, everybody. We are still over Israeli air space. We can start celebrating when the eagle lands in Beirut."

It was 2:15 p.m. The plane was heading north toward Beirut out of the range of the CNN cameras. The flight to Beirut was estimated at twenty-five minutes. It was time to prepare for the arrival of the passengers.

At approximately 2:25 p.m., as the plane approached

the Israeli-Lebanese border, the pilot's panic-stricken voice came on. "Two Israeli F-15 fighter jets are on my tail."

"Stay on course at maximum speed and ignore them," the Chairman ordered firmly. A few seconds later, the pilot was back. "They are signaling me to turn around." He sounded distraught.

"Just ignore them and stay steady on course. Don't make any unusual moves," the Chairman instructed him in a calm voice.

The plane was now in Lebanese air space, but that had no effect on the Israeli pilots. They had been in control of Lebanese airspace for more than a decade, something that wasn't going to change on that day.

The pilot's distressed voice came on again. "They are firing warning rounds in front of my nose. They are going to shoot us down if I don't turn around."

"They are bluffing," the Chairman interrupted him. "You need to stay focused and continue to ignore them. The Israelis won't dare shoot down the plane and murder all the children on board. Stay on course and begin your approach to land at Beirut airport. That's an order!"

As the C-130 swiftly approached Beirut airport, the two F-15s suddenly soared upwards leaving long streaks of white plumes in the clear blue skies as two sonic booms rocked the city.

The thrilled voice of the PLO intelligence chief came through the intercom. "I see them on the local news channel. They are on approach to land at Beirut International Airport."

The dark gray and green wide body of the C-130

came clearly through the monitor. The news crews had situated themselves on a high hill on the landing approach path that provided a very crisp view of the landing in Beirut.

"The eagle has landed with all its cargo," the pilot announced with relief.

International news crews swarmed the airplane, as cameras and microphones stretched to capture the historic, inconceivable event. The C-130 taxied to a predetermined area near the international terminal and came to a halt.

Within seconds, the side door opened and Abu Yasin emerged with both hands up in the air in a victory sign.

"It's time for a magnificent celebration," the Chairman called with elation. "Our warriors are free at last."

The Chairman's loyal staffers lifted him up on their shoulders and paraded him around like a coach who'd just won the world soccer championship. This was the kickoff for festivities to celebrate the enormous success of the operation. It was the kind of operation the world had come to expect from the Israelis, except this time, it was the Palestinians' turn. They had just proved they could execute missions just as well as the Israelis, and that they had matured into an opponent that needed to be contended with seriously. The Chairman had to leverage this success to advance the cause of freedom and prosperity of the Palestinian people.

Ebrahim was already on his way to the airport to supervise the activities and make sure the Israeli hostages were treated with utmost respect and courtesy. He was soon on the phone reporting that all the passengers had deplaned and that the freed prisoners had been separated from the hostages. The hostages were in the process of going through Lebanese immigration and being given temporary visas to allow them to stay until their return trip could be arranged.

The freed prisoners gathered in a special area in the international terminal to receive their temporary residence certificates.

Ebrahim called the Beirut Hilton and ordered red carpet treatment and top-level security for the hostages. Ben Ari and his grandchildren were to be given the prestigious Presidential Suite. Members of the Chairman's own elite security detail safeguarded the hotel lobby and top floor.

It was close to 5 p.m. The Chairman retreated to his quarters and collapsed exhausted on his bed. Soon he would need to start focusing on the next phase of trying to reenergize the peace treaty with Israel. This was the main reason Ben Ari had been picked as a high-ranking hostage. He was known for his moderate stance with regard to peace negotiations with the PLO. He came under criticism frequently from opposition parties and right-wing groups in Israel as being "dovish" and willing to "sell out the country." He was definitely the right official to resume the dialogue and help push the decision process with Harel.

The Chairman took a refreshing catnap to boost his energy. He had much more to accomplish on that historic day, and he intended to enjoy every minute of it. A news conference was scheduled for 6:30 p.m. at the Inter-Continental Hotel, but before he got there, he had an important stop.

He arrived at PLO special operations headquarters where Abu Yasin and his raid team were stretched out on folding beds. As soon as he appeared, they sprang to their feet and huddled around him. This was their ultimate prize, being personally thanked by the Chairman. He embraced and kissed each one of them and expressed his immense appreciation for their great contribution to the freedom of the Palestinian people.

He had a surprise for them, pinning on each of the men the most prestigious medal a PLO fighter could receive for outstanding courage and bravery in battle — the Valor of Freedom. The men were elated with the great honor bestowed upon them, kissing his hand with gratitude.

The Chairman motioned Abu Yasin for a private discussion.

"I commend your flawless performance in delivering this essential victory," he praised him. "I want to thank you for your courage and unconditional dedication on behalf of our people."

He called everybody to attention and then announced the immediate promotion of Abu Yasin to the rank of lieutenant colonel.

The men swarmed around Abu Yasin, cheering rowdily and chanting his name in a steady rhythm. Abu Yasin thanked the Chairman graciously and kissed his hand with deep appreciation.

The Chairman rushed to the Inter-Continental Hotel to address the gathered reporters. He described the mission and its goals and promised that all the Israeli hostages would be treated with dignity and returned to Israel the next day.

The issue of peace negotiations with Israel came up in the question period. The Chairman stated that the Palestinian people were ready for a commitment to a just and lasting peace agreement with Israel. There were no preconditions to the talks, and all issues on the agenda would be open for discussion.

This message was targeted specifically towards the Israeli government's Western allies who could exert pressure on the Israelis to resume peace negotiations. Israel would no longer be able to use the excuse that the PLO was merely a terrorist organization whose only goal was terror and destruction, and that they were not ready to recognize Israel or negotiate the terms of a peace agreement.

The Chairman left the news conference and moved on to a lavish celebration at the same hotel. Ebrahim was in charge of organizing the whole affair. He'd invited the famous Arabic singer, Jahira Al-Nasib, and her orchestra along with a group of belly dancers to entertain the freed fighters and elite troops. She opened by singing one of her famous songs, *"Bukra nekon daula gedidi,"* meaning, "By sunrise we will become a new nation." Even the most courageous men stood there clapping, tears streaming down their cheeks.

Abu Yasin, Ebrahim, and the Chairman were paraded around the hall to the jovial chanting of their men. Plenty of the best Middle Eastern food one could find in Beirut was served. It was the ultimate celebration and a sweet taste of freedom for the recently freed fighters, some of whom had spent over ten years in Israeli jails.

CHAPTER 37

At 9:30 p.m., the Chairman arrived at the heavily guarded Beirut Hilton. He immediately proceeded to the Presidential Suite on the top floor to meet with Ben Ari. He knew it was going to be an awkward beginning, but he was confident he could turn Ben Ari around once the conversation started flowing.

"Mr. Ben Ari," he opened, sitting on the comfortable soft leather sofa in the elaborately decorated suite. "I deeply apologize for having to drag your grandchildren into this mess. We did not have a choice. This was the only way to guarantee the success of our mission. Without you and your grandchildren on board, the C-130 would have been turned into ashes. If you weren't such a close friend of Mr. Harel, surely you and the hostages would have been sacrificed for the sacred cause of antiterrorism."

"You didn't have to drag my grandchildren into this chaos," Ben Ari responded furiously. "They are innocent young kids. The trauma they endured will remain a vivid memory forever."

"I understand your anger," the Chairman continued. "You are well aware that a national struggle for self-determination and independence carries a very heavy price. Your people went through the same struggle against the British in the late 1940s."

The Chairman knew that Ben Ari held several key positions in the Hagana, Israel's pre-independence military organization. He had been responsible for carrying out several bloody guerilla operations against the British in that pre-independence era of Israel's struggle for freedom.

"We never used innocent children as a blackmail tool," Ben Ari snapped.

"You used whatever was at your disposal to accomplish your central goals, and we are doing the same," the Chairman was quick to counter. "But I am here to try to put an end to all the senseless pain and suffering on both sides. This is a very good opportunity for us to have an open, heart-to-heart discussion about how this process can be sustained and how we can turn this dream into reality. I am told there are strong elements within your party who are in favor of continuing the dialogue with us to explore the possibility of concluding a comprehensive peace accord.

"We both know that the economic rewards will be extremely beneficial to both sides. With your technological resources and our abundant labor force, we can turn this region into the technological powerhouse of the Middle East. You surely admit, Mr. Ben Ari, that the potential is limitless."

Ben Ari leaned back on the plush reclining armchair

and closed his eyes. He remained silent for a few long seconds that felt like eternity.

"I agree the potential is there." Ben Ari had finally been drawn into the conversation, "but we have a long way to go and vast obstacles to overcome. Even if my party reaches a consensus to move forward with the peace process, there will be an uproar from the right-wing parties who will label us as traitors and attempt to topple our government. We have our own *mjanin,* you know."

The Chairman was pleased to hear Ben Ari use a popular Arabic word referring to fanatical extremists. He felt it was an indication that Ben Ari was mellowing and opening the discussion. "We have to start somewhere," he said. "We know that there are no guarantees of success, but we ought to give it a very serious try. We can stop the bloodshed, start a productive process, and let your Allah and our Allah help us work out our differences. I am willing to declare a unilateral cease-fire as soon as we agree on a date and location to start the negotiations. We will also clamp down on all the radical factions and suppress any activities they may be planning against Israel."

Ben Ari rose from the armchair. "It sounds like a reasonable start," he said, "but it's not up to me. We live in a democratic state. I can only be the messenger."

"This is all I am asking," the Chairman replied, handing an envelope to Ben Ari. "Please deliver this personal letter to Mr. Harel. It should serve as the first step toward lasting peace."

The Chairman left the hotel at around eleven.

"Take me home," he ordered his driver and bodyguards. He knew that the climax of the past twenty-four hours was still awaiting him — his wife, Leila. Her reward for his victory would be the ultimate, the one he had been looking forward to the most.

CHAPTER 38

As the Chairman leaned back on the soft cushioned leather seat of his heavily armored Mercedes, he couldn't stop thinking about Leila and how intimate they had become.

He imagined the exotic scent of her beautiful body and her gentle hands softly caressing his bare back, releasing all his stress and exhaustion. He would soon be able to let go, sink his body and soul into her welcoming arms, and forget for a few precious hours the daunting conflicts in which he was immersed.

The Mercedes entered through an electronic gate into a heavily guarded underground structure and came to a halt. One of his bodyguards opened his door and escorted him through a set of automated heavy steel doors into a security zone. The structure he called home was built as a combination of a bank safe and a bunker surrounded by heavy concrete and steel armor, and equipped with multiple recognition devices for access control. Fingerprint, voice recognition, and retina scan permitted access only to Leila and him.

This highly sophisticated equipment had been ordered by a prince from oil-rich Abu-Dhabi. An American firm that built secure military installations for the U.S. government had made it for the prince. During a port call on its way to Abu Dhabi, the equipment was "mistakenly" unloaded, and the prince's donation was accepted in return for a promise that his kingdom would not be threatened by terrorist activities for a while.

The interior of the structure was designed as a modern apartment. Past the security zone, it no longer felt like an underground bunker. He walked quietly through a long, wide corridor hoping to surprise Leila as she wasn't expecting him for another hour or so. He entered the first doorway to the right, which revealed a modern kitchen filled with the latest amenities of sophisticated European wood cabinetry and electrical appliances. The kitchen counters and sink looked like they had been recently cleaned and polished, but there was no sign of Leila.

He tiptoed to the dining area, which was designed as an extension of the kitchen with matching furnishings and modern spotlights. The kitchen and dining area floor was tiled with shiny, white Italian marble. Separating the dining area from the spacious living area were carved arches attached to ornamented marble columns on each side.

He walked into the wide-open living area. Leila liked to lounge in the living room and watch a late night TV program as she waited patiently for his arrival.

The living area had a huge mural of the Beirut coastal landscape and its crystal blue waters. It was hand-painted so magnificently that one felt like jumping from the cliff right into the refreshing waters of the sea below. A renowned Lebanese landscape artist selected by Leila to simulate her favorite view of Beirut had created it. Because she spent a lot of her time in the enclosed apartment, the mural provided openness and colors to replicate the outdoors.

Large, rare pictorial Persian rugs sent from Iran by the Ayatollah covered the two sidewalls of the living area. Each rug was artistically woven in its own unique way and displayed a glorious image of significant importance in the history of the Persian Empire. The floor of the living area was made of light- colored wood centered by a huge oriental area rug designed with bright colors and magical figures. This incredibly soft and lustrous wool rug filled the large room with warmth and enchantment.

Facing the mural was a soft light leather sofa modeled after Louis XV classic French style, flanked by two matching lounge chairs on each side. The sofa and lounge chairs were decorated by down throw pillows, hand painted in various Arabian themes. Leila liked to stretch out and relax on the lounge chairs, surrounding herself with soft pillows and focusing her attention on the large TV monitor in the opposite corner. However, she wasn't there this time. He started wondering if she had decided to go out for some reason and all his anticipation was in vain.

Two stained glass French doors led from the back of the living area to a spacious master bedroom suite. In the center of the master bedroom against the back wall stood a king-sized canopy bed decorated by gold tapestry and silk bed covers and pillows. A soft, cushioned wall-to-wall carpet covered the master bedroom floor. Hanging on the walls were several modern paintings by a prominent Italian artist. The ceiling was decorated by varnished cypress beams with a softly colored sheer cloth hanging between the beams forming mysterious shapes of yacht sails blowing in the wind. The bed was made neatly, shattering his anticipation that Leila had gone to bed already.

Two connecting doors led from the master bedroom to a dressing room, which opened into the master bathroom. As soon as he opened the doors, he could sense the sweet smell of rosewater filling the air. He took a long, deep breath and filled his lungs with the refreshing fragrance — heavenly. His worries were unfounded; Leila wasn't going to disappoint him.

Leila emerged beside him and welcomed him warmly.

"I didn't hear you come in, my dear. Were you trying to sneak up on me?"

"I certainly tried," he replied, "I was worried you weren't home."

Leila ushered him gently towards a large round hot tub built on an elevated area of the bathroom. A light mist was rising from the tub mixed with a pungent scent of rosewater that overpowered his senses. Leila undressed him tenderly before he sank slowly into the tub. He felt the shock of the hot water wrapping around his body. The heat and steam were starting to soften his skin, relax his aching muscles, and drain the stress he'd endured the entire day. He sat in the soothing bubbly water for a few minutes with his eyes closed until his body and mind were completely tranquil.

Soon he could sense Leila's exotic perfume and glimpse her shadow as she reappeared through the dimmed lights. Her slender, sexy body was wrapped in a transparent sheer blouse. Underneath, her luscious breasts were bursting out of her low-cut, tight crimson top. She was wearing a matching double-V clinging panty, her tight muscular buttocks shaped like a perfectly carved sculpture. Her tanned body glistened under the dimmed lights as he stepped out of the tub, feeling the excitement rush through his veins.

Leila dried his body with two large warm towels. She kissed him and whispered, "You are in my safe hands tonight. It will be like nothing you ever felt before." He laid down on the crisp, clean white sheets of the bed, and soon the intoxicating aroma of massage oils filled the air. He could now feel her gentle, firm hands piercing into every muscle of his body, squeezing and relieving any tensions left after the hot bath. Leila worked diligently and methodically until his body reached a state of peaceful serenity.

He turned toward her and took her firmly in his arms. He felt the warmth of her body pressing tightly against him, her enticing scent dimming his senses. He kissed her sensual lips with passion and started gently removing the smooth silk sheers off her body. Her breasts brushed against his chest and her muscular thighs tightened against his groin. His hands were gently stroking her back and neck and his lips caressing her favorite sensitive spots behind her ears. Her body shuddered with pleasure as she tried to wiggle out of his tight grip. He ran his fingers up and down her slim spine, sending electric shocks throughout her body.

He knew she loved this preamble, which charged her inner soul and filled her with explosive excitement. He started stroking her back with his fingers, desperately searching for the release clasp of her bra. Those few seconds of struggle with the clasp felt like an eternity, and in his mind, he cursed the designers who always made this task so difficult, yet so thrilling.

When the clasp finally broke free, he felt her succulent, shiny breasts pouring out of her shimmering tanned body against his chest, her excited pink nipples rubbing against him with exhilaration. Leila sat on the bed; he kneeled in front of her, submerging his face between her two beautifully rounded, firm breasts with nipples perfectly centered like pink roses.

He felt in heaven kissing those erect nipples and sucking them like a starving baby. Leila groaned with pleasure, pulling his head in a tight grip against her breasts, her fingers deeply anchored around his lower body. He glimpsed the contrasting tan lines of her beautifully carved, gleaming body. His senses blurred, carrying him to a mystical world beyond the heavens. He felt the blood streaming into his groin, his erection as firm as a rock. He grasped her panties, slipping them down gently. Her muscular, silky white buttocks jammed against him, tightening in a deadly grip around his thighs.

Leila whimpered with ecstasy as their bare bodies

united into one, rocking steadily. "Come to me now, my hero," she whispered into his ear. "You fill me up completely, my brave stallion. I feel you inside every inch of my soul, my courageous king."

He suddenly felt his body explode with pleasure, his brain bursting with meteor showers culminating in the pinnacle of his climax.

Leila's body shuddered, her arms tightening around him as hard as she could. He felt her body pulsating violently in gratification as she too reached the crest of her pleasure. They were breathing heavily, gasping for oxygen as their sweat-covered bodies gradually calmed down and reached a state of total drained relief.

He turned to Leila and kissed her.

"You were right, my angel. I've never felt so good in my entire life. With you by my side, I feel invincible."

"Sh...Sh...it's time for you to rest, my darling."

CHAPTER 39

The Chairman woke up at 8 a.m. Leila had breakfast ready for him. He felt completely rejuvenated and ready to take on the next challenge. He hugged and kissed her goodbye.

"What surprises do you have in store for me tonight, my precious angel?" he whispered in her ear.

She smiled gently, curled her lips, and blew a soft kiss toward him.

"You will just have to wait and see, my brave stallion."

He entered the rear of his Mercedes thinking it was amazing how close he felt to Leila. She had become an integral part of his life, filling his soul with happiness and joy he'd never felt before. Any thoughts of being away from her seemed unbearable.

At 10 a.m., he arrived at Beirut International Airport, where a press conference had been scheduled to bid the Israeli hostages farewell and demonstrate the PLO's commitment to stand by its obligations to return them home safely. Ebrahim had made all the arrangements for an Air France jetliner to be ready at the airport.

The Chairman announced the departure of the hostages into the myriad of microphones placed on a makeshift stage at the airport. He introduced Ben Ari to the press and invited him to answer questions. Ben Ari reported that all the hostages, including himself, had been treated with respect and generosity and that he was looking forward to getting home safely and being reunited with the rest of his family.

Many reporters brought up questions with regard to the prospects of peace negotiations between Palestinians and Israelis. Ben Ari replied that this was something his government had to debate and render a decision upon and that he wasn't in a position to comment further on the subject.

* * * *

Mrs. Shulamit Arditi was sitting in her living room in the town of Zichron-Yaakov off the Israeli Mediterranean coast, her eyes glued to the live CNN coverage of the return of the Israeli hostages from Beirut. The PLO Chairman concluded his introductions, and it was Ben Ari's turn to answer reporters.

"Let them get on the plane and get out of that hell already," she thought to herself. "Every extra second in the enemy's claws could prove detrimental." Her son, Ronnie, a pilot in the Israeli Air Force, had been taken away from her three years earlier, missing in action on a mission over southern Lebanon. She didn't trust these barbarians for even a fraction of a second. They'd refused to provide the Red Cross with any information regarding Ronnie's fate, leaving her and her husband in a limbo and wondering if they would ever see their son alive.

Without warning, the TV cameras turned their focus onto five men dressed in civilian clothes escorted by armed guards. They were marching toward the main podium where Ben Ari was answering the reporters' questions. Before her brain could begin to comprehend what was unraveling in front of her, she saw her son's face gazing into her eyes from the monitor. "It's Ronnie! It's Ronnie!" she started screaming hysterically. "He's alive! He's alive! Bless the Almighty, he's alive!"

Puzzled by his wife's emotional eruption, her husband, Nessim, burst into the living room, Ever since Ronnie had disappeared without a trace, Nessim had been in a deep depression and had gone into seclusion, avoiding any contact with the outside world.

"Look, Nessim!" His wife ran to him. "It's Ronnie! He's alive! It's a miracle! I never lost hope for him. I told you he was still alive."

Nessim gazed at the monitor in disbelief. "It's him! It's really him, my beloved Ronnie, my son, my life, my universe! Blessed be, Hashem is going to bring him back to us very soon."

Five Israeli POWs were paraded onto the stage to the astonishment of Ben Ari. They shook his hand and hugged him vigorously, thanking him incessantly for arranging their freedom. Ben Ari could no longer hold back his tears as the cameras focused on his emotionally charged reunion with his countrymen.

* * * *

The Air France jetliner took off smoothly from Beirut
International Airport, slowly turning south toward the
Israeli border. This was an unusual sight in Beirut.
Jetliners never flew south because the border with Israel
was only a few minutes away.

At Ben Gurion airport, thousands of spectators
jammed the arrivals terminal, impatiently awaiting
the appearance of the passengers from Beirut. They
were cheering, clapping, and singing national songs in
anticipation of the great moment. The heavily reinforced
police units that had been rushed to the airport were
barely able to keep control of the situation.

Upon arrival, Ben Ari, the hostages, and the POWs
were transported to Tel Aviv's municipal square where
thousands more gathered to welcome them and
celebrate the happy ending of their perilous journey.
Prime Minister Harel, government dignitaries, and
high-ranking military officials were there to greet them
with warm, welcoming words. People were singing and
dancing in the street as if it were a national holiday.
The Israeli government had just averted another major
crisis.

CHAPTER 40

In the aftermath of the success of operation Brotherhood of Freedom, the newly earned respect for the PLO and pressure placed by the U.S. and Europeans on the Israeli government facilitated the long-awaited shift in political momentum.

The safe return of Ben Ari and the Israeli hostages from Beirut and the Chairman's last-minute goodwill gesture to release five Israeli POWs provided Harel and Ben Ari with overwhelming public support to press forward and elevate the peace process to the top of their agenda.

Renewed high-level negotiations took place at an undisclosed European location where committees from both sides convened to address specific issues on the agenda. Chairman Aziz sent the teams encouraging messages supporting the progress in the peace process and assuring the Israelis that their security concerns would be addressed in full. Harel promised strong commitments to normalized relations and the gradual turnover of territories to Palestinian self-rule. The peace treaty would be supported by strong economic cooperation between the two nations and financial backing from the international community.

As talks shifted into high gear, Israeli Foreign Ministry officials arrived to try to conclude a draft to be submitted to both leaders for final approval. In an attempt to iron out a few final obstacles that could not be worked out by the negotiation teams, Harel proposed a secret meeting between him and Chairman Aziz to resolve the differences and conclude the agreement.

The following week, a historic meeting was held between the two leaders. Harel was eagerly looking forward to being with Aziz again after seeing him off on his mission close to two decades earlier. He recalled the tall, handsome man with the determined look in his sparkling eyes embarking on his perilous journey without a hint of hesitation, just a smile on his face. He admired Aziz's courage, dedication, and amazing accomplishments of the past two decades.

He also understood that Chairman Aziz had to negotiate on behalf of the Palestinians with tough resolve to prove he'd extorted the maximum concessions possible from the Israelis and hadn't given up on any significant Palestinian demands.

At their first private meeting, Chairman Aziz greeted Harel warmly and shook his hand enthusiastically. "Mr. Prime Minister, I welcome your courage and dedication to a lasting peace between our nations," he opened in almost perfect English. Harel was astounded by his impressive appearance. He was the same tall, slender, good-looking man he remembered, apparently immune to the passage of time. The glistening sparkle in his eyes had not faded even a tiny bit and radiated extreme enthusiasm and eagerness to conclude his Divine duty. Only the speckles of gray hair around his groomed moustache and sideburns proved the aging process hadn't skipped him completely.

Harel responded with equal enthusiasm, welcoming him and expressing his commitment to advance the prospects of peace and help the Palestinian people emerge from despair to self-governance and prosperity.

The two leaders conducted several meetings and spent many hours in privacy to negotiate an acceptable solution to the remaining difficult issues. Harel conducted himself in a businesslike manner, never showing a hint of his total awareness of the identity of the Chairman. They both knew that they could not afford the chance of revealing their former acquaintance, even under the most private circumstances for fear of exposing Aziz. The two men developed excellent working relations and a close friendship that led to the successful conclusion of the negotiations.

Harel presented Chairman Aziz with a beautifully designed necklace created by a renowned Israeli artist, saying, "I am pleased to present this gift to your lovely wife as a token of friendship from Israeli mothers and their young children." The necklace, decorated with shiny diamonds, created a unique representation mingling the symbols of the Jewish star, the Moslem quarter-moon, and the Christian cross.

Both leaders faced the enormous task of presenting the agreement to their respective governing bodies and using their salesmanship skills to obtain final endorsements.

In Israel, the agreement's long-reaching concessions came under strong criticism from right-wing and religious parties who held several demonstrations protesting the agreement. The agreement, however, was finally approved by a narrow margin that included the support of Communist and Israeli-Arab parties, all to the uproar and rage of the opposition. There were widespread claims that because no Jewish majority support existed for the agreement, it was invalid.

Chairman Aziz also faced some objections to the accords, but having eradicated all the extremist groups and garnered the wide popular support of the Palestinian masses, he saw the agreement approved by a wide margin.

The major breakthrough in reaching the historic agreement took other countries by surprise, receiving the immediate blessing and support of the free world. Many countries pledged economic and financial support in the implementation of the agreement.

The Americans, who supported the new peace accords, offered to host the historic event of the signing of the agreement at the White House. The U.S. President presided over the ceremony as the two leaders shook hands in front of the entire world, signed the agreement, and in moving speeches pledged their commitment to peace.

Chairman Aziz was elated; he had just accomplished the most significant objective of his mission, culminating close to two decades of endless struggle and sacrifice.

The arduous task of starting the implementation process of the agreements was his next challenge. He announced an official amendment to the Palestinian National Charter to remove the language pertaining to the destruction of Israel and replaced it with language calling for the two nations to live side by side in peace, security, and harmony. He made the appointment of the Palestinian shadow government official and organized the various ministries to be prepared to take over the vacated territories as was part of the agreement.

Funds to support the transition were pouring in, mostly from Europe and the U.S. Within several months of the ceremonies in Washington, the entire Palestinian government was moved into the territories to take over control of the area from Israel. The Chairman took charge of organizing the formation of a dependable infrastructure to serve as the foundation for the creation of an economically viable entity. He then created institutions to serve the social, educational, and legal functions of the new Palestinian Authority.

Chairman Aziz held frequent meetings and consultations with Harel and other Israeli officials to promote economic cooperation and accelerate the establishment of jobs for Palestinian workers. They decided to build several free trade zones in areas bordering Israel and the territories. These zones would provide incentives to promote the formation of new enterprises and manufacturing industries that would utilize and train labor from the territories.

Aziz tasked the Minister of Education with the revamping of the education system to reflect major policy changes in the Palestinian National Charter. The Ministry of Education strategy was to be modified toward creating a more modern secular entity with less influence from fundamentalist Islamic elements. Emphasis shifted toward the promotion of Western democratic values such as human rights, freedom of expression and the press, free elections, and free enterprise. Increasing the levels of higher education among the population was promoted vigorously to encourage technological advances and create a strong economic backbone.

The Chairman also ordered the removal of anti-Zionist, anti-Israel language from school textbooks, replacing it with an accurate historical account of events using language favorable toward Israel and the Jewish religion.

As progress toward peace moved swiftly, the Nobel committee in Norway announced the award of the Nobel Peace Prize to the Israeli Prime Minister and the Chairman of the Palestinian Authority for their efforts in resolving the Israeli-Palestinian conflict and promoting peace in the Middle East. The two leaders returned to the limelight, receiving well-deserved world-class recognition of their accomplishments.

In new elections held in the territories later that year, Chairman Aziz was elected the new President of the Palestinian Authority in a landslide victory.

CHAPTER 41

As Aziz's fame rose to global attention, his old childhood friend from Iraq, Chaled, noticed that the name of the prominent new PLO leader was identical to that of his long-time childhood friend who had left their neighborhood when he was a young teenager. After investigating the history of the new leader and learning that he'd grown up in Baghdad where he'd attended a Palestinian elementary school and then university, Chaled was beginning to connect the two personalities. A close examination of recent photos of the leader had shown a certain resemblance to the boy he'd spent most of his childhood with.

He recalled that Aziz possessed superior leadership traits from a very young age and had led the local Palestinian clan with bravery and wit. He concluded with a high degree of certainty that the new PLO leader was no other than his old friend.

Chaled and his friends had never understood why they'd never seen nor heard from Aziz again. They'd hoped he would write or visit occasionally. In particular,

Amira was heartbroken after his departure and waited patiently for him to come and redeem her, but not a word had been heard from Aziz all these years.

Chaled thought of Ali, Aziz's old family friend, who'd continued to visit the old neighborhood, and ultimately became Chaled's employer. He went directly to Ali's office to share his exciting news. Ali seemed astounded by Chaled's declaration, questioning him rigorously on how he'd reached his conclusion. Chaled described his evidence, saying he was certain of his revelation and that he intended to call the PA headquarters and try to arrange to meet Aziz.

"Thanks to you, Ali," Chaled said. "I am a generous donor to the Palestinian cause, and the Chairman's door is always open for people with big money."

Ali maintained his skepticism of the PA leader's identity and waited to receive further news from Chaled.

During a state visit by the PA President to Iraq, Chaled attended a PA fundraising event. With a generous donation, he was able to secure a private meeting with the President.

Chaled introduced himself to President Aziz as the childhood friend he'd grown up with in the slums of old Baghdad. At first, the President seemed very confused by the encounter and had trouble placing him.

Chaled started describing vividly some of their childhood adventures. He recalled in elaborate detail the street fight Aziz had had with Suleiman and how Aziz managed to defeat him despite Suleiman's dirty tricks.

"I remember his loud grunt when you whipped his

shoulder with your bamboo sword," Chaled recalled. "Then he tried to throw soil in your eyes to blind you, but you were able to avoid it, make a quick, forward somersault, and dodge his assault. Suleiman stumbled onto the dirt lying there like a beaten bull. We were all cheering for you while his humiliated gang members dragged him back to his rat hole.

"Then there was the time that we used to go to Hassan's sundry store at the street corner. You and Amira kept Hassan distracted, haggling with him endlessly over a package of imported chocolates, while Ahmed and I sneaked to the back of the store and stole candy bars and other delicacies. We used to meet up later at the schoolyard to share the loot and savor the delicious candies.

"Those were real fun days. We were innocent, worry free, adventurous, and completely oblivious to our poverty and inferior living conditions. As long as we had each other, a bed to sleep, food to eat, we were the happiest kids on earth. Sometimes I wish we could relive these wonderful, carefree days. After you left Baghdad, things were never the same."

The President was quiet for a few long seconds, looking at Chaled with a curious stare. Then as if a light bulb had lit up in his brain, he rose and embraced Chaled, kissing him on both cheeks and acknowledging their old friendship. They continued reminiscing about the good old days for several minutes. When Aziz inquired about his old friends and their whereabouts, Chaled filled him in on what had transpired during the years of his absence.

Before the next benevolent donor was ushered to meet Aziz, Chaled looked at him hesitantly. "We were wondering why we never heard from you. Why didn't you come back for Amira?"

"My uncle was a very strict man," Aziz replied. "He did not allow me to leave Basra or write to anybody. I had to work very hard at school and then help with the house chores every day. It was very oppressive.

"When I finally had the opportunity to come to Baghdad to visit you, the entire neighborhood had changed, and nobody knew where you were."

"Do you remember your friend Ali?" Chaled continued. "A few years after you left, Ali became a very successful real estate developer. He helped my family move to a nice suburb of Baghdad and took me under his wing. I became a civil engineer, and have been working for Ali's construction company ever since. I'm one of his top executives now. Ali is on a business trip to Saudi Arabia now, but he sends you his warm regards and hopes to see you during your next visit to Iraq."

* * * *

Aziz was petrified by the sudden appearance of his childhood friend who had taken him so completely by surprise. Denying their acquaintance would have only raised more suspicion. It would have been harmless if it were just Chaled, but Ali's intimate knowledge of Aziz's family history put the PA president in an extremely precarious position.

He'd never dreamt that Ali would maintain relations with his old friends because Ali had barely known them when they were growing up. If Chaled found out the truth about him, he would bring him down without hesitation. Chaled had never forgiven him for fooling around with his sister, and the fact that Aziz had never come back for her wasn't in his favor. Now his entire future hinged on the loyalty of the son of his mother's old housemaid, a man Aziz's father had saved from certain death. He wondered if Ali would protect his life for the second time, for this time the circumstances were very different.

CHAPTER 42

Even though the peace process brought tranquility and signaled the beginning of economic recovery for Israel, the opposition remained firm. Opponents claimed that Harel was giving away Israel's land and security without viable assurances from the Palestinians to keep the peace and refrain from violence. The opposition held several huge demonstrations against Harel and the PLO peace agreement.

Supporters of the government's peace efforts decided to counter the opposition's demonstrations by mounting their own show of support in a major rally for Harel's government and the peace process.

On a pleasant fall evening, tens of thousands of Harel's supporters gathered in Tel Aviv's municipal square to honor him for his courage and wisdom and to reaffirm their confidence in his leadership. Following an emotionally moving speech by Harel, the festivities continued with singing and dancing.

As Harel was ushered to his armored limousine at the conclusion of the rally, a lone gunman opened fire on him, injuring him seriously. Harel was rushed to a nearby hospital where doctors worked frantically to save his life.

The gunman, a right-wing religious extremist, wanted to put an end to the peace process and thought that he could achieve his goal by murdering the Prime Minister. Extremist religious leaders who called Harel a traitor and his government a destructive institution were behind the incitement. During opposition demonstrations, Harel was portrayed as a Nazi officer, the most distasteful image to any individual of the Jewish faith. Some of the slogans called to oust him with blood and fire.

Aziz was spending a quiet evening at home with his wife and young son, Saed. He loved playing with Saed, now an energetic toddler who loved running around and playing hide-and-seek with his dad. When Aziz identified Saed's hideout, Aziz would surprise him, pick him up, and twirl him around, saying, "I caught you, little munchkin. You are my prisoner now. I won't let you go until I get three kisses from you." Saed always giggled cheerfully as he tried to wiggle out of his father's tight grasp.

While Saed was busy playing with his dad, Leila took the opportunity to enjoy a much-needed rest from her busy schedule with her active son, but tonight she suddenly appeared in the living room, a worried look on her face. "Aziz, you have an urgent call from Ebrahim on the red line," she murmured, half asleep.

Aziz rushed to the phone.

"Sorry to bother you, Mr. President," Ebrahim's voice was hesitant. "We just got news that there was an assassination attempt on the Israeli PM. It appears Harel was hit by the assassin and rushed to a hospital in Tel Aviv. We are not yet certain of his condition."

"This is very bad news, Ebrahim," Aziz responded sadly. "I was fearful that some Israeli fanatic would resort to a desperate act after all the political moves to halt the momentum of peace failed." Aziz's mind was racing to analyze the immediate implications of the event. "If Harel dies," Aziz continued, "there are going to be major setbacks to the peace agreement we've worked so hard to conclude and have made so much progress on in the past several months. The Israelis are most probably going to have new elections, and all our hard work could go down the drain."

"That is exactly what the assassin was trying to accomplish," Ebrahim acknowledged. "The extreme right vowed to use any means to try to sabotage the peace process and prevent the Israeli forces from evacuating the territories. Apparently this includes trying to assassinate the PM and topple the government."

"Let's pray that Harel will come out of it alive and we can continue the implementation of the agreements," Aziz expressed his wistful hope. "I will be there in fifteen minutes. Please convene the council for an urgent session to discuss this distressing development."

Aziz updated Leila on the sad news and left in a hurry. He sank into the back of his armored limousine very pensive and upset by the setback. He felt a sense of unique closeness to and admiration for Harel. During their numerous private meetings, they'd developed a very special, warm relationship. Although Harel was entirely aware of Aziz's identity, he'd never showed even a hint of his awareness and always conducted the meetings in a professional, friendly atmosphere.

For Aziz, Harel had become the father figure he'd never had growing up. Harel was older, wiser, and very authoritative. Aziz saw Harel's genuine commitment to improving the quality of life for the Israeli population and to creating an atmosphere of peace and harmony between the two nations. Harel was a very smart, ethical leader, a decorated general who'd fought many wars but wanted to give the new generation the promise of peace and prosperity.

When Aziz arrived at the council meeting room, the council members were just starting to gather. Ebrahim told him that there had been no further updates, but they were monitoring the news closely and would inform him as soon as new developments were reported.

When most of the members were present, Aziz opened the meeting. "I called this emergency council meeting due to some disturbing news that may affect the peace process with Israel. If you have not heard yet, an attempt was made on the life of Prime Minister Harel as he was leaving a peace rally in Tel Aviv. Harel is presently hospitalized in what is described as critical condition. I will inform you of his status as soon as we have more current information.

"This incident may have significant ramifications for the peace process. If Harel does not survive, we may be soon facing new elections in Israel. New elections may bring about a right-wing government that will try to back out of the progress we have worked so hard to maintain over the last several months. We need to develop contingency plans for that possibility and prepare our military to renew the armed struggle if necessary.

"Our main goal will be to continue the negotiations and start the implementation of phase two of the comprehensive agreement that was signed recently at the White House. This will include the gradual withdrawal of Israeli forces from all the major urban areas in the West Bank and the handing over of control of all these areas to the Palestinian Authority.

"It may take some time for the dust to settle from the assassination attempt, so we will have to be patient and considerate of the situation. If a new government is established and refuses to cooperate with us, we will have to apply political as well as military pressure to compel the Israelis to continue the negotiations.

"I would like the political and military committees to convene tomorrow morning to consider all the options and submit their recommendations to me. As for now, we can all go home and pray for Harel's well-being."

At four the following morning, the red phone rang again. It was Ebrahim reporting that Harel had died a few minutes earlier. Even though a team of surgeons had worked around the clock to save his life, the assassin had gotten his way. He'd confessed to the crime, saying he'd acted on God's orders and did not regret killing the Prime Minister.

Aziz was devastated; he felt that his mission was in jeopardy and that he was back to square one. All the years of intense effort and preparation might come to nothing. With Harel gone, he feared a new opposition government could reverse all the progress made to date. If they were willing to murder their own revered leader to avoid peace, what fate would await him as their perceived enemy? Where would this event leave him and the Palestinian people? He would hate to return to violence against his own people and renew the armed conflict with Israel. Also, would he be trapped in his role as PA President without ever having a chance to return home?

Aziz was beleaguered by the many questions flooding his mind and the uncertainty created by the huge void left both by Harel's untimely departure and the new potential threats stemming from his past in Iraq.

* * * *

The assassination of its leader left the Israeli government in total disarray. The moderate government officials who took over for Harel tried desperately to keep the government together, but eventually the weak coalition fell apart and new elections were declared.

CHAPTER 43

Uzi Granit, the Mossad Deputy, had recently been appointed to the helm of the Mossad. His appointment came despite the incident of the private jet skyjacking that had marred his immaculate record. He was a dedicated, hardworking individual with twenty-five years of outstanding service in the organization.

As the new Mossad Chief, Granit was in a superior position to control the actions of his lethal institution. He followed Aziz's rise to the PLO's leadership with much resentment. Aziz's new high-ranking appointment meant that he was safe from the scheming of Mossad assassination attempts, because Granit was bound by the convention that excluded national leaders from being targeted by the Mossad.

However, he'd never forgotten the humiliation he'd suffered in the aftermath of the private jet skyjacking. He'd been so confident in the operation's success and all the indications that his foe would walk down the steps of that jet after it landed. He couldn't stand the thought that someone had outsmarted him and made him look like a fool in front of his men and superiors.

Granit was also embittered by the "progress" made by the peace process. Deep inside he opposed it vehemently, but he had to abide by his government's democratic decisions. He felt that his beloved country was being handed over to the Palestinians with total disregard for the security of the Jewish population. He never trusted the Palestinians or their leaders because he had no doubt that their true ultimate goal was the destruction of Israel and the annihilation of its entire Jewish population, even in the face of President Aziz making far-reaching reforms in the Palestinian Authority, repressing terrorism, and implementing economic reforms that could benefit Israel immensely.

Aziz may have been able to fool the Israeli leadership, but he wasn't going to fool him. Granit was confident that the peace treaty was only part of a planned strategy by Aziz to take over the state of Israel in progressive phases. What the Palestinians and the Arab world failed to achieve by waging war on Israel for almost fifty years they were being handed on a golden tray with a false pledge for peace.

Granit decided to take advantage of the leadership void created in the aftermath of Harel's murder. It was time for him to take matters into his own hands and save his country from future destruction. He recognized that President Aziz had the leadership traits and charisma to advance the peace process and lead the creation of a Palestinian state. Without his uniting force and eloquent political skills, the Palestinian Authority would disintegrate in no time.

It was time for him to get Aziz out of the way and bring the peace process to a crumbling halt. He could easily make Aziz's death look like it had been caused by a rival Palestinian extremist group because of its strong opposition to the compromise peace agreement he'd signed with Israel.

Granit decided to waste no more time and to put the wheels in motion to eradicate his sworn enemy.

* * * *

In the elections held in Israel three months later, the right-wing parties gained the upper hand and were able to form a new conservative government that was opposed to many of the concessions made toward the Palestinians by Harel's government. The new leadership was reluctant to resume direct talks with the Palestinians and used delay tactics to stall the implementation of the peace agreement signed by their predecessors.

President Aziz made repeated attempts to arrange a private meeting with the new Israeli PM, Arie Shomron, but Shomron ignored all of his requests.

Aziz conducted a thorough self-examination of the situation, comparing it to the objectives he'd been assigned upon departing on his secret mission. Before Harel died, Aziz had been very close to fulfilling most of his mission's goals, an outstanding achievement beyond all expectations.

With the reality created in the aftermath of Harel's death, he had felt his mission was concluded. It wasn't his responsibility to carry on forever and deal with the continuous uncertainty of the Israeli political landscape.

He had sacrificed over two decades of his life to the mission. He had missed the opportunity to build a family in Israel that would continue the traditions and heritage of his ancestors. Instead, he was married to a Palestinian woman and raising a Moslem son. What kind of a legacy would he leave behind? This certainly wasn't what his mother had predicted for his future, nor was it what he had expected as the outcome when he'd left on what he'd considered a sacred mission to safeguard and better the lives of his people. He felt trapped in a hopeless role from which he would never be set free. Many restless nights made him so lethargic that he was unable to focus on his daily duties.

Aziz was discouraged by his inability to break the stalemate in the dialogue with the Israelis. He had always been able to make things happen and move the objectives of his mission forward. This was the first time he'd felt completely powerless. He was starting to lose his grip of the situation with no quick solution in sight. He sank into a state of deep depression, exacerbated by the onset of fatigue from many sleepless nights.

During the next several weeks, he started feeling his strength slowly draining out of his body. He developed flu-like symptoms that manifested themselves in general weakness, aches and pains in the joints, coughing, and headaches. Leila urged him to see his personal doctor who ordered a series of blood tests which revealed a higher than normal level of white blood cells. The doctor prescribed antibiotics to fight his mysterious infection.

Leila kept a close watch over him. She kept encouraging him, cooking his favorite dishes, and making sure he drank plenty of fluids. However, the antibiotics weakened Aziz even further. Over time, his illness started affecting his memory and bodily motor functions, which slowed him down considerably and started to impair his judgment. His condition deteriorated to a level that was affecting his ability to govern the PA and make sound decisions. His condition couldn't remain undetected for much longer, which would raise doubts of his ability to lead his people.

Leila summoned his doctor for an emergency consultation. The doctor recommended sending Aziz to a world-renowned private clinic in Switzerland where he could secretly undergo a series of diagnostic tests to determine the nature of his illness. As the clinic treated many world leaders who suffered from varying illnesses, it was geared to keep their treatments in strict confidentiality.

Aziz was very irritated by his debilitating illness. He had always been as healthy as an ox. He never felt so weak or drained out. He asked Leila to summon Ebrahim to see him immediately.

Ebrahim realized the seriousness of the situation and concurred with the doctor's recommendations. He arranged to fly Aziz to Switzerland to undergo a complete physical evaluation. Ebrahim was determined to keep the President's illness a secret in order to avoid instability and prevent possible actions by radicals who would try to take advantage of the situation. He knew that President Aziz's downfall at this stage of the game could lead to the disintegration of the government Aziz had so skillfully put in place. They were finally on the right path to achieving their national goals, and the government was very effective in performing its functions. Aziz's illness needed to be resolved quickly to maintain stability and continue to sustain the progress he had brought to the Palestinian people.

Leila asked to join Aziz on his journey to nurture and support him during his time of dire need, but Aziz told her it would serve his purpose better if she stayed at home with Saed and pretended that everything was normal. Aziz explained that it was vital to avoid suspicion that anything was wrong with him. Officially, he was simply leaving to Switzerland on business to discuss funding for major industrial projects in the Palestinian territories.

Leila reluctantly agreed to her husband's request. As a wife of a Moslem leader, she realized she had to abide by her husband's wishes. She had to play the role of the obedient wife and not appear argumentative.

In Switzerland, Aziz underwent a series of tests at the clinic. The doctors detected some irregularities with his blood tests, but nothing was conclusive with regard to a diagnosis. Expert hematologists were summoned to the clinic to further examine the blood work data and try to make a more accurate diagnosis. After another week of intense consultations and an additional series of blood tests, the medical director of the clinic informed Aziz that they suspected he was suffering from a rare form of blood disease called hypereosinophilic syndrome, or HES, which might in fact be a form of cancer.

"HES develops when the level of white blood cells in the blood stream rises to abnormal levels," the clinic director explained, "The body produces large amounts of white blood cells as a reaction to allergies or certain parasites that may have been introduced into the blood stream. Elevated levels of white blood cells can lead to heart failure and negatively affect other vital organs, often leading to death. HES is a rare disorder, occurring in fewer than one in every one hundred thousand people per year. It also almost always affects men."

The doctors informed Aziz that fortunately, a drug that had already shown promise in the treatment of other forms of leukemia had been used successfully to treat patients with HES. These patients, including some who were very ill, had responded extremely well to the drug, although exactly how the drug kept the aggressive disease under control was still a mystery.

"We are confident that we can use this drug to put your disease into remission within two to three weeks," the director told Aziz, "but we are not always sure how long the remission will last."

Aziz was relieved by the relatively good news. His condition was so grave that he'd almost lost hope of recovery. He asked the director several questions to try to understand the diagnosis and its possible causes as best he could. He was interested in finding out more about patients who had suffered from the same condition and how long they were able to live and function normally. The director promised Aziz to research the matter and to provide him with answers as promptly as possible.

His new drug treatment started immediately, and within a week, Aziz started feeling better. He gained some of his strength back, his facial coloring became brighter, and his appetite returned with a vengeance. He was on the phone with Leila every evening reporting the progress of his miraculous recovery and chatting gibberish with Saed. Subsequent blood tests showed a significant reduction in his white blood cell count, which was edging close to normal. However, the doctors ordered Aziz to stay at the clinic for two more weeks under close observation so he could build up his stamina.

The clinic's director informed Aziz that in eighty percent of the cases, patients with HES were able to resume a normal lifestyle, but they had to remain under close medical supervision and obtain periodic blood tests to make sure they didn't suffer setbacks. Fifteen percent of the patients reported renewed symptoms within several months, but they recovered completely after several regimens of the drug. The mortality rate from HES stood at only around five percent. Aziz was pleased by the director's report, for it gave him high hopes for a complete recovery.

CHAPTER 44

Four weeks from the date of his initial departure, Aziz was back to his old self. His blood work and body scans were completely normal. The doctors released him and he was home in no time, making passionate love to Leila and enjoying his time with Saed.

Aziz felt rejuvenated, almost like a newborn baby. He sensed that he had been given back the gift of life by Divine intervention. He had to complete his mission successfully and not despair in the face of mounting obstacles.

With renewed vigor, he intensified his efforts to restart the peace negotiations with the Israeli government through pressure from the United States and its European allies. He sent envoys to the influential Arab states, asking them to use their power within the U.S. administration to bring the Israelis back to the negotiating table.

He also continued to improve the productivity of the PA governing agencies in preparation for the second phase of the peace accord. These agencies were to utilize the constant flow of aid funds to create new jobs, expand the infrastructure in the Palestinian controlled areas, and significantly improve the living standards of the Palestinian people. This issue had been the central theme of his election campaign, and he had every intention of delivering on his promise to the people.

However, the new Israeli right-wing government stood its ground with uncompromising stubbornness. All Aziz's attempts to renew the dialogue with the new Israeli PM, Arie Shomron, were sternly refused.

It was a complete reversal from the position of Harel's government and the spirit of the signed peace accords. The new government's position with regard to the territories was that this was part of the land promised to the Israelites by God, something that would never change. There were rumors that new plans were underway to expand the existing Jewish settlements in the West Bank, which without a doubt would bring back hostilities and cause a civil uprising.

The new government's position was clearly in contradiction with the mission goals presented to Aziz when he'd embarked on his mission. His main objectives had been to neutralize violence, steer the Palestinians into normalized relations, and create an atmosphere of cooperation and economic prosperity. Now these new policies appeared to be on a collision course with everything Aziz had accomplished so far. They could only lead to escalation of the conflict and renewed violence.

Aziz felt that with the shift in the wind of opportunity for peace, his actions might not represent the best interests of the new Israeli government. His hard labor of more than two decades that had put his very being on the line was no longer relevant to the new leadership. The rules of engagement had been altered significantly. His handlers had no means of contacting him to change the nature of his mission or provide him with a clear direction of what was now expected of him.

This could only mean one thing: for all practical purposes, his mission was over.

He could no longer take responsibility for the killing of innocent Jewish civilians by ordering new terrorist missions designed to revive the peace process. His conscience could not carry such a heavy burden.

If he didn't take any action against the Israelis in the face of the continued stalemate and renewed efforts to expand Jewish settlements in the territories, he would come under intense criticism from his own people, be forced to step down, or be assassinated by his enemies within.

His childhood in Baghdad was back to haunt him, resting against his throat like a sharp *hanjar*. Ali could disclose his Jewish identity at any given moment. Aziz could be arrested for treason without warning and without having a chance to escape. He feared he would face the same fate as his predecessor, Eli Cohen.

Leila seemed to sense his tensions and anguish and tried to encourage him not to despair, but to fight back and take charge of the situation as he'd always done. He was the rock of the Palestinian people, and only he was capable of spinning the wheels, renewing hope, and turning the Israelis around. She urged him to arrange a face-to-face meeting with Shomron and persuade him of the genuine intention of the Palestinian Authority to live in peace and security with the Israelis. "Your wisdom and compassionate personality will convince him that the future is bright for both nations living together side by side. You will build up strong relations with the Israelis and earn their trust. Without you, we are going to sink back to bloodshed, tragedy, and deep despair."

Leila lavished on him her love and affection, and tried to get Saed to re-ignite the spark in Aziz's eyes, but he seemed to shut his thoughts and feelings deep inside, confining them to himself.

In his frenzied search for a way out of his trap, Aziz suddenly recalled the escape route Shaffir had arranged for him. If he somehow could reach Switzerland and access the safe deposit box, he could retrieve his documents and regain his Israeli identity.

He longed for the peacefulness of cultivating the grain fields of Deganya on his tractor, the fresh smell of earth spiraling under the blades of his plow, the cool breeze in the spring and fall, and the searing heat during the summers. He imagined spending time with fellow kibbutz members in the dining room discussing world politics and plans to continue the development of the kibbutz enterprises. On weekends, he would spend most his hours on the shores of the Sea of Galilee, dipping into its serene, sparkling blue waters and letting his body soak in the radiant energy of the sun.

"How long did Shaffir and Harel expect me to stay on this mission?" he asked himself. "They never stated a time frame for my return." With both men gone, he would never know the answer.

"I devoted more than twenty years to this mission," he thought. "It's time for me to come home and be with the people I've worked so hard to protect all these years."

He was hoping that the safe deposit box in the bank in Basel was still waiting for him. He had been told that the Mossad never abandoned its dedicated agents and always kept an open escape route for them.

Aziz decided to leave politics to the talented Israeli politicians and let them figure out a solution to the conflict. He would return to Deganya and settle there permanently.

However, as a person of international fame and the leader of the newly established Palestinian Authority, Aziz faced major obstacles to his return. He couldn't simply disappear from the face of the earth one day and show up in Israel the next. There were issues of how to make his disappearance from the scene appear normal. Moreover, what arrangements could he make for his succession to assure continuity of the progress he had made in normalizing relations with Israel and bringing stability to the entire Middle East?

Aziz thought that the best way to exit the scene would be to somehow stage his sudden death and disappear without a trace. He slowly started formulating a plan to carry out his decision in a manner that would make his demise appear an unfortunate accident.

He planned to initiate a trip to Europe on very short notice. He would inform Ebrahim that he had received an urgent call from the Swiss authorities that they needed to meet him in Geneva at once to finalize funding for a major industrial project. He would board his private Lear jet on a night flight to Switzerland with only his personal bodyguard and pilot.

During the flight, he would slip a dose of a powerful tranquilizer into the drinks of his bodyguard and pilot to sedate them. He would then take over piloting the plane to its destination. While over Switzerland, he would disable the plane's black box and set the autopilot on a course towards the Mediterranean Sea. Using the plane's specially installed emergency ejection mechanism, he would parachute down over the open farmlands of Switzerland.

The plane would lose radio contact with ground control, disappear from the radar screens, run out of fuel, and sink into the deep waters of the Mediterranean without a trace. The incident would be attributed to pilot error or equipment malfunction and he and his crew would be considered lost.

In Switzerland, he would use a disguise and clothing prepared in advance to travel to Basel and retrieve his papers from the safe deposit box. With his papers in hand, he would be able to approach the Israeli embassy in Switzerland, identify himself, and arrange for his return home.

Aziz was deeply torn about leaving Leila and Saed behind. Even though he'd decided to marry Leila for convenience, his emotional attachment to her and their son had grown stronger over time. He knew that his separation from them would be extremely difficult. He wished he could take them with him and start a new chapter in their lives. He was tempted to approach Leila secretly, reveal his identity, and persuade her to join him. He was trying to imagine the look on her face after hearing the shocking news.

Aziz knew that once he revealed himself, there would be no way back, and if Leila reacted adversely, she might expose him. Confiding in her was just too much of a risk to undertake when the outcome might prove very tragic.

After his demise, he was confident Ebrahim would be elected as the new President and take the reins of the PA leadership. Ebrahim was the most qualified leader to take his place. He would be the one to continue the struggle with the Israelis and try to break the stalemate.

Aziz started refining his plan and making the final preparations for its execution. He felt a great relief now that his mind was made up and his preparations almost complete.

* * * *

As the time to carry out his escape plan drew near, Aziz started noticing that some of his earlier symptoms were troubling him again. He dismissed the warning signs as a common cold and was sure they would go away soon. He was eager to get the Chairman-X episode behind him, open a new chapter in his life, and make the most of the years he had left.

Several days went by and the symptoms only appeared to worsen. Aziz remembered that his doctor had told him that the symptoms might return after a while. He recalled the doctor's explanation that the cause of his illness might have been a result of certain parasites being introduced into his bloodstream.

During his Mossad training, he'd learned and practiced methods of eliminating enemy officials by slow poisoning. The poison was introduced through food or drink ingested by the victim over time to make it look like an illness that progressively got worse, leading to a natural death. This method was used to avoid suspicion of the Mossad's involvement in the assassination of such officials. It was a slow kill that brought a lot of pain and suffering on the victim.

Aziz started suspecting that Abu Zayad had somehow been able to penetrate his organization and plant an undercover agent who was poisoning his food. Due to his busy schedule, he ate lunch and most dinners at his HQ. "They must be slipping the poison into my food in the kitchen," he thought to himself. "No wonder I got better at the Swiss clinic. The conspirators couldn't get to me, and the poison started being purged from my bloodstream." Aziz knew that for the poison to work effectively, it had to be continually administered; if it was stopped, the victim could recover.

Before unleashing Ebrahim and his men on the suspects, Aziz decided to test his theory. He started avoiding the foods served to him at his HQ, slipping out of his compound for lunch and eating dinners mostly at home. He also had his food tested randomly several times, but nothing showed up.

When his condition didn't improve even with avoidance of food served to him at his HQ, and the food screening gave negative results, Aziz dismissed his

Abu Zayad theory and concluded that his illness was back.

Leila also was urging him to consult with the doctors at the Swiss clinic. His remission could have lapsed and he might have to get his treatments renewed. This time she insisted on accompanying him on his trip so she could be his nurse.

Aziz was too weak to execute his escape plan and had no choice but to defer it until such time that he would feel better, if there was still hope of one. Ebrahim made all the secret arrangements for his second trip to the clinic. This time Leila accompanied him leaving Saed in the trusted hands of his nanny.

His highly elevated white blood cell count proved that his HES had returned. The doctors started his drug treatment immediately, expecting an improvement within days. Leila nursed him around the clock, staying by his side like a lioness protecting her cub. She kept encouraging him, feeding him his favorite foods that he hardly ate due to a lack of appetite, and hydrating him with plenty of fluids. When he slept, she took short catnaps on the large reclining armchair next to his bed.

Despite his treatment and Leila's nurturing, Aziz's condition continued to deteriorate. The doctors started losing hope, concluding that his case might fall into the five percent of patients who couldn't recover from the disease. All they could do was watch him closely and hope for a miracle.

CHAPTER 45

It was a routine practice for the Mossad to retrieve unclaimed agent safe deposit boxes every several years to reexamine their contents and update any necessary documentation, including cash, passports, driver's license, and other essential papers. Boxes were returned in their original sealed packaging to the Mossad deputy's office for speedy processing.

The Mossad deputy was responsible for opening the boxes, checking their contents with the original list, updating legal documents, adding currency as needed, and if necessary, returning them quickly to the original location. In fact the contents were rarely returned because very few safe deposit boxes were issued, and in most cases, the agents had had to use them at some point when their cover was blown or their mission was over. When it was determined that the agent no longer needed the safe deposit box, its contents were distributed back to the original issuing departments within the Mossad.

When the Mossad deputy arrived at his office one summer morning, his secretary informed him that the

Mossad treasurer was waiting to see him. The treasurer walked into his office and placed a safe deposit box on top of his desk.

"When I ran an audit of our safety deposit boxes last month," he said, "I discovered a record of a box that had been issued some twenty years ago to an agent operating in Europe. It was placed in a bank in Basel, Switzerland. For some odd reason, it had never been retrieved for an update. I asked our people in Switzerland to dispatch it back for examination. I am sorry it took a while to get here, but it's all yours now," the treasurer noted apologetically and left.

The deputy opened the box carefully. He found $10,000 in cash, a passport, an international driver's license, and a second sealed envelope. He looked at the photo in the passport. He couldn't place the person in the picture, even though it bore a vague resemblance to someone he might have known. "The picture has to be over twenty years old," he thought. "I wouldn't be able to recognize this agent." He started wondering what had happened to the agent, why he had never used the contents of the box, and why the box hadn't been emptied when his mission was over.

With increased curiosity, he quickly unsealed the second envelope. It contained several pages folded together. He unfolded the pages, which were well preserved in the airtight envelope. Stapled to the first page was the same photo as in the passport. The first page was titled: Authentication of identity for Colonel (Reserve) Reuben Sasson, Mossad agent. He continued reading the text. 'This is to certify that Mr. Reuben

Sasson, a Mossad agent and highly decorated IDF Colonel, was sent on a highly secret, covert mission to penetrate the ranks of the PLO. Due to the highly sensitive nature of his mission, he underwent several plastic surgery procedures to change his facial features. This letter certifies that the person in the photo attached to this document is indeed Mr. Reuben Sasson. His original identification papers are attached for additional verification of his identity before his surgery."

The deputy quickly flipped through the other documents, which included an Israeli Government official ID card, an Israeli Passport, a set of fingerprints, a certificate of IDF service and discharge, two IDF wartime decoration certificates with medals attached, and a Mossad ID card.

He looked at the photos in the older documents. These looked even less familiar than the first photo he had seen. He was very puzzled by the mystery of Reuben Sasson. He continued reading: "In the event Mr. Sasson's mission terminates prematurely, he will return to Israel and report to Mossad headquarters. Mr. Sasson is to be treated with the utmost respect due a hero who has sacrificed everything in his life for the sake of his country. He is to be fully reinstated with the Mossad and receive a pension from both the Mossad and the IDF. Due to the extreme sensitivity of his mission, all his personal records in the Ministry of Interior, IDF, and Mossad have been removed. However, these papers constitute an unquestionable proof of his original identity."

The document was signed by Major General (Reserve) Abraham Shaffir, Mossad Chief, and stamped with the official Mossad seal.

The deputy recalled that Shaffir had passed away of a heart attack two years earlier so he wouldn't be able to help him resolve the mystery.

In desperation for a quick answer, he picked up the contents of the box and walked it to the office of the Mossad Chief, Uzi Granit.

Granit was surprised by his deputy's unexpected appearance.

"I am sorry to interrupt you, Chief, but I think I have found something of significant importance that is very puzzling. Have you heard of a Mossad agent by the name of Reuben Sasson?"

"I don't believe I have," Granit answered. "The name doesn't sound familiar at all."

The deputy opened the documents and showed his boss the photo on the documents. "Do you recognize the person in this photo?" he asked.

Granit looked at the photo carefully and said, "It bears a vague resemblance to someone I might have known, but I can't place him with any degree of certainty."

The deputy poured the entire contents of the safe deposit box on the table and let the Chief read through all the documents.

"Very interesting," Granit commented looking at his deputy pensively. "I wonder what became of this mysterious Reuben Sasson. Quite a remarkable individual, I must say. Two wartime medals, including the Medal of Valor, are incredibly impressive.

"I don't recall Shaffir ever mentioning anything about him. I agree this mystery must be brought to a quick conclusion," Granit continued. "Why don't you convene some of our veteran officers this afternoon? Let's see if someone can throw some light on the case."

However to the deputy's disappointment, none of the officers in the meeting recognized the person in the photo or remembered the name Reuben Sasson.

The following day, the officer in charge of the Mossad PLO section who had operated cells in Beirut for many years stepped into the deputy's office.

"I just wanted to mention something to you about our meeting yesterday on that Sasson character," he said. "I didn't want to sound stupid in front of everybody. Don't you think that photo resembles that of the President of the Palestinian Authority, Abdul Aziz Al-Wasphi? If you add the moustache and the speckles of gray hair on his temples to the old photo, I would say the resemblance is compelling.

"When I was in charge of the Beirut cell, he was the deputy commander of Force 17. He was a lot younger then, and I remember some of his photos from those days. He looked a lot more like the photo we saw yesterday. We even went after him a couple of times, but he managed to outmaneuver us, the slimy bastard."

"Thank you, I will look further into this," the deputy replied, dismissing the officer. "I will let you know if I need more help on this. For now, please keep your idea to yourself. Not a word to anybody."

The deputy felt like he had been struck by lightning. The man had turned a light bulb on in his brain. He knew that face had looked somewhat familiar, but he just couldn't recall it until the officer walked through his door and threw the crazy idea at him. "Could it be," he thought, with shivers running down his spine, "that Reuben Sasson is the President of the PA? Anything is possible," he thought. "The Mossad's aspirations were always to penetrate its enemy's echelon at the highest level possible." He decided to continue the investigation on his own without involving more people. If this theory could be proven, he would have to inform the Chief, and the Chief would have to inform the PM.

He sifted through old Mossad files and researched the history of Abdul Aziz Al-Wasphi from the time he'd first appeared on the Mossad radar screens in London. He compared older Mossad photos of Aziz with the ones on the recovered documents. The resemblance was astonishing. He looked up the dates for Shaffir's term as the Mossad Chief. The dates matched well with Aziz's first appearance in London.

Then he reviewed the Aziz's records since he had taken the PLO reins. He had tried very hard to eradicate the extremist terrorist groups; he had kept all the commitments on the disengagement agreements. He was working hard on joint economic programs to stimulate the Palestinian economy and improve the standard of living of his constituents. He had revamped the educational system and removed the hate language against Israel.

His overall performance on behalf of the Palestinians and in relation to Israel's expectations was excellent. Israel couldn't hope for a better Palestinian leader, particularly in view of past experiences with the untrustworthiness of past ones. The deputy concluded with a high level of confidence that Abdul Aziz must be the Mossad agent Shaffir had sent on his mission more than two decades earlier. His success in penetrating the PLO was so phenomenal that he hadn't needed to access the safe deposit box all these years.

The deputy went immediately to Granit's office to report his astounding finding. Together they reviewed the information gathered by the deputy in painstaking detail, enlisting the help of Mossad identity experts, and reached the same shocking conclusion: the popular President of the Palestinian Authority was in fact Reuben Sasson, a Mossad master spy.

Granit suddenly turned very pale and looked like he was going to get sick to his stomach. "I have to leave immediately," he barked toward his deputy. "Not a word about this to anybody until I return. I have to take care of an extremely urgent matter. I will be back in a few days. You know how to reach me."

CHAPTER 46

As Aziz became progressively weaker, he fell into a daze fading in and out of consciousness, at times not knowing where he was or who the people around him were. When his condition continued its downhill slide, the doctors had to resort to life support mechanisms to keep him alive.

One night he believed he saw a vivid presence of his mother. She was talking to him with her soft, gentle voice: "Please don't worry *ebni* Reuben, *abdalla el eunak el helluwah,* I adore your gorgeous eyes. Your father and I are here with you. We will never let you down. My prophecy will not diminish — you are already a great leader and protector of our people. You cannot imagine how many innocent souls you have redeemed with your great wisdom.

"The eternity of Israel will never fade, and neither shall you. The angel Gabriel is on his way to save you and raise you above the leaders of other nations. Your wisdom and fame will spread among God's entire kingdom, just as it was during the time of your great ancestor King Solomon. I wish I could be with you, *galbi,* but I am so delighted that the Almighty sent you a wonderful, loving wife to sweeten your life and ease your burdens. No matter what, know that your wife is your *Nasiba,* she is the one meant for you by the grace of God. Don't ever let her out of your sight."

With these words, she vanished.

Through his hallucination, Aziz sensed the image of a tall slender woman with long shimmering hair dressed in a white uniform. She was changing the IV fluids hung over his bed. She looked familiar, but his memory was betraying him as he started losing consciousness again. She caressed his face and hair with her tender hands and kissed him gently on his forehead. Her image quickly faded away, just like his mother's.

Aziz woke up the following morning unsure whether he was in heaven or on earth. The heavily starched white sheets reminded him that he was still in his bed at the clinic. He opened his eyes slowly and saw Leila sitting tensely on an armchair next to his bed. She rose quickly to his bedside, grasping his hand tightly with one arm and cuddling his face with the other.

"How are you feeling this morning, my beloved husband?" she whispered softly, kissing his sunken cheeks and forehead.

"I didn't think I was going to make it through the night," he said with a weak voice, "but for some odd reason I feel somewhat better this morning. My mother came to me in a dream last night and said that I would be getting better very soon. I hope she is right. You were in the dream too. She told me you were my *Nasiba* and never to let you leave my side. I didn't understand why she was saying that. Doesn't she know that I love you with all my heart?"

"Your mother is right, Aziz, you are getting better, and she had a very good reason to tell you about me. Please don't concern yourself with it right now. Every dream has its clues, and you will find out the answer soon. Please get some rest now. I want you to recover quickly."

Two weeks later, Aziz was back on his feet, still pale and weak but on the mend. His doctors informed him that his disease was in remission again but insisted that he take a vacation to rejuvenate before returning to his busy schedule. He and Leila spent a week at a secluded resort in the Swiss Alps away from their hectic lifestyle and nonstop phone calls, alone for the first time since their honeymoon.

On an evening before their departure home, Aziz and Leila enjoyed a lovely dinner surrounded by the spectacular views of the snow-covered mountains, listening to the soft whirling sound of the wind raising icy dust high into the crisp, cool air. After the meal, they retreated to their spacious suite for a relaxing evening. While Aziz was glancing leisurely through a magazine, Leila sneaked into the master bathroom and took a quick shower. She dried her slim, tight body, sprayed on her favorite perfume, and slipped on Aziz's favorite lingerie. Even after having Saed, she looked as attractive and vigorous as ever. She'd kept her slim, striking looks with a regimen of healthy diet and steady exercise.

She reappeared in front of Aziz, who was in bed reading

an article that caught his attention. Upon detecting the exotic fragrance of his wife, Aziz seemed to regain his old composure. He pushed the magazine aside and wrapped his arms around her, kissing her passionately. Leila squeezed her body tightly against him, clutching his head between her hands, lips jammed against his in a passionate French kiss. They made passionate love just as they had before Aziz fell ill.

As they were both lying in bed relaxing from the intensity of their passion, Leila leaned over and started kissing Aziz, whispering something softly in his ears. He couldn't quite make out what she was saying. He tried to listen more attentively. The second time it was somewhat clearer: "It is my pleasure to make your acquaintance, Mr. Reuben Sasson..."

Aziz didn't quite register what he was hearing.

Leila continued her soft whispering, "Yes, Mr. Reuben Sasson, code name Mountain Lion, meet Carmit Arazi, code name Desert Fox. The Mossad sent me to trap you with my beauty, watch your every move, and eliminate you, if you were to become a serious threat."

Aziz had a dazed stare on his face, looking at her in astonishment, unable to utter a word.

"Someone must have been watching over you all this time, Reuben, protecting you from harm and guiding your every step. Destiny rewarded us both, making us think we were making the ultimate sacrifice by marrying our sworn enemies. Instead, we married into our own faith. Saed, too, is born into our faith and destiny. I am so proud of our little angel.

"Reuben, it feels so strange to call you by your real

name, even just for a short while. I always felt there was something very exceptional about you. You always treated me with the dignity and gentle care reserved only for a royal princess. It was very hard to resist your charm, no matter who you truly were."

Aziz looked into her eyes in amazement. He was overcome by incredible emotions. Leila noticed the shiny spark returning to his striking eyes overwhelmed by a swell of tears.

Leila wiped his cheeks gently with her fingers, caressing his face.

Aziz was still gazing at her in disbelief as if she had just landed from out of space. With a broad smile on his face, he said, "I somehow knew that God sent you to be my guardian angel on my perilous mission. I thought I'd married you for the wrong reasons, yet it was all arranged up there. Now I understand what my mother was saying to me in my dream. You are my *Nasiba*, my match from heaven. I love you and our dear son more than anything on Earth.

"Carmit Arazi — fascinating name. Doesn't 'Carmit' mean a vineyard or something? You certainly produced more than your share of delicious ripe grapes to fill my life with sweetness and joy.

"I can't wait to hear your astounding story..."

CHAPTER 47

Leila started unveiling the story of her life: her happy childhood in Beirut, the tragedy that struck her family, her move to Israel, and her career with MI and the Mossad.

"I was the one behind the successful assassination of Saleh in Beirut. I know he was a good friend of yours at the time, but did you know that Saleh was the mastermind behind the hostage taking of the Israeli athletes in the Munich Olympics? The brutal murders of our eleven athletes stemmed from him.

"The Mossad was after him for a while. He was number one on the Mossad target list for the longest time, but he was well guarded and very elusive. The Mossad suffered a major setback when its agents assassinated the wrong person in Norway. It was a case of mistaken identity that led to the arrest and trial of several Mossad agents."

"I didn't know that," Aziz's voice echoed with astonishment. "He never mentioned a word about his involvement in the Munich operation."

"I didn't think you were aware of that since the PLO kept Saleh's involvement in the Munich murders a secret. They knew the Mossad was after him, and the fewer people knew about his involvement, the safer he would be. The success of the Munich operation and enormous publicity it brought to the PLO helped Saleh become the Chairman's favorite commander with a guaranteed path to the top."

"I will never forget the day of Saleh's assassination," Aziz said pensively. "The Chairman and the entire PLO command were devastated by it, including me. I don't believe this was your intention, Leila, but your actions on that day helped boost my own career within the PLO leadership and paved my way to the top."

"I am glad I could be of service to you," she continued. "Subsequent to my triumph over Saleh, followed by several other operations, I was sent back to Beirut by the Mossad Chief and planted as a permanent mole inside the PLO. I was to entrench myself in the organization and wait patiently for further orders.

"When you rose to power, I was instructed to try to court you, watch your every move, and monitor your involvement in masterminding attacks against Israel. I was to make sure you were genuine in your intentions to make a deal with Israel."

"You mean nobody knew that I was a Mossad agent?" Aziz interjected.

"Nobody told me anything," Leila replied. "Granit certainly had no clue. You were the enemy, a Mossad primary target, and my job was to get as close to you as I could."

"I can't believe Shaffir and Harel didn't pass on knowledge of my existence to their successors," Aziz blurted out angrily. "It sounds like I was completely abandoned and consequently targeted by the Mossad. They even tried to hijack the private jet I was traveling on and apprehend me. I always thought I was safe from the Mossad's long arm, but you just proved me wrong."

"It sounds like Harel relied on Shaffir to pass the word along, but Shaffir was determined to protect your identity even from our own people. With their untimely deaths, your secret was buried deep.

"It gets a lot worse than that," Leila continued.

"When you proposed to me, I was taken completely by surprise, shaken by your unexpected move. I had never intended for the relationship to go that far, and I didn't think you were ready for such a major commitment. I needed time to consult with my superiors and digest the implications of such a colossal decision. This was the reason I didn't say yes immediately and asked you for more time.

"I met the Mossad Chief in London, and he talked me into it, knowing that this was something he couldn't simply order me to do. At first, I cringed at the thought of having to marry a Palestinian Arab and become the wife of the Chairman of the PLO. Then, my burning desire for revenge took over. I realized that in my role as the wife of the PLO Chairman, I would enjoy a unique position of power to influence PLO policy and actions at the very top. I could easily extract high-level intelligence by playing the role of your loving wife. I could closely observe your activities and monitor your involvement in PLO planning activities. As your closest family member, I could also easily arrange for your demise if I was ordered to do so, or when I felt it was time to get my personal revenge.

"I knew the Mossad could never get that close to the leader of their most hostile foe. This was once-in-a-lifetime opportunity that couldn't be missed. If I had to sacrifice two or three more years of my life to get my revenge, I felt it would be well worthwhile."

"I can't believe you were willing to sleep with the enemy in total disregard for your personal respect and dignity," Aziz interrupted.

"That is a legitimate issue," Leila countered calmly. "You see, to me this was an act I was willing to follow because of the vows I made to my sister, Vivian, before she died in my arms. Just the thought of being able to smash your skull when I felt like it, as Yael did to Sisera, the Canaanite army commander in the ancient biblical story, was a very comforting and gratifying sensation.

"Mossad female coaches put great emphasis on training me to isolate physical aspects from true emotions. I was prepared to use all the means at my disposal to accomplish my mission, including my physical attributes. Since my personal objectives and those of the Mossad coincided, it was a perfect arrangement. I wanted my revenge desperately."

Leila paused for a brief moment, left the bedroom, and returned quickly with two cans of chilled juice. She handed one to Aziz and then slowly sipped the cool, refreshing nectar from the other can. She climbed onto the bed, sitting opposite Aziz with her legs crossed, giving him her mischievous smile.

"You made it easier for me, dear," she continued. "The gentle tenderness you lavished upon me, your adoring personality, good looks, heart-warming smile, romantic courtship abilities, and without doubt, your passionate lovemaking skills. This wasn't what I was told to expect from Middle Eastern men. It was a gratifying surprise."

Aziz looked at Leila with admiration.

"Leila," he said with a hint of humor, "I must admit that you had me completely fooled into believing that you were only a loving and concerned Palestinian wife dedicated to taking care of her husband. I thought I was the only one fooling the entire world and getting away with it."

"Talk about talented acting: you haven't done badly yourself, Mr. President. Acting is what we were trained to do. It's our job, making people think we are who we pretend to be. It's all about deception mixed with some magic. Making people think that they see one thing while the truth lies deeply under the surface."

"I had the Mossad Chief fooled too," Leila continued. "He thought he was imposing an enormous burden on me by asking me to agree to marry you. In reality, I have been waiting for this opportunity the entire time. I wanted to settle the score, leave everything behind, and start a new chapter in my life."

Aziz gulped down the remainder of the nectar. "This was quite rejuvenating," he thanked Leila, "but I still don't have a clue how you discovered me."

"I was just about to get into that, my dear. I am

sure you are thrilled with your newly rediscovered wife and son and curious to learn how the mystery was unraveled."

Aziz stretched out on the comfortable bed resting his head on a silky pillow. He gazed at the mystifying shapes formed by the colorful cloth cover of the large canopy bed as he waited patiently for Leila to untangle the puzzle.

Leila proceeded to describe to Aziz the events that led to his discovery by the Mossad.

"This is unbelievable," Aziz reacted in a raised voice. "I was relying on that safe deposit box to bring me home. When we reached a long stalemate with the Israelis, I lost hope and considered my mission over. I planned to stage my own death and secretly return to Israel using the papers in that box. That plan could have turned into a real disaster if I had gotten there while the contents were under review."

"And you were going to abandon Saed and me?" Leila protested.

"I didn't think a Palestinian wife and a Moslem son would be very welcome in Israel. Besides, although I hoped you wouldn't, I couldn't risk the possibility that if you discovered who I was, you would turn me in."

"It sounds like a valid excuse, Reuben. I wasn't always so sure that my act was that convincing. The story gets even more complicated," Leila continued hesitantly.

"About four months ago, shortly after Granit was promoted to the helm of the Mossad, I received a message from Carol, my high school friend from London, saying that my father had been hospitalized in a London hospital and that I needed to come and see him urgently."

"Oh, yes, I remember that trip," Aziz recalled. "You phoned me one night when I was working late with my economic advisory committee. You told me that your father was hospitalized and asked if you could leave for London the following morning. I said it was fine, and you made arrangements for the nanny to stay with Saed."

"Yes, this is the trip I was referring to," Leila acknowledged. "I traveled to London once or twice a year to submit reports to my Mossad handlers. I am sure you remember my trips to London to visit my family and do my shopping. I enjoyed my London shopping spree. It was a rare opportunity for me to take a short break from my duties as a mother and the busy wife of the President of the Palestinian Authority. Wearing my wig and sunglasses, I was free to roam the famous London department stores without attracting much attention.

"It was too risky for me to transmit information to the Mossad in any other way. I rarely met any Mossad people on my trips. It was far too dangerous. I dropped my reports into a safe deposit box at a designated London bank, did my shopping, and came back home. If the Mossad wanted to get in touch with me, they had to leave me a coded message that my high school friend, Carol, had called and wanted me to meet her for lunch.

"At any rate, 'Carol' is the code name for a Mossad agent operating in Britain who served as the liaison between the Mossad and me. She was my only contact with the outside world. I wasn't allowed to communicate with anybody but Carol or make any secret transmissions or phone calls for fear of discovery by PLO counterintelligence. This Mossad policy was implemented due to the events that led to Eli Cohen's capture in Damascus in the sixties."

"It sounds like we were both operating under similar procedures," Aziz noted with frustration, "except I wasn't allowed to contact anybody, period. My identity was so well preserved that even the Mossad lost track of me."

"You must have felt so alone with this tremendous burden on your shoulders," Leila told him, identifying with Aziz's exasperation.

"Granit, the new Mossad chief, wanted to meet with me privately to deliver a very important message without the knowledge of any other intermediaries," she continued. "He asked Carol to set up an urgent meeting between us. The day after my arrival in London, Carol scheduled a lunch at a small restaurant outside London. She and Granit, disguised as an English couple, met me there.

"I enjoyed lunch, chatting and exchanging opinions with Carol on the most fashionable London boutiques. After lunch, Carol excused herself, and Granit unveiled to me his ostentatious plan to eliminate you and plunge the PLO into total disarray.

"He told me that these were strict orders approved by the highest authority and that I needed to strictly adhere to all his instructions. I am certain that Granit knew from reading my dossier that the PLO murdered my sister and suspected that I had my own personal agenda to balance the score, although I never revealed the facts surrounding Vivian's murder during my interviews with the Mossad. I feared I would be disqualified from service because of emotional attachments that could potentially impair my judgment.

"I discovered later that Mossad investigators interviewed my family friends in London and learned the details of the incident from them. The subject of Vivian's murder was never raised by any of my handlers, but they must have liked my double motivation factor.

"I was to eliminate you by a gradual poisoning that would cause a slow and miserable death. Mossad scientists had developed a chemical poisoning agent that simulated the symptoms of a rare blood disease."

"Dear Almighty God, you were the one poisoning me all this time," Aziz drew away from her, almost to the edge of the bed. "I suspected some sort of poisoning the whole time, but I was sure Abu Zayad was behind it. After my recovery from the initial illness, I remembered my Mossad training sessions about poisoning techniques used by the KGB and others. I thought it was odd that I got better while I was away and started getting sick again soon after returning home. I started avoiding all the meals in the office and even had my food tested, not suspecting for a second that you could be behind it."

Leila broke down in tears. She wrapped her arms around Aziz, clinging to him frantically, her body shuddering with uncontrolled outbursts.

"I am so sorry, Reuben," she mumbled in a broken voice. "Please forgive me. I didn't know any better. You were a symbol of evil, a villain I was determined to destroy. I came damn close to it..."

Aziz turned away from her to face the window. He lay there motionless, gazing out at the snow-covered mountains in the distance, unable to respond to Leila's pleadings. His mind retraced the events that led to his mysterious illness, probing how despite his strong suspicion he'd failed to identify the source of his poisoning. He realized that most men who had been so betrayed would respond with extreme anger, even violence. But he wasn't most men. For so many years, he had been suppressing his natural emotions so that he could be convincing in his role. Before now, this skill he'd developed had seemed a bad thing that alienated him from his true self, but now it allowed his mind to take control of his instincts.

Leila had been acting under orders, just as he had been — orders that erroneously had come from the same organization that had sent him on his mission. What if she had stood in his way to the Chairmanship? Would he have abandoned his duty, or looked at her death at his hands as just another sacrifice that duty demanded?

He sighed. Another way to look at it was that it wasn't really him she'd been poisoning, but the person he'd pretended to be and perhaps played too well. Once she finally knew the truth, she'd done everything she could to reverse the damage and save him.

After a long time, he turned back to her. "Carmit, I know it's not your fault." He put his arms around her and stroked her back gently. "You were acting under strict orders and following the unrestrained need for revenge in your heart. I can't blame you for that. It's inconceivable for me to think of you, my adorable faithful wife, as a vicious python poised for the final kill, but that is a role you were forced to take. Bless the Almighty for stopping you at the last minute from carrying out the plan. My soul was already on its way to heaven, but they were not quite ready for me up there. I must still be needed here."

He laughed as she snuggled even closer. "I am glad you are on my side now, Carmit. The opposite proved quite lethal to numerous PLO leaders. I was lucky to escape your wrath in time."

"We are both fortunate that you were discovered before it was too late," she comforted him. "I don't think I was ready after all for the role of the President's widow."

"It wouldn't surprise me if the Mossad was planning for you to take over after my death," he speculated. "I think the Palestinian people may be ready for a woman leader."

"That option was definitely not in my cards," she dismissed the idea, "and I don't think anybody would have been able to persuade me otherwise."

They lay quietly together for a few minutes. "So tell me then how you outsmarted me," he said, laughing ruefully.

"My instructions were to administer doses of the chemical agent daily and increase the dose gradually over time. The poison was in the form of a pill that would dissolve quickly in liquids. I served it to you every morning during breakfast, which was the only meal we had together alone most days."

Aziz brushed his smooth black hair backwards with his fingers. "I was wondering how you were able to get it into my system without my noticing anything."

"Freshly squeezed orange juice was always your favorite breakfast drink. I was told it wouldn't change the taste so it was virtually undetectable."

"Go on," he urged her. "I'm finding it very interesting to learn about the fate our Mossad had in mind for one of its oldest agents."

"Granit told me that the initial symptoms, which might take several weeks to show, would be flu-like, manifesting in general weakness, aches and pains in the joints, coughing, and headaches. Over time, the poison was going to start affecting your memory and bodily motor functions, which would cause you to slow down considerably and impair your judgment. It was essential for the doses to be administered continually for the poison to work effectively. Granit also provided me with dissolvable poison pills in the form of Tylenol capsules as a back up.

"When you were too sick to take the orange juice, I was going to give you 'Tylenol' for your headaches. The poison would cause increased production of white blood cells, leaving no traces that could reveal its presence in the blood stream. The blood disease symptoms would show up several weeks later.

"'It will be a slow and painful death for President Aziz,' Granit explained to me. 'We want it to appear as a natural death from a rare blood disease so that there won't be a hint of suspicion that it was anything but that.'

"But when I first started administering the poison, it didn't seem to have the desired impact on you. I started increasing the doses until the symptoms started appearing. Continuing to play the role of your loving wife, I urged you to see your doctor and hovered over you to nurse your illness. In reality I wanted to make damn sure you were continuing to get your 'Tylenol' poison pills and that your condition would soon become irreversible."

"If you and the Mossad wanted me dead so desperately, why did you encourage me to see the doctor?" Aziz inquired.

"There were two reasons for that," Leila replied. "First, I had to continue my act of the concerned, caring wife in order not to raise any doubts about my loyalty. Second, we wanted you diagnosed officially to avoid suspicion of foul play in your death.

"But I came to the point where I started having second thoughts about your poisoning. Your progressive policies were gradually becoming a stabilizing force in Middle East politics. Your dominant personality as a powerful leader allowed you to unite the Palestinian people and clamp down on radical terrorist groups. I felt that your actions were starting to benefit Israel indirectly. Terrorism was down considerably, and peace negotiations had been elevated to the top of the world's agenda. I feared that with you gone, the radicals would gain control of the PA and renew the violence against Israel.

"It was disconcerting for me to witness your pain

and suffering day after day, seeing your strength and resolve diminish gradually."

"So this was the reason I got better for a while your killer's remorse and a moment of weakness. That doesn't sound like the resolute lethal Mossad agent sent to kill me," Aziz remarked.

"I find it hard to explain, Reuben, but deep inside I felt there was something unique about you. You were different from all the previous targets I'd taken out without hesitating. I felt I was going to destroy something good: the best chance for normalization after five decades of bloody conflict.

"I was ravaged by conflicting feelings. I hated you because you represented the thugs that took Vivian's precious life away, yet your resolute actions proved you were a genuine and talented peacemaker. I'm not sure if you recall, but one evening I probed your feelings about peace with the Israelis and whether you were genuine about them or if you were just using the Israeli concessions to advance the armed struggle."

"Oh, yes! I remember that," Aziz acknowledged. "I was wondering why you asked me that question. I decided to tell you the truth, that I believed peace and economic prosperity were in the best interest of the Palestinian people, and that war would only bring more pain and suffering to our community."

"Your answer convinced me to stop your poisoning and see if you could break the stalemate with the new Israeli government. However, by then you were very weak and the doctors arranged to send you to the clinic in Switzerland. The lack of poison, your tough body, and your strong will allowed you to fight back and pull through. The drugs you were treated with had nothing to do with your recovery."

Aziz sat up on the bed looking Leila straight in the eyes. "So how come I ended up getting sick again?" he queried with a piercing look.

"When Granit learned that you had recovered, he was furious. He summoned me to London again, trying to find out why you were still alive. I explained that I wasn't permitted to join you while you were being treated at the Swiss clinic, and the diminishing presence of the poison aided your recovery.

"Granit indicated that the initial poison might have not been potent enough. He provided me with a newly developed substance that had accelerated venomous properties and ordered me to continue poisoning you after several weeks of hiatus. He explained that he wanted it to appear as if your blood disorder was in temporary remission, which unfortunately lapsed after a short while.

"He reassured me again that the orders came from the highest authority and that your elimination would serve the best interests of Israel. He told me that the Mossad had intercepted several internal PLO communications that uncovered your deceptive plot to extort additional concessions from Israel by threatening to boycott the next round of peace talks. This was the reason for Israel's reluctance to return to the negotiating table, he explained.

"He promised that several months after your death, he would orchestrate a scheme to bring me home."

Leila got up, walked to her dresser, and used moisturizing lotion to refresh her face and hands. She quickly brushed her hair, sprayed fragrance over her body, and walked back towards the bed. Aziz glimpsed at her slender body, her shoulder length, vibrant, hair, and her shiny face radiating in the dim light. Every time they were together, it was as if he were falling in love over and over again. She had an incredibly captivating effect on him. It was impossible for him to resist her charm and bubbly personality.

"So this is why it was so bad the second time around," Aziz remarked, his mesmerized gaze locked on her as she came back to bed. "For a while there I felt invincible again, but then it was even worse."

"Well, Reuben, Granit had me convinced the second time. I wasn't going to defy the orders, which he made appear came directly from the PM. I was confident that the Mossad had very reliable sources of intelligence about your intentions and this was why they refused to renew the dialogue with you. I was sure you lied to me when you told me that your intentions towards peace with Israel were genuine. I felt my emotional attachments were clouding my judgment, and that I was wrong about you. My killer instincts were back with renewed vitality.

"The second time I wasn't going to let you get well. I made sure I was at your bedside pretending to be the loyal, caring spouse. I continued to administer the poison diligently making sure you were on your final journey to hell. I wanted you dead so badly that some nights I could hardly resist the urge to remove your life support systems."

"Leila, I find it so hard to believe that you could be that vicious," Aziz teased her, "especially with that innocent, loving look on your face."

"I know it's inconceivable for you to see me that way. I was obsessed with revenge, and I wasn't going to let go until I saw you, the PA government, and the peace accord crumble and disintegrate into pieces in front of my eyes. Hatred and revenge are incredibly formidable forces that can't be mitigated until the plan for vengeance is carried out. Saleh was a small sacrificial lamb I slaughtered on my way, but I wanted to slaughter the entire herd. This was going to be my ultimate act, the purpose of my being, my majestic triumph, finally settling the score with the savage murderers of my innocent Vivian.

"I couldn't sleep a single night without a vision of her sweet, pure face appearing before me, urging me to deliver on my unbreakable vow."

"But you were going to leave Saed behind, with no family to care for him?" he whispered to Leila.

"Reuben, you know how much I love Saed. My motherly instincts wouldn't allow me to leave him even if he was the son of the PLO Chairman. I made Granit promise that Saed would be included in whatever scheme he planned to free me."

"I wish he was here with us in this peaceful haven, away from the tumultuous conflicts of the Middle East," Aziz told her. "I would love to play some of my games with him, sweep him off his feet, cuddle him in my arms, kissing and tickling him endlessly. I can hear his cute giggles as he tries to free himself from my grip and then runs into your open arms when I let go."

"I miss him too. I can't wait for us three to be together. We are so fortunate to have him. He is amazingly adorable and smart. Destiny rewarded us in a very mysterious way for all the sacrifices we've made."

Leila leaned over and brushed her long fingers gently along his face.

"You should have seen my expression when Granit came to meet me in Geneva. I was at the clinic by your deathbed, counting the hours, when I got a call from Carol. She had been looking for me for quite a while. She finally was able to get the phone number of the clinic. She said it was a dire emergency and that I had to meet my father immediately at a hotel in Geneva. I knew exactly what she meant. I left your room, telling the charge nurse that I was going to the hotel to get some rest, but that I would be back that evening.

"I quickly changed, put on a disguise, and took a taxi to the hotel in Geneva. I met Granit in his hotel room. He seemed exhausted, dark circles under his eyes and a pale look on his long, lined face. He looked like he had aged several years since a few months earlier when I'd last seen him in London.

"Granit got straight to the point. 'I have some amazing and equally distressing news,' he said. 'I discovered very recently that your husband, President Aziz, is actually an Israeli Mossad agent. He was planted into the PLO over twenty years ago. His real name is Reuben Sasson, code name Mountain Lion. He is a decorated IDF Colonel and a national hero. His mission was so secret that it was never revealed to us. His creator took his secret to the grave, unable to alert us as to his identity.'

"'He does not know your true identity, and believes that he is married to a Palestinian woman.'

"Suddenly, I got very lightheaded and dizzy. Everything was spinning around me, and then I fainted.

"I woke up with water dripping over my face and into my neck. I saw Granit's face leaning over me, wiping my face gently with a wet towel. He propped my head on a pillow and gave me a drink of juice to help me regain consciousness.

"'I am sorry for not preparing you better for the shocking news,' he apologized. 'You must be fatigued from the endless hours you spent at Aziz's bedside making sure he was never coming back. Due to our recent discovery, your orders are being reversed. Now you must do your best to bring him back to us.'

"It took several minutes for me to gain my composure and start thinking of the implications of this astounding revelation.

"'This can't be true,' I said to Granit. 'Aziz is one of them. He is deeply immersed in their lives and aspirations. When it comes to protecting his people and promoting their cause, there is no one as dedicated and aggressive as he.'

"'You are absolutely right about his conduct, Carmit,' Granit replied. 'This is what makes him the most effective agent ever in our history. Think about it for a minute: how long could he have survived in his hazardous role without doing just that? He is so smart and versatile that he can play both roles simultaneously in a very natural way. We checked his identity with meticulous care and verified the evidence with Mossad records. We are one hundred percent confident of this fact.'

"I was petrified by the thought of the pain and suffering I'd inflicted upon you and the way I'd deceived you so completely for the past several years. I wasn't sure how I would be able to face you and tell you this dreadful story. For all I knew, you could be dead already. When I'd left, you were lying on your deathbed at the clinic, barely breathing. I had no idea how Granit thought you could still be saved. If he had seen you, he would have agreed that it was a lost cause. I was starting to wonder if I was the killer of the most successful Mossad agent in the history of Israel. Then Granit interrupted my thoughts.

"'Carmit, for every destructive weapon we create, our scientists develop an antidote. We made mistakes in the past, and we know that we will continue making mistakes in the future. There always has to be a way to reverse the damage.'

"With that, Granit gave me a small handbag containing several fluid IV packs.

"'You must return to the clinic at once and replace Aziz's IV fluids with these. This is his only chance of survival. I hope he is still with us. I will wait here for a couple of days to see how things turn out.'

"That night, I switched the IV pack of the drug the doctors had prescribed for you with the antidote Granit gave me. You know the rest of the story."

"This is unbelievable," Aziz exclaimed, "a few more hours, and I would have been part of a mysterious history nobody would have ever known or cared about.

"Leila, I can't help feeling shocked and somewhat betrayed by how well you played your part, but I was playing a part as well. You had your orders, and I had mine, and we were both trying to act in the best interests of our country. None of this is your fault. I would never hold you responsible for trying to kill me, though I still find it hard to believe that I was completely abandoned and subsequently targeted by my own agency. We are fortunate that we are both here alive with our family still intact."

"Well, my dear," she said, "now that I know who you are, I feel like a big rock has been removed off my chest. I wasn't sleeping with the enemy, and I don't have to continue the act of the faithful, loving wife while hating every minute of it. I would love nothing more than spending every minute of my life with you and Saed."

"Nothing will make my life happier than having you and Saed by my side until my last day on this earth," Aziz whispered back.

CHAPTER 48

As was his daily routine, Aziz woke up early in the morning. He went into his study where a hidden safe was built into the wall. He opened the combination lock and retrieved a small blue pouch from one of its inner compartments. He removed the gold necklace and pearl bracelet his mother had given him back in Iraq before she'd died. He'd protected the two treasured pieces of jewelry for almost four decades, waiting patiently for the moment he could present them to his future wife, just as his mother instructed him. The moment for which he had longed for so many years had finally arrived. He walked back to the master bedroom where Leila lay fast asleep and gently attached the jewelry around her neck and wrist. His mother's legacy was finally where it belonged.

Leila opened her eyes and looked at him with a gentle, loving smile. She softly caressed the jewelry and said, "I was beginning to wonder who you were saving these for."

Aziz kissed her on her hand.

"Now I know that we are a real family on a divine mission directed by the Almighty himself. Our mission must be carried through with strength and determination to guarantee the safety and well-being of our people at home."

"I have an idea you may want to consider," Leila suggested. "I can deliver a message to Granit to approach Shomron and try to soften his position on the stalemate in the peace process. Granit will inform him of your identity and work diligently to convince him to meet with you and renew the dialogue. We must continue our efforts to bring your mission and mine to a successful conclusion for the sake both of our people and of the Palestinians we have come to know and understand so well. If we fail, the violence and religious incitement will return and transform all the progress you've made into an all-out civil war."

"I like your take-charge personality, Leila, and I welcome your involvement. I've spent twenty years operating in a complete vacuum. Your initiative will definitely make my life more manageable and prevent the inevitable renewal of hostilities should the deadlock persist. Even if I don't order any hostile operations myself, they will start occurring spontaneously when levels of frustration with the present standoff peak. If we don't do something about it quickly, I will be forced to take action or else come under intense criticism and personal threats by radical elements."

The following week Leila left on one of her routine trips to London to deliver to the Mossad the first communication from its lost agent after more than twenty years of silence.

* * * *

Carmit met Granit at a hotel in central London where he'd registered under a false name. He ushered her to a modernly furnished living area where she sat on an upholstered comfortable armchair. Granit offered her a soft drink from the mini-bar and sat opposite her on a couch. Carmit now felt uneasy being alone with him. She knew that his strong feelings for her had never faded away and hoped that he realized that with the emergence of Reuben, there was no longer any possibility of their being together.

She started by delivering a pressing message from President Aziz, who requested an urgent summit with Shomron to try to resolve the current deadlock and move toward renewal of the peace accord. She explained to Granit that if no progress was made within several days, Aziz would have no choice but to order the renewal of hostilities. If he didn't do that, he would likely become the target of an attempted coup by militant extremists aiming to eliminate him and take over the reins of the PA.

"You stand the risk of losing him altogether after the enormous investment the Mossad made to try to influence the behavior of the PA," she stressed. "We almost lost him once. His life, our son's, and my own must not be put at risk again. You have to trust his judgment and respond favorably to his request. He has made incredible progress, and there is no reason to doubt him now. This was the reason the Mossad planted him there in the first place, to try to normalize relations and prevent bloodshed.

"If the government's goals have changed and Shomron no longer feels that Aziz should maintain his PA leadership position, you should call the mission off and bring us home.

"I urge you to meet Shomron at once, inform him of President Aziz's real identity, and warn him of the crisis we are about to face if he doesn't change his mind," Carmit continued her emotional plea with tears in her eyes.

"Carmit, I am very sorry you have been through so much pain and distress in the last few years, and part of it is my fault, but I reassure you that I am going straight to Shomron's home from the airport. I am confident that my arguments will be sufficiently compelling to persuade him to schedule an urgent meeting with Aziz to work out a long-term solution to the crisis.

"Please don't be afraid. After I enlighten Shomron regarding Aziz's identity, I know his attitude will turn around quickly, and everything will be back on track."

"Thank you," Carmit sighed with relief, dabbing her face with tissues she took out from her small purse. "Shomron holds your opinion in high regard, and I know you can change his mind."

"I feel horrible about how events have unraveled for you," Granit continued apologetically. "I never wanted you to go back to Beirut on that horrendous mission. I planned to reassign you locally so that we would have time to plan our future, but the Chief insisted that you should leave at once. I tried to use delay tactics to keep you around a while longer, but the Chief felt that any delays would put your mission at risk. He must have gotten wind of our relations and decided to keep us apart."

Granit paused briefly to remove two more cold drinks from the mini-bar. He placed one in front of Arazi while opening and sipping his own.

"When I learned that the Chief flew to London to persuade you to marry Chairman Aziz, I was heartbroken. Just thinking of you in the arms of our vicious enemy, having to endure this torture and act as if you were the happiest woman alive, made me shake. I couldn't comprehend how you were able to get through it, day after day. When I received the news that your son was born, I was completely devastated and started losing hope for us.

"I waited patiently for a breakthrough, just as I was trained to do my entire career. When I was promoted to the highest Mossad post, I knew that this was my opportunity to set things straight. I came out to meet you, and without consulting the PM, I ordered you to murder Aziz. I not only wanted to free you from the terrible burden laid upon you by the former Chief, but I desperately wanted you back."

Carmit sat frozen on the armchair wondering where Granit was heading with his recap of events.

"When we made the discovery regarding Reuben," he continued, "I suffered a severe personal crisis. Unknowingly I had ordered the killing of our most successful agent for my own selfish cause. I wished Reuben Sasson had never been discovered and that I could have President Aziz killed and bring you back to my arms. I was so distressed, I even considered withholding the antidote and letting him die. I struggled for hours with overwhelming contradictory emotions. Should I sacrifice the life of the agent for my own personal gain? Should I risk the hope of peace and prosperity for Israel and all the accomplishments of this loyal agent in the past twenty years? I finally came to my senses and rushed to meet you in Geneva.

"Destiny kept eluding me, Carmit. I lost you again. Your own destiny led you to Reuben, and now you have Saed, who I am told is an exceptionally bright and cute young boy. I hope you and Reuben will find strength and love in one another and continue to serve our nation in the wonderful manner in which you have done so far. With your ultimate self-sacrifice, you have brought us a period of relative calm, tranquility, and, above all, hope for future generations."

CHAPTER 49

When Granit returned home from his urgent trip to London, he called Shomron and requested to see him right away. The Mossad Chief held such a vital national security post that the PM's door was always open to him.

He met Shomron in his secure home office and started by informing him of the identity of the PA President. Shomron, completely stunned, at first couldn't believe it. "How is it that this is the first time I am hearing of this?" he blurted out angrily. "I thought I was supposed to be informed of even the minute details knowing they can change the course of history."

"We've only come to make this astonishing discovery very recently," Granit responded defensively. "He was planted into the PLO over twenty years ago by Avi Shaffir, the Mossad Chief at that time. Shaffir kept his identity to himself, fearing that if he let the secret out, his agent's cover would be blown. Shaffir never had the opportunity to alert us before he died of a sudden heart attack. We discovered his existence due to a long overdue financial audit of our safe deposit boxes. His identity was verified beyond a shadow of doubt."

"Correct me if I am wrong, but doesn't this character Aziz appear just as zealous as all the rest of them?" Shomron asked skeptically. "He is very aggressive and relentless in his fight on behalf of the Palestinians. He makes far-reaching demands that undermine our national security. How can I trust him?"

"If he didn't do that, he would be dead by now," Granit replied. "He would have been assassinated a long time ago. This is what makes him so valuable. His remarkable talent to juggle both roles so naturally allowed him to survive the turmoil of PLO politics and power struggles. You need to take a hard look at his record since he took power. You must agree that there has been a remarkable shift from the PLO doctrine of hatred, bloodshed, and destruction promoted by his predecessor. We have come a long way in the last couple of years. If we regress now, we will have to deal with the calamities we have faced continually for more than four decades. I don't think the citizens of this country want to return to those days."

Granit paused for a moment to let Shomron digest the magnitude of information he just unloaded on him. He reclined in a high-back leather armchair positioned opposite Shomron's desk and closed his eyes for a few moments of silence.

Then as if he had awakened from a deep sleep, he sat up and addressed Shomron passionately: "President Aziz is our man and our best hope for long-term, normalized relations. I strongly urge you to meet with him without further delay and work a way out of the crisis looming over our heads. Remember, he can be pushed only so far before we're in danger of losing him to the radicals. He walks a very fine line, and we need to give him the time and space to garner the support of his people to normalize relations over time. It's a healing process for both sides that will take a while. He has proven himself again and again during his mission. His accomplishments span way beyond those of any agent in the history of this elite organization. He has sacrificed his entire life for this country and our people. I firmly believe he has earned the right to meet with you. From what I hear, you will not be disappointed."

"You make a compelling argument," Shomron answered, wiping his balding forehead which was speckled with tiny sweat dots. "However, I think you realize how hard it is for me to go through with this. I was elected by constituents who strongly objected to Harel's concessions during the peace negotiations. How would it appear if I meet with Aziz publicly? Many citizens in this country still regard him as a terrorist with blood on his hands."

"I could arrange a secret meeting between you two," Granit replied enthusiastically. "You will get a feel for how you get along with him. If it works out, it will have to become official at some point. However, if you feel that this avenue is not one you want to pursue, I suggest we abort his mission and bring him, Arazi, and their son home. It wouldn't be fair to leave him in a position where he would have to choose between initiating violence against his own countrymen or dying at the hand of radicals."

"I realize that you have been dealing with this issue for a very long time, and your insight is eye-opening," Shomron added. "The fact that he is our man changes the picture entirely. I will take your advice and agree to a secret meeting with President Aziz. Please arrange for us to get together at a neutral location for several hours, and keep it strictly confidential. If anything leaks out, it will be a disaster. I would like you to personally make the arrangements and restrict involvement of others to an absolute minimum. You will accompany me to the meeting so you can finally meet President Aziz yourself. However, the meeting between President Aziz and me should be completely private."

"I will start working on the arrangements immediately. You have my personal assurance of complete secrecy," Granit responded in an excited voice as he left in a great hurry.

* * * *

The Mossad Chief anxiously waited for the PM to emerge from his secret meeting with President Aziz. Granit had the opportunity to meet Aziz briefly and shake his hand. Shomron introduced him to Aziz as his national security adviser. President Aziz had a very impressive personality and a firm handshake. He spoke in a near perfect British accent and was very pleasantly mannered. Granit wondered how Shaffir had been able to recruit this extraordinary individual. He gained new respect for the man he'd once considered his most hated rival. In a strange way, he was pleased that Aziz was able to dodge the long arm of the Mossad. "Surely Aziz is going to make his mark on the PM," he thought.

The meeting went on for far longer than expected. Granit knew this was a positive sign. Finally the two men emerged, shook hands enthusiastically, and exchanged greetings. "I will be in touch shortly," Shomron said to President Aziz as they departed on their return journeys home.

Granit ushered Shomron into the rear seat of an unmarked secret service armored car and sat next to him. In the privacy of the rear compartment, Shomron told Granit he'd had a very productive meeting with President Aziz, finding him not only very reasonable to work with but also extremely witty. "This was definitely a worthwhile meeting, and I want to thank you for your sound advice," he said to Granit.

"I was able to understand his pressing issues, the difficulties he is facing with the present impasse, and the pressures from his critics. He also appreciates my difficulties with the structure of the narrow coalition government, and he will try to buy more time for me to get the government's authorization to restart the peace process."

"It sounds like you hit it off with him and made good progress," Granit commented eagerly.

Resting comfortably against the soft leather seat of the car Shomron stretched his legs. "Yes, indeed," he replied. "Your intuition about him was right on target. There is something extraordinary about this man. His inspiring character, remarkable manners, notable wisdom, and integrity must leave a lasting impression on any individual he meets. No wonder he is so adored by his people and enormously popular in international circles. I could certainly use someone of his caliber in my government.

"I feel he is someone honorable that I can work with and continue to advance toward normalization. But I now have the difficult task of persuading my colleagues of the same."

"I am confident that with a little arm-twisting and your remarkable intellect, you will be able to make a convincing argument to your coalition members," Granit said, expressing his faith in Shomron.

"I hope you are right, I will certainly give it my very best shot."

CHAPTER 50

"My meeting with Shomron went quite well." Aziz informed Leila when he arrived home late that night. "Whatever you said to Granit worked. I was able to penetrate through his rigid façade and pave the way to a breakthrough in our relations. The revelation of my identity must have played a major role in building trust between us. We scheduled a follow up meeting for next week. I also met Granit briefly. Shomron introduced him to me before our meeting."

"I am glad I could be of service to you, dear," Leila commented, brushing her long hair backwards and tying it in a ponytail. "I knew you would win him over and defuse the discord. Somehow I didn't think he was going to call our mission off and bring us home," she said jokingly, applying lotion to her face.

"I wasn't planning to resist such an offer if it were laid on the table," Aziz replied in jest. "I would have loved to take you and Saed to Deganya and continue our lives like a normal Israeli family. It would be so easy to accomplish now that a mere few miles separate us."

"But Shomron realizes what could go wrong in your absence, how peace could crumble without your steady arms holding the reins of the PA," Leila reminded him.

Leila dodged around him with her silky lavender mini-nightgown barely covering her behind. Aziz followed her closely, his eyes fixated on her slick bodily moves with every stride she took. Leila was an artist when it came to capturing his attention.

"The relative peace is boosting his popularity," she continued. "It's an ace he is not going to give up easily. Our mission is not over by any means, my dear. It might not be over in our lifetime."

Leila climbed onto the bed, stretching her body over the downy bedcover, and rested her head on a fluffy pillow.

"You have to accept your destiny as the protector of our people from afar. Your ability to influence the well-being of Israel is much greater as the PA President. If you remove yourself, a successor could quickly change the direction and momentum you have worked so hard to create and return everything to conflict and violence."

Wearing his striped cotton pajamas, Aziz climbed into bed next to her.

"I never dreamed that this mission would be prolonged to such an extent, but I feel fortunate with the twist of events that brought our lives together. We face many challenges and constant risks. We must take every step with extreme caution."

He held Leila by her hand and gazed at the firm, shiny skin of her face, amazed by how she'd kept her youthful looks through years of mounting tensions.

"Although we can't be in Israel," he continued, "our destiny gave us so much. We live as dignitaries and enjoy luxuries reserved for celebrities, and we have a son who could be groomed as the next leader of the PA."

"We are going to have to start planning for his future," Leila agreed. "Saed would need to create continuity in the process and carry your success to the next generation. He will have to prove himself worthy of the role and be elected by the people. You will have to ingrain in his mind the principles and values that have led to your own success. We will start by providing him with superior education to prepare him for his leadership role."

Aziz leaned over and looked deeply into Leila's majestic eyes.

"If this responsibility were left in the hands of others, our days could be numbered."

EPILOGUE

On a scorching hot summer evening in Baghdad, Ali and his wife, Sharifa, were sitting in their lavishly decorated living room surrounded by the whisper of the comfortable, cool air emitted by their central air conditioner. They were watching the evening news and nibbling on dried fruits and salted nuts.

PA President Abdul Aziz Al-Wasphi was being interviewed by the Iraqi national TV on the progress of economic collaboration between Israel and the Palestinian Authority. Only a few weeks earlier, the final peace accords between the Israeli government and the Palestinian Authority had been successfully concluded, with the president consolidating his control over the entire area of the West Bank and Gaza Strip.

"By working closely together, we can turn this region into the technological and economic paradise of the Middle East," the president stated in response to a question by the Iraqi news anchor. "With Israel's advanced technology capabilities and the talented labor resources of the Palestinian people, we can transform this region into the Garden of Eden that was once the dwelling place of our ancestors."

Ali turned to his wife, Sharifa. "What do you think of President Aziz and his grandiose plans for the future of the Middle East? The Iraqi leadership strongly opposes these agreements and refuses to abandon their long-standing yearning to drown all the Zionists in the sea and redeem the Holy Land for the Muslims."

"It seems to me he is the first leader to bring real hope for the future of his people." Sharifa pondered the question some more. "All we witnessed before he rose to power was death, destruction, and deeply routed corruption. What he has achieved with skillful diplomatic maneuvering is so much more than any Arab leader was able to accomplish in decades of armed struggle.

"If nobody murders him first, I hope he will be able to bring an end to the suffering of his people and finally allow them to be masters of their own destiny. Being at the mercy of others for so many years has only brought them misery."

"Well, my dear," Ali reacted, "it may be fine for you to express this opinion in the privacy of our home, but you must be well aware of the dangers such an opinion holds in the eyes of our revered leader."

"I am well aware of the dangers, my dear husband, and I know I can trust you with my secrets."

"Your secrets are always safe with me, my dear Sharifa.

"I don't recall ever telling you that I knew President Abdul Aziz as a young boy. He and his mother arrived here as refugees from Palestine after the war. They were virtually penniless. I helped them settle down in a tiny home in a section of old Baghdad and provided them with their basic needs."

"I never heard that story," Sharifa said, surprised. "It sounds very intriguing. Do you think he still remembers you?"

"I think he will remember me once I refresh his memory. I used to visit him and his mother occasionally to bring them household items they needed desperately. I took a real liking to young Aziz. He was a spirited, bright young kid, and a tough street fighter."

"Ali, it was very generous of you to help them out. You should try to meet him and reintroduce yourself. He just announced numerous new urban development projects for the territories. You should be able to secure a nice chunk of this work for your enterprise."

"That's a great idea, Sharifa," Ali said enthusiastically. "I will definitely plan on doing that. President Aziz certainly owes me a huge favor. Maybe two.

ACKNOWLEDGMENTS

I would first like to thank the several editors who helped me bring this story to its final fruition.

Brooke Smith, my meticulous and responsive editor, helped me put in the finishing touches and get this manuscript to a publishable state. Adele Brinkley, With Pen In Hand editing service, was there to proof and fix lingering errors. Daniel Zitin provided me valuable input while helping me refine the plot and structure of the novel. Peter Porosky gave me sound guidance on adding suspense and tension to my story. Bob Lightman and Lucy Hoopes provided me with the initial copyediting. Finally George Kahmo helped me with Arabic translations.

I received much encouragement and support from many friends and family members who were patient enough to read my initial manuscript and provide me with valuable feedback to make it better.

The Horowitz family: Uncle Sid and cousins Sara and Jay, Randy Levitt, Michael Gittleson, Debbie and

Steve Cohen, Steve Shapiro, Bob Spitze, Margo Cohen, Rick Zitleman, Jeff Gordinier, Donna and Brad Tehaan, and Mike Sager. Finally my writing group at The Writer's Center in Bethesda, Maryland and our talented instructor, Nani Power. Any others, please forgive me if I forgot to mention your name.

I wouldn't have been able to endure this experience without the love and support of my wife, Michelle, and my children Sarena, Jeremy, and Elan, who believed in me throughout this long and laborious endeavor.

I consulted many books, articles and websites during my research for this book, too many to mention individually. I read many books, mostly in Hebrew, about the history and culture of the Jewish community in Iraq in the past century. I visited the Babylonian Jewry Heritage Center in Israel, which I found enlightening and resourceful. Finally I also researched the history of the PLO, its leadership and terrorist activities, in several books, articles, and websites.

ABOUT THE AUTHOR

Rami Loya was born in Baghdad, Iraq. When he was a young boy, his family immigrated to Israel where he grew up and served three years in the Israeli Defense Forces. He continued his higher education in engineering and business in England and the United States.

He drew inspiration for *Chairman-X* from the incredibly rich yet turbulent history of his ancestors in Babylon combined with his own life experiences.

He is the author of a business management book, *Incentive Compensation Strategies for the New Millennium,* published in 2000.

He resides in Maryland with his wife and children.